Praise for *Each of Us a Desert*

"This ambitious, organically Spanish-studded examination of trauma stays adventurous and accessible, resulting in a grace-filled, loving declaration of human value and worth."
—*Publishers Weekly* (starred review)

"Oshiro deftly weaves an intricate, allegorical, and often gory tale within a postapocalyptic desert setting that readers will feel so viscerally they may very well need to reach for a glass of water. A meditation and adventure quest offering solace to anyone bearing an unfair burden."
—*Kirkus Reviews*

"Oshiro leaves mouths parched with their second novel. . . . The writing, akin to an atmospheric, novel-length poem, seamlessly weaving in Spanish and matter-of-fact queer representation, is beautiful to read. Contemplative teens will appreciate this meaningful story about human existence."
—*Booklist*

"It feels like a book that emerged right out of Mark Oshiro's heart, and I mean that viscerally: bloody and precious, intimate and life-giving and spilling over with love. . . . A masterpiece."
—Maya Gittelman, *Tor.com*

"[Like] Lois Lowry's *The Giver* . . . this haunting story will stay with readers just like the stories Xochitl has kept."
—*School Library Journal*

"Part coming-of-age story, part fantasy, this book not only delivers an enchanting tale, but also has some of the most creative world-building happening in speculative fiction right now—all told through a Latinx lens."
—*Den of Geek*

ALSO BY MARK OSHIRO

Anger Is a Gift

MARK OSHIRO

EACH OF US A DESERT

TOR
TEEN

A TOM DOHERTY ASSOCIATES BOOK
NEW YORK

EACH OF US A DESERT

Copyright © 2020 by Mark Oshiro

All rights reserved.

Edited by Miriam Weinberg

Interior art by Ellisa Mitchell
Designed by Gregory Collins

A Tor Teen Book
Published by Tom Doherty Associates
120 Broadway
New York, NY 10271

www.tor-forge.com

Tor® is a registered trademark of Macmillan Publishing Group, LLC.

The Library of Congress Cataloging-in-Publication Data is available upon request.

ISBN 978-1-250-16922-8 (trade paperback)
ISBN 978-1-250-16920-4 (ebook)

Our books may be purchased in bulk for promotional, educational, or business use. Please contact your local bookseller or the Macmillan Corporate and Premium Sales Department at 1-800-221-7945, extension 5442, or by email at MacmillanSpecialMarkets@macmillan.com.

First Edition: September 2020
First Trade Paperback Edition: November 2021

Printed in the United States of America

0 9 8 7 6 5 4 3 2 1

A los que han cruzado

A los que han elegido irse

A los que han buscado una vida mejor

Yo te veo y te levanto.

EACH
OF US
A DESERT

It always began at night, when You had disappeared.

And when You were gone, we came alive.

I am Your cuentista, Solís. I had been raised to take the stories of others, and return them to You in ritual.

But I had none of my own.

I also ran away. I left behind Empalme. Mi familia. You. Myself. And I *ran*.

I should have spoken to You long ago, but I couldn't.

I needed to be free. And I'm not sorry.

So let me tell You a story, Solís.

We met the others at nightfall on the western side of Empalme, past the square and beyond the well. It was where Julio and his men had made their camp over a month ago. We ignored them as we passed, but I could see them watching us as we went by, the fire lighting up their dour, bitter faces. But they said nothing, did nothing, and we joined the rest of the celebration.

Rogelio was there and already drunk, strumming his guitar dramatically while two women harmonized over it all, their voices a complicated dance of melody and sadness. They sang of leaving their husbands behind and making the journey across the endless desert together. "Montamos juntos y nos hacemos uno," Amada sang, almost laughing as she made eye contact with her novia, Carmita.

They were not the only sound in the clearing, as most of los aldeanos were spread around an enormous central fire. This was a celebration of our lives, of surviving another day in the scorched and unbearable world that You left for us. A respite from Your harsh stare. Even without You in the sky, though, las estrellas were many, were brilliant, and they cast a glow over all.

I weaved through the crowd, holding the basket out, offering our tortillas for others. I had helped Mamá make them earlier that evening as You set in the west. We had formed a line behind our home, my parents and I, with my brother, Raúl, at the end, working as the earthy scent of the first burning coals floated up to my nose. Mamá made her tortillas thick and crispy around the edges, la masa blooming into a savory taste on the tongue. She kissed Papá, ran her fingers through his long hair, then yelled at Raúl, who had let one of the tortillas linger on the heat for too long.

It was an important part of our daily ritual. We all took something to our village gatherings. None of it was sold; this was our offering to one another. La señora Sánchez came with her guisado de cabra, and I could smell the spices from across the clearing as she filled bowls with the hot, savory stew. People greeted one another, perhaps not so loudly as usual—our voices thick with increasing worry since Julio's arrival in Empalme.

But we were still here, still alive, and this tradition had lasted for many, many years, since long before I was born. At night, there was a great sense of freedom, but as was usually the case for me, it came at a cost. I had already made my way to the other side of the fire, greeting Lani and Omar, when Rogelio stumbled over, nearly crashing into me. "Cuentista, cuentista," he slurred.

I saw Lani roll her eyes at me. Rogelio was *always* like this.

"Cuentista, I need you."

"I know," I said, exhausted. "But not now. It is barely nightfall."

"I will find you later," he said, smiling, a dribble of spit slipping out of the corner of his mouth.

"I'm sure you will," I muttered.

Lani reached a hand out. "We *do* appreciate you, Xochitl," she said, her light eyes reflecting the fire behind me. "Don't worry about him. As long as he's talking to you, we'll all be fine."

I nodded at her, but bit back what I *wanted* to say. Everyone would be fine; she was right about that. I watched Lani laugh at something Omar had said, and the thought raced through me: *But am I going to be fine?*

Something bumped into my leg, and I looked down to see the

wooden cart belonging to la señora Sánchez, a large metal pot of guisado de cabra in the back. "Disculpe, Xochitl," she said, and she waved at me with her wooden arm, the one she got in Obregán after she'd lost the one she'd been born with. "Would you help me for a bit?"

I smiled at her. I liked la señora Sánchez, and enjoyed her stories of her early days in Empalme, but what I liked most about her was that she never lied to me. "Sure," I told her, and I took hold of the cart and pulled it after her. She greeted the other aldeanos, offered them el guisado, and then moved on.

I kept up as best as I could, saying hello to those gathered around the fire, but otherwise remaining silent. When Ofelia came to get a bowl, she nearly tripped over me. "Didn't see you there," she said, then turned back to la señora Sánchez without another word to me. There weren't many of us in Empalme—we were so far from Obregán to the north and Hermosillo to the south—but most people treated me as Ofelia did. They rarely saw me unless they needed me, and I knew that as soon as Ofelia had to tell me a story, she'd be much kinder.

Now, though, she was locked in conversation with la señora Sánchez, and I didn't matter. "He's going to start interfering with los mensajeros," Ofelia insisted. "And I can't have that. I'm waiting for some *very* important mensajes from my family. I *cannot* have them delayed."

"Perhaps there are more pressing issues, Ofelia," la señora Sánchez said, her mouth curling up in irritation. "Though I sympathize."

"What are we doing about Julio?" she demanded, as if la señora Sánchez had said nothing at all. "Are we just letting him take over our well? What's next? Our food?"

Papá came up to stand beside me. "He's only a bully," he said. "We have enough water that we can get on our own. We'll just bore him until he leaves. Solís will protect the rest of us."

Like instinct, we all made the sign: our palms dragged across our eyes, then passing them down to our chest. A reminder to see the truth, to believe the truth. As long as we kept the truth in our hearts, as long as they all spoke it to me, we would be spared from Your wrath.

But I made eye contact with la señora Sánchez, and she was not thrilled with mi papá's calm. She was *scowling*.

I looked to Papá, uncertainty snaking up my spine. "But what if it gets worse?" I asked. "What if he *does* take more from us?"

"We'll be okay," he said, running his hand over my head, into my long hair. "Just keep helping us tell Solís the truth."

La señora Sánchez cleared her throat loudly. "Beto, I'm not so sure about that."

"There's no need to doubt Solís, señora," Papá shot back.

"Well, you don't have the same history with Julio as I do," she snarled, and I winced.

"Papá, are you sure we'll be okay?" My voice trembled as I spoke.

He ignored me. "Señora, can you speak to the guardians again? Find out if they need anything from us? Or if we're drifting too far from Solís?"

I knew what he meant: Did I need to do a better job? Was there more I could do? But he wouldn't say that directly, only hint at what was expected of me. That's what they all did. I was the undercurrent, the quiet assumption in all their lives, the person they depended on to keep them safe. But would I ever get to be anything *else*?

La señora Sánchez jerked her head to the side. "Why don't *you* ask them?"

We looked in the direction she had gestured.

They stood there, their eyes glowing.

Every aldea, every colonia, every ciudad, had its own set of guardians. You left them behind to watch over us, to act as protectors where You could not. Ours were lobos, giant and towering, who hid in caverns and underground dens during the day, their coats thin and brown, blending in with the colors of the desert. They spoke only to the one they had chosen, and that was la señora Sánchez. I grew up wishing that, as la cuentista of Empalme, I was the one they spoke to.

But as they did tonight, they always stared at me, unmoving, silent.

Papá made the sign, then spoke. "You know they won't talk to me, señora."

She shrugged. "Then don't tell me what I should do."

We moved on, and I gave Papá a sympathetic look as he pulled his long hair behind and tied it off. He always did that when he was embarrassed. As la señora Sánchez served others, I stood there and watched the crowd that had gathered. How many of us were there left in Empalme? Forty? Fifty?

I watched Raúl chase after Renato, his best friend. My brother bounded past me, his round cheeks bouncing, and jealousy struck at me. At least he had someone. Whom did *I* have now? Ana y Quique had left with their parents to travel down to Hermosillo, a journey that would take them a full week. Doro had gone to Obregán last month with her tío, finally ready to continue in the family business.

No one ever came back. They ventured out of Empalme, they found new lives, and then they never returned.

This was my life. I was la cuentista of this place, and I was to remain here, purifying los aldeanos de Empalme, until I passed the power on to someone else in death.

I excused myself and walked around to the eastern edge of the fire. I passed Ofelia, who was complaining to someone else about her mensajes.

I blocked her out.

I stared up at the sky, watched each of las estrellas sparkle into existence. Sometimes, after a particularly difficult ritual, I would lie on my back on the earth, and I would let las estrellas surround me. They would fill every bit of my field of vision, and I would imagine that there was nothing else in the world. Just the desert beneath me and las estrellas above. I was hidden from You, and I would allow the loneliness to settle deep in my body. It was a part of me, one I had no means of alleviating, except for las poemas.

But as I thought of those words I had found out in the sand, I sensed someone staring at me.

After turning around, I locked eyes with *her*. Emilia. She was on the opposite side of the fire, gazing in my direction. I glanced about, and her father, Julio, was nowhere in sight.

There was an empty space around Emilia, as if no one could fathom standing close to her, couldn't bear to speak with Julio's daughter. I watched for a while, saw the others move even farther away.

She tilted her head, staring.

I rolled my eyes. I wanted nothing to do with her.

So I turned around once more and leaned my head upward, my back to the fire, and I watched las estrellas. I stuck my fingers into the waistband on my breeches and felt the edges of the small drawstring pouch I always carried with me.

One touch was all I needed.

I watched las estrellas. They watched me back. I stood like this until my neck ached, until I had drowned out the noise of Empalme. Our nighttime celebration faded around me as exhaustion crept into our bodies, pulled us back to sleep, and soon, Papá was asking me to help la señora Sánchez home. I agreed, but it was mostly because I knew she would keep to herself.

So I enjoyed her quiet presence as I pulled the cart back, the crunch of the wooden wheels on sand the only sound between us.

But I needed to know. As we pulled up to her home, crafted of bricks made of mud, I sighed. "Do you think we will be okay?" I asked. "Have the guardians said anything to you about Julio?"

"No sé," she said. "I have never known the guardians to be so *silent*. And I've lived in Empalme for nearly seventy years."

"Am I doing enough?"

She smiled, caressed my arm with her fingers until they looped with mine. Then she gave me a gentle squeeze. "Niña, sometimes I think you do too much for us."

She took her empty pot indoors without another word, and I walked the rest of the way home, my eyes drifting up to las estrellas every so often. I was alone underneath them.

They comforted me. They always did.

Rogelio called my name. It drifted in our home like a wind, like a lost calf bleating for its mother, and I bolted upright from the floor. He called it out again, and I cast a glance down at Raúl, who slept soundlessly on the ground. As he always did. Nothing ever seemed to wake him, and I sent up a silent prayer to You, thankful that he would not have to hear this.

Mamá and Papá were asleep, too, not far from us, and Papá's soft snoring filled the room. Mamá rustled in her sleeping roll, and I sneaked out while I could. She was the lightest sleeper of them all, but that night, I was thankful she did not wake. I pushed aside the burlap curtain that crossed over our doorway, and he swayed there, his arms drooping at his side, and my name slipped off his tongue again, jumbled together.

"Xochitl."

I stepped out to Rogelio and reached forward, intending to direct him away from our door, but the smell hit me. I choked. Tesgüino, his favorite.

Despite how drunk he was, he still saw me shrink away from him. "Lo siento, Xochitl," he said. "Pero te necesito. He hecho algo terrible."

He slurred all of it, the words coated in alcohol and regret. It was always the same with Rogelio: the sadness. The numbness he sought in drink. The begging. Even if I hadn't been a cuentista, I would still know his secrets. He wore them on his clothing, on his breath, on his face.

I shook my head. "Now, Rogelio? Do I have to *now*? It's the middle of the night."

"I won't make it to morning," he said, and then his eyes focused on me. They were glassy in the bright starlight, and dust clung to the tracks of his tears, road maps of misery and loss.

He knew. Everyone did. Your body told you when your lies, your secrets, the terrible things you had done, were about to take form in our world. Las pesadillas, we called them. Night terrors made real.

I glanced behind him, and there they were. Five men shrouded in the shadows, each of them with their arms outstretched. They were not in solid form, as if the darkness itself had conjured up these beings. At the ends of their arms, blood dripped to the ground from stumps. Someone had taken their hands.

They moved closer.

I stepped back again, shuddered.

It was time.

I was taught that, too. That if a cuentista did not take a story, las pesadillas would gain power, would lash out, would harm others.

So I couldn't wait any longer.

I reached down and grabbed one of Rogelio's sweaty hands. "Ven conmigo," I said, and I directed him behind our home. He shuffled along, and if I had not held his hand, I am certain he would have gotten lost walking those few feet. I guided him toward the firepit in the back, still warm from the tortillas we had made, and had Rogelio sit on a rough cobija placed next to it. He didn't sit so much as collapse on the spot, and then he started humming. I didn't recognize the melody, and then he lifted his hands up as if he held his guitar, and he started playing, and it was one of the saddest things I'd ever seen.

I pitied him. So I sat across from Rogelio, and I took his hands, and I asked him to tell me his story.

As I did, they surrounded our home.

Shuffled toward me, their feet dragging on the ground.

Closer, closer.

I started because I had to. They were almost upon me—and these pesadillas looked *furious*.

This is what I think happened. I don't actually know. I gave it back to You, as I had always done, so I like to imagine what happened as I performed my duty.

He put his hands out, palm down.

I put mine out, palm up.

I placed mine underneath his. I took in a deep breath, and I closed my eyes, opened my heart and my stomach.

He stared at me, and then *he* opened, too. His story was a deluge from his mouth, and as he spoke, they entered my chest. I gasped; that first rush was always the hardest to deal with. Even if I gave You these stories back, I had a sort of memory within my bones of that surge, the passage of truth from one body to another. I had learned long ago how to adjust and settle into the wave of the story, and I guided Rogelio, pulling it out, weaving it into my own body.

"Tell me why you are sad, Rogelio," I said.

"I miss them," he said, and despite that he towered over me even as we sat there, he shrank. He became tinier, a shriveled man drained by his resentment and longing. "They never should have left me."

I bristled. We did this every time. "Why did they leave you?"

There. The story flowed out; Rogelio told me everything. He shared the jealousy, the quiet terror, and the violence. He told me about how he had regretted the money he spent, the gamble he took, the look on the faces of his friends once they realized what he had done with their wages. They simply left one day, and he had begged

Marisol to tell him where they'd gone, and she rejected him every time.

So he went to Manolito's. Bought his favorite bottle. Again. It washed over his memories and shame, eroded the sharp edges.

"I shouldn't do this," he said. "Solís expects better of me. Of *all* of us."

I had it now. With one last tug, I devoured Rogelio's honesty, and the story became mine. It swam within me: regret struggling to surface in a sea of self-hatred.

"Gracias," I told him, and when I opened my eyes, the ritual complete, he was standing above me. He wiped at his mouth, then walked away, leaving me with his regret and guilt.

I had done my duty. What other need did he have for me?

As Rogelio's story filled my body, it jostled for space. It stretched between bones and organs, and I pushed the pain and discomfort down, down, farther away from my heart. I stood and wobbled, trying to separate my own sadness and loneliness from Rogelio's. They were so *similar*, and it haunted me every time. You let me keep that part of the memory; the ritual left me confused, bewildered, uncertain where I ended and where the story began.

I peeked in on Raúl one more time. Still asleep. Same with my parents. If any of them had heard us, they gave no indication.

So I walked. I turned to the north, guided by the glowing estrella that hung over the distant montañas, and I let You take me where I needed to go. I opened myself to the earth. I climbed up the other side of a gully, and the earth spoke to me. I let it pull me to the ground, the dirt biting into my knees and my palms, brief reminders that I was a guest in this body, that at any moment, You could take me away.

His story came out of me in great big heaves, and the refuse poured out of my mouth, sharp and thick on my tongue, and it spilled onto the waiting earth, filling the cracks and seeping deep within. I expunged it all, spat it out at the end, tasted its bitterness. I always remembered that flavor; it lingered beyond the ritual every time. On its way back home, back to You, the truth reached out and tried to take me with it, the shame needling my body, Rogelio's terror my own. I had to fight it; the stories were so desperate to find something to cling to, someone to bond with.

I gave You his story, and You took it back. When the last drop of it fell to the dust, I stood up and it dissipated. Washed away. There was a feeling that remained as the memory floated off. A sadness. Regret. It was fleeting, like something that had happened to me so long ago that I could not recall the fuzzy details.

Then they were gone.

It was the same each time. I wiped the bitterness from my lips, then turned back toward home, the starlight casting me in a glow of purpose. I made the sign to complete the ritual. See the truth; believe the truth. But I could not remember Rogelio's story no matter how hard I tried. It was what I was supposed to do, and it provided safety to Your gente. They could trust me with their secrets because I could not share them. They were always returned to You, and I was left aimless, purposeless as my mind struggled to remember who *I* was.

I collapsed alongside Raúl, much as Rogelio had behind our home, and I curled up on my sleeping roll. The ritual drained me of my energy and of my memory of the story. It would take hours for me to recover, and then . . .

Well, I would do it all over again. Inevitably, it would be only a day or two until someone else needed me, and then I would consume their truth, expel the bitterness into the desert, and forget.

I was Your cuentista, Solís.

I did my best.

I promise.

This is the story that I was told, Solís. Long before Tía Inez gave me her power when I was eight years old, I learned what You had done and what You had asked of us.

You punished us, Solís. Long ago, You became furious with what we had done to Your world. Greed. War. Terror. Jealousy. Strife. You punished us with fire—La Quema, as we came to call it—and You scorched it all. You burned every bit of it, determined to wipe us away. My ancestors buried themselves in the dirt, though, and when fire and devastation rained down on the land that would become Empalme, they felt the heat itching to rip the skin and meat from their bones.

But they survived.

They came aboveground, out from their homes beneath the ash and the destruction, to discover that the earth was blackened, that everything they'd known was gone.

Never again, You told them, Your voice booming over the flattened landscapes, the arid remains. *You must never disrespect my creation.*

This is the story I was told of how las cuentistas were born; You gave some of us the ability to devour the truth of others, and You warned us. We would all know if someone had harmed another, if they had kept their truth from You. The longer one of us went without a cuentista, the worse our pesadillas became. And so we were cast out into the world to ingest what others had done wrong, then return it to You, to the eternal desert. We were spread far and wide, forcing las aldeas to form, each of them around a cuentista. When that cuentista died, a new one would be granted the same power, just as I had been when Tía Inez died and chose me.

We cuentistas were exempt, too. No one took our stories. We did not manifest pesadillas.

We were alone.

I never questioned any of it, Solís. And why should I have? I had never met another cuentista besides Tía Inez; I had never truly ventured beyond Empalme; I had no reason to question anything.

I am telling You this, Solís, because maybe You'll understand. Maybe You will have mercy on me. Because even before all of this happened, before I had to flee Empalme, I knew something was wrong. Why did I not have to tell You the truth? Why were my secrets my own, and why had they never become one of those terrible pesadillas? Why did You not punish Julio and his men, who stole our water from us every day?

I would say that I am sorry, Solís, but I had to.

I had to leave.

I woke in a haze. I always did. The remnants of the story I had
given up swam within me, so when my eyes opened, regret flooded
my mind. What had I done? Why did I feel so terrible?

It took some time for me to collect myself, and I rolled over
to see Raúl and his bushy hair flowing over his face. He was still
asleep, and there was a line of drool over his pillow. I smiled at
that; it brought me home. It reminded me of where I was.

I rose and set about my morning chores—change the waste pot if
it was my day, get la estufa running for Mamá, feed las cabras—while
I continued to separate myself from the residual story. Mamá woke
up in the middle of this, then kissed me on the cheek as she set to
making some tea for herself. She loved this specific mixture of nettles
and rosemary, and the scent of it filled the whole house in minutes.

But I enjoyed our quiet company. She watched me rush around
to get things done. "You hunting agua today?" she asked, stirring
the pot of water. "We're getting pretty low."

"Later," I said. "Have to stop by Lito's first, see if there are any
mensajes for us."

"You spend a lot of time there," she said.

"Lito is my friend," I said, slipping on my leather huaraches near
the door.

"Don't you have any friends your age, mija?"

I stared at her, delivering my accusation silently before saying it aloud. "Like who?"

"Well, what about Ana?"

As soon as the name left her mouth, I watched the realization hit her. She wrinkled up her face. "Lo siento, Xochitl. I forgot."

"Do you need anything else, Mamá?" I asked, hoping to change the subject.

"No. Hurry back, though. I think Raúl wanted to go with you to find agua."

"I know," I said.

"Did you have a good time at the gathering last night?" she said, and I resisted the urge to groan at her. *This again*, I thought.

"Estuvo bien. Food was good."

"Do you remember what you ate?"

It's true that I was often disoriented after giving back a story, but everyone seemed to believe that I lost entire *days'* worth of time, and they always spoke to me as if I were a forgetful child.

"Estoy bien, Mamá," I said. "Promise."

She turned back to the tea brewing on la estufa. "Well, you know how you get."

I didn't want to hate her. It was difficult in those moments to control the rage that surged in me. So I let out a deep breath before saying, "I'll be right back!"

I looked to her before I left, but she was occupied with her tea. Probably on purpose. How could she forget that my friends were all gone? That there wasn't anyone *but* Lito left for me? How could she assume I was so forgetful when she couldn't remember this one thing about me?

I pushed the burlap cloth aside and stepped out as the frustration brimmed in me. It wasn't that I thought my parents didn't care about me. But I couldn't bring myself to tell them how I really felt. Would they think I was ungrateful? Selfish?

I just wanted more. Was that so bad?

I shook off the exhaustion creeping around my eyes and head, knowing I should have slept off the ritual longer. My body ached, and if I didn't get more sleep, it would be terribly sore the next morning. I raised my hands above my head and stretched, and a grunt echoed to my right.

Rogelio's home was only twenty or thirty paces from ours, and I watched him as another snore ripped through the silent morning. His head had dropped down; his chin touched his chest. An empty bottle of tesgüino was tipped over at his side.

I may not have remembered exactly what his story was, but everyone knew he was un borracho. He was probably *still* drunk, even after I'd taken his story. He absolved himself through me, then went right back to it. What was I supposed to do? I only guided secrets out of people; I did not guide them to be a better person. Still, someone should get him indoors before the sun baked him.

I kept walking, the guilt needling into me. I silently resolved to help Rogelio if he was still outside when I came back. I couldn't ignore a clear duty when it presented itself to me. It was an unstoppable instinct in me, to do right by others, even if I didn't want to. And I *definitely* didn't want his smelly breath or his sweaty hands on me again.

María's vacas snorted at me as I passed them. They sat behind a shaky wooden fence whose posts teetered at various angles, as if they were as drunk as Rogelio. I expected to see María tending to them, as the sun had been up for over an hour at that point, gradually baking the world around us. But she was nowhere in sight, so I pushed on toward Manolito's.

My huaraches slapped against the dirt, kicking up dust as I walked, my heart a drum, beat after beat. Not from the activity, but from the anticipation. I came upon the well in the center of Empalme. It was a stone structure, small but dependable.

I gazed at the men gathered there, trading chisme, their long knives resting on their shoulders or against the well. No Julio. They glanced at me but otherwise did not acknowledge that I existed.

I was relieved. This was the best part of my day, and I didn't want them to ruin it. What would Manolito have for me today? What story would he give me?

I passed la señora Sánchez, who was on her way for her daily allotment of water, and I greeted her, too, but we kept the interaction muted and brief. I picked up the pace after that, distracting myself with thoughts about los mensajeros that Manolito employed, who took packages and letters across the punishing desert up to Obregán, sometimes south to las aldeas that rested against las montañas down there. And what was beyond that? I didn't know. But those mensajeros brought with them stories. Not the kind that I took from willing bodies, but those of their travels. Of what Obregán looked like. Of Solado, days and days to the north, so far away that few people ever had stories of that place. We were an isolated aldea, our ancestors few, and Empalme lay between two brutal ranges of montañas. I hoped that Manolito had some chisme he could pass along to me, anything that would make my world seem bigger. He was my only source. Los mensajeros did not *live* in Empalme; they only visited. So few of us had roots here in this aldea. We had a saying: If you left Empalme, you did not come back. As I sped toward Lito's, I wondered if anyone else craved escape as much as I did.

Manolito's mercadito rose above the group of homes built of clay and stone that stood around it, and it was still one of the biggest structures in our aldea. Most of Empalme was constructed of hardened mud, mixed by hand and then left to dry in the baking heat. But Manolito had connections. He *knew* people, people from cities like Obregán or Hermosillo, real places with mercados that were ten times the size of his own, that overflowed with food and wares from all over. His door was lined with some shiny stone he'd been given, but the rest was made mostly of wood from un árbol that grew only in the desert north of Obregán: whitethorn.

I stepped up to el mercadito and raised a hand to knock on it, but Manolito must have anticipated me. The door swung open away from me, and I stood there, awkward, my hand raised in the air. He laughed at me, the sound rushing out of him, his dark mustache drooping at the corners. "Xochitl, buenos días. What are you *doing*?"

I frowned at him, then shook my head. "You're up early," I said, pushing past him into the darkness of el mercadito.

As my eyes adjusted, he gave my shoulder a squeeze, then shut the door behind us. "Los mensajeros," he said. "They just left."

I raised my eyebrows at him. I was shameless, Solís. "Dame el chisme, Lito. I want to know it all."

He chuckled at that, and I shuffled farther in. Ramona sold most of the food in Empalme; everything else fell on Manolito, who stocked anything a person might need. There was a stack of candles, in various colors and shapes, that sat alongside leather water bags. There were books, used and new, that Lito lent out to me if they'd not sold in a while, and I hoped he had something I had not read this time. Clothing, tools for hunting water, tools for hunting for food, building supplies, various pots and pans, rope— there was no real method to the way these things were organized. Despite that, Manolito knew where everything was.

I ran a finger over one of the shelves, and it came away coated in dust. "You need someone," I said to Manolito. "Someone to get you to clean this place more than anything else."

He grunted and walked slowly past me, toward the back of el mercadito, his shoulders hunched forward, his gait lazy. "There you go again, amiga," he said, and he headed for the counter stacked high with mensajes. "Always thinking I need a woman."

"This dust says it all," I shot back. "*You're* certainly not cleaning it."

He looked back at me. "And if I fell in love with someone, they'd get me to tidy up the place? Or they would do it *for* me? Is that your reasoning?"

I flashed him a teasing smile. "Are you saying you *wouldn't* like some company?"

He grunted and pulled the pile of mensajes—folded papers, stiff envelopes—into his arms and began to sort through it, quietly reading the names off the front. He handed me one for Mamá from her friend Xiomara, then asked me to drop off one for la señora Sánchez on my way home. When he put them down and gazed back at me, he groaned.

"I see that look on your face, Xo," he said, wagging a finger in my direction. "I know what you want."

"Tell me a story, Lito. Something new. Something I've not heard before."

He smiled then, a tender expression. He grabbed a wooden stool from beside the counter and patted the top of it, urging me to sit down. I obliged, and I looked up at him with hope. We did the same song and dance every time, and maybe the details were different, but this was our thing. *Ours.*

Did Manolito ever know what he meant to me? What he gave me?

"I *did* hear something interesting this morning," he began, and he would always stroke his mustache, pulling at the ends. "One of my mensajeros—Paolo, you remember him?"

"Tall, super skinny, looks like he could be a cactus?" I stood upright and still, my arms branched upward on either side of my head.

Manolito cackled. "I hate when you do that," he said, "but you're not wrong. Sí, him." He took a long swill from a canteen on his counter, then wiped at his mustache. "I don't know how true his stories are, but he says that miles from Obregán, deep in the desert, he discovered a land that makes your thoughts real."

"Real? You mean like how Solís does?"

He shook his head, and a flash of worry flitted across his face. *What is that about?* I thought, but Lito continued. "No, not like that. He said there is an expanse, a flat land that shines bright as the sun, where everything in your heart spills forth into the sand."

I chuckled. "Did he say it that dramatically?"

"Maybe I embellished a bit," he replied, smirking. "But I've heard stories for years about all the strange things out there. Like las bestias that rule the desert at night. Maybe there's some truth to it all."

"You ever want to leave?"

He gazed at me, Solís, and the panic slipped back onto his face, a brief glimpse of something more, and he recovered again. "Maybe," he said. "I like it here in Empalme. Could do without Julio and his gang, but I prefer standing out in a place like this than being drowned in Obregán. Too many people."

He observed me, his warm, dark eyes tracing the lines of my expression, and he grimaced. "I know you want to go, Xo. It's clear as Solís is true. And one day, you'll get out of here, and you'll change the world."

"But why not now?" I said. "Why am I always too young to see more? To experience more?"

"You're the eldest, Xo. Maybe your parents don't want to let you go yet."

I sighed and grabbed los mensajes for la señora Sánchez and Mamá. "Gracias, Lito. For listening."

I made to leave and he cleared his throat. I watched him shift his weight to his other leg, his eyes downcast. I knew immediately what he wanted; I'd seen too many people treat me the same way. So I didn't force him to say it.

"Today?" I asked.

He nodded.

"Is there any chance it can wait until tomorrow? I just listened to Rogelio yesterday, and I'm exhausted."

"It hurts, Xo," he said. "I can feel it. It's close to breaking free, and . . . I'm worried."

I stepped toward him. "About what?"

"What pesadilla Solís will show me."

His shoulders were pulled in as if something were dragging them down toward the ground. And there, in the shadows of el mercadito, it hid. Behind a shelf. It was hunched over, shy and nervous, but it was there.

Its eyes opened. They were bright red.

"Can it wait until tonight?" I asked, staring at it. "We're almost out of agua, and Raúl wants to go with me."

Lito still wasn't looking at me. "Por supuesto," he said, his voice soft and afraid. "Gracias, Xo. I know this can't be easy, but we appreciate what you do for us."

Maybe that was the reason I liked Lito so much. He was one of the only people to say things like that to me and mean it.

"Gracias, Lito. ¿Hasta luego?"

"Until then," he said. He raised his hand in farewell, and then he finally looked at me again.

He was terrified.

Something pulled me out of el mercadito. I knew what it was, and I scurried beyond the door, out into the heat, and to the place that would make me feel safe again.

The land spoke to me, called me forth, and even though I did not have a story to return to it just yet, it seemed to know that I needed the solitude after my interaction with Manolito.

I headed to the east first, toward a patch of mesquite that smelled rich and vibrant in the middle of the day. The sun bore down on me in an oppressive heat, but I was resilient. Alive. I stuck a hand into the waistband of my breeches, felt the edges of the brown leather pouch tucked there, and a thrill rushed up my arm.

I needed them. Again.

I had been doing this more and more lately. I would tell my parents that I needed to take a story, to return one to the earth, and I would be gone for hours at a time. They claimed to understand me, but they understood only the need for the ritual. They didn't get how much I needed to be away from home; away from all the responsibilities and the sad, needy faces; away from feeling stuck in a life I never chose.

So I would walk. Usually, I didn't pick a direction, but I needed shade right then; the sun was still searing the exposed skin on my arms and my face. I kept my breathing even, wiped sweat off my forehead, took my steps carefully so as not to trip on the uneven ground. Without water, I couldn't last long outdoors. This was the closest spot, and it was where I'd found the first of the two poemas, the words etched onto paper with coal.

I had been hunting for water weeks earlier, and I thought that You were guiding me to a new source. I rarely went to the east, but as I walked in that direction, it was as if something had looped twine around my heart and kept tugging me. *Closer, closer*, it said, and I obeyed. I always obeyed, always did what I was told. I was the dutiful daughter, wasn't I? The one who honored her parents, the one who kept herself available to all in case las pesadillas were close.

But this was different. I was good at hunting water, at picking up the signs Papá had taught me, but the earth shouted at me, guided me farther east, until I was in the shade of a thick patch of mesquites. The sensation was so similar to my ritual as a cuentista, and I let the power take me to the dirt, and I dug down until my fingers hit leather. The force ripped through my body, knocking me back, and the ground bit into my elbows. But the pain was nothing compared with that spark, that rush. My heart raced as I pushed myself forward, and I tenderly reached out, ran the tips of my fingers over the little pouch again, and my whole body shook.

I unearthed it.

I consumed it.

That first time I read la poema, I couldn't make sense of the words. They were too real, too close, and I dropped the scrap of paper back to the earth, stood up, and walked away from it. But it sang to me, called me back, and I returned, devoured it over and over.

I found another the next week, just to the north of Empalme, buried next to a saguaro that was missing an arm. Aside from Manolito's stories, they were all I had of the world outside Empalme, the only glimpse of a life that wasn't constrained and controlled.

And so I visited the place I found the first one as often as possible.

The earthy scent of mesquite rose up to me, and I lowered myself to the ground in the shadows of los árboles. I pulled the pouch from my waistband and removed one of las poemas. I delicately placed it on the ground. The corners were wrinkled and folded from being stuffed under my bedroll, tucked into the band of my breeches or under the loose stone in the floor of our dwelling, and the coal ink had smeared near the bottom. But it was still there, each letter ending abruptly, as if the person who had written this was in a rush.

I placed two small stones on either side of the paper, weighted it down so it would not blow away, and I traced the letters, my fingers just barely above it, and I read it again. And again. And again.

cuando estoy solo	when I am alone
existo para mí	I exist for myself
cada paso	each step
para mí	for me
cada aliento	each breath
para mí	for me
cada latido de mi corazón	each beat of my heart
para mí	for me
cuando estoy solo	when I am alone
estoy vivo	I am alive

They called out to me, each of the words a sharp and piercing glimpse into myself. How had they done this? How had they known what I felt out here, all alone? I read it again, allowed it to fill me up, to know me, to *see* me.

There were prickles on the back of my neck, a dull ache settling in behind my eyes. I lost track of the time, but my body was reminding me that I could not be outside for much longer. Night would fall soon, and I had duties around the house before the meal began and You disappeared. I folded the paper gently, returned it to its hiding place, and then got to my feet, the sweat pouring down my back.

Doro was long gone; Ana y Quique had departed recently, too. All my friends, except Manolito, had left me behind. I hadn't felt this alone in a long time. But as I made the journey back home, back to my family, I was alive in that solitude. I was full, satiated by the knowledge that someone out in the world understood me.

It never lasted long enough.

I made it back home right as the sun was in the middle of the sky. Your warmth, Solís, spread over the land, filling in los valles, shadows stretching long and deep. I stopped by the home of la señora Sanchez first to drop off el mensaje; she gave me some dried manzanas she had made as a thanks. I was chewing on one of them as I approached our home.

Rogelio was thankfully nowhere in sight.

Raúl greeted me on the other side of the burlap curtain, nearly crashing into me before running off again. "I'm almost ready!" he cried out. "I just need my hat."

Papá was standing near la estufa, using his hands to ball up some leftover arroz from the night before. "Anything for us?"

I handed him el mensaje from Mamá's friend, and he examined it briefly before setting it aside. "Some of los viajeros from the south are scheduled to get in tonight," he said. "Your mother is out back already."

A pang of disappointment struck. I knew I'd be too exhausted after Lito to join Mamá, but los viajeros were a spectacle. They journeyed all over the endless desert, making camp in various aldeas y pueblos, bringing with them items they'd collected from other places, food that we had not tried before, and . . .

Stories. They brought stories. So many of them, more colorful and strange than anything Paolo or the other mensajeros had. Maybe I could do both. Maybe I could take Lito's story, visit Mamá, and *then* perform the ritual. . . .

It felt like too much. So when Raúl came back, his wide-brim straw sombrero sitting atop his head, I tried to focus instead on our hunt, to keep my mind off the anxiety pulsing in my veins.

"You two be safe," Papá said, kissing us each on top of our heads.

"We will," I said. "Be back in a couple of hours."

He blew me another kiss, and I stuck my cheek out, pretending to catch it there. Raúl tugged me out the door, though, his excitement overflowing. He then grabbed the two buckets and the water-hunting tools set out for us. "Come *on*, Xochitl!" he called out, dragging me by the hand.

After Julio and his men took over the well and started charging la comunidad to withdraw water, some of us devised our own means of surviving. It was extra work, but it also meant that sometimes our family could go days without seeing Julio.

Raúl and I settled into our walk after I glanced briefly at the stone pit and waved at Mamá as she pulled warm tortillas off the grill. I fought to keep up with Raúl, who was not nearly so tired as I was.

I shrugged it off. We fell silent, and the heat filled the desert. There were others in Empalme who swore that the sun rose without a sound, but I still think they are wrong. The sound of sunlight is the gentle scurrying of lizards and mice, desperate to find shade and comfort. It's the earth, groaning and creaking as it wakes up, as the moisture within it is pulled away, cracking and breaking the soil. It is the scratching echo of our feet pressing into the sand and dirt, of sweat dripping off us into the dust.

I fought the urge that came suddenly upon my body. I wanted to start running, toward las montañas to the north, to find las bestias. The mysteries. The land of thoughts come to life. My body was full of desire and longing, Solís. What was I supposed to do? Continue ignoring it? Every time I ventured into the desert to return a story, to hunt water, or for food, it haunted me. *Every. Time.*

I switched the bucket I held from one hand to the other, then made the sign—see the truth; believe the truth—hoping it would calm down my thoughts. Raúl's hand flung out and stopped me and—

There. On the arms of a tall, green saguaro sat una paloma, gray and delicate. It pecked at the rough hide, and we held our breath, now as motionless as the towering cactus, and then we saw la paloma lift into the air, its wings beating, and dart off to the north.

Raúl and I exchanged a quick glance, and a smile curled up on his lips.

We followed.

Papá had taught us that life in the desert was a sign of water. Other creatures couldn't live without it any more than we could. Normally, Papá and I braved the heat to find underground sources. There used to be a well to the east of Empalme, but bandits had ransacked it and destroyed it a couple of years ago. But I had gotten so good at picking up the signs of hidden agua that I usually did it alone these days.

I was grateful to have Raúl at my side that morning, though. We sprinted toward a patch of mesquites, and I was already panting and dripping sweat by the time we reached it and saw the colorful branches. There was no sign of la paloma anymore; it was much quicker than we were. But the smell leapt to my nose, and I knew that these árboles were *alive*, thriving in Your heat. There *had* to be water somewhere here, and I let go of my caution. I dropped to my knees at the foot of the nearest árbol and pulled out la pala that Papá had given me long ago. It was made from a thick branch of paloverde and a sheet of iron that had blown off someone's roof one night. I plunged la pala into the ground, the dry earth fighting me every time it dug deeper and deeper. Soon, I could see moisture seeping around the sides of the hole I had made.

Raúl slumped to the ground under the flimsy shade of the mesquite. "That was quicker than usual," he said, still out of breath. "You want to do the first bit?"

I nodded at him. "Rest," I said.

And then I got to work.

I got another foot down in the hole before there was a sizable pool of water at the bottom. I stuck my hand out and Raúl passed over the cloth used for extracting water. I dropped it into the puddle and let it soak up some of the water, then squeezed it out into the bucket. I repeated it: Drop. Soak. Squeeze. Drop. Soak. Squeeze.

"I'm going to Ramona's again today," Raúl said after a long silence.

I squeezed more water out into the bucket. "What for?"

"See if Renato is around. Or if Ramona needs any help."

Drop. Soak. Squeeze.

"Just stay away from Julio and his men," I said.

He dismissed me with a wave. "He's not going to pick on me. He doesn't even know I *exist*."

"Well, make sure you don't announce your presence to him, ¿entiendes?"

He didn't say anything else, and my stomach grumbled in the growing heat. I kept at it, trying to focus on the task, but my thoughts wandered quickly. What if I just stood up and left? What if I floated away, like una paloma, to be free? Would that be possible for someone like me? Or would I have to take stories every day for the remainder of my life? The thought pressed down on me, pushed me into the dirt, and it was harder to lift my arms, to wrench the water from the cloth, to accept that my whole life was written out for me.

"Want me to take over?"

I sat back, sweat pouring down my head, dripping into the dirt. I'd been working so hard I hadn't even noticed that the bucket was nearly full. "Please," I said, handing him the cloth.

He lifted his eyebrows, wrinkling his forehead, but didn't say what was on his mind. He grabbed the cloth from me, then scooted over to the hole I'd dug. But before he started, he looked back to me. "¿Te sientes bien? You seem a little . . ."

He didn't finish. He dug deeper and went silent. Drop. Squeeze. Soak. Was I that obvious? I took pride in being able to hide so much of myself from the others. Aside from Manolito, no one really knew about my desires. And *no one* knew about las poemas.

"I'm just tired," I said, which wasn't a lie, not after taking Rogelio's story the night before.

Raúl smiled back, and then he began to work on filling the second bucket. While he did so, my mind took flight. I thought of las poemas, letting hope spring in me. I knew them both by heart, and the second one floated up from my memory, poured into my body, filling me with its power:

Este mundo de cenizas	This world of ashes
no puede contenerme	cannot contain me
No hay paredes	There are no walls
para detenerme	to stop me
Soy libre.	I am free.

By the time Raúl finished and the two of us began to haul those buckets back to filter the water, I was aching with desire for las poemas to be in my hand again. I knew I'd have to wait until no one was looking to get at them, but it was like a terrible itch spreading over my skin. I *had* to see them.

Raúl was talkative on the walk back, but I responded only occasionally, mostly to let him think I was paying attention. I wasn't. I kept repeating the phrase in my head:

Soy libre. Soy libre. Soy libre.

I wanted it more than anything. To be free of these responsibilities and rules and expectations. I wanted my *own* life.

Mamá was trading chisme with Papá as he worked to prepare el almuerzo for us. She took the buckets and said that she was proud of how much water we'd gotten, that she'd filter out the dirt and the rocks in a few hours. She had too much to do before los viajeros arrived. She kissed me on the forehead. Told me she loved me. Papá blew another kiss my direction.

I loved them back. I really did. And yet, as I sat down on my sleeping roll, stretching out my legs and my arms, my fingers grazed over to the loose stone. I ran my fingers over the edge of it. Wiggled it a bit in its spot. No one was looking, so I quickly removed the stone, stuffed the little pouch in there, and then covered it again.

I lay back, exhaustion taking over me. I had to rest before I saw Lito that night. I needed to recuperate.

I needed to feel less isolated.

And I needed to know who wrote las poemas.

But I was all alone there in Empalme, with no hope of ever escaping it. I closed my eyes, and I could not wait for You to sink out of the sky, for las estrellas to return.

I saw Julio again that evening before I arrived at Manolito's. I'd passed the home of la señora Sanchez, and the sun was a sliver on the horizon, glinting off the metal of her roof. I wasn't paying attention, and then he just *loomed* there, seated atop an enormous brown horse.

He was lanky and tall enough as it was, but as he glared down at me, his patchy facial hair a shadow on his face, he was a giant. Unfathomable. Impossible. I had seen few horses in my life—they were too challenging to own and care for in a world so harsh—and so it made him look even *bigger*.

Yet here he was. It had been only a month since he and his men arrived in Empalme, but he filled the space left behind by all those who had traveled to the north or to the south for work or for a better life. There simply weren't enough of us willing to make him leave anymore, not when he and his men carried such sharp sabers and knives.

I stilled when I saw him. He paused, only briefly, casting a wicked glance at me, up and down, and then I noticed her—

Emilia.

She sat behind him, and her glare was somehow more stern than his. She had the same long, flowing black hair as him, the same sharp, angular features. Her brows furrowed as she looked at me with an expression that said it all: She was above us. She would not dare to lower herself to our level.

I did my best not to react, even though I found I could not tear my eyes away from her.

But they were gone, just as quickly as they had ridden into view. All I heard was the gentle plodding hooves of the horse, and I waited until they faded away before I continued on. Neither of them looked back at me. Was I unworthy of their attention? I was relieved to be able to get to Manolito's unbothered. I was still tired from the previous night, and the thought of giving back another story weighed my body down.

But this was what I was supposed to do. I couldn't refuse it any more than I could refuse to breathe or drink water.

El mercadito was different as night began to fall. It was not nearly as welcoming; it rested in the shadows of the buildings around it. I pushed open the door and was greeted by the sounds of a loud negotiation. Ofelia had her hands placed firmly on her hips. Manolito looked up at me, then sighed before focusing on Ofelia. "There's nothing I can do," he said. "It's not under my control anymore."

Ofelia's shame spilled forth when her eyes locked with mine. It was obvious that I should not have heard this conversation. "I'll be back, Manolito," she said. "They can't do this to me."

She turned up her pointed nose at me as she passed by, but I could see the worry lines near her eyes, on her forehead. It was a mask, an attempt to make herself seem strong and powerful to me, but her eyes betrayed her.

Manolito sighed again as the door slammed shut. "Sorry, Xo," he said. "It's a difficult time for a lot of people."

I stepped forward to his counter and extended my hand when he let the words perish. "For you, too, ¿no?"

We'd done this many times before, and yet Manolito always got so bashful before he gave me a story. He knew I wouldn't remember it the next day, but that didn't seem to matter to him. He'd refuse to make eye contact, would treat me as though I'd already judged him as inferior. He briefly grasped my hand, then let go of it and rushed past me. "Let me lock the door," he said, and he dropped a thick wooden post across the doorframe to keep the door from swinging inward. The darkness settled amid the dust and silence as he stood there, his back to me.

"Xochitl," he said, unmoving. "Please don't judge me."

I watched him. His shoulders heaved upward as he breathed. "You know I can't," I said. "That's not what I do. I judge no one." I moved away from the counter, toward Manolito. "You tell me your story, and I give it back to Solís. We are all cleansed by Them if we see the truth, believe the truth."

His eyes were red and raw. "You can't tell anyone."

An anger hit my chest, branched outward and down my body. "I never do, Lito," I said. "I *can't*, even if I wanted to. So please, don't say that again."

He closed his eyes and shook his head. "Lo siento, Xo." His eyes flicked open, still bloodshot. "I'm afraid."

I reached out to him again, and this time, he took my hands as he was supposed to, so I could become the conduit he needed. "Please, talk to me, Manolito. Tell me your story. I will forget it, as I always do, and you can change. Be better. Make Solís *proud*."

Another deep breath from Manolito. Another jolt of fear, and this time, I could feel it as it passed down his arms and into me. It was the sign I needed, the one that told me that the connection had been made.

It was time.

Let me tell You a story, Solís.

Manolito was born back when Empalme was even smaller, still growing, and still desperately clinging to life in an arid nothingness. Only a few generations had survived La Quema, and Manolito was now the fourth born of his lineage since You took away our world.

This was before Julio, before his men arrived from some aldea in the north, and long before we had to pay someone else to access our own water.

Yet Manolito had never seen anything like Julio's ominous appearance. The man had ridden into Empalme the week before with a party of nearly ten men and Emilia. They took up a spot on the south side of la aldea, out where the homes were sparse. Manolito kept track of them as best as he could, but they were barely seen that first week. Sometimes he would catch them inspecting parts of la aldea—particularly the well—but they otherwise kept to themselves. They never came out at night to celebrate surviving another day, to surround themselves with the light of las estrellas or to bask in the sound of los aldeanos laughing.

And then one day, as Manolito was walking away from the well with a bucket full of water, they descended.

They moved in as though it had been coordinated. Poor Ofelia, who happened to have arrived moments before to retrieve agua for herself. Julio placed his saber at Ofelia's throat. "This well is ours now," he said, "and I will not hesitate to spill blood over it."

Manolito almost believed it was a joke until he saw blood dripping from the saber, watched the dry earth drink it down. Where was the blood from? Whom had he killed?

Julio's men swept into la aldea and claimed every empty home, left behind by those who had set out, looking for work and new adventures in Hermosillo or Obregán. After that day, two of the strangers were permanently camped near the well, and they demanded payment: Food. Drink. The coins used in El Mercado de Obregán. Anything we had that we could spare. It seemed unreal, impossible.

Until la señora Sánchez tried to take her weekly portion of water.

And Julio lifted his saber into the air and severed her arm below the shoulder.

We knew he was serious then, and a terrible pall settled over Empalme. Some of us found ways to avoid him by hunting water on our own. But Manolito found that Julio increasingly relied on him, not only for supplies but for information, too. He had Lito's mensajeros running errands for him, traveling to Obregán for tasks that were kept a secret from Lito. It became clear that Julio was not a temporary problem. He was planning on *staying* in Empalme.

Manolito did not know whom to tell or how to prove it. It was an instinct, a feeling deep down that Julio was digging in for the long haul. How could he stop it? How could he save Empalme from a man who demanded so much?

The package came a couple of weeks ago. Paolo had left it behind and said that it was important that Lito deliver it as soon as possible, that there would be a second shipment coming that would require this first one. Manolito did not understand what that meant, but he accepted the task. He knew that it was better to find Julio in the mornings, when the drink was wearing off. The first time they spoke after Julio had harmed la señora Sánchez, Julio became furious that Lito had not sought him out. He had run his long saber over Lito's knuckles, asking him which finger he'd like to lose the next time.

So he resolved to deliver the wooden crate the next morning. Easy enough. It wasn't terribly heavy, so Lito left it alone. He stuffed it on the shelf under the counter, and then a day passed.

Two.

A week.

Two weeks.

He knocked it off the shelf yesterday morning, and it tumbled to the ground, tearing open as it did so, and they spilled all over the floor: tiny glass vials that shimmered in the low light. Manolito panicked. He wasn't supposed to read any of los mensajes; he never opened anyone's packages. But it was so tempting, Solís. Manolito had never seen anything like this before, and curiosity burned in his mind. What were these for? Why did Julio need them?

He left el mercadito that night and headed straight for the one person who would know more about this than anyone else: Marisol, la Reina del Chisme, as she was known in Empalme. Manolito dashed to her home, descended down steps carved into the earth, but she turned him away almost immediately. "I do not cross Julio," she said, setting aside her stitching. "No matter what you are paying."

"But I just wanted to show you—"

"No digas ni una palabra más," she said. "I don't even want to know."

"I'll do anything," he begged. "I can—"

She pointed to the door.

He returned to el mercadito, returned the box to the counter, and was no closer to understanding what was going to happen in Empalme. He picked up the vials that had rolled over the floor. It was just *there*, sticking out of the box, and Manolito picked it up, unfolded it, and began to read el mensaje addressed to Julio.

He shouldn't have read it, Solís.

He folded it back up, stuffed it in the crate, and tried to reassemble the container as best as he could. It was hopeless, too broken ever to reconstruct. He hoisted it up off the counter, walked it out of el mercadito, and marched straight out into the desert. He didn't stop until he was sure he wouldn't be seen. Then he set a single lit match to an edge of the wood, then another, then another, and it caught fire, a thick smoke rising into air, and he panicked. He would be seen. He would be *caught*. So Lito rushed back home, to the tiny room underneath el mercadito, and he waited.

And waited.

And waited.

Manolito begs for Your forgiveness, and he hopes that his truth absolves us of Your wrath. He was weak, he knows it, and he will never betray You again.

He shouldn't have read it.

But he did.

And he can't do anything about it.

The letter was wrinkled around the edges, the script hasty and messy, as if someone had written it under duress. They wrote to Julio of their success, of the delivery they were taking south, under the light of las estrellas, away from the gaze of You. They were determined to avoid suspicion, and they would be in Empalme in a few days.

Then, the person wrote, the bloodletting would begin.

La aldea would be controlled.

And the letter writer had included one last touch of devotion in the end.

The final line read, "My beloved cuentista, Julio, I long to make you proud. You will not be disappointed."

They were coming for us.

"Lo siento," Lito rasped, and sweat dripped down his temples. "You cannot tell anyone."

I couldn't breathe. I couldn't think straight. Lito's terror thrust into every open space of my body, and panic rolled behind it. These emotions rushed through my body and nearly overwhelmed me. I held back a scream, pushed the story down.

I heard something rustling behind me. My head spun around, and Lito's pesadilla was there. It closed those bright red eyes, and then it shrank before me, until it was nothing but the shadow behind a shelf.

The vials.

They were gone, just like Lito's pesadilla.

But something is coming for us.

I turned back to Lito, and his shoulders were pushed back, his head held up higher, and relief radiated from his body.

He had given his burden to me.

He was free.

Soy libre, I thought.

"You have to give it up soon," he urged me, wiping at his damp forehead. "No one can know. I'll try to stop him, but . . . but I don't know what to do. And I'm afraid he'll find out."

I clutched at my chest, Lito's terror and my own becoming one.

No. *No.* What did this mean? Why did Julio want our blood? What was he going to *do* to us?

I wanted to ask Lito more, to tell me what else he knew, but he helped me up and was gently guiding me to the door.

He was free.

I couldn't get the words out. I couldn't say anything. His fear was overwhelming, and if I didn't get it out of me . . . I didn't know what would happen. Would it overpower me? Would I become unable to do anything but give in to the fright? Would I fail Empalme, too, like Lito already had?

This was my burden. My duty. I would give up this story . . . and then I would forget. I would forget *our own destruction.*

"Gracias, Xochitl," Lito said, and when our eyes locked, I saw pity in his own. "I know this can't be easy, but I feel so much better." He smiled. "I don't know what we would do without you."

The door closed in my face. The fear ate at me.

I walked out into the desert. I didn't know what else to do.

When You leave our world, there is a sound to the sunset, too, and I dropped down to the earth as You dropped behind the horizon to the west. I had not journeyed far out into the desert, as I usually did to complete the ritual.

I became still as I remained hunched over there, and that's when the desert woke up. Las lagartijas, las serpientes, los ratones, los conejos: all of them emerge from their hiding spots, and the ground comes alive with their footsteps, with each rustle of feathers or fur. A rattlesnake slithered from behind a saguaro to my left, regarded me, and did not perceive me as a threat. I was motionless. I became a part of the ground, of the sky, of everything around me.

I could feel Manolito's story within me, swirling deep in my gut, and his fear flowed up into my throat, a flood of emotions that were not mine, but which I still recognized.

There are no emotions I do not empathize with anymore. For a cuentista, there is nothing new under You, Solís. Empalme has been giving me stories since I was a child, and then I return those stories to the desert, to You.

I have felt it all:

Regret. Anger. Distress. Sadness. Hatred. Envy. Disappointment.

I may forget the details, but I know that those in Empalme have felt every emotion imaginable. I knew what mi gente suffered with in their lives. At least, I *thought* I did.

Except—Julio and his men.

They had been a mystery to me, and not only because I did not know where they had come from. Probably from another aldea, some other place they stole from and exploited. They had refused our rituals and our guidance, and they didn't care if we were worried that You would return and scorch it all out of existence again. We were superstitious and silly to them, and that's why Julio had said we deserved to be conquered. "You are all like this," he slurred to Papá one morning during that first week he arrived; it was also the last day that we relied on our weekly portion from the well. "The last aldea I controlled, they were just as weak as you. Waiting for Solís to save them." He brushed his hand across the face of mi papá. "Their god didn't show when I slaughtered them all."

Was he telling the truth? Why did he choose us? Was this a test, Solís? Did You want to see what we would do?

I thought of that as I let You pull me down, down. And then I knew I was ready.

I slowly leaned forward, close to the ground, felt the dirt and stones tear into my palms and knees. I pressed myself closer to the earth, hunched over, and Manolito's story was ready to leave.

It churned within me, and then it poured out of my mouth, into the nooks of the desert, deep into the dirt, and it was filthy, thick, bitter. I coughed as it exited me, and I lost the weight of it. I rolled back, wiping at the acidity as I panted, and stared up at those estrellas far in the distance, their brightness twinkling at me.

Manolito's story was gone, sent back to You, and I shook.

I trembled there on the desert floor, exhausted by the experience.

————

Except that didn't happen.

I remained hunched over the ground, the story churning in me, climbing up my throat, but . . . The vials. I couldn't believe it. What did they mean? What was the second shipment? *What is coming to Empalme?*

I had intended to give his story to You, to give up the burden and Lito's fear and my own knowledge of it all.

I leaned down closer until my mouth was nearly touching the dirt. I let the story move again, and a burning sensation crept up my throat and—

It slid back down.

Nausea swelled up from my stomach and threatened to spill everything out, but I stopped the story from rising again. It fought me, barbs of fear jutting out into my body, and the sharpness of it caused me to cry out, but I couldn't. I couldn't give this up.

The vials.

The second shipment.

And then the last thing.

A word—a title—a hope that seemed impossible. That should have *been* impossible.

Maybe it was selfish. Maybe I should have ignored it.

But Julio is a cuentista. How? *How?* And he had *left* his aldea? How was that even possible?

I knew my decision was wrong, but it was still mine. So I rose from the ground and felt the story drop lower in me. Manolito's emotions churned. An anxiety threaded my ribs, stitched terror to my insides, but I couldn't give his story back to You.

I kept it. I'm sorry, Solís. But I had to—You'll see.

But as I stumbled away from the desert, my bearings a horrific mess, I already knew I had to start lying.

Immediately.

Omar was leaving the well, and I tried to rush past it, hoping that he wouldn't see me, but he called out my name. *Twice.* He jogged toward me. "Lo siento por molestarte," he said, "but I was hoping you could help me."

"Sure," I slurred, and I tried to avoid making eye contact.

"Are you okay?"

I looked up at him, at his short-cropped hair and high cheekbones, at the concern etched into his face. The thought popped into my head in an instant.

He knows.

I choked back a cry, then covered my mouth. "Sorry," I blurted, and the lie rolled out so easily that it unnerved me. It was as sudden and natural as the paranoia swirling inside. "I just finished . . . just did the . . ."

"Oh, Xochitl," he said, his hands up, palms out. "I had no idea. This is a bad time, I can see that now. Can I get you anything? Do you need water? Do you know where you are?"

I narrowed my own eyes at him. "In . . . I'm in Empalme?"

"Sí, you are," he said. "We all know how bad your memory can get sometimes."

My face twisted into a glare, but I recovered. "Gracias, Omar," I said. "But I will be fine."

"Do you need me to walk you home?"

I shook my head quickly. "No, no, I know where it is."

He knows.

His eyes looked over my face again, and he smiled. "I'll find you tomorrow," he said. "Get some rest, Xochitl. Y gracias por lo que haces."

Then he was gone, another shadow heading toward the nightly fire.

He knows.

I tried to push it out of my head, out of my body, but my own fear spiked in my gut. When it did, it met Manolito's own. The two twined together, and I had to crouch over, let my nausea pass.

I had now kept a story for longer than ever before.

And I was *terrified.*

I pushed myself east, toward home, and exhaustion threatened to pull my eyes shut, but I kept going, my pace brisk, but as I came upon my home, I stilled.

I couldn't go in.

They would know.

Ya lo saben.

My hand grazed the edge of the burlap cover in the doorway, and another spike of terror raced down my arm.

I had to face them.

There was an iron pot on la estufa bubbling, and Raúl was deep in conversation with Mamá. Papá stood to the side, rolling a ball of masa over and over, his muscles flexing, and he winked at me as I walked in.

"You finished?" he asked.

I walked over to him, let him kiss me on the forehead. "Sí, Papá. All done."

I rubbed at my eyes and yawned. I didn't have to fake the exhaustion. It hit me fiercely, a rolling sensation that merged with the guilt. Was that *my* guilt or Manolito's?

"Mi hija obediente," he said. "We're so proud of you."

They know.

I smiled, or at least I tried to.

What had I done? I had never heard of a cuentista keeping a story. We just didn't do it. We wouldn't dare betray the promise we made to You.

Would we? I had known only one other cuentista: Tía Inez. And she had passed on mere hours after she gave me her gift. Her *curse*. I didn't know what it was anymore.

What had I *done*?

And was Julio *really* a cuentista? How had he left his aldea without abandoning his people?

I shuffled over to my sleeping roll. Mamá said something then, but I curled up, turned away from her.

Raúl was at my side. "Do you want to eat first?" he said. "We were going to meet the others at the fire."

I shook my head. "No, hermano. I just need to sleep."

"Déjala sola," Mamá ordered. "You know she needs her rest."

They know, they know, they know.

I let the exhaustion take over my body. I did not dream. I woke up in spurts that evening and into the night: once while the others were still awake, again a few hours later when our home was dark and silent. They must have been at the fire, at the nightly celebration.

Each time I awoke, Manolito's story moved inside me, as if it were burrowing deeper, finding a better place to hide.

I fell back asleep, and I didn't awaken again until the warmth of the morning pulled me into consciousness. Raúl was snoring softly this time, and I let the sound of it—the normality of it all—convince me that everything was fine.

It was not. But my anxiety was not as bad as it had been the night before. Instead, it was a gentle pulse near my heart. I lay there, staring up at the ceiling, and I breathed slowly, in and out, waiting.

Nothing happened.

No.

Nothing *had* happened.

I pushed myself up on my elbows and looked about our home. Raúl was still asleep, and I could hear Papá snoring in the other room. Was Mamá up? Would *she* know?

I breathed slowly again.

I had done it. I had kept a story for nearly half a day and . . . I was still alive. You had not punished me. You had not scorched the earth again. We were surviving, as we had always done.

Nothing has happened.

There was a muted sense of dread deep within me, but as I kept myself busy, I was able to ignore it. I emptied our pot of waste in a hole behind our home near the old jardín and covered it up. Then I lit la estufa while the others still slept. I brewed nettle-and-rosemary tea for mi mamá, and then I made a large desayuno for myself—huevos from the chickens that María kept, leftover frijoles and tortillas with fresh green pimientos fritos Papá had grown. Sometimes they were shriveled from the heat, but they still stung my tongue with their bite.

Mamá was the first to rise, and as I gave her tea and el desayuno, she told me about los viajeros, where they had come from, and where they were headed to next. She said that they had given our nightly celebration a much-needed burst of joy. "I almost forgot Julio was even here," she admitted, sipping at her tea. As I stood there, watching her braids swing back and forth as she spoke, the mention of Julio's name brought all the panic right back.

They know they know they know she knows she knows SHE KNOWS.

I told mi mamá that I wanted to get a head start on some other chores before it got too hot out. As I finished dressing, I caught her staring at me. Her gaze lingered on me longer than I wanted.

I left quickly and hunted water again, brought back another bucketful a couple of hours later. I focused on every dig with la pala, every squeeze of water into the bucket. It was a necessary distraction.

The vials.

The shipment.

La cuentista among us.

What was I going to do with this? What *could* I do? I couldn't confront Julio by myself, not about his plans or his secrets. And I couldn't tell my family. How would they react?

Would they still love me if they found out I had defied Solís? That I might have doomed us *all*?

But the story from Manolito haunted me. I tried so hard not to think of it, but it was too easy for all his emotions to come rushing back to the surface.

So when Papá asked me to accompany him to Manolito's once I got home, I nearly broke. It was hard enough keeping this secret from those I knew and loved, even from random aldeanos. But from Lito *himself*?

I sputtered a response. Papá tilted his head to the side, and his eyebrows furrowed in concentration.

If I didn't go with him, he'd become suspicious. He already was, wasn't he?

I had to keep the lie going. *Just a little bit longer*, I told myself. Until *what*, though?

You burned me. The sun felt so specifically targeted on my skin that I started to convince myself that You were about to destroy me. When we got to el mercadito, I asked Papá if I could stay outside while he negotiated for some new tools.

"Isn't he your friend?" he asked. "Don't you want to see him?"

The lie came to me, and it was too close to the truth. "I do, but . . . I took his story last night. I think maybe he needs a little space from me."

Papá nodded while smiling. "You're so considerate, mija."

He kissed me on the top of my head.

His love had never hurt me so badly.

How was I going to keep this up? How long could I last when his words were like knives in my heart?

I was initially thankful when Ofelia came rushing up to el mercadito just after Papá went inside. It gave me a chance to think about something else. "Is he busy?" she asked, and she pushed her long hair out of her face.

"Papá is in there. They might take a while."

She examined me. "We haven't spoken in nearly a year," she stated, her eyes crinkled up. "Do you have time?"

The relief was gone. "For a story?" I said, my voice hesitant.

"Por supuesto. I have no other need to talk to you."

Well, at least she was honest. I couldn't say that for myself, though, and another bout of panic ripped through me. What would happen if I took another story? I couldn't give hers back; wouldn't Lito's follow it? The immensity of what I'd done was undeniable. I had no idea what the ramifications of this choice would be.

"Right now?" I said hesitantly.

"Do you have anything better to do?"

She had a point, and it made me dislike Ofelia even more. I didn't want to do anything for her or make my situation more complicated.

But what choice did I have? I could deny her request, and it would be only a matter of time before people became suspicious. If I accepted and then returned her story, I would lose Lito's in the process. Was I really supposed to give up what I had learned?

Perhaps. But I couldn't do that. I just *couldn't*.

I took her story, Solís. She told me the truth about her interaction with Lito the day prior. Her older sibling had cut off contact with her, believing that Ofelia had objected to their imminent marriage. Ofelia believed that she *had* to attend the wedding. She had not apologized for calling her sibling's partner ugly and unworthy of their love, but Ofelia was just being *honest*. Why couldn't they see that? So every day she went to Lito's, and every day, there was not an invitation waiting for her. "I hate them," she told me. "I hope their wedding day is ruined."

She left me to drown in her ire. As I gasped for air, I looked up, saw Ofelia roll her eyes at me. "Do you have to be so dramatic about this? You'll give the story back, and we'll all be fine."

As she walked away, I thought her shadow was a little bit longer than it had been, a little bit more alive. She disappeared behind a home to the east.

Solís, how often did mi gente do this to me? How often did they tell me their stories, only to be completely oblivious to what they had done wrong? Had people *lied* to me in their stories before? How could I even know? I always forgot them when I returned them to You.

I stood up from the ground and dusted my breeches off, and Ofelia's anger brushed up against my own. What if this wasn't the first time someone had treated me like a solution to *their* problems? How would I ever have known that when You took my memories from me each time?

Papá came out to find me panting and sweating profusely. Ofelia was gone, but he knew what had happened; he'd seen me in this state before. "Already?" he said. "I was gone only a quarter hour."

"She was quick," I said, but added nothing more. My parents knew better than to ask me about the stories, and so Papá guided me home, his hand on my back, full of love for me. But would he still love me if he knew the truth? If he knew how I really felt? If he knew what I had done?

I lied. Again. I told Papá that I needed to return Ofelia's story sooner rather than later. I wanted to visit the mesquite patch, to drown myself in those beautiful poemas, so I set out to the east.

I couldn't make it. My heart was beating too fast; sweat poured down my temples. I normally thrived in the early morning heat, but right then, I was convinced it was punishing me. I stopped and caught my breath under the shade of a paloverde, then headed home.

They bought the lie I told them, Solís. They didn't question what I had done at all.

I tried to fill myself up on carne frita and cebollitas that afternoon. But the two stories inside me had destroyed my appetite. I pushed my food around my plate, ate what I could, and then told my family that I needed to sleep more. They all understood. None of them questioned me. This was how it was after the ritual, wasn't it?

When I woke up the next morning, the guilt was gone. I lay on my roll, the sounds of the others sleeping all around me, and the warmth of the morning sun inching into the doorway.

I was still alive. Unpunished. The world had not fallen apart, had not been razed by fire.

Maybe I hadn't made a terrible mistake.

The day oozed by, slow like the sap of the aloe vera, and nothing happened.

No fire from up above.

No damnation from You.

Nothing happened.

But as Your heat swept over the earth, the threat loomed.

Something is coming.

I couldn't talk to Manolito about it. If I went to el mercadito, he would know the truth about his story. He had trusted *me*.

But would he have told me a terrible secret if I *weren't* our cuentista? Even if it had lessened his own burden?

Did *anyone* actually trust me, or did they trust the role that You gave me? It was more clear than it had ever been: Empalme sought me out because of what I offered *them*. Were any of these people friendly to me? Eager for my company when a pesadilla was *not* following them around?

I just started walking. My body seemed to drag me toward el mercadito, as if Lito were calling it home. Sweat left a sticky film over my skin. I had made a mistake. I had to give up these stories, or You would destroy us all.

But what if Julio is going to do the same?

I stumbled into the main square where the well was, adrift. Lost.

Pulled by guilt and fright and the terrible dread that, somehow, *I* was the one who had set this monstrous event into motion. I was the catalyst, the spark of fire that would consume us all.

What have I done?

But *she* was there.

Emilia.

Next to the stone well, heaving up a bucket of water, and she turned her head to me, locked eyes.

My heart jumped.

Her long hair flowed behind her, and her cold gaze was much like that of her father.

Julio . . .

The idea was tantalizing, como un sueño, como una flor. It unfolded before me.

There was one person in Empalme who did not know that I was a cuentista, but who knew that Julio *was*.

I approached Emilia, and she stilled. Her face—that angular nose, her high cheekbones, her dark brown skin—twisted in anticipation. What was she expecting of me? I thought of the other night, of how we treated her. Maybe she thought I would serve up more of the same.

I walked up to the well. Made to say something.

"The guard will be back in a second."

I raised an eyebrow. "What?"

"The guard will be back," she repeated, and her voice was plain, uninterested. "I can't let you take any water."

I shook my head, both at her and at the assumption she had made. Irritation flared; who was she to say something like *that*?

"I'm not here for water," I said, low and angry.

"Then what are you here for?"

The fear bloomed again, and I felt Lito's story, pressing up against my heart.

"Where did you come from?"

She tilted her head, as she had done the last time I saw her. "From far away. To the north."

"But *where*? Obregán?"

She set the bucket on the ground, and an urge flashed in my mind: *Take the bucket and run.*

I ignored it. Emilia was still staring at me, her brows furrowed, her nostrils flaring. Was she *angry* with me? For what?

"No," she said. "Farther."

How far? I wondered. What else was beyond Obregán?

"What do you want?" She spat it at me.

"Your father," I said, and I said it like a curse. "What is—?"

"I don't want to talk about him," she shot back. "Is that all you people discuss?"

I gasped.

And the words spilled out.

"Well, it's not as if you give us much else to talk about."

She scowled again. "What's *that* supposed to mean?"

"Do you do this all the time? Play innocent and pretend you don't know what Julio is doing?"

Now it was her turn to look wounded. "I didn't say—"

"I came to talk to you." Rage simmered under my skin. "I thought you might have something interesting to say. Guess I thought wrong."

And then I began to walk home.

I did not look back.

But I was no closer to discovering what horror Julio was about to bring down upon us.

As I walked, I felt certain that she was somehow still staring at me, that those piercing eyes of hers watched me disappear into Empalme.

Papá was home when I returned, my skin warm from Your heat. He was fiddling with something near la mesa, where we gathered and ate our meals during the day, when it was too hot to stay outdoors.

"¿Estás bien, Xochitl?"

I had my hand up against the wall. I lifted my head and smiled. "Just having one of those days, Papá," I said.

He crossed the room, his long hair flowing. "Mija," he said, and I nearly broke. The softness in his voice rounded off the jagged edges of my pain. He put his hand to my chin, gently raising it to look at me. "Is there anything I can do to help you?"

He knows he knows he knows.

I almost told him, Solís.

I almost let it all spill forth.

I almost gave him my story.

He looked upon me with love, with an attempt at understanding, with a desire to know what ailed me. Mi Papá, so certain, so dependable. I could tell him, couldn't I? Wouldn't he understand me?

I didn't try.

Instead, I gave him the lie: I was tired. I had more stories to take. I needed to rest.

I lay on my bedroll as he went back to whatever he was doing.

My fingers traced the edge of the stone in the floor, beneath which sat las poemas.

Soy libre.

I wasn't. Not even close. I was trapped here, trapped in Empalme, trapped in the decision I had made.

I wasn't ever going to get out.

This was how my days passed.

I hunted water.

Drop. Soak. Squeeze.

Raúl came with me a couple of times, but he suspected nothing. He was his usual boisterous self. It was easier and easier for me to hide the truth. The stories were nothing more than a dull pain, a distant reminder of what I had done. I kept to myself, too. The fewer people I was around, the less possible it was that I would be discovered.

In the evenings, they still came for me. The first time, I was convinced that You knew somehow. That You had sent me more stories to test me, to see how full I could become before I burst.

But for days afterwards . . . nothing happened.

The stories crowded up inside me, each of them still alive, still yearning to be free. Manolito's cuento burrowed behind one of my ribs, in a place so deep that I couldn't reach it without tearing myself open. I tried to muster up the courage to go see him, to talk to him. Maybe he would understand if I told him the truth. But it was too terrifying, and I couldn't lose the only friend I had left.

He wouldn't be for much longer, had he known. I convinced myself of that. And as I did so often with Papá, I accepted the lie rather than face the truth.

Empalme changed so quickly in those days. I doubted what I had done every time someone looked at me, their gaze resting on my face for too long. They stared at me differently. Was I imagining that? I couldn't be sure, but the paranoia—mine or Manolito's, maybe both—won out every time.

Ofelia came again. She told me the same story as before, and I
knew then that she had done this to me, over and over, that she
had used me not to pass on the truth to Solís, but to exonerate herself. I listened; I took her story; it was a crumb compared to Lito's,
but I could still feel it.

Omar was next; he had managed to hold off la pesadilla for a
few more days, and in a strange way, I appreciated that he *tried*.

But then he told me he had cheated on his husband, and while
he said it, his eyes went red and glassy. He said he was sorry, that he
wouldn't do it again, that he would try harder this time. I held him,
and a thought popped into my mind: He had done this before, too.
He would do it again. Was he really sad? Was he performing for
me? For his own heart? Did I ever question this before when I took
his story? I couldn't be sure, and the thought enraged me. What
was I to these people?

What was I to *myself*?

The stories piled up, rooting into their hiding places in my gut.

Lani, with her short hair and her disarming smile, told me that
she had cheated her assistant out of her earnings by blaming it on
Julio's men.

Lázaro had stolen from Ramona. He did not feel that guilty
about it. But his pesadilla had grown too large and he could no
longer hide it. It was an enormous lobo with teeth like razors, and
it slunk away once Lázaro was done telling me the truth.

When I slept, the stories rose in my mind, bursting into mis
sueños like unwanted guests. They reminded me of the betrayal.
The guilt. The anger. I awoke frequently in those days, coated in
sweat, slick with my own guilt. I pushed it down by telling myself
that this was worth it. All I had to do was get the courage to go to
Manolito and then . . . what? How could I convince him to give me
the information I needed without revealing what I'd done? I hadn't
considered that, so instead, I stopped going to Manolito's. I couldn't

bring myself to do it, to face him, because he would know the truth if he saw me.

By the end of the first week, I was convinced everyone knew.

And I had no solution to it. Nothing except . . . go to Manolito. But *how*?

And then Raúl came home late one afternoon, when I had so many stories rumbling inside me that I couldn't tell which was which, and he was drenched in sweat, out of breath, terrified.

I had been home alone, reading la poema again:

> cuando estoy solo   when I am alone
> existo para mi   I exist for myself

I was filling myself with the solitude offered by la poema, my eyes tracing patterns over the cracks in the ceiling when Raúl burst inside. I snatched at la poema and hid it. My hand was under my bedroll, clutching la poema tightly, and I was convinced that Raúl had caught me. But he was too panicked to notice the obvious, so when I stood up, he didn't look down to see the hole in the floor and the missing stone.

"It's Manolito," he huffed, and he bent over, his hands on his knees, trying to catch his breath. "You have to come, Xochitl!"

"Take me there," I said, and I looked back, quick as I could, and hoped that no one would come home before we did.

He pulled me out the door. "They found something—Julio's men," he said. "Something in Manolito's mercadito."

Dread ripped my heart down to my feet. No. *No.* This couldn't be a coincidence, could it?

I wanted to believe it was, but they all awoke at once inside me, a painful rush of noise and emotion.

They know they know they know

We ran as fast as we could toward the center of la aldea, toward the well that Julio now controlled. The well where the town had once gathered.

Our feet pounded on the dirt, kicking up dust with each step, and we said not a single word to each other. Not just because of our shared terror but also because of the silence that sat around us.

Raúl put his arm out and slowed me as we approached the well. The dark iron pump jutted out of the center of it, and a long shadow stretched toward the east.

Julio and his men stood in that shadow. I stilled and nearly missed Manolito, who was curled up at the foot of the well, most of his body out of sight behind it. His hands were behind his neck and his head.

Julio raised a hand. "Leave him," he said. Then he brought two fingers up to his mouth and used them to whistle, high and long. By the time he dropped his hands down, his mouth was curved into a devious smile.

"It's time," he said, his voice echoing in the clearing. "If you are watching us now, it is safe for you to come out. This display is for everyone."

The central plaza of our aldea was lined with homes, and I saw Ofelia pull aside the cloth of her doorway across the square from us. She delicately stepped forward, reluctant to commit more than a step. Julio waved at her, almost as if she were a friend, and she allowed herself another step.

I saw others, peeking around corners, hiding in their doorways, and Raúl and I remained where we were. I didn't want Julio to see me.

It rumbled into the square, a covered wooden cart that wobbled from side to side over uneven dirt, the wood creaking and groaning as it came upon us. I had never seen one as tall as this one, but I *had* seen the person who clutched the reins.

Emilia.

Her jet-black hair draped over her shoulder like the expensive silk wraps you could buy in Obregán, and it ran down to her lush leather boots. She wore them well; they *suited* her.

I hated her. I hated that she did everything Julio told her to, that she didn't protest *anything* he did. She was a conqueror like him, wasn't she? She played her part in all of this, and our interaction days earlier had soured her even further in my eyes. But the fact that she did nothing, that she never intervened? That made her unforgivable to me.

She stepped down from the cart and joined her father at his side, a scowl twisting up her sharp mouth as she looked up at him. She seemed to be *thriving*.

"Empalme has been mine," Julio announced, and his voice rang out in the square. "And I am done with it. It is time to return it to all of you."

"What does he mean?" Raúl whispered. "'Done'?"

I shushed him and watched Julio walk over to Manolito, reach down, hoist him up. "Manolito, you stole something from me."

I don't know whose guilt ripped a chasm in me. My stomach dropped, a stone that pulled me toward the ground and compelled me to give up their stories to You.

I couldn't. *I couldn't do it.*

"I didn't do anything," croaked Lito, and he wiped something from his mouth. Redness. Blood. "Please, let me go."

"Will you tell me the truth?"

Lito looked up. Then he looked out at us.

Then he looked at *me*.

He was broken. His brows shot up.

I shook my head. I had not told his secret to anyone! How did Julio *know*?

Lito let his breath out. "I don't know what you mean. Please."

Julio shook his head. "I want everyone to see that I gave Manolito a chance. You cannot say I am not fair."

"How is any of this fair?" Raúl whispered.

I ignored mi hermano. My attention was rapt on the terror unfolding.

"Manolito," Julio said, and then he knelt before him, his hand out, stretching toward Lito's head, "tell me a story."

No.

No.

"What?" Manolito jerked away from Julio, but one of his men held him in place.

Julio's hand rested on Lito's forehead.

"Tell it to me."

It wasn't a request.

It was a *demand*.

And Lito's eyes rolled back in his head, and he started choking, and then the screaming filled the square, something guttural and primal and terrible, and then he suddenly stopped.

His eyes focused on Julio.

And he started talking.

His words were without emotion. Without the playful, singsong tone I was used to.

"I dropped your shipment," Lito said, and his face was lifeless. "And I saw what was inside it. After I read the note that came with it, I took it all out into the desert, and I burned it."

Lito collapsed.

Julio smiled.

"Gracias," said Julio. "For telling me the truth."

Raúl swatted at me. "Xo!" he whispered, my name sharp on his tongue.

I looked down. I had been squeezing Raúl's arm so hard that I left a mark behind.

I knew then how Julio had done this. How he conquered the places he'd been.

He had figured out how to use his power as a cuentista to *steal* stories.

And if he was able to get that out of Lito . . .

"Whom else did you tell?"

Julio's words chilled me. I fell back onto the dirt, and I tried to scramble away, but—

"Only our cuentista," Lito said. "And she always gives our stories back. I promise."

The pall of silence was unbroken. I saw nearly everyone. Omar. Lani. Ofelia. Ramona. La señora Sánchez. We watched. We waited.

"Please, just let me go," Lito begged.

Julio shoved him toward the wooden cart. "I will," he said. "I'll give you a head start if you want."

Manolito studied Julio's face. "Are you serious?"

Julio nodded, all smiles again. "One last thing before you go," he said. "I grow tired of being defied. And as my final gift to you, Empalme, I will show you what I am capable of."

He slammed an open palm on the side of the cart. "¡Libéralo!"

The rear creaked open as one of Julio's guardias yanked on it. It leapt out, striking the ground, its paws thundering in a terrible chorus. The muscular bestia dug into the earth, its snout long and terrible and upraised, sniffing, growling, snarling. There were two gnarled horns protruding from its head, and its fur was thick, black and gray, and Julio knelt down before it and pulled something from a pocket in his breeches. Lito tried to scramble backwards and out of the way, but one of Julio's men held him in place.

It flashed. Your light shimmered off it, Solís. I had never seen one of them myself, but I knew it was the vial that Lito had *told* me he destroyed in a fire. How? Had Lito told me a lie?

Julio reached over, pulled out Lito's arm, and slammed the end of the vial into it. He screamed in agony, and then—it was over. Lito breathed heavily on the ground.

Then Julio reached out to the creature, and he held up the vial. Red.

It was now full of Lito's blood.

"Mi sabueso," he said. "Are you hungry? Are you aching for the blood?"

He twisted something on the end of the vial, tipped it forward, and el sabueso jumped up, lapped at the blood that it could, the rest of it plummeting to the dirt. Julio stood, holding the vial upside down, Lito's blood dripping to the dirt.

"Run, Manolito," said Julio.

Lito did not hesitate. He pushed himself upright, and he ran, so quickly that his arms flopped back and forth, trying to gain more momentum.

Then he was out of sight.

El sabueso sniffed at the blood on the ground, tasted it, lapped at it, and then it *changed*. It lifted its snout to the air, then growled. Its head jerked to the north. Its gaze was focused, razor sharp and—

El sabueso bolted.

Someone screamed. Julio smiled, wider and wider, and his men, gathered around him, laughed and laughed. One of them, clean-shaven and baby-faced, shouted out and raised his saber high. "¡Más rápido!"

Emilia was stone still, her expression blank. She didn't care.

"Xochitl," Raúl said, and this time, I had not noticed how hard he was gripping *my* hand. "Should we leave? I'm *scared*."

But I had to know, Solís. I had to know. Was this my fault? What was going to happen?

I put my hand on Raúl's arm to signal him to stay, and el sabueso was gone, gone, far away from us. A thick silence dropped over la aldea, one of terror and anticipation, and it smothered us. We waited. And waited. And waited.

They know.

Why? Why did that thought arrive in my mind? It made no sense, but I couldn't push the paranoia down.

His scream was a wail, and it ripped the silence apart, and then it was cut short. Raúl gasped next to me, and a whimper followed, and I tried to cover his mouth to get him to stay quiet, but he shook out of my grasp.

I heard ripping.

Tearing.

El sabueso trotted back, its jaw clamped over something, and then I couldn't stop the cry that rushed from my throat as la bestia passed by Raúl and me, couldn't stop the sobbing that broke through, couldn't believe that el sabueso held an arm, torn ragged from a shoulder, still oozing blood onto the ground, and then it dropped its prize at Julio's feet, its jaw stained scarlet with the blood of my friend.

My *only* friend.

Julio smiled again. "I missed you, mi sabueso," he cooed, dropping down to give la bestia affection. "It has been too long."

El sabueso, its body twisted and wrong, nuzzled Julio's hand.

Julio had his arm behind Emilia, embracing her, and the two of them looked upon the remains of Lito.

"I am tired of your little aldea," he announced, "and Manolito here tried to hide his theft from me. I leave you with this gift."

He picked up Lito's arm, and the eyes of el sabueso followed it. Then he dropped it into the well, and the splash of it hitting the water echoed back up to us.

Julio said something; I didn't hear it. My eyes were locked on the remaining puddle of blood on the ground, all that was left of mi Lito. Raúl was begging me to leave, but I couldn't move at all. A new realization formed inside me, gripped me tightly:

We were being punished.

No.

I was being punished.

I had wronged You. I had defied You. And this was Your revenge.

But I couldn't stand there and do *nothing*. Despite the pounding of my heart and my body as both screamed at me to run away and hide from the horror, I stepped out into la plaza. I moved forward, then rushed at Julio, and none of his men saw me, and I knew it was foolish, knew that I was making a mistake, but I couldn't let him leave unscathed. I collided with his back, my fists raised, and I let out my grief and my anger. He pitched forward and stumbled, but his men snatched me from him.

Rage filled me, and I felt someone's—Ofelia's, perhaps—churn in my gut. This wasn't *my* fault. It was *his*.

"What have you done!" I screamed.

Julio wiped dust and dirt off his breeches and smiled. "Who are you?"

"You killed him!" I seethed. "Why can't you just leave us alone?"

He strode toward me, but I jerked away from his outstretched hand.

"You're smart to fear me, chica," he said. "And to fear my touch."

"Xochitl!"

Raúl's voice rang out in the clearing, and he rushed forward even as I shook my head at him. *No, no, no!*

"Leave her alone!" Raúl shouted, and another man held him back with a hand on his chest.

"Raúl," I panted, "turn around and go back home, okay? Go back home to Mamá y Papá."

He puffed up.

Put his hands on his hips.

Sneered.

"You disrespect las cuentistas," he said, and my stomach dropped. "You are nothing like mi hermana."

Silence.

Please, no.

"So you are la cuentista of Empalme, ¿no?"

My mouth was a tight line. I said nothing. But the stories . . . oh, the stories awoke again in me, twisting around in my torso, trying to find a new place to hide.

"Manolito told you what he knew."

I remained resolute. I would not give him what he wanted.

"And you did nothing to stop me."

"How could I?" I shot back. "I gave your story back that night, back to Solís. As you are *supposed* to."

I tried to sell the lie by spitting on the ground. It was only a little bit true. I despised Julio and what he had done. But was I in any place to judge him?

"You have no idea of the power that you have," he said.

He reached forward.

I tried to force myself backwards, but his men held me in place.

"Don't," I slurred.

"I want your story," he said.

His fingers grazed my cheek.

It was all he needed.

It was all he could *stand*.

EACH OF US A DESERT

Because a spark tore from my body, a burst of magic that I had never before felt, and Julio was thrown back. He hit the ground and his breath rushed out of him, but this was not an act of protection.

It was a warning.

Julio stood openmouthed, his eyes wide. "Mi cuentista," he muttered. "You still have them."

I shook my head, coughed out a protest.

"You keep them as I do."

"No, that's not—"

"Did you figure it out, too?" he said, and his eyes were alive with lust, with joy. "Do you know the truth?"

You knew.

They *all* knew.

A numbness settled over me as I heard the murmurs around me, as I heard Raúl softly crying, as I accepted that the truth was now out in the open. My gaze followed the line of blood in the dirt, right up to the well, and then I looked up and—

Her dark eyes were locked in mine. Still. Expressionless. They drilled into me. She saw me. Then her face twisted in . . . was that disgust?

"Is that true, Xochitl?"

Ofelia. She rushed toward me, put her hands on my arms and shook me. "Did you keep them?"

I didn't know what to say. I looked for Raúl, and his bushy hair had fallen over his eyes.

He was still crying.

"Look at me!" Ofelia cried, and she dug her nails into my skin, but I couldn't focus.

They were all moving in toward me.

Closer.

Staring at me.

Realization growing like dawn on their faces.

"We *trusted* you," Omar said. "We don't have a choice. We *have* to tell you our secrets!"

I couldn't look at him. I cast my eyes down, but there it was.

Manolito's blood, pooled at my feet. All that was left of him.

Was this my fault?

When I looked up, they had mostly surrounded me. But Julio was still smiling.

"She's yours," he said.

Then he walked off, Emilia at his heels.

My panic burst, and I couldn't be there any longer. I spun around and ran as fast as I could, silent and terrified, and every step pulled my stomach further down in shame and guilt. They called out after me, yelled my name, demanded the truth. The only living part of Manolito was inside *me*. His story twisted, and now my guilt was my own.

I had done this, hadn't I? I thought. We were not supposed to lie. We were not supposed to hide from You. And I had not given Lito's story back, and You had punished him.

Hadn't You?

Were the others next? Ofelia y Lani y Omar . . . I had their stories inside me, and it was only a matter of time before they were taken away . . . and then me.

I had to find Mamá y Papá. They would understand me, wouldn't they?

I ran faster, ignoring the sound behind me. I was determined to make it home.

If Empalme didn't kill me first.

I was nearly home when I saw them. Huddled together, arguing, and Mamá was furious, inconsolable. I couldn't tell what they were saying, but when Papá looked up at the sound of our approach, his expression told me everything I needed to know.

They had seen Julio's display, too.

I stood there, swaying, and I couldn't bring myself to get closer. *I did this*, I thought. *I brought this upon us.*

"No, *no!*" Papá shouted, and he knelt down as Raúl plunged into his arms. "Tell me that isn't true, mija! Please!"

Mamá sobbed. "Xochitl, he was lying, right?"

Mamá examined my face as she came close. What could she see upon it? Did she know what I was thinking? I couldn't tell, but her eyes searched me, over and over, and I tried my best to shove it all down. To hide in plain sight.

But she knew the truth. She knew that Julio had not made anything up.

"How *could* you?" she said, her voice low, hurt. "Inez told you how important your power is. Why we need it."

"But, Mamá—" I began.

Papá loomed in my vision. "Please tell me you've given them back now. That Solís has cleansed us."

I couldn't look Papá in the eye, but I longed for that touch of his. His tenderness. His understanding.

I started crying, and I worked up the courage to look at him. His hands hung at his sides. No touch. No comfort.

"Xochitl," he said, barely a whisper. "What have you done?"

Raúl sobbed, and it was a bitter, distraught sound, one that echoed outside our home.

He would not come near me.

The three of them gathered, facing me. I had no means to explain my decision. I had kept the story because I thought I could change what was coming. I had made a mistake, and now, Manolito was dead.

That night, my family ate dinner in silence. No one else had come for me, as I had feared—I didn't know why, but I couldn't really process it all. I can't even remember what we had; it all blurred together. No one said anything to me, even though I could tell they all ached to. I caught them glancing at one another, as if daring someone to break the terrible quiet first.

They could not bring themselves to do it.

I helped Papá clean up after dinner, still silent, still tormented by everything racing through my mind. Hadn't others done so much worse than I had? Wasn't Julio's murder of Manolito a far more terrible thing? Solís had not punished him. I couldn't believe that what I had done was so unforgivable.

And Julio had corrupted everything it meant to be a cuentista. He *stole* stories out of the bodies of others!

Where was his punishment? How had You let him survive—and thrive—for so long?

There was a voice at the door. I thought it was Rogelio, come to ask me to absolve him once more, but it was la señora Sánchez, hunched over, and she coughed, her white hair pouring over her face.

Papá rushed over to her and tried to help her, but she waved him away. "I won't be long," she said, "but you need to know, Beto."

"Know *what*?" Papá said.

"They're gone."

"Julio?" Mamá said. "Did they finally leave?"

She shook her head, then wiped at the tears on her face. "No, Lupe," she said. "The guardians. Los lobos. They're all gone."

"That can't be true," Papá said. "*Gone?*"

"Their den is empty. The blood has dried." She paused, sucked a breath in deep. "We might be alone out here."

Papá glanced at me, and I must have looked miserable because he asked la señora Sánchez to step outside. She gave me one last look before she did.

Raúl sidled up to me. "Are we going to be okay, Xochitl?"

"I'm sure we'll be fine." Another lie. "This will all solve itself soon."

Each lie easier than the last.

"Why did you do it?"

Mamá was standing behind Raúl and shushed him. But I knelt down before him, ruffled his bushy hair. "Do you trust me?" I asked.

"Always," he said. "But aren't you supposed to give the stories back?"

"I found out the truth about Julio," I said, "and I wanted to do something about it."

"But you didn't."

His words were a fist to my chest. He didn't mean to be cruel, so I gave him a weak smile. "I thought I could do something."

Raúl smiled back. "You'll figure it out," he said. "You're our cuentista."

He meant it as a sign of solidarity, as an expression of hope.

It felt more like a *curse*.

When Papá returned, he didn't want to talk about what else he had spoken of with la señora Sánchez. He made for the back of our home, and Mamá followed him. Their voices were muffled but sharp. They were arguing. About what? I never found out.

I lay down on my sleeping roll and tried my best to ignore them. I could hear Raúl next to me, trying to do the same thing.

My mind raced, uncertain what the immediate future would hold. I brushed my fingers over the hiding place in the floor, las poemas so close to me. I wanted to find the person who had been able to reach inside me so delicately, so wholly.

But that wasn't *me*. I had my whole life mapped out before me. Take, consume, return. Tuve que honrar a Solís. Proteger mi aldea. Amar a mi familia. That was it. I protected others, but who protected me? Who listened to *me*? Who cared about the things that made me scared, worried, or angry?

How could I tell any story of my *own*?

They knew. Whoever wrote las poemas, *they* would know why I had done what I had done. They would understand the deep well of emotions that churned in me. They would understand my curiosity when I learned what Julio was. They knew what it was like to feel contained . . . and they had broken *free* of that.

Soy libre.

I had to know. I had to know why these words held such an immense power over me.

I had to leave.

There was one person en la aldea who could help me. I took a waterskin bag, filled it halfway with water from my hunt the day before, and then looked upon Raúl. I couldn't tell if he was actually asleep or pretending to be.

I left my home and was met with the cool air of the early evening. You, Solís, were nearly gone from the sky, and the soft glow was settling in. Soon, las estrellas would light our path at night. Would we still have our celebrations? I wondered. Or had Julio ruined that? Had *I* ruined that?

How could we celebrate when Manolito was dead?

I walked to the west. I went straight for Marisol, one of the last people ever to talk to Manolito.

She would have the answers I needed.

I had not seen Marisol during Julio's terrible display, and by the time I crossed over Empalme—down dark alleys, cutting through abandoned plots of land, wary of how quiet and eerie the evening was—I worried that this plan wouldn't work. What if Marisol had left la aldea already? What if I was truly stuck here? What if los aldeanos got to me first?

Marisol had come far from the north, from a distant aldea with a name I did not know, whose people had survived La Quema by burrowing deep into the ground. I had heard Marisol tell of her upbringing there, of the complicated network of tunnels that kept la comunidad safe from the scorching sun during the day.

Maybe she had left Empalme and gone home.

Maybe this was a horrible idea.

What am I doing?

These thoughts tormented me as I came upon her home, dug into the arid soil. Only a small bit of it sat aboveground. If you didn't know where it was, it was impossible to see at night, even in the glow of starlight. Rogelio was known to trip over the edge of it and fall asleep on the roof after our celebration until the baking sun forced him to seek shelter in the morning.

That night, though, Marisol was sitting on the edge instead, and her lit cigarillo glowed in the darkness, its ember orange, red, sparkling. She took another long drag from it, lowered it to her side. "¿Qué quieres, Xochitl?" she asked, and her voice was deep and musical. "What can I do for you?"

Marisol knew things. People. Places. That was her role in Empalme. She was one of the few who regularly traveled in every direction, and she brought information back with her. La Reina del Chisme. Who had work available in the surrounding granjas? What was the latest chisme out of la capital? Which aldeas were still thriving? Which had died out? If you had a question, you could pay Marisol, and she was dependable. For the right price, she could give you an answer for practically *anything*.

Her features came into view as I stepped up to her. Her hair was bushy and full, and her tight curls fell dramatically down the sides of her face, most of them gray and white. She was stunning, really, but it was the feeling I got from being around her that captivated me the most. She seemed so sure of herself, of her place within the world. As I was born to be a cuentista, she was born to be La Reina del Chisme. And in an existence so scattered, so desperate to cling to life after La Quema, information was valuable. *Powerful.*

She had been here for nearly fifty years, before my own parents had been born, and it was hard to imagine Empalme without her.

And now I needed her. After all this time, I had a reason to talk to her. To ask the questions.

"I need to leave Empalme," I told her, choosing to be as direct as possible.

"And go where?"

I hadn't thought that far. "¿Obregán?"

She smiled, blew smoke out of her nose, and it was so intoxicating to watch. "Ay, niña, you cannot make that journey. Do you think you can survive the desert and its horrors all on your own?"

"I have to," I said. "I don't have a choice."

She laughed, a throaty sound that cut through the silence of the night. "You always have a choice," she said. "We often don't like what one of the choices is, so we ignore it, pretend it is not there."

She blew more smoke out. "Why must you leave, Xochitl? Why are you not asking your parents for help?"

"You don't know?" I said. "Were you not here?"

She squinted at me. "I know everything."

"So you saw what Julio just did?"

The ember flickered in front of me, and seconds later, she blew smoke up into the air. "Did what?"

"Manolito is dead."

The cigarillo stopped moving. "Dead?" More smoke. "Don't joke with me, Xochitl. I don't find that funny."

"I'm telling the truth," I said, and then a pang of guilt hit me. *Maybe about this I am*, I thought. "Julio killed Manolito for stealing from him. He's a cuentista, and he took Lito's story right out of his body." I paused. Swallowed. "And then he had him torn apart by this creature that could track him. With his blood. He called it 'un sabueso.'"

The effect was instant. Her cigarillo hung in the air, and it burned down as she stared at me. Her dark eyes were wide, so intently focused that a chill rushed over me. "Marisol? What is it?"

"Esa palabra," she said. "Otra vez."

"Sabueso," I repeated. "Julio brought it out and—"

The cigarillo plummeted, tumbled over the ground, and Marisol swore. "I have to leave," she said. "Now."

She reached out and grabbed my hand, and a piercing pain shot up my arm. "Let me go!" I shouted, and I tried to yank my hand back, but she only held on tighter.

"Xochitl, you need to take my story," she said. "You can't let them get me."

"What are you *talking* about?"

She dropped down to her knees, nearly pulling me down with her. She had both my hands in hers, and they were slick with sweat.

I had never seen her like this. Marisol, La Reina del Chisme, now looked more frightened than even Raúl had earlier that night.

"Marisol . . . ," I began.

"Take it," she said. "Then you'll know."

I took a step back. Marisol had *never* sought me out in all the years I had been a cuentista. She said she had her own that she used, somewhere in Obregán. Why now? Why did she have to ask me *now*?

"I *can't*!" I screamed. "You don't understand—"

"It won't matter," she said. "I have seen los sabuesos before, and they only bring devastation."

I breathed in deep, and when I said, "Tell me," her terror burst up through me, up my arms and into my body. It was one of the quickest connections I had ever made with someone during the ritual, and her desperation to tell me the truth flooded my body and—

Let me tell You a story, Solís.

Marisol never wanted to leave her home. She had been born underground, had lived her life in the complex tunnels and chambers of Solado, the tradition she was taught to survive Your rage. It was a land far, far to the north.

Her fathers, Josué and Ricardo, had let her run the tunnels, and she spent her days getting to know the other people who lived underground with her. She would come home late in the afternoons, and she would tell her parents about all the stories she had been told that day. Josué in particular loved hearing them, and he would sit with Marisol in his lap, asking all the right questions, always interested, always loving. Even Ricardo, who worked overnight to help collect food for his aldea, soon became enamored with how much information Marisol was able to get in only one day.

They were the most knowledgeable family in Solado, and Marisol thrived most when she sat quietly, listening to the words and stories of those around her.

She stayed there for years, and it became her responsibility to teach the other children: about how to farm underground, when best to harvest vegetables, which aldeas nearby were best to travel to for supplies. She told stories, of a sort, to explain to others what it was like to live in Solado.

She never thought they were perfect, that they had no problems. Solado had to depend on Carmilo to the north for meat and cotton. While it was not forbidden to go aboveground, it was highly discouraged, and Marisol could recall only a handful of times that she stood on the earth itself, gazing up into the sky, at Solís and Their light. She had seen las estrellas at night even less, as angry bestias roamed the land above when darkness fell. Sometimes, if you crept close to the entrance, you could hear the creatures above them, snarling and growling outside.

But Marisol loved la comunidad. She loved the ways they survived in a universe that seemed so hostile and frightening. She loved her place in Solado, and by the time she was twenty, she was *trusted*. Believed. It was told that Marisol could get anyone to open up to her in her presence.

And it was around that time when they had ruined everything, stole it all from her.

They came in the night. She had her own home by then, carved out of a tunnel on the end, and she heard the shouts. The echoes. The snarls. Marisol sat upright in her bed, her heart beating in her throat.

A shadow passed by the entry. It was impossible. They wore masks with elongated snouts so no one could see their faces. Long white cloaks flowed behind them, stretching their shadows into frightening shapes. Every bit of their skin was covered. They seemed to be from some other time, some terrible place.

At first, she believed she was dreaming, and then she heard the screams, heard the tearing of flesh, and then she saw *them*.

They skulked behind their monstrous owners in the passageway, and the shape seemed impossible. She rose from her bed to get a better look, crept slowly to the edge of her door, tried to stay quiet, tried not to scream in panic, and she watched as they dragged a man out of his home. He fought, hard and fierce, and then a knife sliced at his arm, and one of the creatures jumped, stuck its snout in his blood.

There, in the light, she saw what had descended upon Solado. Their eyes glowed, and their bodies were twisted, dark, their snouts so terribly long, the horns on their heads hideous and sharp.

Then . . . they fed.

The man was nothing more than shredded remains, a sickly pile of gore and blood, when los sabuesos lost interest in him.

She kept her mouth covered, backed away from the door, and tried to make it back to her bed, an irrational thought consuming her: If she buried herself underneath la cobija, it would all disappear. This was a dream. She could wake in the morning, and it would be nothing more than her imagination.

Then a shadow from the doorway fell over her.

La bestia stood motionless, then twisted its misshapen, nightmarish head to the side, that awful snout filling Marisol with dread, and then it took a step forward.

These people conquered Solado. They stole la aldea from its inhabitants in only a few hours.

But that was not what haunted Marisol, what drove her to Empalme. No, when that *thing* stepped into her home, Marisol leapt up and knocked it aside, shoved into it hard with her shoulder, and she rounded the corner, into the passageway, past carnage, past destruction, past those she knew and loved and respected as they were torn apart.

She did not stop for their screams.

She did not stop for those who begged her to help them.

She was so afraid, Solís, and she couldn't think. She just *reacted*.

Marisol was close to the entrance to Solado, so close that she could see the glowing light of las estrellas seeping down below.

He called out her name.

"Marisol! Marisol!"

She stopped, spun around, saw Ricardo, the light from a torch behind her reflecting off his bald head.

He was pulling himself forward on his arms. Something was wrong with his legs, something she couldn't make out, something she could focus on and—

They were missing.

Redness trailed behind him.

"Mi amor," he slurred, "please help me."

Another voice. It rang out from farther along, echoing to her.

"¡Mi sabueso siempre te encontrará!" the voice declared. "You can't escape."

She cut back a sob.

"Mi amor," Ricardo said, "just a hand, please."

He extended it.

She was so afraid.

She saw its eyes before anything else, glowing behind her papi.

And her body pushed her, pushed her away from him, yelled at her to keep going, to save herself, and she obeyed it, Solís, and she heard Ricardo's voice rise high in horror.

Then it was cut short.

Then: nothing.

She ran. She escaped. She didn't even try to stop them.

Marisol begs for Your forgiveness, Solís. She is sorry. She is sorry that she buried this story within her, that she waited so long to tell the truth, but she ran. And ran. And ran. She left it all behind a generation ago, and she started a new life in Empalme.

And she now believes it all came back to her.

You came back to her.

She told me she was sorry. Over and over again.

Her ragged breath tumbled out of her, and she was covered in sweat. I was, too, and some dripped into my eye, stinging me as I tried to stay upright.

"Lo siento," she said, possibly for the hundredth time, and I knew she wasn't saying it to me anymore. There was a piercing regret now living in my stomach, and it joined all the others in a wave that overwhelmed me. I tried to steady myself on Marisol, but she could barely stay still beneath me. "I have to leave."

And so did I. Yet as I stood there, Marisol huffing nearby, her words settling within me as nausea clung to my throat, the same thought penetrated the haze.

I wanted to leave—because I couldn't do this anymore.

Marisol's guilt tore at me, but I ignored it. How was this my life? How was I expected to consume such horrible traumas over and over again? Now that I had kept so many stories inside me, refusing to give them to the desert, Empalme no longer looked the same to me.

Mi gente were suffering. Not just from men like Julio, but from You, Solís. From the terror of potential: at any moment, You could take everything away from us again.

No matter how hard we tried, no matter how much we improved

or survived, You could finally decide that You had had enough, and then, You could wipe us all out. All those attempts to keep Empalme safe, every story I took and gave back to You . . . was that ever enough? Was our nightly celebration pointless, a lie we had agreed to believe?

How was that any way to live? How could we ever thrive if we were so gripped by terror?

There was a longing inside me, one that had been building for years, slithering up like the rattlesnakes that hid in the barrel cactus and under the baking stones. Maybe it was selfish of me to want more, but I had to choose for *me*. Would Empalme be plagued with pesadillas if I left? Would they finally be punished for their misdeeds?

I couldn't make this my problem anymore.

If I gave those stories back to You, I would forget everything. I would forget about Julio, la cuentista who had survived Your wrath. I would forget the true shape of Empalme, the vivid portrait of suffering that had now formed within me.

They would not forget, though—what I had done or what they had tried to hide in *me*.

I had spent the past week lying, but how much of *my* life was a lie?

Marisol stood, and I knew then it was time to change.

"Tell me how to get to Obregán," I said, and my voice was no longer shaking, my heart was no longer uncertain, my spirit was no longer afraid. "Tell me now, or everyone will know."

She shrank away from me. "I could take you," she said. "If Julio is still here, I can't—"

"He and his men left already," I said, cutting her off. "They're gone. You don't need to leave. But I do."

Her eyes flashed open, and she brought herself upright, wiped at her eyes. She still seemed so much smaller than she used to be. "Follow me," she said, and she led me into her home.

I had never been to Solado, and I did not know if Marisol's home was an exact imitation of that place, but I still gasped when I descended into the main room. Her home was so much bigger than I had expected. Since she had only tiny windows up near the ceiling, she used candles, set deep within recesses along the walls, to provide a haunting glow. There was an intricately woven cobija hung above her bed, full of bright colors that collided with one another. She crouched down and pulled out a wooden box from under the bed, then searched through it.

I was still gaping at the inside of this structure when she spoke. "Less exposed to the sun," she said without looking up. "So it doesn't heat up so much during the day."

I had nothing for her; her story flashed within me, and then I was inside: inside that room in Solado, deep within the earth, as if the memory were my own.

"It reminds me of home," she said, and then she looked up, her eyes raw and shining. She rose, and she stuck her hands out, a small leather purse cupped inside them. "Take it," she said, lifting one of my own hands and dropping it there. "It's the least I can do."

I balked at her. The purse was heavy with coins. "I don't need—"

She raised a hand to stop me. "Take the road out of the north side of Empalme. Follow the trail across the hills and gullies, and as long as you're heading toward las montañas in that direction, you'll be fine. The path up and over is between two saguaros. They are mirror images of each other. Los Gemelos. It's the only way across that won't kill you."

"Kill me? What do you mean?"

"You don't want to know," she said, and then she was pushing me toward her door. "Please, I need to be alone."

"Wait!" I spun around to face her. "Julio . . . how did he do it?"

"Do what? ¿El sabueso?"

I shook my head. "No, not that part."

"You'll find out soon enough."

I balked at her once more, unsure what that meant. "But how did he leave his aldea? How can someone like that abandon their purpose as a cuentista?"

She tilted her head to the side, examined me. "You are not who I thought you were, Xochitl," she said. "You remind me of who I used to be."

I didn't know if that was a compliment or an insult. "You have to know," I said.

"If you want to find more cuentistas, go to El Mercado de Obregán. Head to the northwest corner. You'll know when you see them. They might have the answers you need."

She grabbed my arm as I turned to leave, and this time, she had the advantage. "I don't know what you've done," she said. "But are you prepared to pursue this path that's laid out before you?"

I smiled and said nothing. I walked out of her home.

I floated home. Empalme was unfamiliar to me, as if I had never spent any time walking its dusty streets. A darkness sat over la aldea like a shroud, and the shadows grew. I trusted nothing in that terrible silence. Were the others afraid of what would happen next? How long would it be until we reclaimed our rituals and routines? Until we would begin to pour out of our homes once You left the sky? Until Rogelio would serenade us with his mournful voice? Until la señora Sánchez resumed roasting maíz over a fire, handing them to the children and warning them of how hot they were, only to watch them ignore her *every* time?

Would all return to normal once I left?

Yes, I told myself. That had to be the solution. If I left, if I took this plague, this *curse*, away from them all, they would be fine.

At least I hoped that was the case. Empalme was silence now. No fires, no meals together, no joy, and no fiestas.

No Manolito.

The only sound was my breath. The beating of my heart.

Cada latida de mi corazón.

This was for *me*.

My home had never felt so empty. They were all asleep except for Papá, who sat up against the far wall, reading something. He looked up briefly, nodded at me. Raúl's sleeping roll was next to him, and he had one hand gently running through Raúl's hair.

I smiled at him, drank some water, and then dropped down onto my sleeping roll on the floor. By the time I hit the ground, the decision was made. I would leave in the morning, before the sun was out, and I would tell no one.

I closed my eyes.

"Xochitl."

His voice was barely a whisper. Through the darkness, I looked back to mi papá.

"¿Estás bien?" he asked.

It was his question for me. He never meant it as small talk. It was so common that I could imagine his face, even though my eyes were shut. He did this thing where his eyes opened up, became affectionate, and I crumbled right there, convinced that all my plans had disintegrated in an instant.

I swallowed. "Estoy cansada," I said.

He believed me. He didn't move from his spot, and as I drifted off to sleep, I heard him say, "Te quiero mucho, Xochitl. I don't always understand you, but we'll get through this."

I was asleep before I could reply. I was thankful for that, because if I had started talking to him, I would have told him that I was leaving.

I woke only a few hours later, and I almost gave up all the stories again. As consciousness stirred in me, so did all those competing emotions—anger, sadness, regret, fright—and they fought for space in my body. If I thought about Manolito's lie, about his act of destruction, guilt and terror jolted out to all my appendages. I sat up and saw that Papá had fallen asleep in the exact spot he'd been earlier.

I knew that I was leaving—leaving him. And Raúl. And Mamá.

What price was I going to have to pay? And would You exact that price from them instead of me?

Should I leave? I asked You. I raised my hand, put fingers over my eyes, over my heart. *Is this what I am supposed to do?*

When it first began to fall, I did not know what the sound was. It was like thousands of grains of sand had been dropped from on high, and they bounced off the roof of our home. Shadows filled most of the room, so I watched the still forms of mi hermano y mi papá, and I thought of waking them, to ask them to experience this alongside me.

Instead, I pressed my palms into the ground, levered myself upright, and slowly walked to our doorway. The smell hit me first: something sharp. Bitter. Dust kicked up from below, and tiny pockets appeared in the dirt. I stuck a hand out and—

Rain!

I lurched forward and felt the droplets, hot and thick, pelt my body, and I *laughed.* When had it last rained? When had You last blessed us with something so beautiful, so necessary?

I lifted my head to the sky, and I opened my mouth. The bitterness hit my tongue, and I choked, spitting it up and returning it to the earth, and I raised my hands up to my face.

Darkness. The rain was *dark.*

I ran my hands down the blouse that I'd fallen asleep in, and they left a stain across the front of it. A brand. A sign. It was *red*, a deep, terrible scarlet, an impossible color.

Blood.

Somehow, I knew it was Manolito's blood. Blood on my hands, on my body, covering every inch of me.

I stumbled back indoors and peeled off my clothing in a panic. After I wiped at my skin, I left everything in a soggy pile by the door and stood, naked and afraid, wishing I could bathe and scrape this filth off my skin.

The others slept. I dressed again in clothes that were clean, free of those horrible stains, and I curled up on my sleeping roll, far away from my family.

Had it begun? Was this a curse? Cuentistas were not supposed to suffer from pesadillas, but . . . what was that rain? How was it possible that Lito's blood had fallen from the sky, had soaked through my clothing?

I did not sleep for the rest of that night. I kept waiting for the end to come.

As dawn approached, los pájaros became chatty, chirping and singing to one another. It meant it was time for me to go. They shrieked
and sang as I rolled up my sleeping roll and walked as quietly as I
could toward the food stored on the other side of the room. There
was a leather pack on the wall, and I took that; Mamá used it sometimes when she journeyed to Obregán, but she hadn't used it in a
while. She probably would not miss it.

Would she miss me?

No, I told myself. *Don't think that.*

Because if I did, I wouldn't leave. And I *had* to leave.

I glanced at Papá, and then . . . my gaze fell to the pile of clothing I'd left by the door.

Unstained. Damp, crumpled, but still clean.

I could still taste the blood in my mouth, could still sense it
running over my skin.

I refused to leave them with my curse.

I packed some dried meats and fruits, wrapped some leftover
tortillas in paper and took those, and then grabbed one of Papá's
goatskin bags, the ones he'd purchased from a viajero years ago.
They were sturdy and kept water cooler than anything else, and I
didn't know how long this journey would take.

How long *would* I be gone? What if I didn't find what I wanted in Obregán? What would I do after *that*?

Doubt needled at me, and every time, I had to swat it down, stuff it further inside me with the stories.

They were awake, and they reminded me of all the horrible possibilities that awaited me.

I sneaked back to my side of the room and stuffed some clean camisas and undergarments into the bag, just in case this took longer than I expected. I had no real time to consider anything else, so after my sleeping roll went in last, I closed the bag, and looked back on my family.

It wouldn't take much time to tell them goodbye, and I wanted to. But I couldn't linger any longer, couldn't be pulled back to who I once was.

One of the buckets for hunting water sat by the door. I grabbed la pala that Papá had made me and put it under the sleeping roll in my pack.

As I pulled aside the burlap covering on the door and quietly rushed outside, someone grabbed my arm.

Mamá.

"Xochitl!" she said, her voice a harsh whisper. "Where are you going?"

What was I supposed to tell her, Solís? I had lied so many times, and I could have added another, but when she looked at me, her eyes were inviting. She had both her braids laid over her chest and down to her waist, and they shone in what little light there was that morning.

"I have to leave," I blurted out. "I need to go, Mamá. To find something."

I left the rest unsaid: I need to escape. I need to flee from my own pesadillas. I must find *myself*.

She sighed, and I expected her to order me back into our home, to explain everything to her, but she merely reached out, ran her hand over my face from cheek to chin. "You know, we've been waiting for this day," she said.

"Who?"

"Tu papá y yo. Estás inquieta, Xochitl. You can't ever seem to stay in one spot. You're always moving, even here in Empalme. You have a drive in you that we might not understand, pero lo vemos."

My eyes blurred. "Mamá . . ."

"Just tell me one thing, Xochitl." She wiped at the tears on my face.

"Anything."

She sucked in a breath deeply. "Will you come back? Please tell me you are coming back."

"Por supuesto," I said without hesitation.

But did I mean that? Did I really intend to return?

She didn't ask me about being a cuentista. She didn't ask me about the stories. She stared at me, her eyes glassy, her mouth curled in a bittersweet smile.

Would Empalme *let* me return?

Mamá kissed me on the forehead, held me in her arms briefly. Then she gently pushed me off her. "Go, Xochitl. Find what you've been looking for."

"Gracias, Mamá," I said. "I'll be back."

I walked off, trying to ignore the stone in my throat, the one threatening to make me sob. She knew. Not all my secrets, but she knew more of my struggle, my lies, than I had let on. The guilt was back. Had I judged them all too harshly? Would they have accepted me, asked for my story, if I told them the truth about my sorrow?

No. It was time to go. I *had* to.

I became a solitary procession of endings, of goodbyes, of finales. How long would it be until I saw all of this again? Was this the last time I'd see Rogelio's porch, his battered guitar resting against the wall near the front door? Was this the last time I'd see Lani's cabras, who munched on refuse and dried grass? Would I ever see la señora Sánchez again? María?

Or would it all be unrecognizable? Would I be a stranger to these people?

I couldn't stop, though, and there was an uncanny momentum within me. Each step took me farther from home, and each step felt *right*.

I passed the town square, and it was empty. No one from Empalme, no trace of Julio or his men. It seemed that they really did leave. We had some rebuilding and healing to do—someone would have to fish out Manolito's arm from that well—but at least I got a brief burst of relief at knowing that I was not leaving Empalme while it was under Julio's control.

I picked up speed, comforted by this thought. Beyond Marisol's, there was a thick, chaotic patch of crushed wood, still smoking, blackened, demolished. I gasped and tears leapt to my eyes. The remains of Manolito's mercadito crackled every few seconds, but most of the embers had died out.

Julio must have destroyed it before he left la aldea, a final act of violence and spite. Whom would he visit his terror upon next?

Why didn't You stop him?

A crackle. A scrape against the dirt.

My eyes locked on the smoldering ruins. I listened, went still, reached into my training as a hunter, made myself as motionless as possible.

Nothing.

I turned slowly, kept my feet rooted to the ground, and to the south, there stood Emilia, tucked up against the side of one of the homes, the light falling onto her face, and she was staring directly at me.

Our eye contact was brief, but she pierced me with her gaze, so cold and tense. How? How was she still here? Had Emilia's father sent her back to get me?

I glared at her, a ferocious hatred for her and her father burning through me. Let her try to get to me. Let her try to stop me from leaving. She was good at that: doing nothing at all.

Then watch me, Emilia.

I walked away. That walk became a run, and I was beyond el mercadito, beyond Marisol's, beyond so many places and people in Empalme that I had known since I was a little girl, and when I got to the gate on the northern edge of la aldea, I flung it open, let it slam shut behind me, and I did not turn back for a long, long time.

I ran, Solís.

From Emilia. From Julio. From Empalme.

From everything.

I don't know for how long. Ten minutes. Maybe twenty. I ran because I had to, because I wanted to put distance between myself and Emilia, because I had to get as far away from Empalme as I could, lest I change my mind. If she was supposed to track me down, I wanted to give her as difficult of a job as possible.

I slowed only when my chest felt as if it would burst. I climbed up the side of a short hill, then finally gazed in the direction that I had come. Empalme was nothing but a speck behind me, a dark brown mound in the distance, the only sign of life in any direction. The mountain pass that Marisol had instructed me to take was hours to the north of me, still short and manageable at this distance, but I swung back around. No clouds of dust rising from the ground. No one on the clear, flat path back to Empalme, nothing. No one followed me; no one was chasing me down.

So I didn't stop.

Out here, the land stretched farther than I could see, and the horizon, shimmering and shining in the morning heat, held possibility. When I moved toward it, secrets were revealed. The earth could give you patches of mesquites, the unwavering arms of the saguaros, the pointed branches of the paloverdes.

I'd learned long ago from Papá that the desert could also give you an illusion, its own magic, a trick of the mind and of Your land. I was taught that if we did not please You, You would fool us. You might let us believe in the oasis we saw where the sky met the earth, and You would pull us miles off course, until finally, we would return to You.

I had to keep a clear mind, and so I kept my breathing regular, something Papá had taught me from his trips to Obregán. In, out, in, out, in a constant rhythm. I kept going. Every doubt I had was burned away by the sun, by the distance I put between my old life and . . . this.

What was this? What would this become? Who would *I* become?

They ran up to me then, and I was so convinced that my mind was playing tricks on me that I only glanced at los lobos and kept walking. I had seen lobos in the desert many times, and they were skittish bestias. They did not attack humans unless given a reason to. But one of them—large, with fur that was the color of sand and dirt—bolted in front of me, and finally I *heard* them.

You are la cuentista, they said.

I stopped walking, stilled by the realization washing over me.

The guardians.

They had not left after all.

"I am," I said, my voice shaking. They had *never* spoken to me in all the years I'd been in Empalme. Never spoken to *anyone*, really, except la Señora Sánchez and elders before her.

You are leaving, they said, and they sat on the trail in front of me. The others—their coats varying shades of brown and gray—assembled behind the largest one. They all stared right at me, but only one of them spoke to me.

We will take care of Empalme, they said.

"But la señora Sánchez told us last night that you had left us," I countered. "That you had abandoned us."

That is not our way, they said. *We only hid from the one who attacked us.*

"He is not from Empalme. And he is gone."

We know.

I took a step forward, and I knelt in front of them. "You will stay?"

Empalme needs our help while you are away. Until you return.

I grimaced. "I am not so sure I will."

They regarded me, saying nothing. *You will return, and you will change it all.*

They moved off to the east. What did *that* mean? I had no time to ask. They left me in the dirt, under Your heat.

They left me alone.

They left me *free*.

I continued to walk to the north, continued to push out every fear that cropped up, every bit of terror that hid within the stories I had. There was a comfort in knowing that our guardians had not left us, but I still had to distract myself in order to remain hopeful.

So I imagined myself with wings, great big brown appendages with sleek feathers, and I thought of pitching up and down in the air, watching the land pass below me. Flying over montañas, over valles, wherever I wanted.

Wherever I wanted. An hour later, I glanced back.

Empalme was out of sight.

No mound, no speck of dust, nothing.

I was farther out in the desert than I had ever been, and each step was a choice, was a conscious decision, was an act of freedom.

No one was telling me to take a story. No one was telling me that it had to feel good to be needed. Every bit I moved forward plunged me further into the utterly unknown.

For the time being, no one was looking over my shoulder, no one was expecting anything of me, and I got to choose *whatever* I wanted to do.

Soy libre.

The sensation dripped down with each bead of sweat.

Each step I took.

Each breath that filled my lungs.

I was supposed to be free.

I was supposed to choose myself.

Manolito visited me before el mediodía.

I knew the desert played tricks on the mind. I was focused on breathing evenly, breaking my routine only when I had to direct myself around saguaros or down into small ravines. I remained careful not to lose my footing, and I kept an eye on las montañas to the north so as not to drift too far from the trail that ran toward it.

I remembered Marisol's instructions: find Los Gemelos.

As the sun's heat spread over my skin, I started thinking about my time as a cuentista. The elation I felt over my newfound freedom—and the guilt of my failures that pierced me—finally gave way to something new. *What are You to me?* I wondered. My only connection to You was these stories, the refuse that poured out of my mouth, bitter and thick, and into the earth. They were my responsibility.

But Solís, You had remained silent my entire life. I was Your cuentista, but what were You to *me*?

More and more sweat dripped down my face. I stopped every quarter hour to take a small drink of water, then continued on. I was the only sound in every direction. Who else would be foolish enough to walk for miles and miles during the hottest part of the day? Not the creatures that thrived out here. Even they knew this was the time for resting, for hiding, for disappearing.

But not me. I was alone out here.

Soy libre.

He stood off to the side, his form nearly hidden behind a thick saguaro trunk, and it was only the flash of red, the blood from where his arm had been torn off, that caught my eye. I had almost missed him.

Don't trust it, I told myself. *It isn't real.*

I spun my leather pack around to the front, then unlatched it so I could get some water. I was starting to sense the pressure building, first behind my eyes, then on the back of my neck. I'd been under the sun for a long time, and my body was trying to warn me to rest, to drink water, and that's why it sent me the bloody image of Manolito.

At least that's what I tried to convince myself of. I settled my bag on my back again, pushed on farther and—

He

was

right

there.

Standing so close to me now, blood oozing out of the stump where his arm had been, and his torso was a terrible mess. I averted my eyes from whatever hung out of the gash on his stomach and choked back a horrified cry. I couldn't afford to lose what little I had managed to eat over the last half day. That would bring me closer to death.

He was there again in front of me. I shut my eyes and walked. Felt nothing. Opened my eyes.

He was still the same distance from me.

"What do you want?" I asked, my voice shaking. "Did Solís send you?"

"You have to turn back," he said, or at least, that's what it *sounded* like. When his mouth opened, they poured out: both the words and maggots. A sign of rot, a sign that Manolito had become a meal for something else. Where was his body? Is this what he looked like now? The insects tumbled to the ground, piling upon one another, then his tongue, split on the side and shredded, half consumed by el sabueso, drooped to the sand.

"Go back," he slurred. "You must."

I was firmly planted where I stood, but when he took a step toward me, I tumbled, fell back onto my elbows, a new pain bolting up my arms.

"Lo siento, Lito," I said, softly, barely able to speak. "Lo siento que te pasó."

"Go back," he oozed.

"I can't," I said. "I can't go back there. I can't let them pay the price for what I've done. I have to find out what's in the desert. What's in Obregán."

His head tilted to the side as if he was considering something. "You were warned," he said, and he took another horrible step toward me, and from where I lay sprawled on the ground, I could see that his right leg was barely connected to his body, that it was held by sinews of tendons and muscle, that he might fall apart right there.

Lito reached down. His hand—those cold, bloody fingertips—brushed over my cheek.

"You will see me only one more time, Xo," he said. "And it will be before you admit the truth."

For just a flash, I saw *him*. Lito. The man I knew, who told me stories of Obregán and the desert beyond, and through that bloody, mangled face, he came back to me. "I'm sorry I didn't tell you," he said. "I should have told you everything."

His whole form collapsed, as if he had never been there in the first place, and a hot wind gusted around me, sending ash—what remained of Manolito—into the air.

He was gone.

My stomach lurched, but I ignored it, desperate to keep the food down. I sucked in a breath, tilted my head back, let it out.

I was still alive. I was still here. So I stood up, and I brushed myself off. I forced a little water down, and then—

I kept walking.

Was that You, Solís? Or something else? Did the guardians send him to me?

I pushed away so much uncertainty on that day.

Most of all, I tried to ignore the fear that You were still watching me.

It would have made more sense to walk during the night, when I could be hidden, but I was alone. And I had no knowledge of where I was going. So I kept walking, with only those poemas in my heart.

As terrible as Julio was, he, too, had been a cuentista—and he was evidence that what I was told as a child could not be true.

Soy libre.

Did You understand me? Or did You think I was a fool?

I believed in myself despite everything that told me not to.

Is that really so bad?

I picked up the pace at first, a desperate attempt at escaping the spot where Lito had appeared and then turned to ash. My legs wobbled, but despite the scare, I remained determined. I *had* to keep going. Was I running from guilt and shame? Maybe.

Maybe deep down, I thought that if I walked faster, I'd never have to accept that I had kept all those stories, that I had played a part in accelerating everything. Mamá *had* said that they expected me to leave. Had they known that I would betray Empalme, too?

I kept my eyes on the trail ahead, about ten paces or so in front of me, because it helped me feel like the landscape was passing much quicker than it was. Your heat cut straight through my skin, seemed to cook the bones and muscle and tendons that held my body together. It was a piercing sensation, like terrible knives shooting into me. But I didn't complain. I said nothing when my monthly cramps rushed into my abdomen, and I grimaced as they forced me to stop and breathe deeply. They passed for the moment, certain to come back, and I kept going.

The land bled into itself, repetitive in a manner that made it difficult to tell anything apart. I hadn't passed that patch of prickly pear before, right? And that mesquite or those ocotillos were new, ¿no? Las montañas *seemed* closer, but there was no way to tell. Browns blurred into dull greens; each hill or shallow valle barely

differed from the others; the saguaros stood still, bearing witness
to my passage, acting as silent judges on Your behalf.

And I kept walking,

and walking,

and

walking.

I wasn't sure how long I'd been gone.

My head throbbed, and each pump of blood sent pain to my
temples, down the back of my neck. The journey stretched out
before me, and it occurred to me that this could all be endless.
Impossible.

It was a silly thought, one I discarded by laughing so my whole
body shook. "Stop it, Xochitl," I told myself. "It's the heat. You
were foolish enough to walk during the hottest part of the day.
You've done it before. Do it again."

I had not spoken in so long that it was soothing to feel the
words emit from my throat. I took another drink of water—nearly
a quarter of it gone, I noticed—and swallowed it gratefully.

I cleared my throat and recited la poema from memory:

Este mundo de cenizas	This world of ashes
no puede contenerme	cannot contain me
No hay paredes	There are no walls
para detenerme	to stop me
Soy libre.	I am free.

I *was* free. It was a terrifying thought, but I let the power grow,
and it sent a chill down my arms, raising bumps, and I welcomed
las poemas. They always did this to me. Whoever wrote them
didn't just understand me. It seemed that they had reached far

across the desert, dipped their hands into my heart, and removed the tiniest bit of my spirit. They folded it into each of these lines, and that's why they pulled me. Called to me. Kept me hopeful. How was that possible? How could words on a piece of yellowed paper have such an incredible spell over me?

The sun was dropping to the west. I continued to the north, and I kept las poemas in my mind, allowing them to cool and comfort me, and then I looked up. How much time had passed? How far had I gone?

There was nothing recognizable behind me.

Ahead of me, there was a haven of árboles, thick and lush, the mesquites in bloom. There was ironwood there, too, the flowers a delicate lavender at the tips of its branches. Two gray palomas flew overhead, another sign that I had found a place that was alive. That had *survived*.

The patch was about a half hour short of las bajadas, the thicker growth that you find at the bottom of most montañas, but I could see shade as I approached. Shade. *Relief.* I stumbled briefly in excitement, because I needed a break to refuel, to relieve myself, to stop moving.

I kept the respite short because I still had a climb ahead of me, and it would be the highest I had ever ascended. I'd survived the heat so far, but climbing would only make Your heat feel worse.

A sound.

Soft. High. A sound so rare, so impossible, that my own heart leapt at the very chance that it was not my imagination. I stilled, as I did when I hunted for water, and adjusted to the silence of the desert so far from home, and *there it was again*.

A quiet trickling.

Water.

I took off at a full run, and my legs struggled to keep up with my own excitement. I plunged through a mesquite bush, and its branches whipped at me, striking my arm, scratching and tearing at my skin, but I didn't care. It was louder now, the sound of water rushing and falling, and I pushed deeper into the thatch and emerged into a clearing, shaded and dim, and then I was on all fours, my face planted in a stream, my long hair dripping at all sides of my head, resting in the water, and I drank, deep and long and full, and it was *real*. My head flipped up and I gasped for air, and I couldn't control the tears that began to run down my face. *How, Solís?* I asked You. *How is this here? How has no one in Empalme ever found it? How had we not known?*

I couldn't stop myself. I drank again, my belly mostly empty, so when I filled it up, nausea forced me to stop. I let my pack fall off me, rolled over on my back, and panted, trying to keep it all down, but it didn't matter. I had found relief from the heat, and it felt like a blessing, as though You had judged that I was on the right path.

The joy spread. My breathing slowed, a calm settled over me, and I sank into the earth, letting it accept me as I accepted it. We both benefited from each other; it was what mi gente had taught me. We all knew that one reason Solís had sent La Quema was because of the violence that humanity had subjected the earth to. It was why I gave the stories back to the desert first before they were sent home. The earth deserved our contrition, too.

But in that moment, the earth loved me, and I loved myself.

> cuando estoy solo   when I am alone
> estoy vivo   I am alive

I rolled over and pushed myself up, then removed my blouse, then my huaraches, my short breeches, my undergarments. There was a small spot of blood on the cloth padding there, and I was thankful that I had not bled too much so far. In all of this chaos, I had lost track of the days.

I set my clothing in a neat pile next to the stream, and I stepped into it, surprised at the depth at first, at the coolness of the water, and another step brought the water level up to my knees, then another dropped me down to my waist, and then I curled up and submerged myself, rubbed at my skin, cleansed my body. I then brought each item of clothing into the water, scrubbed them, too, until they no longer smelled of sweat and the odor of exertion. The dirt and dust came out, and I removed most of the stain of blood on my padding. As long as it was clean, that was all that mattered.

Before I dressed, though, I lowered myself into a squat, then eased myself backward so that my head rested on a large, smooth stone in the middle of the stream. I relaxed, let my arms float free at my side, rested my legs against the riverbed, and I imagined that I was part of the water, como un pescado. They lived in water, and now I did. I became a part of a new world, and I was thrilled by the transformation. My body adapted to the temperature, to the newness of freedom.

Soy libre, I told myself.

I lay in the water until I could feel the call of exhaustion. I wanted to sleep there, but I was too far from my destination to make this my temporary home. I had to keep moving. I finally sat up, thanked the stream for allowing me to become a part of it. I walked toward the edge of the clearing and squatted, relieving myself. My urine did not smell strongly, and it was nearly clear. I was pleased. This oasis had helped me stay hydrated, and as I dressed, pulling my damp clothing over my body, I quietly thanked You, Solís.

All my doubt and fear was gone. I was on the right path.

I feasted as quickly as I could on some tough but flavorful cabra that Papá had seasoned and dried. I dumped out the goatskin bag and refilled it, then stuffed everything back into my pack. At the edge of the clearing, I gazed back once more on this paradise. The shadows sat delicately over the ground, the rocks cascaded gently downward to the west, and los árboles bent over the stream, yearning to touch it. If I went back home, I would tell Empalme that there was a source of water a half day's walk from la aldea. They would appreciate that.

I glanced down and saw the outline of a boot print, the toe facing toward the water. It made me smile. This place had blessed someone else, too, and I sent another prayer up. *Solís, please continue to allow this place to give la gente hope.*

I made the sign. See the truth. Believe the truth.

I was much more careful getting out of the oasis. I stepped through the stream, soaking my feet one last time, then exited the other side, pushing past mesquites and other squat bushes I did not recognize. Once the shade faded, the heat pressed upon me, tearing the moisture from my skin, and within a quarter hour, only my breeches were still slightly wet. A spot of dryness appeared in my throat, and I thought back to that stream, and I turned to catch one last glimpse of it.

The trail behind me was flat and straight. There was no oasis behind me. Just the endless, stretching expanse of the desert.

The dirt trail, dry and wide, rose from the ground, up into the curled nooks of la montaña. I stood motionless at the edge of las bajadas, and I traced its path with my eyes. But then it tucked behind ridges and out of sight.

The summit seemed so very far away.

I couldn't look upward. Papá taught me that, to keep my eyes a few paces ahead of myself so that I could maintain a solid footing, to spot holes and ridges so I didn't trip, and to keep the illusion of distance at bay. I passed through las bajadas, greeted the silence and the ironwoods and the mesquites and the skyward-reaching saguaros. I was the only thing that moved, the only sound at all. My leather huaraches scraped against the dirt, my breath lightly huffed out of my mouth, and you could hear the sloshing of water in my pack.

Nothing else.

I was alone out here, and I had never felt so alive.

How did la poeta know that? How did they know me so well?

Las bajadas were short, and I passed through them swiftly. It amused me that I was climbing closer to You as You dropped in the sky.

I looked for the cacti that Marisol had told me to find. They stood on either side of the path, mirror images of each other. Each

of the saguaros had the low arm facing the other, and the arm on
the outside was stretched high.

Los Gemelos.

I was on the right path. I took a deep breath and passed my
hand across my eyes—then stopped.

And then I started to climb

and climb

and climb.

It was a gentle ascent at first, and half an hour later, I hadn't
made as much progress up la montaña as I had wanted. My pace
was steady, my pulse was not pounding in my head, and I had kept
my breathing even and regular. But then the trail veered sharply to
the left and I wished for the slower climb.

The trail was wider here, and it must have been so carts and
horses and mules could pass one another. But I saw no one else on
the horizon. I stuck to the side farthest from the edge, unnerved by
just how far down I could fall if I didn't watch where I was going.

Each step was a reminder of my choice; each step was a deliberate move away from home. I accepted it. And I paid the price, but
I did not mind. My legs started to ache—a dull, constant pain—
and I took a brief break to drink more water, which was still cool. I
broke my own rule, too, and glanced up toward the summit. I had
maybe conquered a third of the path. But I was still high enough
that the tallest árboles en las bajadas were tufts below me. The trail
was a direct line to the south before it snaked off in the distance.

Was that it?

Empalme?

Was it only a brown speck from up here, a tiny impossibility? Is
that where I came from? I squinted and tried to focus on it, but I
was too far. I could not make out any recognizable details. Would
it have been easier to see at night? The desert stretched forever to
the south, to the distant montañas in the west, to low hills in the

east, and there was nothing. No other aldeas, no other granjas, *nothing*.

A panic gripped me, tightened around my heart.

I couldn't go back now, at least not until the next morning. Empalme—if that was it in the distance—was so very far away, and I would need to make camp soon if I was going to stay safe from—

Everything.

I'd heard all the stories growing up, but they were just *stories*. I had never seen anything unusual at night. Conejos, lobos. Owls and lizards. Plenty of mice. But what of all the stories? What of los cuentos of two-headed bestias and creatures the size of ten humans?

Then again—I had never been past the safety of los lobos before, either.

I looked down the trail, and I thought I saw Manolito, tucked behind one of the thicker saguaros, and when I shut my eyes tight and opened them again, I saw nothing. Was the doubt playing games with my mind? Was the heat getting to me?

I drank more water.

I kept moving.

I rounded more corners that looped back on one another so consistently that even though I'd walked a thousand paces, I still hadn't progressed that far up la montaña. The incline was not so bad, but my muscles twitched, an early warning sign that cramping could arrive soon. I drank more water. Ate another strip of meat. Briefly squatted to relieve myself again.

More yellow. Not a good sign.

The sun was near the horizon to the west when I finally noticed that the heat was beginning to fade away. It was gradual, and my mind was focused on the climb. I wiped at my arms, felt the grime of salt and sweat, and I wished for another oasis. I wanted to bathe the filth from my skin, douse my body and wash it all off, and a flash of memory came to me: the deluge. The blood. The blame and the guilt. Were they mine? Or was Lito's story awakening in me, desperate to be set free?

I pushed it back down, I walked farther away from Empalme, and I did not look back.

This was the only way that wouldn't kill me. That's what Marisol had told me.

I hoped she was right.

Then the vista came upon me so suddenly that I only noticed it when the pressure on my legs faded. I looked up and gasped, mostly out of *relief.* The land had flattened before me, and my legs knew that they were done for the night, and I collapsed right there, lying flat on my back and panting, an elation ripping my insides, then slipping into joy.

I had made it. One impossible part of this impossible journey just became real. The joy spread through me, and I gripped the dirt, connected myself to what I had walked, and I lay there as You began to fade, to drop beyond the horizon, and darkness slid into the world.

While You were gone, we were unseen. This was why we celebrated at night, under the stars around us. We were hidden. Unwatched. Free. My breathing slowed, and I urged my body to stillness, listening.

Silence was back, but this time, it held the anticipation of possibility. What would awake? Who would join me?

I slowly lifted myself with my palms, then pushed, my legs and arms aching, and I ignored the pain, the muscles screaming in my body. Your light was nearly gone from the sky now, and the darkness was so calming, so welcoming. The shadows that stretched from the rocks and árboles were not intimidating. Se sentían como amigos. I looked up, hoping las estrellas would come out soon, would bless me with their gentle twinkling.

Not yet.

I walked slowly across the vista, toward the north, hoping Marisol's information was right.

It sprung from the desert like an eruption, as if the earth itself had spat it out in a fury of creation. Lights sparkled from unknown sources, and what buildings I could make out all seemed to lean against one another. How were they so tall? How were there so *many*? It was as if you could fit a hundred versions of Empalme within it, and somewhere, in that mangled, complicated mess, las cuentistas waited for me.

La Ciudad de Obregán. It was finally within view.

It felt silly to think about how little I had seen of the world, but as I stood on the edge of la montaña, what else *could* I consider?

There was una ciudad awaiting me, a place so monstrous and large that it must be un sueño or a trick of the mind.

But it wasn't. Papá had been there once, as had Marisol, and yet, their stories paled to the reality. Nothing compared to the actual sight, and this was in the evening. What would it look like in the daylight?

A part of me wanted to let that mysterious pull guide me to Obregán. I had to resist, though, because while I may have been foolish enough to journey during the heat, I refused to risk my life when las bestias took over at night. It was possible that all the stories were exaggerations, that it was all just a myth. Still, I needed rest. I needed to get some energy back if I was going to face El Mercado de Obregán.

Was an answer really that close?

Was this worth it?

I stayed on the north side of the vista, spread out my sleeping roll, and then walked far enough to the east so that I would not be relieving myself close to where I slept. I dug a hole in the ground with la pala, then used it, making sure to cover it back up again when I was done. I cleaned myself and my hands off with a little water that I could afford to wash with, because now I was so close to another source.

I fell back down on my roll once I had finished, and my whole body thrummed with a soreness, the kind that got even worse after a night of sleep. I wasn't looking forward to that, Solís, but I was sore because I had *chosen* to be.

I ate again, but this time, Obregán, my destination, was in sight. I devoured a decent portion of the food I had brought, saving some of it, just in case.

I could have built a fire, maybe roasted a few of the vegetables that I had packed, but I didn't want to bring more attention to myself while I was alone. So I ate quietly, listening as the rustling around me revealed how many other creatures woke in the darkness.

Like the time immediately before sunrise, los pájaros called to one another, their chirps high and joyous. A crackling in the mesquite bushes revealed a small brown conejo, its ears pointed up, alert and wary. It hopped off and ducked into a hole near the whitethorn that stood near the passage south.

Then las estrellas arrived.

Night was here, and I was free of You.

A relief flushed my body, and I lay there, on my back, watching each of the twinkling lights appear, one by one. From here, up on top of esta montaña, there was nothing else I could see. Las estrellas surrounded me, enveloped me, were my entire world. A light in the darkness, a light without you.

A life free from being a cuentista.

Soy libre.

There was no one here, begging for me to take their hands in mine, to take their stories into me. No sneers, no scoffs, no expectation that I would do as they asked or else the entire aldea would suffer. The pressure in my bones lifted, and I had never been so light. I could have floated up into those stars, become one myself, a brightness to guide others, to give others hope.

I could not recall another evening spent like this.

There was more rustling, more crunching of leaves. I sat up and tucked my legs under me, thankful for how much it stretched me out, and I remained still. There was a scratching to my left, and I moved my head as slowly as possible to see if I could spot what was coming my way.

There was nothing.

A snap.

Still soft, muted by distance, this time to the south, beyond the lone whitethorn.

Probably un conejo, I told myself. I focused my gaze on the south, on my past, and I allowed the darkness to settle, to sketch out the lines of the whitethorn, the mesquite bushes, the barrel cactuses that were clumped on the ground and

something

was

right

there.

At first, I thought it was another saguaro, but as I traced the outline cast in the starlight that grew above me, *it moved*.

A slight twitch on the right.

I moved as slowly as I could, reaching with my right hand toward my pack, inching the clasp open, then thrusting my fingers in until the cool wooden handle of la pala was there, its edge sharp enough to pierce flesh.

If I put enough force behind it.

I pulled it in my lap, careful not to make a single sound, not to make any sudden movements. I stopped again and watched, my eyes gliding over the edges of the dark shadow that stood there.

I tensed.

It moved. *Again*. No trick of the shadows and darkness, no magic of the mind. I watched the figure move in my direction. Did it know I saw it? Was it toying with its prey? Did that mean *I* was the prey?

It moved into the clearing on the vista, and as it did so, the figure became clearer.

Human.

Was that worse? I didn't know.

Una pesadilla? Had Manolito come for me as he had promised? No. That wasn't it.

Who had followed me? Or was it a stranger, from some other aldea, trying to make the passage north; someone who had merely stumbled upon me by accident? But human or not—there was always something worse out here. Marisol had warned me. Was that warning now true?

I took a risk, Solís.

And I did it because I had to *choose*.

I bolted upright, la pala pointed directly at them, and I said, clear and loud: "Stop! What do you want?"

I wondered briefly if I'd been fooled, if they were even there, but then they moved so quickly that before I could even react, before I could raise la pala and save myself, she had her arms on my shoulders and they shook and jerked, and I cried out.

"You have to help me," the girl said.

She made a sick and pitiful sound, something between a sob and a yelp of pain. She dropped right there on the ground, became a heap, and her breath was ragged and panicked and horrible and she didn't stop. "Get me away from him," she spewed, and her hands were on my legs and my feet and I tried to escape, but she held me so *hard*, Solís.

"Away from *whom*?" I yelled at her.

She choked, spat something up, and then looked up at me, her cold eyes visible in the starlight.

I knew those eyes.

"My father," said Emilia.

Emilia rolled onto her back, a single burlap sack flung to the side, and continued to cough, and it shook her entire body. She began to gurgle, and I just *moved*. I hated seeing her, I hated the terrible possibilities that she brought with her, but she sounded like she was dying.

I danced away from her grip and retrieved my goatskin bag. By the time I went back, her eyes, glassy and red, were focused on me. I could see more of her, and her outfit—black breeches, a flowing camisa that used to be tan—was filthy, torn, and there was a dark stain running down one side of it. Blood? And was it hers?

I stuck a hand behind her head and gently guided her up so that she could take a few sips of water. She drank too fast, began coughing up again, but then she slowed down, taking only a sip or two, swallowing, and then repeating it until her thirst was quenched.

"I need you," she said.

I frowned at that and moved slightly back from her. What if this was a trap? What if Julio had sent her to track me down, to take me back to Empalme? A story rolled in me: Lito's. He was warning me, telling me not to trust her. Or was that my own natural suspicion?

I couldn't tell.

"Why are you here?" I asked her. "Why did you follow me?"

"Let me tell you, please," she continued, and she reached out gingerly, grasped me lightly by the right hand. "Let me tell you a story."

I yanked my hand from her and rose. As I backed away, I said, "No! You're just trying to *trick* me! Leave me vulnerable!"

"Please," she begged, and the coldness was gone. What was that in its place? *Fear?* "Give me this one thing, at least. Then you'll understand." She lifted herself up, rested on her elbows, and her piercing eyes bore right through me. "This isn't a trick. I *promise* you."

I shook my head. *No*, I thought. *She's with Julio. It's a trap.* I focused on the spot where the trail met the southern edge of the vista, hoping that I could see someone coming.

"You think he's coming, don't you?"

I looked down at her. "Who?"

"Julio," she explained. "You think I'm here for you, don't you?"

I wrinkled my brow up in response.

"You keep looking behind me. Like you're expecting someone."

I sighed. "Can you blame me? After what he did?"

"But I did something, too, and I can't go to Julio. Not anymore. I have to clear my conscience before I continue on. And you could help me."

"Why would I do that?" I stood up then and I walked away from her, taking the goatskin bag with me. This was foolish, and despite how exhausted I was, I *had* to leave. There was no way this was anything other than a ploy to keep me distracted. Julio was bound for us, and I was not going to let him catch me. I would lose myself in Obregán, and I would leave this entire nightmare behind.

"I can help you."

I scoffed at her. "No, you can't. Not with what I need."

"I'm sorry about your friend," she said, her voice in a high, pleading tone. "What my father did to him. But that's not what I meant."

I packed up my sleeping roll but kept la pala close.

"I can help you with something else."

Don't listen to her, I told myself.

"I know someone en mi aldea who can take your power away."

I stilled.

My breath was caught in my throat.

"She offered it to my papi before he chose his path. Before he became corrupted."

"You're lying," I said, and I couldn't control how shaky I sounded. The idea was *offensive*. "There's no way that's true. You can't give this up! No one can."

"I know it can happen," she insisted, and she stood and came toward me, her hands up. "My friend Ivan used to be a cuentista. He is the one who gave the power to Julio."

"No!" I threw my hands up in the air. "And he did so *without* dying?"

Tears spilled down her cheeks. "Ivan fell in love with someone, someone who needed him, someone who understood him. So he sought out our curandera—Simone—and she did it for him. She said it could never be reversed. And Papi volunteered to take it on. He . . ."

She didn't finish the sentence. Her gaze dropped down, and her bottom lip quivered.

"He *what*?" I moved closer. "Emilia, what did he do?"

"I have to tell you my story," she said.

"But I don't know if I can!" I said, my face twisting in frustration. "You heard the truth back there." I pointed to the south, toward Empalme. "Those stories . . . they're all still inside me."

"Please," she pleaded once more, wiping at her tear-streaked face.

She was manipulating me. She *had* to be. If a pesadilla threatened her, then maybe I should leave her be, let it claim her for all the times she never bothered to stop the brutality of her father.

But it was so hard. This was what I had been told to do. It was *all* I did. And kneeling there, in front of someone who seemed so desperate, I didn't know how to say no.

No matter how far I had run from Empalme, I was a cuentista. I knew nothing else.

"That is all I will do for you," I said, and my voice was flat, threatening. "After I am done, you will tell me where to find Simone, and then I'm leaving."

She nodded quickly. "It's not a trap," she said, and maybe if she hadn't always been so cold, I would have felt pity for her. She sat up, her hair now tied in one long braid down her back, and she still trembled when she held her hands out. A panic threaded through my veins, and I told myself that if this was a trap, I was probably surrounded already.

Was I wrong to be curious? Was I wrong to want to know why she had followed me so very far, without any supplies that I could see?

I reached out. Put my palms faceup. Emilia put her hands in mine—they were wet with sweat, and now I could see that her arms were covered in a dark substance, dust and dirt caked on to it. Blood.

Whose blood?

"Are you ready?" I asked her.

She nodded.

"Tell me, Emilia. Why are you here?"

Let me tell You a story, Solís.

Emilia was born far, far to the north, in a place she was too young to remember, and then she was taken to a land of devastation when she was still an infant.

She grew up in Solado.

Julio never forgave himself for what had happened. They came at night, dressed in strange pale outfits with monstrous masks on their faces, and then, when Emilia's family awoke, they were underground, in a new home, one that was forced upon them. Her family learned the hard way that this was how they took you: under the cover of night, while you slept, when you were most vulnerable.

They had a name, one given to them by the original inhabitants of Solado, those who had survived the initial attack:

Los pálidos.

The ones who wore the pale vestments.

Emilia's mother, Alegría, told her stories of where they had lived before: among los árboles, the cover of the leaves shielding them from the heat of Solís. Whenever she spoke of this place, her eyes sparkled. Emilia could tell she missed it.

It was nothing like the tiny room they inhabited in Solado.

All their homes were carved out of the underground passageways. They were cool and dark, which Emilia loved. It was all she knew. But her parents were haunted by the low ceilings, by the lack of sunlight, by los pálidos who now controlled their lives.

Julio believed that he had been weak not to defend his family, and it was not long before his time in Solado transformed to bitterness. He should not have been asleep, he reasoned, or he should have woken up when los pálidos came to steal them away.

No matter how often his wife, Alegría, or Emilia told him there wasn't anything he could have done, he still believed with his whole heart that he could have saved them.

Alegría, however, adapted. She had a daughter to raise, and Emilia grew up with a mother who taught her many things, but of them all, the most important was how to *thrive*. "This is not enough," she told Emilia once when she was little. "One day, I will get us out of here, mija. I promise you. But until then, you must feel *alive*."

She taught Emilia weaving, which came naturally to Alegría, but Emilia struggled with it. Alegría made colorful, vibrant serapes, taking inspiration from the layers of rock and sediment they found deep below the ground. These caught the attention of los pálidos, the strange people whom they never saw without their ghastly outfits. It wasn't long before they realized they could make money off Alegría's work, and then she was given a privilege few enjoyed:

Alegría could leave Solado.

So Alegría was allowed back aboveground, and Julio despised his wife for the freedom. He felt *he* should be the one

allowed out so he could begin to plot their escape. But Alegría
assured him that this was meant to be, that she would find a
way to free them all.

But Emilia's father never truly believed her, and his acidic
resentment grew and grew.

Alegría's time was split: she would spend weeks weaving
down below, then would go away for days at a time, only to
return with stories of the land around Solado. "Solo era ce-
niza," she told Emilia. "Solís took Their anger out up there.
It really is poison."

"How do you survive, Mami?" Emilia asked.

"Los pálidos give me their masks," she explained. "They
are uncomfortable. But they keep me alive."

One morning, Alegría sneaked Emilia through the tunnels,
past the crops and other homes and the large hall for meeting others. She showed her daughter the exit she always used
whenever she left their underground world. She walked Emilia
back slowly, forced her to memorize everything she passed.

"One day," she told her, "you may need to leave. I want you
to know how."

Emilia did not understand, but she obeyed.

Alegría gave her daughter stories. She taught her about
their old home, of the forests that seemed to stretch up to las
estrellas, of all the growth that had sprung to life after Solís
set the world on fire. "I miss seeing the sky," she admitted.
"The blue. The sun. The way the light filters through tall
branches."

"Is the sky not blue anymore, Mami?"

"Sí, mija, it still is," she said, stroking Emilia's hair. "I just
don't see it that much."

"What do you see? What is above the earth?"

She told her. Of aldeas near and far, of those who lived

aboveground in the sun and heat, who hunted water, who lived en las montañas. She told her everything she could.

She even said that the land above Solado was destitute, that Solís must have punished the original inhabitants with a unique fury.

Whenever Alegría was home, Emilia was inseparable from her. They weaved together; Emilia learned how to use a loom; Alegría taught her how to tie back her hair quickly and efficiently. They were constantly at each other's side.

And Julio came to resent that, too.

Five years ago, Alegría disappeared. She was taken aboveground for a delivery, and she had kissed Emilia on the forehead before leaving. "Hasta pronto," she said. "I'll have a surprise for you when I return."

One day became two.

Became seven.

Became a hundred.

Julio began to drink again.

Emilia clung to hope for a long time. Success kept Mami away, she reasoned. Each morning, she expected that when she opened her eyes, Alegría would be back at her loom, weaving a new, more colorful design, and she would welcome Emilia with open arms and a story.

But it never happened.

And Emilia sank deeper into her grief.

It was around this time that strange creatures began to haunt the passageways in Solado. Sabuesos, they were called. It seemed to be a rumor at first, but not long after Alegría disappeared, Emilia was certain she saw one in the fields, stalking behind rows of maíz. She tried to tell her papi about it, but . . . well, Emilia's father had his own life to live.

This was how it went: He tended the fields during the day, harvesting food that mostly went to los pálidos. Then, Julio would leave in the early evening to go find his friends, and Emilia knew he would not return until he was even more drunk, even more resentful. He would come back and shower Emilia with kisses and affection in apology. Then he would gently pick at her, criticize her, remind her that she was not her mother, and then the yelling would begin. He hated that Alegría had left, he hated that he was not so talented as she, he wished he could have sold the serapes instead, and it happened over and over and over again.

Emilia missed her mami terribly, but it was not until Alegría was gone for over a year that she realized she also missed her best friend.

So Emilia stopped talking. What was there to say to Papi anymore? She could only apologize so much for something that was out of her control. So when the guardian appeared at her door—in the form of un perro, a long, lanky creature with dark, short fur, black spotted with gray—Emilia assumed the worst. Her mother was gone forever, and they had come to take her next.

But the guardian said nothing. They sat next to Emilia, curled up against her when she cried herself to sleep that night, and every morning, she awoke to the guardian at the foot of her bed.

Was she chosen? Emilia had no idea. But every day, that guardian—whom she named Luz—stuck by her. Luz accompanied her when she started to work in la huerta, a place deep in one of the caverns where children first began to pay their dues. It was the most time she spent around los pálidos, and it gave her a sympathy for her father. They were a *miserable* people.

"It's why they wear those damn monstrosities," Papi had explained after her first shift picking manzanas and carrying baskets full of them to another part of Solado. "Apparently, Solís punished them worse than everyone else, and the light of the sun is deadly to them." He laughed at that. "They think they are owed the world."

After weeks of the difficult labor, with only one day to herself, Emilia began to talk. She told Luz about what little she remembered of Alegría's stories of their old home, then told her about her mami. Luz sat there and occasionally tilted her head as if she was listening. Emilia appreciated it, and so she told more stories, often while she was collecting fruit that had fallen to the ground. She shared her fears and her anxieties with Luz so frequently that years passed before she realized she had not sought out Ivan. Why would she need a cuentista when she was telling the truth to her guardian?

And then Emilia started making up stories. She imagined a life outside of Solado, outside of all this labor, outside of wishing for her mami to come home. As the years passed, she stopped thinking it was possible, but her stories kept alive the tiniest sliver of hope. Maybe her stories could come true.

It was less than a year ago that Julio burst into their home, panting and sweating. He said nothing at first. He bundled some of his clothing together, brought them up to his nose, sniffed. Stuffed them in a bag. He laughed, then looked up at her. "I am finally free," he said, and Emilia's heart sank. The joy dripped off him. "And we are leaving this wretched place."

"Leaving? For *where*?"

"Didn't you hear? Simone has given me a *gift*."

Luz rose from the floor; the fur on her back bristling.

Tienes el poder de una cuentista, she said.

As long as Luz had been by her side, she'd said nothing to

her; this was the first time Emilia had ever heard that voice, deep and sensuous.

"I do," said Julio, and a wicked smile spread over his lips. "And I already used it, and now I know how to leave."

Do not go with him, Luz said. *He will corrupt everything*.

"She is *my* daughter," Julio sneered. "She will do as I say."

"What do you mean by 'using' your power, Papi?" Emilia pushed herself up from her bed. "What have you done?"

He crossed the room quickly, unnaturally. "Don't you get it, mija? No one has ever used it as *I* have."

"I'm confused. How did you—?"

"Ivan," he said. "Ivan wanted to be with his man, and Simone needed a volunteer, someone she could give the power to instead."

Luz growled again. *You are supposed to be pure of heart*.

"It doesn't matter," he said, his voice giddy. "Because Simone believed me."

He threw an empty bolsita at Emilia then and ordered her to pack. Emilia knelt and ran her hands over Luz's head. "Luz, what's happening? Is this real?"

Unfortunately. There was a chilling pause. *Emilia, mi amor, you must not go with him*.

Emilia clutched at her chest. She trusted Luz unconditionally, but she still could not believe that she was speaking aloud. She wanted to do as she was asked, but she found herself gazing up at her papi, lost in her confusion.

"Me and my men . . . we are heading south," Julio told her, caressing her chin, and then he moved on to her clothing, started piling them on Emilia's bed. She grabbed at him to stop him, and he swatted at her as if she were nothing more than an insect. "It is time for me to stop waiting around this place for your mother to bring us our fortune."

Emilia was terrified, but no matter what Julio said about Mami, she stood up for her. "But how can you—?"

"I'm done waiting," he said, and the smile he wore on his face cut her down.

"Papi, we *can't* leave," she begged. "What if the stories are true? What if the land above us is poison? What if we die because we don't have protection?"

He ignored her, as he always did.

She held on to Luz as her father's men—Emilia did not even know their names—came into her home. She screamed as they grabbed her arms and legs and yanked her out into the passageway. Luz began to howl, then leapt at one of the men, tearing at his forearm, determined to reach her.

The last thing Emilia saw of her home was one of those men looping a rope around Luz's neck and holding her back. Her guardian pulled fiercely on the rope, yapping and howling and crying out, and then Luz was gone, lost around a corner.

Emilia was wrested from her home that night, and, under the cover of darkness, she left the land of devastation. Just before she was taken aboveground, her face was wrapped tightly in a rough cloth; she was told that this was for her protection. She could not see much at all, and her voice was gone from all the screaming, but she paid attention. She watched as they stepped out into the arid land above. With each foot forward, the ground crunched underneath her. She listened to Papi talk to the others of what they could do now that they were free. What Julio would be able to accomplish as a cuentista.

They threw Emilia on the back of a pale horse, tied her in the saddle. She did not fight much. Where could she go? She tried to see what she could in the light of las estrellas, but the eerie glow filled the land with shadows. She passed

out then, mostly from terror, her head against the horse's
neck, her eyes focused on those impossible twinkles of light
above her.

Las estrellas.

She awoke in the back of a wooden cart, one that rumbled and bounced along a dirt trail, and the sun was just
beginning to rise. She lifted herself up, and the sight of the
desert made her gasp. The hills unfolded around them, the
landscape stretched out in every direction, and panic filled
her. She had lived her entire life trapped, enclosed, with
ceilings and walls she could reach and touch at all times.
There was a thickness in the air from Your heat, and she ran
fingers over her arms, her face, down her legs, felt the moisture along them, the way sweat beaded on her skin, and she
sucked the air deep into her lungs. It did not poison her. She
did not collapse, she did not plunge to the ground and clutch
her chest, *she did not die.*

She was still alive. What *else* had she been lied to about?

Emilia saw her father ahead of her on a light brown horse,
but he seemed uninterested in her. They journeyed in silence,
and she did not know what direction they traveled. South, as
Julio had declared? West? East? How far had they gone to
escape the land of ash?

By the time You were firmly in the sky, she had prayed to
You. Asked You to tell her what was happening. But You said
nothing. Julio and his men—she counted nine of them—instead
spoke of what awaited them in each new aldea. Riches. Glory.
Power. They spoke of a time long ago, centuries before La
Quema, when there was a dignity in control, a respect gained
from taking what you wanted. "That is what our masters taught
us," Julio said, riding alongside the cart. "We are done pleas-
ing Solís, mija, so you can stop praying. We are done living by

all these rules, in all this guilt, and we are done waiting for a
god to speak to us. We will speak to *Them*."

She wanted Luz back, Solís. She didn't care if Julio left
them both to do whatever he wanted. She just wanted to see
Luz's soft face and her brown eyes.

She wanted to see her mami, too, but she knew that was
impossible.

They traveled all day, and Emilia experienced the true intensity of Your burning. There were no shadows, no caverns to
duck back into when You became too hot. It drained her, and
her skin was tender and red the next morning. But still they
pressed on, and by mediodía on the next day, they arrived en
la aldea of La Palmita, and that was the first time Emilia saw
death. Julio led them to the center of La Palmita and slaughtered a woman who was stretching out hides to dry in the sun.
She watched as Julio's saber was lifted in the air, the way it
swiftly dropped down, the spray of red, the scream cut short
as the act repeated. When the woman's son tried to stop Emilia's father, one of Julio's men stuck him with a long blade, then
laughed as he squirmed and shook on the ground.

La Palmita was theirs now.

But this display was not enough. Emilia watched in horror
as Papi called out to the man curled up over the bodies of the
woman and the boy that he had killed. He ordered the man,
whose long, scraggly hair was coated in the sweat of terror, to
kneel before him. Then Julio placed his hand on his head, and
with no hesitation, the man was telling the truth: admitting
his crimes. His misdeeds. His betrayals.

And then he told Julio where he could find the food stores
for La Palmita.

"I am now your cuentista," Julio announced. "And you will
not defy me."

Emilia couldn't remember how long they stayed there, how
many people Julio and his men killed in that first aldea. Time
passed without any meaning or sense, and the days bled together like the pile of corpses left in the plaza of La Palmita.

You said and did nothing, Solís. So they continued.

As soon as they got bored, after they had stolen everything
they could, after la gente de La Palmita resorted to hiding
in their homes to avoid any contact with Julio and his men,
the terror finally ended. Julio gathered what he could—all
the more richer, all the more certain that he was on a divine
path—and led his men to their next conquest.

Emilia went with them. She could not see any other options.

They would travel again, farther and farther each time,
and then they would descend on a new aldea like a swarm,
using their violence and Julio's power to take everything.
Emilia became numb to death, and she prayed to You to give
her a way out of this. She wondered whether she had done
something wrong, if she had kept some horrible secret from
You, and this was how You forced her to pay the price. Her pesadilla had manifested as Julio, her immorality born as this
journey of violence.

You did not answer her.

She moved from aldea to aldea, drifted from one display
of horror to another, and she had no means of stopping the
monster her papi had become. She soon lost track of how long
it had been since she left Solado. A month? Two? They never
traveled long before they found a new aldea, a new comunidad to terrorize.

And then she came to Empalme.

Julio did not tire of death, but she realized that he was
spending longer and longer in each aldea, treating them as
if they were a game to be played. She watched as they qui-

EACH OF US A DESERT

etly moved into Empalme; she watched Julio plan what to take control of; she watched him slice off the arm of that poor woman; and then she watched him wait. He said he had a new idea, something that news from the north had convinced him was possible.

So they stayed. This was uncommon, as Julio rarely lasted more than a few days in any single place. But in Empalme, with the well firmly in his control, the friction did not dwindle.

Emilia was consumed by an immense pity for los aldeanos de Empalme. She had seen so much suffering before, but these people . . . they did not fight back like other aldeas. They believed that Solís would protect them, would *save* them, and they hid in their homes, avoiding Julio and his men, as if he would fade away if they ignored it all. It filled her with a terrible sadness.

She refused to show it, though, because she knew that if Papi saw even a shred of sympathy on her face, he would lash out at her as he had back in Solada. So her face became as a mask, a cold, terrible thing, and she buried her feelings deep inside her so that they were a tiny stone, one she could ignore, could pretend wasn't even there.

And then Julio struck back.

Oh, Lito. Emilia had watched it happen, knowing that, once again, there was nothing she could do to stop it. Should she have defied Julio? What other choice was there? She had never seen un sabueso up close; they had existed in the shadows for so long. Yet here one was, and its power was so much more terrifying than she could have ever expected. When it returned with Lito's arm, she refused to look at it.

Julio had not touched her since they left Solado. Not one embrace, not one graze of the fingertips, nothing. But now his hand whipped out, grabbed her by the back of the neck, and he forced her to watch the carnage.

Emilia decided, right then, to leave. She had no idea how to survive on her own, how to subsist on the land, how to thrive under Your gaze, but she couldn't stay anymore. She couldn't be a part of this, and she knew that as terrible and frightening as it was, she *did* have a choice.

That night, she wore her lightest clothing to bed, hoping it would keep the heat off her body. She waited to sneak out until after Julio, drunk off tesgüino, ordered his men to gather their supplies and begin packing for the next aldea. Somewhere to the south, he had said. There was more to conquer.

He had never smiled wider at her.

She did not escape that night, however. She wanted to make sure Papi was long gone, that he would not come after her, so she found an abandoned home and buried herself in old clothing and rags. She waited there, the stench of rot and decay unbearable, until Empalme became quiet again.

When You appeared in the east the next morning, and she was confident she could finally leave, she bolted from that shack, desperately hoping that Julio was not looking for her, and headed for the north gate, and—

She found me trying to escape as well. She was terrified, too, Solís, and in her mind, I was going to reveal her to Julio, a final act of spite so that I could depart unscathed. But she watched me run off, let me get ahead of her, and then she began to follow once it was safe. She took it as a sign and obeyed the feeling that gripped her, that compelled her toward me.

She lost sight of me a few times, unable to see my fleeing body as I crossed over hills and down into ravines. She knew this sudden plan made no sense, that there was no real reason to follow me. But she saw a girl fleeing for her life, and it felt like a sign, as though You were telling her that she was not alone. Here was someone else, shunned by those around her, alone in a crowd, and she believed that, at the very least, I would understand.

She always found me, no matter how long she went without a glimpse of my long hair, my dusty clothing. She thought she had lost me for good when I climbed las bajadas, but then she whispered another prayer to You.

That was her, wasn't it, Solís? It wasn't Lito hiding behind a saguaro. It was *her*.

But her journey was even more fraught than mine. Emilia had a visitor, too: la mujer de La Palmita, who stretched her hides in the sun, who spilled her blood on them as Julio sliced her down. She walked behind Emilia as she climbed la montaña, and she wouldn't speak. She tried to keep her eyes ahead of her, and then she looked back again—

She *shouldn't* have looked back, Solís.

La mujer, nameless and bloody, opened her mouth wide, wider, until her jaw cracked, and a hand reached out of that gaping hole, and then an arm, and the hand grabbed at anything, hooked its fingers on the woman's ear. He pulled himself out of her, covered in the remains of his own mother, and her body collapsed in a heap and poured into the cracks of the trail. He stood up, and there was the long blade, still stuck in his stomach, and he looked down at it.

Then at Emilia.

Then he pulled it out.

Then he showered her with blood, so much of it that it filled her mouth, hot and bitter, and she couldn't breathe, couldn't scream, and she fell to the road and clawed at her arms and her throat, and then

then
It was all gone.
The woman,
her son,
the blood.
Except for her arms, where Emilia had clawed at herself,
and as she bled, she blamed herself. She blamed herself for
what someone else had done.
And then she found me.

Forgive her, Solís. She didn't know. But she is here now, and she wants You to protect her from Julio, after all those years when You didn't.

How could You let this happen to her? How could You allow such horrible things in Your world? If You were powerful enough to destroy us all in one blow, one burst of fire and fury, then why could You not take care of one person? One situation? One impossible problem?

Did You ever care about her? Or did You think she had to suffer in order to become worthy of Your attention?

She gave me her story.

And *I* listened.

When she finished, the breath wheezed out of Emilia's throat. My arms pulsed with anger, with terror, with resentment, with longing, with all the emotions Emilia had given me, and they were a terrific chaos inside. Her story was a living thing, and it felt Lito's, Marisol's, it knew the same horror of los sabuesos, of feeling trapped and alone; it clung to the bitterness of Ofelia, to Omar's guilt. I sat there on the ground, closed my eyes, ingested this story, let this new truth that felt so at home with its companions make a place within my body.

Solado. That was where Marisol was from. It was the land that was stolen from her people.

As Emilia's fear and regret clamored for space inside even as they attached themselves deep in my belly, I knew I would have to keep this story, too, and not just because I had kept all the others. Emilia's anger was too familiar. Her desire for freedom was too close to my own. *I was so wrong about her.*

And I now had information I needed. Simone. Simone could give my power to *someone else.*

"I'm sorry," Emilia said, and her voice faltered. She swallowed. "I had to tell someone. I had to tell *you.*"

I nodded at her, but I kept my distance. I had misunderstood her. I had seen Emilia's coldness as something to avoid, to despise.

I had been so, so wrong.

I wanted to reach out to her.

To comfort her.

Was this catharsis? Validation? Were the stories pushing me to do this?

But I did nothing. I couldn't let myself get near her at all, not in the way that I wanted. How was I worthy of that?

She could not trust me. I was a liar.

I couldn't trust myself either. Her story was so familiar to me: Her life had been a lie. She had been trapped. But she had *escaped*. A selfish desire to keep the story, to examine it, to understand it, swept over me. How could she possibly appreciate that?

Emilia was overflowing with shame; I saw it in how she clung to herself, in how she made her body smaller, how she shrank in the hope of becoming invisible.

"Have some more water," I told her, passing her the goatskin bag.

She nodded.

Emilia looked at me with such earnestness, Solís, and I hated it. I was seeing her as a means to an end, to gaining my own freedom. And I shouldn't have done that.

I did it anyway. It was so easy.

I scooted back a bit, then stood and walked to the west toward the farthest edge of the vista. From where I was, Obregán glowed to my right, but the montañas stretched as far as I could see that night. I lowered myself to the ground, coughed a few times, and the stories roiled in me, ready for their journey back to the earth.

No, I told them.

As soon as the ritual began, it was over. I held them there with my willpower, urging them to reach into my body and hold tight. I had done as much for days now, and it was so much easier now than it had been that night after Lito's ritual, when I had made my fateful decision. I just needed to make sure the stories would stay where they were: within *me*.

A deer, its coat the color of the desert at night, soft blues and grays, appeared to my left. It raised its head, and its antlers twisted in every direction, small thorns jutting off the sides of them, a tangled mess, and its eyes glowed green.

We both were still, and then it turned and slowly trod away.

I gulped, wiping at the sweat now forming along my hairline. I watched the deer fold into the shadows, then shook off a creeping sensation along my skin before heading back to Emilia.

She looked up at me as I returned and handed me the goatskin bag. "Everything okay?" she asked.

I nodded. "A little drained," I said, and I drank.

"You were so *fast*," she said.

I drank again. "What?"

"It's like you were made to be out here. I could barely keep up with you while you were climbing la montaña."

I shrugged. "Papá taught me well, I suppose."

"I have a proposition, then."

I passed her the goatskin bag, but she did not drink from it. Those eyes—which I had regarded as cold before—bore into me, dark and mysterious. She was trying to see into my heart, wasn't she? To see if she was safe to suggest what she was about to say.

"I'm listening."

"I have something you need," she continued. "Simone. I can take you to Simone."

I frowned. ". . . but?"

"I want to go with you."

I shook my head. "Mira, no te conozco, Emilia. I'm sorry for what has happened to you. But until a few moments ago, I thought you were one of the worst people I'd ever met."

"I know how to get to Solado. Do you?"

I grimaced, well aware that she had a point. "No, I don't."

"Then you need me, too."

"Wait, why do *you* need *me*?"

"I don't know how to survive out here on my own," she replied, gesturing around her in the darkness, her brown skin illuminated in the starlight. "If you help me, I'll help you."

I lowered myself to sit across from her. "Tell me, then," I said. "Why do *you* want to go back to Solado if the place is so awful?"

"Luz."

There was no hesitation on her part as she uttered the name. I gazed into her face, saw the tracks of her tears over her cheekbones.

She was serious.

"You're going to go back for her?"

"They took my guardian from me," she said. "And I just know it—I feel it in my heart—Luz is still alive."

She went silent, and her shoulders drooped. "They took my best friend from me."

"And you'd go to Solado to get her back? And introduce me to Simone?"

"Without question," she said, gazing back up at me. "You help me, and I will do the same for you."

Una vida sin el poder de una cuentista. I couldn't imagine it. No more stories. No more responsibilities I did not ask for. No more exhaustion. My freedom from Empalme . . . what if that could last *forever*?

It was too irresistible.

So I did not resist it.

I put my hand over my eyes, then over my heart. "I'll do it," I said.

"Gracias—" Emilia began, her eyes lighting up with relief.

"But we go to Obregán first."

She squirmed. "Shouldn't we keep going?"

I scoffed at her. "First, we are not going *anywhere* right now. I'm exhausted and I need to sleep."

"No, I meant—"

I raised a hand to stop her. "I know what you meant. But I need to get supplies in Obregán, and there are some people I need to see." When she frowned, I continued. "We do it my way, or we don't do it at all."

"Bueno," she said. "I brought some things, but I don't think it's enough."

She paused.

Hand over the eyes, then over the heart.

The sign.

See the truth; believe the truth.

It meant that she was telling the truth.

The pact was sealed.

"And you're sure you know the way to Solado?"

She hesitated. "Sí," she said. "Not precisely the same way we came here, but I know how."

I let my suspicion pass. She had a solid motivation to get to So-lado, and Julio had not sprung himself on us. She was most likely telling the truth. And it wouldn't make sense for her to guide me to the middle of nowhere, because . . . well, she would die, too.

"We'll get there. Together."

"Together," I repeated.

A warmth flooded my chest, pushed the stories further down.

"We leave in the morning," I said, trying to ignore the sensa-tion. "You have any agua left?"

She nodded. "Not much."

"Let's use yours to clean you off. Shouldn't be too far tomorrow to get more."

Emilia was still shaking as she sat there, so I dropped myself down beside her, took her canteen, and poured a tiny amount into my left hand. "May I?" I asked her, and she held out her right arm to me, nodding, and I used the water to wipe the blood and dirt off as best as I could.

I poured more water into my hand, then took her left hand in mine. I ran water over it and gazed up at her. Her eyes were locked with my own. They were dark. Soft. Vulnerable.

If she knew the truth, she wouldn't be here.

I ran my hand up her left arm, toward her elbow, and then she jerked away, tucking her arm close to her body, and wouldn't look at me.

Why is she afraid of me? I thought.

And the darkest part of me—my terrible doubt, those terrible stories—answered back:

Because you deserve it.

"I'll do that," she announced, and she took the canteen back. Just like that, we returned to coldness. To what we had been a day earlier.

To being strangers.

"Fine," I said, and I walked to my sleeping roll and lowered myself to it, eager to get some sleep before that night got any stranger. A few minutes later, I heard Emilia's footsteps near me.

"Gracias," she said, but I did not turn to look at her. "For helping me."

She rolled out something next to me, not too close, and I heard her body settle on the ground. I was facing Obregán—there was a light in the sky above it—and I counted some of las estrellas that still shone brightly. Emilia's breathing slowed, and she fell asleep shortly after that. I was aware of how close she was, but I didn't move, didn't turn toward her. As my heart raced, I spoke the words to her, like a prayer to the desert, to the night and las estrellas:

"You're welcome."

I slept.

I dreamed of Mamá.

We were outside our home, behind it, and the sun was setting. As it sank in the west, Mamá twirled. She spun in a dance, her black hair parted down the middle of her head, and it flowed evenly on either side of her face. She called out my name in a musical whisper. *Xochitl! Xochitl!* She would reach for me, but every time I stretched out, we couldn't touch. We couldn't close the chasm between us. She spun farther and farther, and I brought my leg up to step forward, but I couldn't move in that direction.

She danced and danced and danced, away from me, away from my outstretched arms, and she sang my name the entire time.

Xochitl!

Xochitl!

Xochitl!

I could not answer her.

Then I dreamed of Papá. We were in the center of Empalme, and he floated out from our stone well, his arms crossed in front of him, cradling a baby swaddled in a colorful serape. He wouldn't look at me. "Papá!" I called out, but his eyes were trained on the infant he held, and he rocked him, cooed at him, raised a finger and brushed it over the face, and somehow, I knew it was Raúl.

He made a gesture with his hand, beckoned me toward him, and this time, I could move with ease, and so I slunk over to Papá, and he peeled back the serape, and I screamed and screamed and screamed, and then he dropped Raúl's head, a tongue fell from the mouth of mi hermano, and Papá laughed and laughed and laughed—

I awoke covered in sweat. I sat upright, and Emilia was curled up, unmoving, unaware of my terror, and the world was still and silent around me. I remained there, my eyes adjusting to the darkness just before dawn. The stars around us were so far, so distant, and I watched them disappear, a handful at a time, and then the horizon to the east glowed.

Brighter.

Brighter.

You awoke. You gazed upon us.

It was time to move.

I gathered up my things and packed them away first, then knelt beside Emilia. I hesitated for a second, uncertain about touching her at all given her response to me the night before. So I rubbed the edge of my huarache in the dirt loudly. She woke, her eyes shooting open as she rolled onto her back.

"Were you watching me?" she said sleepily, rubbing at her eyes.

"No," I said, too quickly. "Yes. I mean . . . I felt bad waking you up. But we need to go."

She smiled, and the angles on her face no longer seemed as vicious as they had in Empalme. "Should we make a fire? Maybe make some food?"

I looked to the east. "No," I said. "We should start heading down. I've got some dried meat and fruits, and we can eat those, and then we'll go."

I left her to pack as I headed for the whitethorn so I could relieve myself for the morning. I passed Emilia on the way back as she was headed to do the same. I waited for her on the end of the trail, my eyes locked on Obregán in the distance. More shapes were appearing as the sky lit up la ciudad: towers. Buildings that rose impossibly from the ground. Creatures soaring through the air, taking off from atop structures and then circling over Obregán before heading to some unknown destination.

"¿Estás lista?" Emilia called out, and I waved her over. She had her burlap bag slung over her shoulder and I wondered what was inside it.

"Not much farther," I said, pointing toward our destination. "We'll figure out where El Mercado is once we get there."

The idea of a "we" was strange to me, but Emilia said nothing. She nodded at me, then gestured me to lead the way.

I couldn't allow myself to get comfortable with this notion, this idea that I was one to be followed. But I also realized that I was no longer alone.

cuando estoy solo   when I am alone
estoy vivo   I am alive

I would have to adjust.

I was used to Empalme and to open space. I could cross our whole aldea in a quarter hour, and I knew everyone who lived within the boundary of our gates. I had reason to; at some point or another, each person came to unload their stories on me. But as we descended toward Obregán, the very idea of that ciudad perplexed me.

The sun rushed out over el valle, and with each turn in the road, la ciudad grew closer. I saw more of the flying creatures, and some seemed to have wingspans bigger than houses. How did those buildings not tip over and crumble, taking others along with them? I could see carts and horses and people on foot, almost all of them slowly scattering away from Obregán in every direction, though only a few were traveling toward us. Few visitors from Obregán ever made the journey to Empalme. We were probably just as much of a mystery to them as they were to us.

We continued to walk in silence, and my sore muscles were thankful that they did not have to do so much work. I spotted a large herd of something—perhaps cattle—leaving the eastern side of Obregán, heading off into the endless expanse of desert. I watched them for a while until they were nothing more than a speck on the horizon, and I wondered if others experienced this perspective. Were we all specks to one another in this isolated, empty world?

A man passed us on his way up about an hour into our descent. He waved to us in greeting. His name was Martín, and he was returning to his husband and son, making the long journey to the southeast to his aldea. Batopilas, he called it. I had never heard of it before. His cart was stacked high with grain for los aldeanos back home, and he asked us if he could sell us any. I gripped the coin purse tucked into the waist of my breeches, then shook my head.

He bade us goodbye, and his horse kicked up dirt as it pulled him up the hill. He would be alone for days.

I glanced over at Emilia, who kept her gaze straight ahead, her expression featureless. Did she like being alone? Her story rumbled in my gut, and her emotions pierced me. She had not truly been alone until she escaped Julio.

I shivered. Parts of her life were so strange to me, so unfathomable. Like Solado. Living underground. Having a guardian choose you. But then the other stories awoke, scrambling for validation, to be noticed, and I pressed a hand on my stomach, trying to calm them. How many lives had I understood before I gave them back to the desert?

As we neared the bottom of the road an hour later, there were more people. Some were climbing up the pass by themselves, either on burros, in carts pulled by horse, or on foot. There was a small camp set snug into a fold en la montaña, and I saw a boy, brown and joyous, run away from his mamá as she tried to feed him. He hid behind a tent staked to the ground with wood, canvas stretched over the posts to block out the sun. Did they live here? Were they taking a break before continuing on elsewhere?

The range of possibility spread in my mind, and I was struck by how little I had known of the world. I grew up aching to travel to Obregán, yes, but there were so many other aldeas beyond it. How different were they? Who else had chosen to leave their home? Were there other cuentistas out there who had given up their duties, who had defied You?

My life was full of stories. The ones given to me in ritual. The ones told to me. Those inside my body felt real, living. But what of all the oral traditions told to me by Mamá, Papá, Tía Inez?

What if those stories were *wrong*? What would that make me?

The last stretch of the road was flat, and the sun was now coming over the edge of the very pass we'd just descended. It shone brightly over us, and sweat beaded on my forehead. Obregán felt more and more intimidating as we approached it. I could not understand and appreciate its size from the top of la montaña. Down here, it was obvious that many of the structures and buildings en la ciudad were as tall as twenty or thirty homes stacked on top of one another. Somehow, they remained as still as the saguaros.

We were close to the southern entrance when I asked Emilia if we could stop for a moment. I stepped to the side of the road and stood there, staring, unable to fathom how many things there were to look at. La Ciudad Obregán was so high, so wide, and I could now see people leaning out of windows, some shouting at others down below or hanging clothing to dry. The sound, even at this distance, was like nothing I had ever heard. Obregán *hummed*, a magic of sorts passing through these people and this place. Or was it even magic? A creature snorted behind me, and I jumped, turned to see some massive bestia with thick, curly hair, two gnarled horns jutting out from its head. It nuzzled its owner, who walked alongside it, then snorted at me again as the two went on their way.

"What is *that*?" said Emilia.

I stared openmouthed.

There was too much to take in. We moved toward la ciudad, right as a group of children, their skin various shades of brown, rushed past us. It was instinct more than anything else: I reached out and grabbed Emilia's hand. I didn't even realize I had done it until I looked to her and saw that she was staring down at our fingers clasped together.

I pulled mine back, but she shook her head. "No, it's okay," she said. "Just so we don't get separated."

She grabbed my hand this time and pulled me toward Obregán. We walked together into that surreal place, and it was as if a thousand conversations were buzzing in my ear. I heard my tongue being spoken, but plenty of others floated past. There were thick accents that made the words hard and angular, other inflections that seemed to slow down time. A man with a small cart of sizzling meats gestured to us, then let loose a long string of syllables and sounds I had never heard before. I couldn't even tell what kind of meat it was—or what lengua he spoke—so I smiled and shook my head, and then—

The smells. La carne frita hit me first, savory and sharp, and then a stench of waste, most likely from some creature nearby. Then something new. Floral? Was that garlic? Solís, there were so many new scents; how many more would I discover?

My stomach called out as more of these smells taunted me, tantalized me. I looked to Emilia, whose gaze was stuck on a woman selling freshly made pan and tortillas. She smirked when I caught her in the act.

"Looks like we have the same idea," I said.

"Should we get food before we find El Mercado?" she asked.

"Maybe," I said. "My stomach certainly wants to."

We were right on the edge, just past the arched gates, which stood wide open. Los guardias sat on pillars and overlooked those coming and going, their eyes falling on us briefly and slipping right off. We must not have been worth their time. People continued to rush past us, some wearing long cloaks and colorful wrappings on their heads. A couple of men with heavily jeweled fingers and ears, sharing chisme in some strange language, looked the two of us up and down before moving on to wherever they were headed. Two women rushed by in wooden sillas propelled by the power of their own arms, and they wheeled around a crowd and disappeared. People spilled out of a large gray stone building to our right, and I couldn't catch more than one or two words of their conversation. They passed by us as if we weren't there. I watched a woman stroll by with a large clay pot perfectly balanced on her head, and she was communicating with a friend using only her hands.

And the buildings! I leaned my head back as I walked, staring up at the towering impossibilities that loomed all around me. I couldn't see the tops of some of these structures. Someone bumped my shoulder and knocked me out of Emilia's hand, and I tried to scowl at them. But they slipped right back into the crowd, gone as fast as they had come.

"I've never seen so many people!" I said.

Emilia squeezed my hand tighter. "We're close," she said. "Follow me."

I let the crowd take me and Emilia, surround us, make us a part of it. As I walked, first to the east, I couldn't focus on any single thing around me. A quiet anxiety festered in me, the fear building up as people shuffled past, touching me as they did so. Their shoulders brushed mine; a woman placed her hand on the small of my back as she squeezed past, and I kept crashing into people walking toward me. How did anyone ever learn to navigate all of this? How did a person hear conversations over the noise? How did anyone ever memorize all the streets and the alleys? I had been here for so short a time, and I was already completely disoriented.

I was also *elated*. I could go where I wanted. Do what I wanted. See what I wanted.

So I walked, my hand in Emilia's. We tried to keep the pace of the crowd, moving through the shadow of a massive building that appeared to lean over the road. It did not topple over, and no one else seemed alarmed by its tilting presence, so I did my best to accept that it was safe. I reached my free hand out and ran it along the smooth stone at the foundation. It was cool to the touch. Where did they get something like this? How could a stone be so *big*?

It filled me with a childish embarrassment. I knew so little about *everything*. The world of Empalme was so tiny. I had been told that Obregán was enormous, but that could not have prepared me for *this*. And if *my* world was still so small, what else awaited me on this journey? The shame rippled my own foundation, sent heat into my cheeks.

What was I *doing*? How did I ever expect to survive a journey I knew nothing about?

I shook off the feeling and breathed in the air and energy around me. Obregán was alive. Alive during the *day*. I was used to silence, to the heat pushing us back indoors, away from one another, until we spilled out of our homes once nighttime returned. That was not the case here. The people rushed about, unafraid of and unconcerned with You.

They thrived in *spite* of You.

From the stone structure, we moved toward another building, this one capped with a gold dome shimmering in the sunlight. At the top, a small tower reached up into the sky, and there was someone up there, in a tiny window, looking out at la ciudad. The steps leading up to the entrance were covered with people, most of whom were listening to a man in a long flowing white robe. His gray beard swayed as he looked over the gathering.

"Beware of the path that strays from Solís!" he shouted. There was a murmur at this that spread throughout the crowd. "They will surely punish us again if we fail Them! Heed the warning given to us from Hermosillo!"

I didn't understand what he meant—once again, I was lost in my own ignorance—and so I focused on the crowd that drowned out his words. Emilia tugged on me and—

"Heed the wisdom of Solís, Xochitl! Tell the truth!"

I whipped around and stared at the man in the robes, but he wasn't looking in my direction. Neither was anyone else. He was still preaching, his audience rapt and hungry, and I shivered.

"What is it, Xochitl?" Emilia said, sidling up to me.

I scanned the crowd again.

Nothing.

"Never mind," I said. "Let's keep going."

I sped up, ignoring the other voices I heard: The curses from those I bumped into. The conversations floating by. The stories I ingested, each now struggling to find a way up and out of me, each one telling me to turn back, to go to Empalme, to stop this silly game, to spill them into the earth and back to Solís and—

No. *No.* I could not go back.

On the next corner, near the crossroads, there was a wooden sign. It directed people to various buildings or sights, but the only one that mattered to me was in bold lettering: EL MERCADO DE LA CIUDAD OBREGÁN. It pointed east and slightly to the north, and my heart began racing again. I was here. I was *close*. What would I find in El Mercado? What would las cuentistas be able to tell me?

I took the lead, and I pulled Emilia forward. Much as Obregán had risen out of the earth at the top of la montaña, El Mercado de Obregán now towered in front of me. There was no end to it in either direction from the corner where we came to a stop, and the white roof—stretched canvas and cloth, blocking out the sun— was a beacon in the desert.

I had to do this, Solís.

Northwest corner, I told myself, Marisol's directions echoing in my head.

I stopped before the entrance.

"You found it," said Emilia.

I chuckled. "Just followed the sign."

"Maybe," she said, and she let go of my hand. "Vámonos adentro, get some food. And then we should probably get going as soon as we can."

She wasn't wrong. But my hand, damp from the heat and from my nerves, twitched at my side.

I missed holding hers.

So I breathed in deep, and I entered El Mercado de Obregán alongside Emilia.

The din rang and crashed all around me. Sounds bounced off the stone walls, merged with one another, and I tried to take it all in. There was a stall directly to my left, and three people were shouting, trying to negotiate over the roots and vegetables displayed on the counter, all the produce shaped strangely and specked with dirt. The man under the blue awning yelled numbers at the patron on the other side, who consulted the third man, who then offered another number back. My gaze fell to the stall next to it, its colorful blusas stitched with bright patterns. More smells, more sounds, and I looked to my right.

The aisle stretched beyond where I could see, overflowing with people.

Everything competed for space: Bargaining. Conversations. Children yelling. Someone singing sad songs loudly over guitars and an accordion. It was a roar that filled my head, that rattled my insides.

I walked slowly to the east first, pressing in between people, muttering apologies over and over again, but no one else seemed to care about how close everyone was, that people had to basically squeeze tight to one another in order to get anywhere. The stalls were at least organized in rows, so I quickly figured out each section as I passed through it. I moved from los granjeros to what I assumed were cures for ailments of the body and mind. A young woman with skin like the thorny mesquite branches reached out to me, urged me to try her herbs, told me that they would give me a better night's sleep. She was stunningly beautiful, and I listened to her as she listed off other products, other remedies for sale. There were avocado leaves for inflammations of the nerves and skin, jacaranda for upset stomachs. I wanted to keep talking to her, but Emilia nudged me, then jerked her head to the west.

After the herbs and curanderas, I pushed through an area with smelly pens full of bizarre creatures and livestock. A two-headed vaca stared at me with only one set of eyes. Smaller creatures like the guardians of Empalme yipped at me from their wooden crates, and eager jovencitos knelt down to pet them through the cracks and holes, letting them lick their hands and faces. Their fur looked soft, sleek, and inviting. Then there was a row of pájaros in cages, tweeting and chirping at everyone, some of them able to speak whole words and phrases in their high voices. A woman leapt out of a chair in her stall and thrust a small blue pájaro at me, and it perched in her hands, tilting its head from side to side.

I waved a dismissal at her, and then passed through the area marked ROPA. Then COMIDA. My stomach cried out again as the smells hit me, tempted me to make a stop. I took a sharp turn to the north once I neared the end of El Mercado, and the food changed again. From vegetables fritos and fresh fruit, I walked past stalls with raw meat ready to be butchered. There were small pockets of masa frita, stuffed with all sorts of items, and I knew I would try those. A person was selling bowls of guisado de cabra with an aroma that made my mouth water. Dried fruits, nuts, sea-food . . . it was all there.

"Okay, we have to eat *something*," said Emilia.

We tried a small bowl of some sort of guisado overflowing with vegetables and thick brown sauce that was savory and creamy at the same time. Halfway through it, I spotted another booth that sold pan frito, and it made the perfect partner for the guisado. We stuffed ourselves while standing off to the side, watching the flow of people.

There were so many of them.

And then there was me and Emilia. In this entire place, she was the only person that I knew.

But I didn't really know Emilia either. I glanced over at her, watched as she ate her food hungrily. Was she starving? Nervous?

I tipped back the bowl and downed the guisado, then took the remaining pan frito to sop up what was left. "Vámonos, Emilia," I said. Maybe she *did* want to get going sooner rather than later.

She said nothing. Just nodded at me, wiped at sweat forming on her brow, then grabbed my empty bowl. I watched as she returned it to the merchant who had sold us the guisado, then jogged back to me.

The color had drained from her face, and she did not look well. "Are you—?"

"Vámanos," she said. "I'm ready when you are."

We headed north at that point, suspicion gnawing at me. Why did she want to leave? We tucked ourselves between groups of people, squeezing towards the northwest corner. There was too much to look at, too much to smell, too much to process. So I kept my focus singular. I had one goal here.

And then:

A wooden post.

A sign carved in large letters.

CUENTISTAS.

More than one?

I tried to make sense of yet another new reality, another sign that I knew so little. Stalls were bunched up along the wall, heading toward the east, dramatic curtains draped in front of them. Some curtains were pulled shut, while other booths stood open, with people hanging out of them and calling to those who walked by, promising to take their stories, return them to Solís.

There would have to be more than one here, ¿no? At least that made sense to me. There were so many people in Obregán, and a single cuentista would find it impossible. But then I walked to the closest stall, one without a curtain pulled across it, and a man stood up from a chair, smiling at me, his hands stretched out toward me.

"Niña," he said, and a part of me bristled at the term. I wasn't *that* young.

"Espero que puedas ayudarme," I said in my own tongue, and his smile went even wider.

"You are from the south?" he said.

"Sí," I said. "Empalme."

"Ay, muy lejos. And you and your woman traveled all that way together?"

I whipped around. "Oh, no, señor," she said. "We're not—"

"Está bien," he said, his hands up. "Do you need your story taken, niña?"

"Me?" I shook my head. "I was hoping—"

"Before you go any further, we should probably negotiate my fee."

"Your . . . I'm sorry. Your *fee*?"

His features twisted in confusion. "¿No entiendes?"

"What *fee*?" I asked, and I couldn't help my voice pitching up in shock. "You're not supposed to do that."

"I don't tell you how to run your affairs," he said, shaking his head at me. He grabbed the edge of the curtain. "You would do best not to disrespect me."

He dramatically pulled the curtain shut.

The notion bewildered me. People in Obregán paid *money* to tell their stories to las cuentistas? *Why?* The thought had never crossed my mind. This was my duty, and it was important to *everyone*. I would never dream to deny a person peace with Solís because they couldn't pay me. And what of las pesadillas? Las cuentistas kept them from harming others. We didn't make a *living* from it.

I stumbled backwards, the impossibility of it all radiating through every inch of my body.

She came out of the booth to my right, sidled up to me so quickly that I yelped when she appeared. She wore a veil, hooded and dark on the inside, stitched with colorful vines and flowers on red fabric on the outside. Her brown eyes were cold, and she had smeared something dark, like charcoal, around them. "Niña," she cooed, and she took my hand, "let me help you. Let me intercede on your behalf for Solís."

I shook my head. "No, no gracias."

She ran her fingers over the top of my hand, but there was no warmth there, no good intentions, and I shivered.

"I don't think she needs this," said Emilia.

"Do you not believe in Solís, niña?"

"Por supuesto que sí," Emilia replied.

"I can tell she is troubled. For a small fee, I can take her story, return it to Solís, give her peace."

"I would never pay you," I said, spitting the words out in ire. "I've never known a cuentista to take money for this."

"Many people do not have cuentistas in their aldeas or pueblos. They must travel here for help."

I shook my head again and started to walk away. "I don't need you," I said. "I'm a cuentista myself."

Her hand dashed out and grabbed mine. "Even better," she said. "For even cuentistas need someone to listen to their stories. And you're in luck: Soledad is *the* best cuentista in all of Obregán."

"We don't tell our stories to anyone!" I scolded. "And who is Soledad?"

"I am," she said. "And you won't find a better cuentista here." She let go of my hand.

"We have to go," I said. "We have a long journey ahead of us."

"It will only take a few minutes," said Soledad. "Let me give you a sample, if you will. To show you what I can do."

I gazed into her coal-stained eyes. "I need something else," I said. "I don't think you can give it to me."

I should have left.

She held my hands, and I felt it: The pull. The urge. The pathway opening.

This woman needs to tell me something.

The stories rose.

They needed another story to bond to, to feel less alone.

Soledad guided me toward her stall, and Emilia gasped. "Xochitl, what are you *doing*?" she cried out. "We really need to go."

But I didn't listen. Something told me to be right *here*.

I followed Soledad into her space, and she closed the curtains behind me, shrouding us in darkness. She lit a candle on her wooden altar, then motioned for me to sit on the floor on the pillows spread about. Emilia burst in, and the brief flash of light distracted Soledad. "¡Ciérralo!" she barked at Emilia, who obeyed her, then shot a glare in my direction.

Soledad sat across from me, her scent overwhelming the space. Lavender. Something earthy and smoky. She smiled and pulled up the sleeves on her tunic after removing her veil. She set the veil aside and then stuck her hands out. "Breathe with me," she said. "Dame tu nombre, niña."

"Xochitl," I said, taking a deep breath, then laying my hands on hers.

"Close your eyes and focus on my voice," she said, and her voice dropped in volume. "Think about your story, Xochitl. About what you want to tell me. About what you *need* to tell me."

I closed my eyes. Maybe Soledad would make her connection first, but I suspected she would soon spill forth the truth to me.

Nothing. There was no sensation. No opening, no calling of my own story within me. Which wasn't surprising; we did not give up our own stories. It just did not happen.

I opened my eyes, saw that Soledad had hers still closed.

Nothing.

I withdrew my hands. "Soledad, it's not working," I said. "I don't feel anything yet."

She opened her eyes now. "You have not begun to tell me your story yet," she said. "Start talking, and as you tell me the truth, I will take it inside myself."

I balked at her. "That's . . . that's not how it works."

She chuckled at me, waving her hand in my direction as if to swat away this opinion. "You must not be as experienced as I am. I've been doing this since I was your age, niña."

"But are you *sure* this is how it's supposed to work? Do you do it differently here in Obregán?"

This time, her brows arched together in frustration. "Such disrespect for someone so young." She stuck her hands out again, a forceful gesture of spite. "Then show me. Show una vieja how it is done."

There was a bitterness in her voice. I did not say anything in response, though. I slowly put my hands out, palms up, and stretched them toward Soledad until they were close to her. She sighed and placed her fingers on top of my palms, then slid them down toward my wrists, and she cried out, a loud, piercing sound. Her emotions surged forth into my body, plunging their talons into my skin, and they flooded me: shock and terror and regret and shame and—

I need to tell You a story, Solís.

Her name wasn't even Soledad. She was born in Obregán, one of many people whose parents were from the surrounding aldeas, but who chose to leave their homes to find a life in a place better than their own. They were from Batopilas, the same aldea as Martín, and they arrived in Obregán the night before Soledad came into the world screaming and crying. They named her Jovana, and she grew up in a place of chaos, of possibility, of survival.

And then they died.

It was sudden, in the middle of the night, not long after she turned ten. Their bodies were stiff and cold when she woke, and no matter how many times she shook them, they never responded.

She never found out what happened to them.

She was younger than Raúl, Solís, and You took them from her. Did she deserve that? Was she supposed to suffer, too, as Emilia had, so that You could find her worthy?

Her parents' families were all back in Batopilas, and she was just a child, una jovencita. She had no means of understanding

the journey she would have to make, all to get back to a place
she had never known.

So she stayed in her home and she slept a lot, and every time
she woke, she would check to see if her parents were still in the
same spot. It was like that the next day and the next and then
the smell became too overwhelming, and she went next door
to see if Delfina could help make her mother and father come
back. Delfina was short and hunched over, and she looked as
though she could be someone's abuela, but she had no children
of her own. And when she saw Jovana at her front door, telling
her that her parents smelled weird and could she please help
wake them up, Delfina knew what she would have to do.

So Jovana went to live with Delfina, though in those early
months, she would wake up and go back to her home, hoping
to find her parents alive and well, ready to welcome her into
their arms. The home was always empty, always as cold and
lifeless as their bodies. She finally had to stop when another
family moved in. They did not take kindly to someone asking
to see her dead parents.

It wasn't long until Jovana settled into her life with Delfina, who worked in El Mercado selling pottery that she made
by hand. Delfina, her hands knotted, her hair white, began
to fold esa jovencita into her life as best as she could. She invited Jovana to help her with little things at first: like carrying
freshly made pots from the studio to the windowsill to dry.
Like teaching Jovana to shape the pots as she spun the mud
and clay. Soon, that sad girl filled her spirit with Delfina, who
never made Jovana feel like anything but her own daughter.

Jovana met her first cuentista while wandering around,
trying to find a suitable meal for herself and her new mother.
Her name was Soledad, and she was gorgeous, haunting,

irresistible. Jovana had never met anyone so tall, who commanded the attention of those who cast their gaze on her. She coaxed Jovana into her stall, brushing aside her black hair, which was so long that it swept across the floor.

Jovana sat before her, her hands out, and Soledad took her story. She told her everything: of her life while her parents were still living, of Delfina, of the creeping loneliness that invaded her late at night as she wished for a different life.

When the telling was over, Jovana felt lighter. More *alive*. "Puedes ser una cuentista, también," Soledad had told her. "It is a lucrative practice, and there is always someone with guilt in their heart."

"Lucrative?" Jovana had asked. "What does that mean?"

Soledad held her hand out and demanded that Jovana pay her for her services.

She learned her lesson the hard way that day when she returned to Delfina without food, then had to lie about where the money had gone. Delfina had just shaken her head at Jovana and told her that everyone makes mistakes, that she would have to be more careful next time so that the money did not fall out of her pocket. She did not seem to suspect that Jovana had lied, and for some reason, that hurt Jovana more.

Yet she couldn't stop seeing Soledad. The woman allowed her to sit in her stall, hidden behind a curtain in the back, while Soledad took desperate customers, pried their secrets out of them, then charged them modest prices to do so.

They always paid.

They always came back.

She never gave any of those stories to You, but what did those people know? As far as they were aware, Soledad was one of the most sympathetic and understanding cuentistas in

Obregán. She never judged others for what they had done, what they had felt, who they were. When those customers left her stall, they were alight with the hope that they could become better, that they would stop doing You wrong.

This continued for years, and Jovana found herself spending more and more time hidden in Soledad's stall. Delfina never bothered to ask where Jovana would disappear to; she always welcomed her back.

Jovana shared this with Soledad one day, and Soledad smiled. "It is rare to meet someone so unconditionally good," she said. "But Delfina is an exception. Most people are hiding something, and if you promise them good fortune in the eyes of Solís, they will admit it to you."

She brushed her hair back, and then she said, "Come. It is time for me to show you the real power of being a cuentista." She ran her hand lovingly through Jovana's hair. "You are ready."

She swept Jovana away, into El Mercado, and they headed for the section where the jewelers flourished, where everything arranged on the tables and racks glittered and sparkled and shimmered. Soledad found one of the stalls where all the gems were a stark, deep red, and the jeweler—a man named Márquez—greeted Soledad with a smile. "What do you have for me today, mi cuentista?" he said.

"How much?" She held her hand out, exactly as she had done when she first tricked Jovana.

"What is your story worth?"

"It is worth nothing to *me*, Márquez," she said, her voice syrupy and lush. "It is more a matter of what it is worth to you and your business." Jovana watched as Soledad glanced dramatically to the left at the vendor next to them, then back at Márquez. The other man was deep in conversation with a potential customer.

Márquez said nothing. He reached under la mesa, then dropped a small cloth bag into Soledad's outstretched hand. She did not count what was inside, but merely tucked it into the folds of her cloak. She leaned forward.

"Ignacio has been stealing gems when you go to relieve yourself."

His face changed—a flash of shock—and then he relaxed. "Gracias, Soledad," he said. "Your gift is eternal."

As they walked off, Jovana heard a sharp yell and spun around. She watched as Márquez left his stall, reached over Ignacio's mesa, and ripped the man into the aisle.

Then he slashed Ignacio's throat. Blood spilled forth, as red and deep as the gems that had been stolen.

Jovana looked back at Soledad, who wore a subtle smile. She was twisting the bag of coins in her right hand.

When the time came, years later, Jovana began to take stories, too. She added her own flair: she lit candles, she waved expensive oils about her, and she wore paints and coals on her face to allow people to think she was something more than she was. Soledad grew proud of her, and she let Jovana start to take just one story each day. She was often given the easiest ones, but one story per day became two, and then together, they sold the myth that Jovana was Soledad's long-lost daughter, reunited through the power of Solís and the art of las cuentistas.

She spent more and more time with Soledad. One day, she packed a small bag in Delfina's home while Delfina was at El Mercado, and after she left, she did not return. Soledad gave her a small cama in her own home, on the northern edge of Obregán, and Jovana dived into her new life, her new destiny.

More years passed. She forgot about Delfina and what that woman had done for her. So when Jovana walked by a stall in El Mercado and Delfina sat there, her face twisted in shock, it took a moment to remember who la vieja was. Jovana drifted forward, a smile on her face, and she stretched out her hands. "Do you have a story to tell, señora?"

Delfina jerked her body away from Jovana and said nothing. Jovana never saw Delfina again.

Years passed again, and then one day, Jovana knew she was ready. The people of Obregán, of aldeas near and far, were desperate to see "la madre e hija," las cuentistas reunited by the power of faith, and both were busy taking stories, selling salvation, and using those stories to give themselves a life of comfort and extravagance.

But Jovana knew she could get even more. She knew she could *be* more if she eliminated her final obstacle. She found the solution in Cruz, a man who crafted fine metal blades and knives, who had given his stories of volatile rage and anger to Soledad for years. Jovana found him at night, when El Mercado was still open but much quieter. He was drunk, as he usually was when he'd had a bad day of sales. He was unaware that it was not the quality of his work that drove people from him, but his demeanor.

Jovana knew that he was perfect for this.

She walked up to his display, and he grunted at her. "Tell Soledad I have nothing for her today," he said. "Maybe next week."

"I'm here for *you*," she said, and she fluttered her long lashes at him.

He grunted again. "Not my type."

"I have a story for you, Cruz."

He raised an eyebrow. "No soy cuentista. And I have Sole-dad. What use are you to me?"

She looked around her, to sell him on the idea that what she was about to say was a secret. "I took Soledad's story."

He said nothing; his eyebrow was still raised.

"I have not given it back to Solís, because . . . well, it doesn't feel right to. Not when I know what she did."

"Chica, please tell me what this has to do with me."

She leaned in.

She breathed out.

"She has never returned your stories to Solís. She kept them all."

Then she leaned forward, even closer. She told him a small detail, something that she herself had heard Cruz tell Soledad barely a week ago, while she was hiding behind their stall.

He didn't move at first. Then he set his drink down and stood up. He looked at her, his face blank and unresponsive, and then he reached up and picked the longest, sharpest blade off his wall.

Jovana stood there for nearly a quarter hour. Waiting. Then she slowly walked back to Soledad's stall, each step powerful, sure. When she entered it, Cruz was long gone. She stepped over the body, then picked up a sage candle that rested on Soledad's—no, *her*—altar. She licked her thumb and used it to wipe away the splash of blood that had trickled down the side of it.

I think I'll change my name, she thought.

She is sorry, Solís. But only now. Only because she got caught.

Soledad crumpled there, sobbing and wheezing, and she kept saying that she was sorry, that she had thought los cuentistas died out, that I had to tell Solís that she was never going to do this again.

But I remained motionless. I had kept stories. They surged in me again: Lito's terror, Marisol's guilt, Emilia's rage. I had not returned them either. Did it matter that I had not made money from them? Did it matter that I was not turning one person against another for my own gain? How was I any better?

How had she not been punished, when it felt so obvious to me that You were punishing me?

That emotion overpowered them all. A rage, pure and fiery, ran through my veins, overpowering the others.

What was real anymore? Were the stories of Solís y los cuentistas even true? Was *everything* in my life a lie?

I tried to say something, but the words would not form on my tongue. I swayed as I stood, my world spinning around me.

Soledad cried out again, implored me to stay, to teach her what she did wrong. "Please," she said. "Don't leave me."

Emilia was still standing there, shaking as she tried to hold me upright. "We have to go," she said.

My head was still swirling and reeling, still trying to process what I had learned.

"What do you want? What can I give you?" Soledad stood and searched her altar. "More coins? Please let me give you something."

"You don't have what I need," I spat out, the anger finally getting the best of me. "How could you? How could you take something so sacred and *ruin* it?"

She spread her arms, and her cheeks were still wet and puffy from the tears. "At least let me try to make things better, señorita. *Please.*"

She held her hands up to me.

It was so pitiful.

But was I any *better* than she was? Hadn't I lied, hadn't I kept secrets from those who loved me?

I looked at that portrait of misery and regret.

"Xochitl, *please*." Emilia tugged on my arm. "We have to get going *now*."

"Do you need a coyote?" Soledad asked. "I can get you one. A guide. Are you going north?"

Emilia and I stilled.

"What do you mean?" I asked.

"Eduardo!" she yelled at me, and spit dribbled out of the corner of her mouth. She didn't even seem to care. "If you keep this to yourself, I will tell you where to find Eduardo, and I'll make sure he takes you on, free of charge."

"What's a coyote?" Emilia asked.

I looked to Soledad, as I wanted the answer, too.

Soledad seemed to think she had an opportunity to win us over; her face lit up with excitement. "A guide," she said. "There are many of them here in Obregán, all willing to guide you to any aldea in the world . . . for a price, of course."

"And this Eduardo can take us to Solado?" I asked. I had some money that Marisol had given me. Perhaps it would be wise to use it.

"I know the way," Emilia reminded me, cutting down my

excitement. She pulled on my arm once more. "Are you able to move? Because we *have* to."

"Please," Soledad said. "Let me send you to Eduardo. Or to another cuentista. Anything, *please*. Let me be la cuentista you need, Xochitl."

"I don't need you," I said. "And unlike you and your mentor, I keep my secrets."

She begged me profusely, her hands running up and down my arms, and my skin crawled as she did so.

"Vámonos, Emilia," I said, hoping my dizziness would pass.

But Soledad held me tightly. "Can you teach me?" she asked, imploring me with those eyes of hers. "Can you show me how to be a cuentista?"

I didn't answer. I got away from her as fast as I could.

The sounds of El Mercado rushed back in. More cuentistas offered their services, but I ignored them, too. *Why did Soledad say she believed we had died out?* Did las cuentistas of Obregán all behave the same? Was it all an elaborate lie?

My world continued to expand. Bigger and bigger, and as it did so, I felt smaller. Less consequential. Less like I mattered. Less like all the stories I had ever been told about Solís were anything more than that: just *stories*.

I didn't know what sort of person I was if all those stories weren't real.

By the time we got out of El Mercado de Obregán, You were straight up above me in the sky. I was surprised by the sight of a group of children standing under a torrent of water being pumped from an old stone well off to the side of the road I was on. I watched as an older man, his hair graying and hanging down his back, laughed at the children, then stuck a metal canteen under the stream. Water was available everywhere here. No hunting for it, no worries of thirst.

No Julio.

I did my best to blend in, to seem as though I knew what I was doing, and refilled my goatskin bag as casually as I could, then motioned for Emilia to do the same.

"We didn't get supplies," said Emilia. "Only a meal."

"I know," I said after taking a deep drink of water. "I just needed to get out of there."

She nodded. She understood.

Did she, Solís?

Because as I waited for her to fill up on water, I wasn't even sure I understood myself.

A flash of a memory hit me:

Emilia, swaddled and terrified, being taken aboveground, learning that los pálidos had lied to her people.

Maybe she understood me better than I ever thought she could.

We walked, my mind buzzing, and I didn't know what to do next. I let Emilia lead me for a while, and she paused next to a red structure that was built of some sort of clay, smoother than what we used in Empalme. I could smell salvia from the nearby doorway, and the aroma calmed my nerves. I breathed it deeply, letting it fill my lungs, imagined it running through my veins and to every part of my body. There was a man in another of those wooden chairs with wheels, and he waited behind another man who was being fitted with an arm, much like the one that la señora Sánchez had gotten.

This was a center of healing, and enfermeras flitted about from person to person, asking what people needed, then taking some of them indoors, while others received medicinas or potions before handing over coins or trinkets as payment.

Did Emilia need something from this place? I looked to her, and she was paler, sweat dripping down her face.

"Emilia?" I stepped closer to her. "¿Estás bien?"

"Hold on," she said, annoyed.

I closed my eyes and took another deep breath of the salvia. *I am going to find Simone*, I told myself. I had to. I couldn't turn back empty-handed at this point, not after all I'd gone through. I allowed my anger at Soledad, at the stories I'd been told, to swim through me. It was refreshing to have a focus, something to direct my ire at.

"Should we get some supplies?"

I opened my eyes. Emilia did not look any better. "Probably," I said. "Let me think."

"I don't know that we have much time."

I frowned. "Are we in a rush?"

She was breathing harder than before, and her next words were quiet. *Frightened.* "Oh, Solís, help me."

"Emilia, what is going on?"

"We need to go *now*."

The last word was a blunt force, and I backed away from her. "I am confused. Is something wrong?"

"Please, Xochitl. NOW." She clutched her hands to her chest and winced. Then her eyes bulged and she spun about, like she was trying to find something.

"Can you just tell me what—?"

"He's here."

I stilled. A chasm ripped open between us.

No.

No.

My instincts had been right. This was a trap after all. There was only one person she could have been referring to:

Julio.

"How do you know?" I yelled, and all the calm that the salvia had given me was gone. "Where is he? *Where?*"

"No, no me entiendes," she said, and her speech was sloppy, the words slurred as they came out of her mouth. She wiped at her face, and her eyes were red, blurring and glassy with tears, and she wouldn't stop *moving*. She shifted from one leg to the other. "I can sense it."

"What are you talking about, Emilia? Sense *what*?"

She stepped closer finally, and the tears were now spilling over. "We don't have time, and I wish I could tell you my story, but—"

"But you already *did*!" I said.

"I lied!"

It was as if she had slapped me. She might as well have.

I grabbed her hand, intending to guide her from this place, to hide her in Obregán, where Julio could not find her—but it all rushed into me the moment I touched her.

No ritual, no prayer. I cried out, and fear and regret bolted up my arm and—

It was impossible.

And yet—

Emilia had watched me run off from her the morning before, saw me far in the distance, but she did not follow me. Not at first, not as she had told me the night before.

She went *back*.

She had seen my pack and realized what she forgot; she did not want to venture out into the desert without supplies, without food or water or clothing. So she rushed back to the place Julio had stolen from someone in Empalme. Most of her life had been spent underground, and she had not learned much from being with her father aboveground. But she knew that without food and water, she would die.

There was little left, but she found a burlap sack in a corner of the home, some dried fruit, and a canvas canteen. It was enough. Enough to get her to wherever I was going, enough to allow her to follow me and the foolish plan that she'd assembled only minutes before. She grabbed a small hunting axe off the wall, stuffed everything into the bag, and as she made for the door, she felt a hand in her hair, pressure on her scalp, and she screamed, shattering the terrible silence of that place.

"Did you think you could *leave* me?" Julio shrieked, and he flung her down on the ground, and she looked up at his towering form. He teetered in front of her, his body a mass of rage and tesgüino. He fell briefly himself, used the wall to push to his feet, and she scrambled away from him, farther into the house.

"No, Papi," she whimpered. "I was afraid, and I was going to find you and—"

"Don't lie to me, mija," he slurred. "Where were you going?" She said nothing, paralyzed with terror, and he shrieked at her. "*Where were you going?*"

"Away!" she yelled back. She had never before raised her voice at this man, had never dared to risk facing his wrath, but she was so *tired*, Solís. She was tired of cowering in fear. Of keeping to herself. Of believing that *she* was the problem. "Anywhere but *here*! Anywhere without *you*!"

He swayed again, blinked, wiped at his mouth. "Then go," he said after a silence. He waved at her as if she were a stray animal. "Leave."

There was no longer any emotion in what he said. She stared at him, could not believe that he had given up on her, but it wore off quickly. She lifted herself from the ground and moved forward, one step after another, her eyes locked on him, and she stepped past him, to the door, to her freedom and—

His other hand whipped out, and there was a puncture on the underside of her left arm as cool metal bit into her skin.

She strained as hard as she could.

It ended.

He let go of her, and she spun around.

Glass. Metal. A vial. He held it up in the low light of the morning, and he examined it. "I'll give you a day," he said. "You're free to leave now."

Horror swirled through her. "What have you *done*, Papi? ¡Soy tu *hija*!"

Julio ignored this. His old smile came back—sinister and raw—and he directed it at her. "There's something you don't know about los sabuesos, about their magic," he said, his tone informational, as if this were something she'd find interesting and entertaining. "I have wanted one for so very long, but los pálidos . . . they had very few of them left. But now I know how to make them."

A malicious grin lit up his face. "Something happens when they are created and corrupted. They have a pull on their prey. When they get close, their victim feels like they cannot resist. They run *toward* los sabuesos."

He chuckled. "I wonder if Manolito met his fate with open arms."

He sealed the vial, turned away from his daughter. "You have one day, Emilia. Goodbye."

She sobbed loudly, but she couldn't stay any longer. She ran out the door and did not look back.

She lied to me.

I lied to her.

That's all this was: nothing but *lies*.

Emilia let go of me, gasped for air, and then she just *moved*, brushing past me, and she thrummed with energy. "Now you know," she said, ignoring the look of confusion on my face. "And I feel it right now, Xochitl. It's *beckoning* to me."

I followed. I followed because I had no time to think through a plan, to consider that it was dangerous to be *anywhere* near Emilia. All I could see in my mind was Julio. I began to frantically look around the crowd for his sinister form, his twisted mouth, the sound of el sabueso. But there were too many people. How did people ever locate *anyone* in this place? My gaze jumped from one person to another, from odd headwear to flowing cloaks, from dark skin to light, from thick curly hair to straight black cascades like my own. No Julio. No sabueso.

How did she do that? How did she give me her story without the ritual?

"They're closer!" Emilia sobbed out. Then she lifted a shaking finger and turned back toward me as I caught up to her. "That way. They want me to go that way."

Then she took a step in that direction, walked right into me, kept pushing. I put my hands on her shoulders and tried to steady her, but she continued to walk, crying as she did so, and I almost lost my balance. "Emilia, *no*! Stop it!"

"I can't help it!" she wailed.

Another step.

Then she screamed.

I followed the gaze of her wide eyes.

There, right as the crowd parted, I saw them.

They were at the end of la calle.

Julio.

Then, at the end of a leash made of a thick rope:

Un sabueso.

Emilia kept pushing against me, and I uttered a low moan. "Emilia, we can't go that way, we have to—"

I shoved her in the opposite direction, and a growl rumbled over the sound of Obregán.

I spun back, tried to find them in all those people, and we found one another.

Our eyes locked.

Julio smiled.

He dropped the leash.

I grabbed Emilia's hand, harder than I had ever grabbed another person, and I yanked her. My voice became shrill and horrible as I begged her to trust me, to believe in me, and I started *running*. I guided her north and we ran

and ran

and ran.

I heard the snarling first, then the screams that echoed from the already noisy crowd. I risked a glance back. I shouldn't have. El sabueso—the same black-and-gray one from two days earlier—leapt up and bit at the throat of a man who had crossed its path while entertaining passersby with card tricks. He dropped the cards to the ground, and his hands shot up toward el sabueso to block it, but too late. There was a tear, a spray of red, and the man clutched at his throat as he thrashed on the ground.

By the time I stopped looking, he had stopped moving.

I kept my head up as we ran, held back my own tears and my own terror, and I forced Emilia forward while she repeatedly jerked me toward the oncoming sabueso. We passed a recess in the brick-and-stone wall of a building to our right, and a few people were tucked into it, smoking cigarillos, and they called out to us in slurred accents, asking where we were going. One of them stepped out into the road to continue flirting, and then el sabueso was on his leg, and we kept running, ignoring the sounds of death behind us. I pulled Emilia into an alley and she thrust her hand out and tried to stop herself on the wall of the building.

"It hurts," she gasped, clutching at her stomach with her free hand. "It's like something is trying to tear me apart if I go the wrong way."

"We have to hurry," I said, then stole a glance back, and it gained on us, its maw and horns stained red with blood and gore, and at the end of the alley, la ciudad lived on. It continued, unaware of what Julio had unleashed inside it. We burst out onto another busy calle, full of merchants peddling trinkets, ropa, and food, and a man with skin the color of the desert sand led a large white horse across the road.

The idea was terrible.

I had to do it.

I ran toward the horse, and el sabueso poured out of the alley behind me. I gripped Emilia's hand and I led her directly in front of the horse, spooking it, and as I had hoped, it reared up and whinnied loudly, causing its owner to curse at us in an unfamiliar language.

As its front legs fell back to the ground, the horse saw el sabueso bearing down upon it, and it rose again, tried to strike la bestia with its hooves, and *it worked*. El sabueso growled at the horse and went for one of the back legs, then darted out of the way. But it was a futile thing, and suddenly, el sabueso was on the horse. It tore into flesh, and its snout was now deep into its body. Blood and entrails spilled to the dusty road, and bile surged into my throat.

I had never heard a horse scream. I won't forget it.

It became easier to run, knowing that el sabueso was busy, and the farther we got from them, the less Emilia tugged me in the opposite direction. My head had started to pound, but I refused to give up. I couldn't let Julio get her.

We ran. We twisted around people, we ignored the people shouting at us, and we *ran*.

I had been betrayed, hadn't I? Used for Emilia's own end, used to get her to safety, and she didn't care. She wanted me for what I could offer, just like everyone else back in Empalme.

What was true? What was merely a story? Was Simone even *real*?

I had come so far and fallen right into the same pattern all over again.

Why did I care so much? I had known Emilia for less than a day. She had just *lied* to me and put both of us in danger. I wanted to leave her behind. I entertained the thought: El sabueso wasn't after *me*. I could cut away from Emilia, disappear into the crowd, and it would be over. I didn't need her. *She* needed *me*.

But I couldn't do it. I couldn't make a decision like that. It felt wrong, yes, but . . .

Julio was real. His *power* was real. And someone had *given* it to him.

There had to be someone to take my power away.

And maybe I could use Emilia back in order to get what *I* needed.

Emilia tugged me toward the left, tugged me hard, so hard I nearly fell over. "This way," she said, and I yanked on her arm, my frustration finally overflowing.

"No!" I yelled. "We can't double back."

"I've been here before!" she said, and the fury welled up again.

Another secret? Another story she'd failed to tell me?

But there was no time for interrogations or for my anger. She quickly guided me to the east. "I know a place," she huffed out as we ran, "where the smell should hide us."

What did *that* mean? Did she know something about how el sabueso tracked her that she *wasn't* telling me?

She guided me, and I didn't want to, but I followed. We dashed down an alley, came out near a building that had to have been some sort of school. There were children playing outside it, and they laughed and cheered at us as we ran. My heart leapt at the thought of el sabueso finding one of the children, but we cut around a large fountain spewing water high into the air, and the moment passed.

But then the screams broke out behind us. Had an attack happened?

Emilia was now sobbing, stumbling step after step as we ran, leading me farther east, past more buildings that leaned into la calle, as if they were waiting for us to fall and would crumble upon us once we did. The effect was disorienting, and I swallowed down my nausea, the stories, the terror.

She pointed toward a nearby structure. "¡Allá!" she cried, and she slowed, for an instant, and I had to pull her along. "It's calling to me, el sabueso," she sobbed. "Please, keep moving. Get inside the gray building!"

The stench hit me first, and I coughed hard and spat on the ground, nearly pitching forward. It was the worst thing I'd ever smelled, something bitter and sharp, and tears sprang to my eyes.

"Get inside," Emilia ordered, then stuck a hand over her mouth. "It should mask my scent long enough."

Long enough for *what*? "But el sabueso—"

"Just *go!*" she screamed.

I did what she asked.

The building was tall, not so high as most of the others, but still bigger than everything in Empalme. I didn't recognize the substance it was made out of; it was like smooth mud, but a pale, pale gray. I had my hand over my nose as we pushed through a wooden door and—

People.

There were people here.

A woman stood up, her clothing in tatters, her hair patched with gray, and she raised an arm to me. "No, you cannot just—"

She stopped.

"Emilia?"

The door slammed behind me, and Emilia rushed past. "Chavela, I'm sorry for the intrusion, but we need to hide."

Chavela shook her head. "Emilia, chica, we can't—"

The others—children, adults, an elderly couple—crowded around Chavela as there was a loud pounding at the door. I cried out in alarm, and it all happened so fast, so terribly fast. Chavela yelled something at the others—in a language I had never heard, the words quick and clipped—and they scurried away from her. A tall man with his hair in multiple tight, dark braids lifted a board in the floor, and they all disappeared below.

Pound.

Pound.

Pound.

"Emilia!" yelled Julio, and I heard el sabueso throw its body against the door again. "You cannot escape us!"

Emilia's burlap bag slipped off her shoulder, and as it hit the ground, its contents spilled out across the floor. Clothing. Dried fruit. Her canteen.

The axe.

Emilia began to take steps toward the door. "I can't stop," she sobbed, and it looked as though she was fighting her own body, her own willpower. "I can't stop it."

I dropped my pack and fell to the floor, my knees banging against the wooden boards. I went for the axe and gripped the wooden handle as the door burst in.

As light spilled into that giant room.

As Chavela called out something in that language of hers.

As Emilia cried.

As I scrambled to my feet.

I ran forward.

El sabueso charged.

Snarled.

Growled.

Opened a mouth stained red with the life of others.

Leapt up off the ground.

Aimed for Emilia's throat.

And I aimed at *it*.

The axe landed between el sabueso's shoulders, bit deep into muscle and tendon through the dark fur, and la bestia shrieked as I slammed it to the ground. It tried to stand up, but its front legs no longer worked. Julio was motionless, silent, and he watched as I placed a foot on el sabueso's head, right between its horns, as it whimpered and snapped at me, and the axe was in the air again, and all I saw was Manolito's panic on his face, before he tried to escape his terrible fate, and when I brought it down, el sabueso went silent. Blood sprayed on my huaraches.

It trembled.

It went still.

And Julio burst into a rage.

The axe clattered to the ground, and Emilia did as well. The spell was broken, the magic gone, and I watched her wilt and deflate before me. Julio wailed and dropped to el sabueso, now in pieces, and his voice was tortured. "What have you *done*, puta?" He dropped the head to the floor. "Do you know what this cost me?"

I rushed to Emilia's side, lifted her up from under her arms, and her relief burst into me, set my heart racing again. *How can I feel that? Why is she open to me, so vulnerable?*

Emilia coughed, spat on the ground in front of her father. She wiped at her face, stood up straight and tall, no longer leaning into me for support. "Is that all you care about, Papi? How much this cost *you*?"

"Watch your mouth, mija," he shot back, and he took a step toward the two of us. "Or I'll bury you."

Chavela appeared suddenly, placing her body between us. "I need you to leave," she said to Julio. "This is not your home."

"I take what I want," he said to Chavela. "And I'll take your life, too."

He raised his hand up, as if he was going to take Chavela's story. Emilia sobbed and moved behind me. But Chavela did not wince, did not react. "Go ahead," she said. "You wouldn't be the first man to hurt me."

His arm dropped. His patchy facial hair twitched about his face as he frowned, and I could see him working something out. He had not expected resistance. He never did. Emilia's story roiled up within my gut, and I doubled over as it thrust barbs inside me. I choked, nearly spat it out then. All her emotions poured into my body: Her fear of Julio. The pain he put her through. Her intense loneliness.

I stood upright, my eyes blurred by tears, and Julio was still there, examining me. His face—all those angles, all that hatred—was familiar to me, as though it were part of a long memory of mine. But it was Emilia's memory, layered into my own through her stories.

I was terrified of him.

The force of this fear trembled throughout my body as he continued to stare at me. "What is wrong with you?" he said.

Chavela put a hand on my back. "Chica, do you need agua?" she asked, her voice soft and concerned.

"Emilia," I choked out. "Where is she?"

"She left you."

My gaze snapped up to him. He was *smiling*.

I spun around.

There was no one there.

This space was so much larger than I had realized, and I searched the room, desperate to find Emilia, to see her shadow, to see *anything*. There were sleeping rolls scattered around, cooking supplies on the southern edge of the building, some tools hung on the walls to the east. Most of the place was bare.

And Emilia was definitely not in sight.

"You're lying," I said, using Chavela's arm to keep myself steady. "She wouldn't."

"She ran away, like she always does," he said. "She is a coward."

No. Impossible. Why would she leave me here?

"You were a friend of his, weren't you?" Julio stepped forward.

I shook my head and moved back, Chavela at my side. "I don't know what you're talking about."

Another step toward me. "Manolito. Did you like what I did to him?" He grinned, and his mouth turned up in a sinister curl.

He unsheathed his blade, one of the smaller curved ones that his men always carried, and it shone in the bright light cascading in from the open door behind him. "I don't like liars," he said.

"Señor, *please*," Chavela said. "Just leave. Leave this place. Déjala en paz."

"You know what's wrong with this world?" he asked, moving

closer and closer. "You all wait. You wait for someone else to solve your problems. You don't want to take a chance and—"

He was so certain. So lost in himself.

So he did not see the shadow fall over the open doorway behind him.

He did not see the axe raised up and to the side.

It whisked through the air.

It landed in his neck.

His eyes went wide.

His tongue lolled about in his mouth.

His hands went up to the blade now buried deep in his flesh.

He ran fingers along the edge.

Felt the blood leaking out of the torn skin.

Then he pitched forward, and Chavela and I screamed as his body hit the ground hard, and he twitched there as el sabueso had, and she stood there, a shadow in that brilliant light, and she panted.

He tried to roll over.

He stilled.

His life leaked out.

And Emilia walked over to her papi, her face a cold mask, and she ripped the axe from Julio's body, ignored the spray of blood, then looked up at the two of us.

"Emilia . . . ," I began.

"Don't," she said. "Just help me carry the body out."

She set the axe aside and grabbed his legs, dragging him toward the door, and Chavela and I silently followed.

Julio was dead.

I had forgotten about the stench, how the heat seemed to press up against us so fiercely. Chavela had one arm, I had the other, and the three of us dragged him through the dirt. To the east. Toward the source of the smell.

There was a large pit, dug deep out of the earth, and I watched as a man upended a large waste pot over the edge, and the contents tumbled down the side, into the depths below. It was deep enough to fit an entire home. There was so much refuse piled at the bottom, and insects buzzed and flew all around it. I coughed again, and Chavela raised her free hand to make Emilia stop. We set Julio's body on the ground, and then she dug into her tunic until she produced a small glass vial. "For the smell," Chavela said, and she put a couple of drops on her finger, then approached me. She dabbed it under my nose, and an intense floral scent invaded me, made my eyes water. She did the same for Emilia.

Emilia took a breath, then gestured with her head. "In he goes," she said.

Maybe I should have protested. Or said anything. But my body and my mind were numb, unable to fathom what I had witnessed. So I did as I was told. We set Julio on the edge of that pit, and Chavela backed away. She grabbed my arm as I moved toward Emilia.

"No," she said. "Let her do it."

I watched as Emilia stared down at his lifeless body. She didn't say anything, and her face was as unreadable as ever.

She put her foot on his torso.

She kicked out.

And he rolled down, his arms flopping about, and he landed facedown in a pile of human waste and refuse.

Emilia stared at him, then walked back to the building we had come from. I couldn't move, stilled by my own confusion. She came back out, the body of el sabueso cradled in her arms, and she tossed it over the side, and it rolled down to meet Julio's body. Her clothing—already filthy from her journey—was now covered in blood and remains, stark flashes of red that stained the fabric. She spun quickly and made for the gray building once more, her hair following behind her.

She looked eternal and terrifying.

Chavela took my hand and led me inside. My eyes went up to the ceiling, to the long blocks of wood that crossed above me, to the high windows that allowed light into the place. Chavela let go and headed back to the removable board in the floor, stomped on it three times. "Navarro! It's Chavela," she shouted. "We're safe now."

I looked for Emilia. Where had she gone?

They came aboveground. The tall man with the long braids was first, and he knelt to help the others up. A couple of children came up next, and I realized that they were twins, and I thought of Los Gemelos, and it seemed so very long ago that I had walked between those saguaros.

"What is this place?" I said as Chavela approached me, a canteen of water in her outstretched hand. I took it and drank the cool water down, then sniffed. The smell was not so bad indoors, thanks to the floral oil that Chavela had given me, but the glory of Obregán seemed to have skipped over this place. I was reminded of the homes that had been abandoned over the years in Empalme, and a memory struck:

Emilia. Cowering in rags in one of those empty homes.

"It's where we live," Chavela answered, and shook me free from Emilia's story. "El olvidado."

"El olvidado?" I took another drink from the canteen. "I don't understand."

"Obregán is a big place," said Navarro. "And some of us fall through the cracks. No familia. No homes. No one to catch us."

"How is that possible?" I asked, and the people who had been hiding beneath the floor spread about, going back to their lives as if nothing had happened. "You have *no one*? Nowhere else to go?"

"Life is complicated, chica," said Chavela. "I came here with my family years ago. They're all gone now. Dead, or moved on."

"I came here for work," a man said, his face folded with wrinkles. "It dried up. I found my way to this place." He gestured around him.

I heard a boot scuffle on the ground, and Emilia was there, standing in the door her father had destroyed. She stepped forward into the space, out of the bright light of day. Her face was drooping with exhaustion, her gaze far in the distance, in another world, in another time.

"Emilia?" I stepped toward her, a hand outstretched. "Do you need help? Can I clean off your clothing?"

She gazed down, examined the mess, pulled it back and forth, then looked back up to me. "It's stained," she said, her words clipped. "Ruined."

I took another step. "I know. Can we help you?"

"What do I do next?"

Her story awoke again. Loneliness. Panic. They intertwined within me, reached for her. I pushed them down.

Next? I couldn't answer that for her. I barely knew what *I* was doing. Who *I* was. What the future held for *me*.

But I hesitated too long. She looked back down, then said, "I need something else. I'll take some food, too."

She walked out the doorway.

"Emilia!" I called, and I chased her out into the brightness. "Emilia, stop!"

She slowed and turned her head toward me.

"Please don't leave," I said, and a memory from her story flashed in me: Alegría leaving for the last time and Emilia not knowing she'd never see her again. I clutched my stomach. "Talk to me. I need to know."

"Know what, Xochitl?" she said. "There's nothing more to tell. I gave you my story."

"You *lied*."

I had not intended to blurt it out, but once the words flowed from me, they sat between us, pushing us apart, widening the chasm.

"Do you think you deserve the truth?" she shot back. "Is that what I owe you?" She came toward me, crossing the divide in a few furious steps. "You think because you're a cuentista that you *deserve* everything there is to know about me?"

"No, I don't think that! But you *just* killed your father in front of me! And none of this would have happened if you hadn't lied to me about him chasing you!"

Her features twisted in anger. "I don't owe you anything, Xochitl. I only have to get you to Simone and that's it." She fixed a scowl onto her face. "We'll leave tomorrow."

She stormed off. I watched her leave; she had twisted her hair into two braids that bounced off her back. Then she disappeared into the crowds of Obregán. Gone.

Sweat lined my skin, and I stomped back into the building to escape the sun, to get myself farther from Emilia with each step. Hadn't I just helped her? Hadn't I killed something to save her? She used me as a cuentista, and now she wanted to throw that in my face?

Chavela was inside the doorway, and I sagged a bit when I saw her, my own shame rising up. She *had* to have heard us. But she smiled at me. "You need somewhere to stay tonight, chica?"

And just like that, Chavela's kindness wore down my ire. "For the night, I guess," I said. "We have to leave in the morning. Have a journey to make."

There were two people next to the iron pot, and the savory smells hit my nose. They kissed each other, then continued cooking as we moved past them. "Anyone is welcome here," she said, "as long as they can contribute something."

I pointed toward the entryway I had used earlier. "Let me clean up . . . the mess," I suggested. "And I can help with a meal if needed. Or hunt for water."

Chavela chuckled at that. "One good thing about Obregán is that no one pays for water. I'm sure you've seen the public fountains and wells. They're for everyone. But cleaning . . . that will help."

She got a broom for me, as well as a bucket of water. She added a few drops of another oil to the bucket, and a sweet, sour scent filled the air. I washed off the boards and swept away the gore as best as I could, and it wasn't long before I noticed that the stench from the refuse pit was completely unnoticeable. Navarro stayed silent as I cleaned.

"You're passing through, ¿no?" Chavela asked me.

"To Solado," I said. "Where Emilia is from."

Navarro used a broom to push some of the filth toward the door. "Ah, sí. Solado. We know."

I frowned. "From Emilia?"

"She has told us stories," said Chavela. "She always said she was going to go back for Luz."

"Well, she's taking me there," I said.

Chavela looked at me without speaking. She did not ask the obvious, though.

"Where did you come from?" Navarro asked.

"Empalme. You heard of it?"

He nodded. "From the south. Not so far as Hermosillo, pero . . . eso es muy lejos."

"Why so far, Xochitl?" Chavela asked. When I lifted my eyebrows at her, she held a hand up. "I heard Emilia say your name."

"Are you visiting Emilia's home?" Navarro said.

I knew I couldn't tell them the truth. They were still strangers to me. So I pushed away the urge to let it all come forth, to finally be true with someone.

"Something like that," I said.

Chavela took the broom from me. "You'll be in good hands," she said. "She's a good soul, that Emilia. You can trust her."

I frowned and opened my mouth to respond.

"I can only say this," she continued, raising a hand up. "We met once, me and Emilia. And I could tell from her stories that he was not good to her, that something horrible had happened. She will need to deal with this, Xochitl, and she's going to need someone to help." She paused. "Even if that means giving her some space."

I nodded. That made sense, but . . .

Why did it have to be *me*?

I cleaned off the ground as best as I could, and Navarro threw another bucket of water over the stain, which had dulled in vibrancy. He told me to let it sit awhile, so the three of us gathered in the shade on the eastern side of the building, and we talked for hours. They told me more about how they had come to Obregán, why they stayed, what the world was like outside the desert. "I've never been to Solado," Chavela admitted, running her fingers through her long gray hair. "But I've heard it's beautiful, in a terrible sort of way."

"We've been losing a lot of people to that place," said Navarro. "It's opened up some work here, which is good for a lot of us."

"Do you think you'll ever go to Solado?" I asked, drinking down more water, thankful that my headache had finally subsided.

Chavela shook her head. "I love it here too much. Look at what we have! This place is so alive, so vibrant, so interesting." She laughed then. "Además, soy una vieja. I don't think I could make a journey like that. You're young. You seem like you can handle your own."

But could Emilia? Or would she continue to rely on me?

When night fell, las estrellas above Obregán had to compete with the lights of la ciudad. We were still in the same spot, our backs against the wall of the abandoned building, the building of el olvidado, and I leaned my head back, took in the twinkling starlight. They had never quite looked like this, because I had never seen them from this place.

It was new. And I appreciated that.

Emilia came back as we stared at the sky above us, trying to find the brightest star. I almost missed her, but she paused before she darted around the edge of the building.

"Go," Chavela said. "Talk to her. *If* she needs it."

Inside, most of the people were curled up on their sleeping rolls, and a few of them were quietly talking to one another. Emilia stood next to her own bag, which Chavela had moved to the eastern wall. I approached her carefully, as her back was to me. "Emilia . . . ," I said, trying the name out on my tongue again.

She didn't react. I stepped closer.

"How are you?"

It was such a weak, ineffective question, but I didn't know what else to say, what else could break through the wall between us.

She had on different clothing: camisa and breeches, both of them the color of wet dirt, a shade or so lighter than her own skin. But those elegant boots were still on her feet, and I wanted to laugh. They seemed so impractical.

I took a risk. I lifted my hand, let it graze her shoulder. She let me lay it there for a bit before she twisted away and focused on unpacking. "We should get some sleep," she said. "Since we need to leave in the morning."

She wasn't wrong, but the way she said it brought all my anger back. "Bueno," I said. "We'll leave just after dawn."

Emilia didn't look at me. She stretched out on her roll, then turned to face the other wall.

I wanted to know more. I had so many questions about her, her lies, her need for me. But as I unrolled the thick cloth on the ground, the memory of what she said prickled my skin.

I don't owe you anything, Xochitl.

I had lied to her, too. I was overflowing with secrets. And Julio would have gone after her even if she *hadn't* lied to me. Why had I said otherwise? Why had I been so cruel? My stomach rumbled at the memory, and I feel asleep to a deep shame. I was not who Emilia thought I was.

I was worse.

Chavela woke me up the next morning with a gentle nudge in the side with her foot. I had slept soundlessly: no restless tossing and turning, no sueños. When I sat up, I looked to my left.

Emilia and her things were gone.

Disappointment ripped through me.

Images filled my mind:

Alegría leaving.

Omar on his bed, staring at his husband asleep next to him.

Manolito standing over the burning remains of Julio's shipment.

They were so vivid, Solís. Is this what happened when a cuentista kept stories? Could I now recall these events as if I had actually experienced them?

I rolled onto my back, stretched out my sore muscles. I faced a whole day of travel with Emilia, and I had no idea where we were going. I lay there, unmoving, unmotivated. Should I do this? Should I venture out into the horrible unknown with someone who was basically a stranger?

"There are some warm tortillas and frijoles by the fire," Chavela said, and I looked in her direction. "Relieve yourself out back, and then get some food in you before you leave."

I ran a hand over my belly, unsure whether the pain I felt there was the stories or my monthly cramps. "Gracias, Chavela," I said,

standing up. I did as she said, relieving myself in a small pit that
opened up into the larger one. I returned to el olvidado and greeted
some of the others, many of whom were readying themselves for a
day of seeking work. I packed up my belongings, and Chavela was
waiting for me near the northern entryway.

"There's one of our public wells a few streets over," she said, taking my hands in hers. "And I want you to know . . . " She smiled at
me, dropped one of my hands, and then reached out, caressing my
cheek. " . . . you are welcome here, Xochitl. I don't know what sort
of journey you are on, but this place will *always* be here for you."

Chavela's eyes sparkled. She meant it, Solís. She offered me a
home, a place I could have as my own, and she barely knew me.
What did it take to trust someone else like that? How had she maintained such goodness of heart after seeing so many terrible things?

Maybe it was a choice. Maybe we all had one.

I told Chavela that I would get water and return to wait for Emilia.
Then I walked out into the sunlight, out into the crowds of Obregán.
It was so easy to vanish into the flow of people, and that left me with
a new sense of isolation. It didn't matter that there were so many
other souls around me. As I walked eastward, people brushed past
me, never casting anything more than a quick glance, and then they
continued on their way. I meant nothing to them.

El olvidado.

It made sense now, how people could become forgotten in a
place this large.

I refilled my goatskin bag with cool water at the well Chavela
had described, then let it pour over my head, trickle down my
back. I shook it off.

You can do this, I told myself.

"Xochitl!"

I spun around, and Emilia was running toward me.

My heart flopped at the sight of her. Was that excitement? Fear?

Both?

"Chavela said you were here." Emilia bent over slightly, trying to catch her breath. "I . . . I didn't want you to leave without me."

I raised an eyebrow at her. "Emilia, I don't know where I'm going. I *have* to go with you."

"Oh." She traced a pattern in the dirt with her boots, both of which were now coated in a fine dust. "Right."

The city moved around us as we stared at each other. People rushed by; a bell rang in the distance; shouts echoed off the walls. The din was overwhelming. Smothering.

"We just have to—" I said.

"I think we—" Emilia began, interrupting me, and then we both smiled, laughter spilling afterwards.

"You go first," I said.

She grabbed my hand—my heart fluttered again—and she pulled me off to the side, closer to the red clay building and out of the way of the streaming crowd.

"I'm sorry," she said. "This has been . . . a lot. A lot to deal with."

"I know," I said, combing my hair out of my face.

"And I didn't expect any of this to happen. I never thought I could stand up to him, not after everything he'd done."

She continued to run the toe of her boot in the dirt. I knew exactly what she was referring to because . . . well, her story was still alive inside me. It shivered deep in my stomach: Loneliness. Abandonment. Terror. She had been so afraid to act, and . . .

. . . . she felt *guilty* about it, didn't she? She was convinced she could have done more, and done it earlier.

"But you did it."

Emilia looked up at me.

"He's gone. El sabueso is dead. You're *free.*"

She nodded. "I just . . . I just *acted.* I didn't really think about it. I grabbed the axe after you dropped it, and then got behind him and . . ."

Emilia gulped, and then she focused on a spot on the ground. I let the horror pass, let the reality of what she'd done sink into her. She breathed in deep, then looked back to me.

"What was it you just said?" she asked.

"Uh . . . well, I said that he's gone. And you're free."

"I never have been," she said. "I was stuck beneath the ground in Solado. Lied to. Trapped there. And when I was freed from that place, he kept me in his clutches."

I squeezed her hand. "No longer."

She let go and rubbed at her face. "So . . . what do I do *now*? What do you do when you're free?"

I hadn't figured that out for myself. And was I free? Was I liberated from what held me back? Not yet. I had one thing to do, one thing left to accomplish.

"You do what you want," I said. "And it seems to me that you want to find Luz."

"I do," she said, breathing out in relief. "I know it's going to be dangerous to head back, but I can't leave her behind."

"Vámonos," I said. "We need supplies. And I need to know more about Solado."

She hoisted her sack farther up on her back. "I'm sorry that I took out my frustration on you. I don't know why I reacted that way." She paused, then narrowed her eyes at me. "Sometimes I feel drawn to you, and I don't know why."

That flutter again. Did she feel it, too, as I did? It made no sense to me. I hadn't known Emilia that long, but . . . was I drawn to her as well?

Heat rushed into my cheeks and I looked away. "Don't worry about that," I muttered, then changed the subject immediately. "Well, let's pick up some food. How long is the journey north?"

If she wanted to talk more about what she'd just revealed to me, Emilia did not make it clear. Maybe she was thankful to discuss something else, because she jumped on the change of subject. "A few days if we don't take long breaks," she said. "We stopped a lot on the way down, but that's only because my father visited so many settlements."

She went quiet then as I guided us back to El Mercado de Obregán. La ciudad was as alive as it had been the day before, as was El Mercado. We squeezed through people negotiating at the stalls, stopping only to try some colorful pastries from a panadería. Full of sweetness, we perused the available food. I picked out mostly things that wouldn't spoil in a few days, that would keep our energy up and help us on the journey to Solado.

At least I assumed the journey north would be difficult. Since I had left home, I had already traveled farther in a single day than I ever had before. I had walked for hours, and if Emilia was correct in her estimation, I had more of those days ahead of us.

But . . . how sure of that was she? How did she *actually* know the route back to her home?

I didn't question her aloud, and with our bags full of supplies, we joined the procession out of Obregán on the northern road, following behind a couple of carts loaded up with fresh vegetables and grain. We walked in silence as the tall buildings gave way to smaller ones, as the shadows shrank and disappeared, as people turned off the main road toward their destinations, wherever they lay.

It took us nearly an hour to reach the edge of Obregán, and I could see enormous montañas in the distance. Here, the homes were spread farther out, laid closer to the ground, and there were more animales roaming about, like cattle, cabras, and perros. I saw camisas strung out to dry in the morning heat, children playing together, running between houses.

We observed it all in silence, two strangers awash in our unfamiliarity with the world around us. I knew that it had to be uncomfortable for Emilia, who grew up in the shadows beneath the ground, to see children free in the open air. But it was strange for me, too, because life in Obregán did not seem constrained. People were free to come and go as they pleased. They were not bound to stay in one place.

And then Your presence, Solís, was so minimal. I barely heard Your name. No one seemed to be terrified by the presence of las pesadillas. Where were they? Were none of the people here tormented by their refusal to admit the truth?

Why were the stories around You and las cuentistas so *different* in Empalme?

There was a final well next to the northern gate to La Ciudad de Obregán, and we slaked our thirst and refilled our waterskins as one of los guardias watched us. I expected him to say something, to demand payment, but he gave us a curt smile before he focused his attention on the north.

That was *it*.

With my goatskin bag full and Emilia's canteen overflowing, we left La Ciudad de Obregán.

We crossed the boundary into the desert, which stretched before us, las montañas far in the distance. Your heat bore down on us as You climbed the deep blue sky. It was always hot during the daytime, but I could tell that today would be particularly intense.

And I had no idea where we were going. Just . . . *north*.

"Did you and Julio follow a trail to Obregán?" I asked, once we were well beyond the gate.

"For the most part," she said. "Whenever we found a new aldea, we stopped . . ."

She didn't finish her sentence. She didn't need to.

"So . . . should we retrace your journey? How much of it do you remember?"

Emilia gazed off to the north. "That's not really necessary," she said. "We just have to head in the right direction, and Solís will help with the rest."

I smiled at first; it was a charming answer. But then she started straying immediately from the wide road that led out of Obregán.

"¡Oye!" I called out. "Emilia, where are you going?"

She glanced back, then pointed to the northeast. "We need to head that direction," she answered. "Hay una granja por ahí."

I approached her. "How do you know that?"

"Solís tells me. I just *know.*"

I rubbed at my eyes. "Are you being serious, Emilia?"

"I can't describe it," she said. "I know it sounds odd."

I was Your cuentista, Solís. And yet here was someone You apparently *spoke* to. You had been silent my whole life, leaving me to ponder Your mysteries alone.

There was no reason for her to lie; dying in the desert was not something she craved. So, I *had* to believe, despite the resentment building in me. What made her special? I wondered.

No matter. Because if Simone could give me what I needed, then this journey would be worth it.

So I accepted what she told me.

"Okay, then here's your first real lesson," I said. "It is very easy to get lost in the desert, even if you can see your destination."

"But they're montañas and—"

I raised my hand to stop her. "Even then. Unless you truly know the way, you shouldn't stray from trails and paths. They exist for a reason."

"Which is?" she asked, scrunching up her face.

"Things can bleed into one another, start to look repetitious.

Even worse, as Solís sucks the water out of you, you can . . . you can *see* things."

"Things?" She pulled her canteen out and took a small drink. "What *kind* of things?"

"You never really know," I answered. "The mind can imagine all sorts of images. Fresh agua. Árboles. Animales. They seem real, but they are not."

"How do you know what's real, and what isn't?"

"Hopefully, we won't reach that point," I said. "But we can't just leave the trail like that. Give me a general sense of direction, but let's stick to the road for the most part. I don't know what we'll encounter otherwise."

"I won't disappoint you, Xochitl," she said. "I promise."

I gestured in front of me to the path that snaked to the north, and Emilia led us, moving at a steady pace. She seemed to be turning over the idea in her head, so I decided to change the subject.

"What's at la granja?" I asked, my voice pitching up in worry.

"That's where we can camp tonight. There's a man who hosts those who travel the desert, who will let us rest so we don't have to face the desert at night."

Now I was shaking my head. "*What's in the desert at night?*"

"I've only heard stories," she admitted. "I was told not to roam the desert once Solís leaves the world."

As we set off up the road from Obregán, I wasn't sure this was such a good idea. I had skills to survive in the desert, but would I survive the things I did *not* know?

I went with her anyway, Solís.

We walked for a long while, Solís. Hours. The road from Obregán snaked mostly to the north, rising and falling in gullies formed by rare floods. We had the same ones outside Empalme, and every time we dropped into and climbed out of one, I wished for rain, for the sensation of water falling from the sky and coating us, washing away the grime and dust and fear from our bodies.

We got no rain.

You were near the midpoint in that vast blue sky when I finally looked behind us. Obregán was merely another speck on the horizon, so small and inconsequential that it blended in with the rest of the desert.

Were we all like that to You?

The hills came upon us next, a gentle rise followed by a dramatic drop down into a ravine. This calmed me, if only because I no longer felt so exposed to the rest of the desert, and it allowed me to breathe in the beauty around me. I sucked in the dry, arid air, and it warmed my lungs, and I examined the plants and rock formations as I passed them. Barrel cactus and verbena. Mesquite and indigo. Lots of flat leaves and green hides with sharp needles to keep predators at bay. I took another drink of my water, and I let You spread over me.

We did not talk much, even if I wanted to. I was worried about exerting myself too much in those first hours, especially since I had no idea how far away la granja was. I hoped that they grew food there, that perhaps we could have something fresher than the dried fruits and meats I had purchased with Marisol's money in El Mercado.

Lito's. The thought of el mercadito, of the burnt husk that remained, of his blood sinking into the sand, pushed me deeper into my loneliness.

I wondered what Emilia was thinking—she seemed so far away. I wondered if she was feeling the same gnawing sense of doubt that I was.

I broke that long silence as I saw Emilia swallow down more of her water. "I should teach you something else," I told her, and she slowed to walk by my side. "In case we need it."

"Need what?" she asked, wiping at the sweat that poured down her face.

"Agua. In case we run out."

She frowned at that. "I hoped that we'd be able to find some, or maybe run across someone who could tell us more."

She really *did* need me, I realized then. Those were pretty terrible odds. So I explained it to her, how to recognize patches of life in the desert, how to dig down into the soil deep enough. We had only limited tools with us, but even with some cloth or fabric—anything that could absorb water—we could filter out most of the dirt, enough to drink and keep us alive.

"I hope we don't *have* to do that," she remarked when I finished. "But at least I know where to look."

I did not say that I agreed with her. It kept me looking as if I wasn't afraid.

Even though I was.

I ignored my aching muscles and joints as they called out to me to stop moving, to give in to exhaustion. I couldn't. I thought of the promise of Simone, of the chance that I could give up this power and these stories and choose a life of my own. It kept me moving past the patches of prickly pear, past the dry bushes I had never seen before that broke when you touched them, leaving pieces behind, past the countless holes dug into the earth where creatures burrowed to hide from Your heat.

When we reached what would be the only incline of the day, You were beyond el mediodía, and I believed that I had not sweat so much in my entire life. Any of my skin not covered was layered in dust, thick and sticky. There was a large black stone at the bottom of the trail before us, and I waved my hand at it. "I need a rest," I said.

I let my pack fall to the desert floor, then leaned up against the stone. I didn't even care how hot it had gotten in Your light; my legs were thankful for the rest.

Emilia sat on the other side of me, but I closed my eyes and allowed myself to fall into the darkness of my own mind. The two of us had not spoken in a long time, and I assumed that meant we were still on the right path. But I also wasn't sure what to say. I felt we were in a better place than we had been the night before, but I still didn't know much about her. Who was she? What was she like outside of what we had experienced over the past day? Should I even bother getting to know her? What if she stayed behind in Solado? How would I get back home? Was I going to return as I had promised Mamá?

There was too much unknown, too much hanging in the balance.

I filled myself up with food and water, then left to go relieve myself behind a paloverde. When I returned, Emilia was ready to go.

"I need to know something," I said. "Before we go any farther."

Emilia shifted from one foot to the other. "What is it?"

"What happens at the end?"

She frowned. "What do you mean?"

"When we get there," I explained. "We go to Solado, and you find Luz, and I find Simone, and then . . . what? Will you stay there? Am I to find my own way back?"

She shook her head violently. "I can't stay there. Not one more day."

"But what of your friends? What about Simone?"

Emilia stayed silent, her gaze focused to the south, then said, "I don't know if you'll understand this."

I stepped closer to her. "I'll try," I said. "I have to try. I have to know that I'm not taking a one-way trip."

She focused those eyes on me. Piercing, as usual, but not cold. They were alight with a fire, an intensity, a conviction.

"Once you've been free, you can't go back to it all." She pulled her braid in front of her shoulder, and she ran her fingers up and down the tight lines of her hair. "I need to find Luz. And then . . . I have to leave. I can't stay there anymore."

It was like hearing my own thoughts coming out of her mouth. Hadn't I felt just as she did, but about Empalme? Hadn't I desired to leave for so, so long? Maybe this was *meant* to be a one-way trip. Maybe I wasn't supposed to go back home.

"Then let's keep moving," I said. "And if Solís is truly guiding you back to Solado, then They must want me to complete this journey, right?"

Emilia nodded. "They drew me to you, didn't They?"

I had nothing to say to that.

So we climbed.

We crested the hill as You were finally dropping toward the west, and I paused to take another drink of water, short and calculated so as to preserve as much of it as I could. "I know you've been do-ing it," I said to Emilia, "but make sure that you're taking regular sips, even if you don't think you need it."

"Why?"

I drank down deep; half my water was already gone. "Because

it can sneak up on you. It's better to keep a regular schedule than not to drink for an hour and start to suffer the ill effects of too little water."

She grimaced then. "I don't really know what those are," she said.

"The big one to pay attention to is your temperature. You'll feel extremely hot, you'll sweat more than you ever have in your life, and your skin will feel like it is burning."

Emilia sighed. "So . . . what I'm feeling now?"

"Probably," I said, smiling. "It's awful out, I know. But when your head starts pounding, or there is a dull pain behind your eyes, let me know. That's the start of something worse."

She drank more water as I gazed behind us, first down at the trail we had ascended, and then up to el valle before me.

Most of the hillside was bare save for a tall ironwood. It was far off the main trail, and as I stared at the lone living thing on the side of la montaña, I spotted another trail, this one jutting off toward the west. How many of them were there in the desert? How many criss-crossed with one another? Where did they lead? How many others had stood atop this same montaña and realized how very tiny they were in Your world?

I crossed over to the other side of la montaña where Emilia stood, and I suddenly understood why we were heading to la granja.

The land to the north was *fertile*.

The next valle stretched before us east to west, and it reminded me that we were a resilient people. After La Quema, we still rebuilt our lives. I had heard of las granjas grandísimas in the north that supplied most of the south with the food that kept us alive. I never dreamed that I would see them. But there they were, so immense and huge, rows of greens, browns, and yellows tucked up against one another, lined with the irrigation ditches that caught rainwater from las montañas and delivered it down to the fields. There seemed to be no end to them in either direction.

220   MARK OSHIRO

This was where our food came from?

It felt holy. Hallowed.

In spite of the punishment You gave us, we survived.

"I remember seeing this for the first time," said Emilia, breaking my concentration. She pointed to the north. "Only I saw it from those hills."

"But your people grew your food," I said. "There are few crops in Empalme. So we rely on las granjas."

She nodded. "It must be a lot to take in."

I excused myself then and headed for an ironwood on the western edge of the clearing, hoping to relieve myself. I had squatted down over a hole I dug in the dirt when I felt it.

The tug.

The twine around my heart.

The *pull*.

I ignored it at first. I had to be imagining it. But the sensation flared again. I stood up and yanked my breeches back into place, then swayed there, trying to breathe through it.

It was happening. The same feeling I had experienced that day hunting water. I carefully stepped to the west, beyond the ironwood. Another step, another tug. I gingerly moved closer, and then something brought me to my knees. I dug in the dirt immediately, without removing my pack, and my fingers plunged into the soil, dry and tough, and I could feel it caking underneath my nails, but I couldn't stop. The edge of something hard, like leather, poked out of the hole, and I pulled on it, then dug it out further.

Another little pouch.

Another poema!

I did not immediately tear open the pouch, despite that I wanted to. No. I *needed* to. But this was too good to be true. How had I found one of these so very far from home? Was this a trick of the mind? Had I failed to drink enough water?

"Xochitl!"

I spun at the sound of Emilia's voice. She crunched through the underbrush, moving toward me much quicker than I expected. I tucked the second pouch behind my back and into the band of my breeches.

She appeared. "You finished? It may look close, but we still have a long walk to Jorge's."

"Who is that?" I said, hoping I didn't sound too out of breath.

"He owns la granja. Well, the one we can stay at."

"And you've stayed there before?"

"Close enough," she said, frowning. "My father didn't trust him, so we made our own space on the other side of the fields of maíz. But I got to talk to Jorge. Nice man. I think he'll be pleased to see us."

She headed off ahead of me, and I took the chance to run my fingers along the edge of the pouch. The leather was more worn than the others, softer, inviting me to open it up.

And it was definitely real; this was not my imagination.

How long had it been here, buried beneath the ground? Years? Had no one ever found it? Was I *meant* to discover it?

There was no time to read la poema, though, and when I relieved myself and rejoined Emilia at the head of the descending trail, I felt I was about to erupt from joy. She lowered her canteen and squinted at me, and I didn't care how obvious my excitement was.

She examined me, then smiled. "You as happy as I am that we're going downhill now?"

"Don't let it fool you," I said. "It is easier on the legs, but you still need to drink agua. The heat isn't any better on the decline."

She nodded. "Gracias, Xochitl," she said. "I'm glad you're here."

My insides twisted up at that. So I chewed on some nopalitos as we descended. A dull ache settled behind my eyes, the first warning that I needed more water, but we were heading to a place that shimmered in greenness. I did not worry about preserving water for the next day, so I allowed myself a number of big gulps until my belly sloshed when I moved.

I reached into the band of my breeches.

I brushed my fingers over the edge of the leather.

I reminded myself again of what I was doing.

I was seeking freedom from this curse.

The pain would be worth it.

The stories that I held had been quiet for most of the day, but at the thought of purging myself of this power, they awoke, if only to find a place deeper within my body to hide.

It would not be much longer before I was free.

I clung to that idea. To *hope*. I ignored the pain—the throbbing in my head, the cramps in the lower half of my abdomen, the soreness that settled over my legs—because there was a purpose to this all.

"Do you have a plan, Emilia?"

She swallowed the nopales she had been chewing on. "¿Para qué?"

"After."

We rounded another switchback on the trail, our soles pounding against that packed dirt. She wiped sweat away from her eyes before answering. "To see the world," she said. "As much of it as I can."

"How?" I asked. "I always hear how dangerous it is in the desert. Don't you want to settle down somewhere? Build a new home?"

"I've basically been in one place my whole life until maybe a year ago," she said. "I'm not ready for something like that. Not yet, at least."

I had been in a single place for sixteen years. There was a part of me that understood what she meant, but it was still a discomforting idea, something jagged that rubbed me raw the more I thought about it. Could I spend my life traveling the desert? I thought of los viajeros, who traveled from aldea to aldea, selling and trading and giving stories. That was their normal.

Maybe it was time for me to change my perspective.

You were far in the west by the time we made it to the bottom of la montaña, and we were shrouded in its shadow. Emilia was now more sure of where to go, and she directed me to skirt the edge of the nearest field, the ground a deep brown, green sprouts of something shooting toward the sky, reaching up to You.

We came upon two new fields split by the road, and there were some sort of beans growing to the left, calabazas to our right. My mouth watered at the thought of a calabaza cut open, roasted over a fire until the seeds were a dark brown. Mamá would add azúcar to them as they cooled, and we would eat the flesh out of them while watching las estrellas come out.

I missed her. It was a brief, fiery thing.

It passed.

Because while I missed home, I knew I had left for the most important reason of all: to become *myself.*

My mouth dried out quickly, though. You were falling past the horizon and Your light was fading, yet the air lacked any moisture or relief. I longed for the oasis again.

I sipped at my water as we came upon another crop, this one with stalks that rose high above us. The leaves were browned on the edges, burned from the heat, but they were still green and thriving otherwise. A few ears of yellow maíz poked out here and there. It survived as the rest of us had.

"It's easy to get lost here," Emilia said, "so stick close, Xo."

Xo.

I liked the sound of that. Lito had been the only one in my life to call me by that name. But this felt *right*.

So I reached out and grabbed her hand, and she twisted around and smiled.

"Now I get to be the teacher," she said. "Since I've been here before."

Emilia guided me forward, between two rows of the towering stalks. The leaves were rough around the edges as they brushed against my bare arms. The rustling was the only sound, and the shadows from the setting sun were long, haunting. I had no sense of where I was or where I was going. All I had was Emilia, holding me tight, pulling me forward.

It was long before the edge of the crop came upon us, opening up to a clearing.

I should have felt relief as I looked upon the flickering light that danced in front of the dark outline of some large structure. There were people there gathered around a fire, and they turned to see who was approaching.

Emilia had done it. We did not get lost at all, and she'd accomplished it without a guide or a map.

She had done it, Solís, as promised.

But then an anger filled me. Emilia was telling the truth, which meant that You really *had* guided her.

Why?

Why had You chosen her when I had been so loyal to You for half my life?

Emilia eagerly ran toward the flames, toward the person she apparently knew, toward certainty. I watched her greet and hug a man, saw her turn to the others and introduce herself, and this all seemed so easy for her.

I shoved the anger down and kept it to myself. These people wouldn't understand me. And I feared that ultimately Emilia wouldn't either.

When I walked up to the fire, Emilia turned and then waved me over. There were six others by my count, mostly men and one older woman, a young boy clinging to her side.

"Let me introduce you, Xochitl, to everyone else," Emilia said.

There was Jorge, tall and wiry, his face seemingly stuck in a goofy grin. These farms and fields had long been in the family, and Jorge's mother had passed them on to her children before she passed. She had taught the twins how to till the land, how to rotate out crops, how to use every drop of water that fell from the sky, ran down from las montañas, or lay deep within the ground. He explained to me over dinner that night how more and more people were passing through his fields, getting lost in the maíz, as they tried to find work or new homes in the surrounding desert. He decided to open his home and his lands to them, and for the past three years, this had been a safe haven for those who traveled.

And then there were those who traveled.

Rosalinda, short, round, who never drifted far from her son, Felipe. He had her curved face, her big cheeks, her thick black hair. They had been traveling for over a month, had come from Hermosillo, had escaped something that Rosalinda would not explain, and I knew not to ask her about it.

There was Eliazar, a flash of gray in his hair, his beard full and long, his smile infectious and joyous. He was much more eager to talk, more willing to spill the details of who he was and where he'd been. He had been walking for over a year, had come from El Mar, far out to the east, a place I'd only heard of in stories that seemed magical and impossible.

Then there was Roberto y Héctor, who sat close together, stealing glances at each other, always touching, their gaze dancing off the rest of us. Roberto reminded me of Papá: tall, long, flowing hair, with a wide chest and dark eyes. Héctor was smaller, his face long and sharp, and he wouldn't make eye contact with anyone.

They smiled briefly. They said hello. That was all.

"There's agua over near the house," Jorge announced. "Take as much as you need to drink, but no bathing."

I nodded at Jorge, and that smile of his spread across his face. "Gracias, compadre."

"And where do you come from, señorita?"

He asked this as I sat next to Emilia. I hesitated. Maybe it was smart to keep things to yourself, but we were so far from my home. There was a freedom in that; no one here knew who I was, what was attached to me. What I had done. I could choose to be who I wanted to be, how I wanted to present myself.

"Empalme," I said. "It's about two days to the south."

"Ah, someone else from the south," said Rosalinda. "Bienvenida."

"And are you seeking something? Someone?" Jorge asked.

I looked to Emilia, who simply inclined her head.

"Someone," I said. "In Solado."

At the mention of Emilia's home, Héctor bolted upright. The motion was so quick that it startled me. He opened his mouth, as if to say something, and panic spread over his features. He glanced back down at his partner, who reached up and held his hand, guided him back down. Lips quivering, he sat. Then he whispered something to Roberto, too low for any of us to hear.

"Not now," said Roberto. "They won't believe us anyway."

"Believe you about what?" I said.

A silence fell over the group. Our attention was on Roberto and Héctor, who seemed to shrink before us, as if they were willing themselves to be smaller.

"Te dije que te creo," said Jorge, his voice soft, his grin gone. "Does it matter if they do?"

The rest of us looked at one another.

"I feel like I missed something important," I admitted.

"Niña, we all did," said Rosalinda, and she stroked Felipe's hair as he lay with his head in her lap. "What's wrong with Solado?"

Emilia was shaking her head. "Why were you two going there?"

"I heard there was work," said Roberto, and he ran his hand up and down Héctor's arm. "It ran out in our aldea, so we headed north to find something."

"Oh, we found something," Héctor spat out. "Don't go to Solado. You'll never make it."

"I'm *from* there," Emilia said. "We'll be fine."

Héctor's mouth dropped open. "You're going *back*?"

"*We* are," I said, sticking my legs out in front of me and bending forward, thankful for the stretch it gave my muscles. "She has something to retrieve, and I have someone to see."

"You'll never make it," repeated Héctor, shaking his head, still not looking at us. "You can't go."

"We'll be fine," said Emilia. "I've lived there. I know how to keep us safe from los—"

Now Héctor lifted his head, and his eyes bore straight into Emilia, straight into me. "That's not what I mean. You won't make the journey itself."

"¡Ya basta!" said Roberto, and he tugged his partner closer to him. "You're just scaring them."

"After what *we* saw? What *we* went through?" He scoffed. "They *should* be scared."

Jorge walked up to the fire, maíz in his hands. "Enough of this talk," he said, then looked at me. "Some people don't make the journey, Xochitl." He began to place los elotes on an old metal grating over the fire. "They turn back because it's too hard, too long, or . . . well, they start to see things."

Ah. The heat. I knew about that. But as I nodded at Jorge, Héctor stood again. "None of you believe me," he said. He glanced down at Roberto. "I expected you to support me, but you're a coward, just like it said you were."

He walked away from the fire, off toward the fields to the east. Roberto gave us an apologetic look, but said nothing. He chased off after Héctor, and left us to ponder what this had all been about.

What had they seen? Why was Héctor so convinced we wouldn't make it? What had told Roberto that he was a coward?

The maíz crackled and popped as it cooked, and Jorge started to hand it out after adding spices, butter, and some sort of white cream on top of it. When he handed me an ear, I realized how hungry I was.

"Gracias, Jorge," I said, taking the food from him.

"It's what I do," he said. "Solís be willing, I help where I can."

We raised our free hands and covered our eyes and then our hearts.

"Don't pay too much attention to them," he continued. "I've been hearing stories for years."

"What kind of stories?" asked Rosalinda. Her son, who had remained quiet during all of this, was staring with his eyes and mouth wide open. Rosalinda gently tapped his chin with her hand. "¡Qué grosero, Felipe! ¡Cierra tu boca!"

He did, but he kept staring.

"I never know how much to believe," Jorge said. "Mi familia . . . we have always been en este valle. Tending las granjas. The fields. The crops. There's livestock to the east that my twin sister manages. I see her only a couple of times a year, she's so busy." He went quiet, wistful. "We don't leave this place. There's too much to do, and now that I help others . . . well, there's not a whole lot of time to go exploring."

Jorge spread strips of some sort of meat over the grill, seasoned them liberally, and flipped them over to do the same for the other side. We waited, eager to hear what he had to say next.

"So I take it all in," he continued. "Los cuentos. I hear what people have to say. And I don't know if the heat of Solís makes people imagine things or what. But something happens between here and Solado. People . . . see things."

"What kinds of things?" Felipe's voice was high but soft, his attention rapt, focused entirely on Jorge.

Jorge knelt in front of Felipe, and his smile lit up his face. "It's nothing you need to worry about," he said. "You're brave, aren't you?"

Felipe puffed up his chest and nodded.

"And you're traveling with your mother, ¿no?"

Nodded again, harder this time.

"And neither of you will let anything happen to the other one?"

"Never," Felipe said.

"Good." He ruffled Felipe's hair. "Then you'll be fine."

When Jorge returned to the fire, I nudged Emilia. "Did anything ever happen to you?" I asked.

She shook her head. "No. I was with my father as we traveled south." Then she pursed her lips. "Things happened, I guess. But it was always *him* that was happening."

"So will we be safe?" I asked.

No one responded.

We looked to Jorge.

"The more of you there are, the better chances you have," he said. "You're all heading north for various reasons. Why not travel together?"

It wasn't a bad idea. But where were the others even going?

"I would feel better if we had all of you," Rosalinda said. "It's been me and Felipe for a long time, and . . . it would make me feel safer."

"I've been alone on my journey," said Eliazar. "I could use the company."

"I don't mind," said Emilia. "As long as I'm not taking anyone into Solado with me and Xochitl."

"And what of the others?" I said, gesturing with my head toward the east, where Héctor y Roberto were last seen.

"I don't think they're going to continue on," said Jorge, and he started passing out some of the meat he had cooked. "Not after what they saw."

"And what exactly did they see?" said Eliazar. "Tell us. We can handle it."

Jorge shrugged. "The truth."

There was a terrible silence after that. "What does that *mean*?" I finally asked.

"That's what Héctor said. He said, 'The truth came to us, and it judged us.'" He shrugged again. "It spooked them out so much, they came back."

We had nothing to say to that.

We settled in, spreading out our sleeping rolls, and Rosalinda spoke to her son in a soft, purring voice. Felipe was stretched out on his back, his eyes up to the sky.

Did these people celebrate at night, as we did in Empalme? It felt strange not to, but I guess we all did in our own way. We had eaten together. Now we were sprawled out, our eyes on the stars around us, and I finally felt calm. Comfortable. The stories had gone quiet; perhaps they were frightened by what Jorge had told us.

The truth awaited us in the desert.

What was *my* truth? What had I not yet revealed?

I thought of Manolito's warning. I'd see him again when I was about to admit the truth. Would that be soon? What had I lied about?

So much, I thought. I had lied so many times in Empalme. Would this be a reckoning?

Perhaps. Perhaps I would finally face Your wrath after defying You. Perhaps You wouldn't let me succeed in my attempt to rid myself of this power, to find a life outside of Your control.

I reached down then, dug around behind me until I felt the edges of the little leather pouch I had found earlier, then pulled it out.

I needed this.

I needed to know what I had found.

I stood nervously. "I'll be right back," I said to Emilia. "Just have to relieve myself and take care of a couple of things."

"¿A dónde vas, Xochitl?" Jorge called out.

I pointed to the south of us. "To the edge of the field. I need some privacy, that's all."

"Don't go too far," he said. "It's easy to get lost out there."

My ecstasy flared, and I did not listen to the aching soles of my feet or the dull burning in my legs. My body may have wanted me to stop, but my soul was calling out for the next poema. I *had* to have it, had to feel it wrap its arms around me, had to know that someone else out there knew who I was.

At the edge of the field, just out of sight of the others, I crouched down and set the pouch on the ground, then carefully untied the leather strings. They were still coated in dirt, but that didn't matter. Whatever was inside was pure. It was exactly what I needed.

I slipped the paper out of it, felt the sharp edges, how thick it was, and I could see the writing in black coal, the curved, delicate letters . . . Oh, it was them, it was the same person!

I read the words under the starlight:

Cada una de nosotras es una desierta	Each of us a desert
solitaria y vasta	solitary and vast
quemada	burned
nos estiramos por siempre	we stretch forever

I fell back, and it swept over me, and I lay supine on the earth, my gaze up at the sky, and I repeated each of the words aloud, felt their sharpness and meaning on my tongue, and I said it all again.

Each of us a desert.

Weren't we all?

Weren't we all so vast and solitary inside? Or was it just me?

No, it wasn't. There was someone else out there who understood me, who knew what it was like to feel this unending loneliness, to be empty within.

We stretch forever.

What did that mean?

I let it tumble in my mind, and as I did so, they awoke.

They stretched.

They yearned for more.

We stretch ourselves: to fit within the roles we are given. To make ourselves look better to those around us. To convince one another that we are good people in a world so vacant.

Each of us a desert.

My back was against the cool dirt, and my heart was satiated. Quenched. As if I had drunk an entire well's worth of water.

I walked back to the camp in silence. I looked up, and there was a long flash of light that burst across the night sky. We saw them sometimes, distant estrellas moving across the darkness, and they were considered a good omen, a sign of blessed fortune to come. I nudged Emilia, who was gazing up as well. "Did you see that?" I said.

She shook her head. "See what?"

"Ah, nothing," I replied, and I smiled at her, thankful that she was here. That I was here. That the others might be joining us on our journey in the morning.

Maybe it was not so strange that Emilia believed so fully in You. I had my doubts about You and Your love, but at that moment, surrounded by possibility and hope, it was easier to believe.

I curled up and faced away from Emilia, the fire crackling behind me, the conversations dying out.

"Where did you go, Xo?"

Her voice was soft, barely louder than Rosalinda's snoring or the crackling fire. I didn't say anything at first, because unconsciousness was pulling at me.

The fire sparked louder. "Nowhere," I told her.

Emilia said nothing more. The fire calmed down, and I passed into sleep.

I woke the next morning, alive with hope.

I watched Your light slowly bleed into the sky. Los pájaros were chatty and eager, though, and I knew they wouldn't be for long. I could feel Your heat entering the world, Your embrace clinging to my body. I was calm.

Sore and aching still, my muscles protesting the very thought of another day of walking, I was ready to continue on. My destination was clear: Solado. You had guided us here, so maybe Emilia was right. You wanted this to happen.

Maybe You were as done with me as I was done with You.

Rosalinda was already awake and was stirring something in a metal pot over the fire.

"We're leaving in ten minutes or so," she said. "Get some food and agua, relieve yourself, and then we go."

"Mami says we should get as far as we can before el mediodía," said Felipe, waddling back from the well with a bucket of water.

We. I guess we were all headed north together.

I returned to the edge of the field to duck behind a few stalks to relieve myself. I was thankful that my urine was clear; that was a good sign at the start of the day. I pulled up my breeches and then passed Felipe, his round face bouncing as he rushed to the maíz, panic twisting his features as he hurried to relieve himself.

I laughed at that, then rejoined the group. I packed as quickly as I could and munched on some leftovers from the meal that Rosalinda had prepared. We took turns refilling our waterskins, and as I was nearly finished, I looked up to see Jorge, his hair disheveled, staring at me.

"They left already," he said, and when it was clear I didn't understand, he shook his head. "Roberto. Héctor. To Obregán."

Eliazar dumped dirt and some water on the fire, and it steamed and smoked. "We will be fine," he said. "There are now five of us. We will make it."

"Make it *where*, exactly?" I asked. "How long will you travel with Emilia and me?"

"I don't have a specific destination," said Eliazar. "I'd like to find a new home someday, but right now . . . " He picked up his pack and slung it over a shoulder. ". . . I'm just walking. Searching for something."

"We *are* looking for somewhere to settle down," said Rosalinda.

"There's a camp beyond las montañas that we should try for," Emilia said. "It's pretty far, but if we make good time today, I think we can make it."

I gazed north. "Beyond *those* montañas?"

They seemed so terribly far, Solís, much farther than we had traveled the day before. And that was *before* the others had joined us.

"We have rested well," said Eliazar, as if he could read my thoughts. "I think we can make it. We've made it this far, ¿no?"

I wanted to believe him. I *chose* to, because what was the alternative?

I didn't want to imagine that. This journey had a purpose, and I told myself then that I would do anything to make it.

"There's another well beyond the end of la granja," said Jorge. "Stop there. Fill up again, as much as you need. I don't know of any sources of agua to the north, aside from those deep in the ravines of las montañas." He scratched at his head. "And that's half a day away."

"Thank you for letting us stay," said Emilia. "May Solís look down upon you with joy."

We headed out to the east at first, cutting through the fields as we had done the night before. When we popped out at the other end, Emilia directed us north on a worn trail. For the next hour, the stalks were tall enough to block out Your light, and so we all walked as close as possible to them, relishing every moment in the shade.

The fields eventually ended, as did the shade. We were silent again, focused on making good time to the well, trying to ignore how bright the sun was. The land shimmered in Your light, and the desert spread in all directions, a ceaseless brown punctuated with the arms of the saguaros and the branches of the occasional paloverde. Low bushes sat still on the ground. We were the only creatures awake anymore, as most had scurried to find shade as You moved through the sky.

We were a defiance, weren't we? We made the deliberate decision to be under You when most hid in the darkness. I don't think we appreciated that then. No, Emilia and I were focused entirely on the walk: putting one foot in front of the other, taking sips of water every quarter hour, making sure our footing was good as we climbed out of gullies.

The pain came back before we reached the well, though, and I felt the stories awaken. It was becoming harder and harder to determine whom they belonged to. Each emotion blended with the next. Who felt regret? Was it Lani or Lito? Which story belonged to the lonely one? Was that Emilia or Ofelia or me?

A spike ripped through my lower abdomen, and I clutched it, trying to breathe through the pain.

Just walk, I told myself. *Focus on the end. Because this* will *end.*

"¿Estás bien, niña?" Eliazar asked, reaching out as I rubbed my belly.

"Only a cramp," I said. "I bled the other day, so it's probably that."

He nodded at me. "Do you need a break? Some agua?"

I shook my head. "No, no, we should keep going."

I massaged the spot for a few minutes as we walked, and I caught Emilia looking back at me, trying to disguise it in a stretch.

I smirked.

She winked at me.

A new sensation filled my belly, one that did not belong to any of the stories, but was mine and mine alone.

Desire.

She was so beautiful, Solís. It had taken me a while to admit that, but I did not let it bloom into anything else. This was not the time. Emilia had her own life to live, and after Simone, I probably would not fit into it.

Still, it was nice. To desire someone.

The sun was firmly in the sky when we made it to the stone well. After Felipe filled up on water, I shamelessly dipped my head under the stream of the pump. I let the cool water pour over me and wiped at my skin and the stickiness that still clung to it. We filled up our stomachs again with enough water to make us burst, and Rosalinda laughed when Felipe burped loudly. The sound echoed out into the desert.

There was one lone field of maíz out here and perhaps the only shade for a long while. The others were talking and joking when I made for it. "¡Ya vuelvo!" I called out, and Emilia raised a hand in acknowledgment.

I didn't know why I went in that direction, Solís. I moved to the east, through the stalks, letting the leaves scrape at me, and I assumed the pressure down below meant I needed to relieve myself again. But then I was moving quicker and quicker, pushing past the maíz, and something ripped into my arm, tearing the skin, and I didn't care.

There was one here.

La poeta had left another one.

I plunged to the ground and tore off my pack, then pulled out la pala, and I was furious, almost sick with elation as I dug into the earth, deeper and deeper, and there it was, another drawstring pouch, the leather as worn as the previous poema, and then it was in my hands.

Excitement ripped through me as I opened it and saw the wrinkled edges of a scroll. I unfolded it, let my eyes course over the writing scratched into the paper, committed them to memory as fast as I could:

Veo el sol y veo Solís.	I see the sun and I see Solís.
¿Pero quién me ve?	But who sees me?
Me estoy escondiendo en	I am hiding in
las sombras	the shadows
En el dolor	In pain
Solo quiero ser vista.	I only want to be seen.

I rolled it up, stuffed it back into its pouch and my pack, but I was repeating that last line, over and over again, soft like a whisper, like a prayer to You.

Solo quiero ser vista.

I only want to be seen.

I had been nudged back onto the right path. Esta poema was proof of that. I was closer to the truth. I had to be.

If You did not want this, You would stop it.

Right?

I wore a smile on my face as I returned to the well, filled up on water, replenished myself with hope.

The five of us walked in a line, snaking across the land, toward las montañas.

Each of us a desert, alone and vast.

We were alone together, at least.

There were few árboles of any kind beyond la granja and the fields, and the shade that had protected us in the early morning was now gone. We could hide behind the tall arms of the saguaro that poked up from the earth, but if you got too close to them, they would leave you with a painful reminder that they were prepared to defend themselves against invaders.

The newest poema ran through me, and I continued to recite it to myself, devouring its power, and the cramps that had tormented me faded away in its wake. I was lost in my head when I realized that Felipe had slowed down to walk next to me. "Can I ask you a question?" he said.

I snorted. "Isn't that a question?"

He frowned. "That doesn't count."

"Go ahead," I said, giving him a smile.

"Where are you from?"

"Empalme," I answered. "You ever heard of it?"

He shook his head, cheeks shaking. "No, I haven't. How far is it from Hermosillo?"

"I have no idea," I said. "This is actually my first time away from home. I've never been to the south."

"Never?" he said, his tone disbelieving.

"Felipe, please," said Rosalinda. "Don't bother her."

I smiled once more. "He's not, I promise."

"Why didn't you leave?" He used the back of his hand to wipe sweat off his forehead. "Didn't you want to go anywhere else?"

I caught Emilia's eyes widening. Children had a way of cutting right to the bone with a question. Felipe didn't know any better, though; he wasn't trying to be cruel.

"I wanted to go all sorts of places. But I wasn't allowed to."

"Did you make your parents mad or something?"

This time I laughed out loud. "No, Felipe, not like that."

I paused.

Should I tell them? I thought.

I was far from Empalme.

What could it hurt?

"Soy cuentista," I said. "So I was the one who took care of my aldea."

Felipe gasped.

"A real cuentista?" He reached out, put his fingers on my arm, then yanked them back. "Mami! ¡Xochitl es cuentista!"

"I heard," she said. "Since I *am* right behind you, mijo."

"We didn't have one."

I stopped.

Right in that spot.

Rosalinda ran into the back of me, and I nearly tumbled to the ground.

"Dímelo otra vez," I said.

"¿Qué?" Felipe had turned around and was walking backwards, facing me.

"¡Otra vez!" I cried. "You had *no* cuentista?"

"Well, *no*," Felipe said. "We didn't deserve one."

"'Deserve'?" My legs wobbled. "What does that have to do with anything?"

Eliazar, who had brought up the rear of our group, now joined me on the other side from Emilia. "That's not how it works," he said.

"I know," I responded. "Every aldea has one . . . don't they?"

He shook his head, took a long drink from his waterskin. "Not at all. There's only one born every generation."

"A *generation*?" I scoffed at him. "How is that possible? How can anyone survive like that?"

"Survive?" It was Eliazar's turn to look confused. "It's not about survival. They can save lives only if they absolutely *must*."

"But what of las pesadillas?" I said.

They all stared at me, unmoving, confused.

"The stories that come to life?"

Emilia shook her head. "I don't know what those are."

"Do you need más agua, Xochitl?" Felipe asked. "Maybe you're tired."

I stared at them, the impossibility spreading through my body, reaching the stories, startling them awake, and I gritted my teeth.

Cada una de nosotras es una desierta.

And we were all so different.

I stumbled toward two tall saguaros without speaking to the others, my mind reeling, the ground shaky under my feet.

They weren't lying.

They couldn't be.

Who would lie about something so important?

But how could all of this be true? Your heat pushed down on me, and I almost gave up right then, Solís. I almost brought myself to the earth to return all those stories to You. The bitterness was in my throat, on my tongue, threatening to pour out of my mouth and drip down the front of me, seep into the dry and arid dirt. Why shouldn't I do it? Why was I so set on keeping them all within me?

Giving up would be so easy.

I bent over.

My knees found the earth.

My hands next.

They rushed up—

"Xochitl!"

Her voice stopped me. Shoved the stories back down.

"Xochitl, are you okay? Are you—?"

I looked up, tears streaming down my face, the refuse at the corner of my mouth. I wiped at it, saw the dark liquid on the back of my hand, and I nearly lost it again. Emilia said something, something I couldn't make out, and I gazed back up at her. Her angular face was even more sharp with worry, and I collapsed back, and the bitter taste of the stories slid back to my gut, then spread out, finding somewhere to hide.

"How?" I choked out. "How can this all be true?"

"I don't know," said Emilia. "I thought it was strange that you were stuck in Empalme, but I never said anything. We had many cuentistas in Solado."

"*What?*"

The faintness came back. I took off my pack and dug through it for the goatskin water bag. I knew it was reckless and foolish, but I poured some water over my head and let it run down, let it shock me and cool me.

"Xochitl, do we need to stop?" She knelt before me, ran her fingers over my face. "You're burning up."

"No," I said. "We can't stop. Not on account of me."

"No, I meant—" And then she sighed. "You don't have to push yourself so hard. It's okay if you take a break."

"And slow us down?" I shook my head. "We have too much ground to cover today."

Emilia offered her hand, and I pulled myself upright, wiped at my face. "Emilia, how can this all be true? I mean . . . someone has to be wrong about Solís."

She shrugged. "Maybe we all are."

I couldn't stop thinking of that as Emilia gave me some of her water. What if none of us knew what You wanted, Solís? What did that mean for our world?

For this journey?

"We should get going," I said. "If we're going to make it to our next stop."

The two of us rejoined the others, and Rosalinda wore pity on her face. "Xochitl, we don't have to—"

"No," I said. "We can keep moving."

"¿Estás bien?" Felipe asked. "You were crying a lot and it looked like you were sick and maybe you should take a nap."

"Felipe!" Rosalinda gently swatted at him. "You don't always have to say what's in your head."

"But why did she react like that?"

I gave Felipe a smile, hoping that it would convince him I was fine. "I had been taught something very different about us. About las cuentistas."

"So your aldea *doesn't* deserve one?" He scratched his head. "I'm confused."

Emilia guided us back to the main trail as we spoke. *All* of us. Rosalinda explained what Felipe had been referring to, how her people believed that only deserving communities who had pleased Solís were gifted with a cuentista, and they were *born* into that aldea.

"But how can that work?" I asked.

Rosalinda, who walked alongside me, shook her head. "I don't know that I think about it like that," she said. "It just *does*. Those of us in Hermosillo know that we must be better, so that Solís will bless us."

"Then . . . your cuentista is a *child* when you get one," said Eliazar. He sighed. "How is that fair to them?"

"I was a cuentista at eight," I said. "I had to start taking stories once Tía Inez passed on the power to me."

"You can't pass on the power," said Felipe. "Solís is the one who decides that."

"But I *know* it can be done," Emilia countered. "I've seen it."

"Ay, I'm lost," said Felipe. "None of this makes any sense."

That realization killed the conversation, and the only sound reverberating across the desert plain was our boots scraping against the earth. It truly did not make *any* sense. My life had been so rigid in Empalme. But the rules that had been used to control my life, to make everything defined and perfect, were not even *true*?

I slowed down, letting the others move ahead of me until I was alongside Eliazar. He had not said much during my outburst, but what he *had* said was interesting to me.

"So, only one in a generation?" I said to him.

He ran his fingers through his long beard. "That's what I was raised to believe," he said. "I had to travel to see a cuentista if we needed healing. They were living in a place to the west. So I often went years without talking to one."

"*Years?*" I balked. "But . . . how did you deal with las pesadillas?"

He played with his beard some more. "In general? Ay, no sé, señorita. You can't really control them, can you? You get them when you get them."

"No," I insisted. "Only when you are not honest with Solís. They take form. They become real."

His eyes lit up at that. "Ah, you mean the things you see when you become consumed with dishonesty?"

I nodded at that. "That sounds familiar."

"They're rare." Eliazar stumbled briefly but caught himself before I could reach out to grab him. He waved me away. "You have to be truly lost to Solís for that to happen."

I did not know how that was possible. I had grown up *seeing* las pesadillas. They lived in the shadows, gained form the longer a person did not give up their story. So why was this not the case for the others?

The anger came first, and I remembered Ofelia's rage, the sense that she'd felt betrayed, that she'd been left out. Her memory spread out in my mind: She read the note, felt the rejection, stormed to Lito's in fury.

It only made me more mad, and it poured out from my chest, radiated into the rest of my body, flooding me like the gullies during a terrible rain.

And then Eliazar brought me back.

He cleared his throat. "Xochitl," he said.

No.

I knew that tone.

I had heard it so many times.

I *couldn't*.

"I have not been honest in a long time," he continued.

My feet were stones, impossible to lift.

"I have sought out others, but . . ."

I was so full, so overflowing with the stories of others, and they swirled and churned inside me, eager at the prospect of another one joining them.

"They could not help me."

My abdomen hurt, and I clutched a hand there, begging the stories to return to their slumber.

"I've been wandering for so long."

I couldn't do it.

"Later," I said, the word draining out of my mouth as if it were the bitterness and refuse of a story being given back to You. "Ask me later."

Eliazar smiled.

A hand over the eyes.

Over the chest.

"I am so glad you are here," he said. "Solís must have wanted you to help me."

I was so very far from home, and yet . . . I couldn't escape it. I couldn't escape the role that had been forced upon me. I thought I was safe. They were not from Empalme. They were not my responsibility.

But You knew, didn't You? You knew I was trying to escape from what had been forced upon me.

I vowed right then to make it to Simone at any cost.

The heat weighed heavily on my face and on the bare skin of my arms, and there was a precision to it, as if You were shining on me and *only* me.

But I resisted.

Maybe Eliazar and the others saw me as nothing more than a cuentista, as a means to their end.

But I was choosing to end this.

This was *my* decision.

And I had never been so alive in my life.

I breathed in that freedom, and I was overflowing with purpose. It was not the one that had been assigned to me, that had dictated my life. It was my own.

No hay paredes	There are no walls
para detenerme	to stop me

I kept an eye on Eliazar as I walked; he had begun to slow down, and I worried that the heat was getting to him. I spoke to Rosalinda for a little bit when she saw me massaging another cramp in my lower stomach and fell back to match my pace. She told me that if we found la garra del diablo, she would brew me a tea that helped with monthly pain. The roots of the plant made for a bitter taste, she explained, but it would be worth it.

I did not tell her the other reason for my pain.

As we talked, I sipped at my water, which had remained cool despite the heat. I did not want the tightness in my head to come back. I reminded Emilia of the same. This was, after all, the reason she asked me to come, to help her survive this trek.

She said nothing about whether we were heading in the right direction. *Perhaps You are still guiding her*, I thought. I wasn't sure I actually believed that anymore.

Rosalinda told me more about her life, how they made tortillas out of a white flour where she was born, and Felipe often interrupted to add in his own bits to her stories. He made reference to an escape; Rosalinda shushed him, and they did not speak further of it. No matter; the talking passed the time and kept our minds off the heat, off the persistent fire in our muscles, off the fear that we would be walking forever.

Maybe this was our punishment. Nuestra pesadilla. To walk and walk and walk and never know if it was going to end.

There was a rustling overhead, and when I looked up, a brilliant flock of palomas flew by. They spun and twirled together, and the others gasped at the sight of them. Eliazar said this was a good omen, a sign that we were still on the right path.

Perhaps. And perhaps You were teasing us, reminding us that we did not have the gift of flight, that we were forever bound to the earth, that we would live and die down here.

We pressed on.

And I kept these thoughts to myself.

Why did You punish all of us, Solís? If You despised what humanity had done to Your world long ago, why punish all those who came *after*? Why not wipe the slate clean, start over, and fix the mistakes from the first time around? Or do You not believe that You made any mistakes, that all of this was *our* fault?

If Your creation was perfect, then why do we do such imperfect things?

I was told so many stories, and the farther I walked from Empalme, the less real they became.

I was born to a body meant to help others. But I am so selfish, Solís. I give and I give and I give myself: to You, to mi gente, but why did You put me in a body with such unending desire? That wants so much that it cannot have?

Raúl was impatient.

Mamá had a temper.

Papá could disappear into himself and forget that anyone else was in his life.

Then there was Manolito, who had so many secrets. Or Rogelio, who drank himself into a stupor to dampen how much he hated himself. Or Marisol or Lani or Soledad or Emilia or Omar, who all lived imperfectly in an imperfect world. Or los pálidos, who had stolen an entire aldea from those who had built it up.

I now knew the secrets You purged from my body every time I completed the ritual. Maybe that was the point of it: I forgot because if I remembered, I would know the truth about this whole rotten system.

They had broken the rules of Your world, and I was there to fix them, to repair them so that our nightmares would not become flesh, would not destroy us. I existed so that You wouldn't burn us up again.

But there was so much more, wasn't there? Obregán was full of people who appeared not to believe in You, at least not as I did.

Yet they stood.

They sold Your power.

They were unpunished.

How was this fair? Just?

Were we isolated by design? Did You stick us so far apart because if we met one another, if we compared all these stories, we would figure out the truth?

It feels strange to say this to You, but I have to.

Your world is imperfect, Solís. It is designed to make us feel misery, designed to make us doubt ourselves, designed to force us to choose between one terrible thing and another. What are we supposed to do? How do I make You happy when it is so very impossible to be happy for *myself*?

It is hard to tell You this next part. But I have to. I have to tell You the whole story.

I hope You are still listening.

You were sitting tall above us when Eliazar first fell.

He had been walking nearest to Rosalinda, who was talking to me about Hermosillo. Felipe was pestering Emilia with a million questions about Solado. They both seemed to be enjoying it despite the terrible heat.

The land was flat, and las montañas were finally closer to us. It would not be long before we started our ascent for the day. Eliazar was quietly listening to our responses when he stepped wrong, his foot grazing a large rock he had not seen, and he pitched forward. Rosalinda was quick, and she caught him before he hit the ground. He slowly lowered himself to one knee, panting. I stuck out a hand to steady him, and my fingers lightly brushed against his neck.

He was cool. Sweaty. *Soaked* with sweat.

It was bad for the body to suffer a drop in temperature like this. "Drink some agua, Eliazar," I insisted. "Catch your breath."

Rosalinda crouched down next to him and handed over her canteen. "Have some of mine," she said. "It's still cold, and I don't need as much as you do."

He thanked her with a nod of his head, then brought the canteen up to his mouth. Some of the water trickled out and down his chin, running along his neck and beard and then soaking into his already drenched camisa.

"Más," Rosalinda ordered.

"Are you sure you don't mind?" he asked.

"I'll be fine," she said. "Please, señor."

Emilia and Felipe had backtracked to us. Both of them looked tired, too.

"¿Qué pasó?" Emilia asked. "We're still making excellent time, so we can stop here."

Eliazar held a hand up, and Rosalinda and I helped him rise. He swayed in place, then gave us a goofy smile. Such a warm expression on his face, but when it faded, there was a sadness there, a soft edge to his brief joy. He looked to me, and his mouth curled up. "Could I have a moment alone with you? Before we continue?"

No, I thought. *No, I know what this is! I can't do this!*

Emilia must have seen the panic on my face. "Eliazar, are you sure this is the time for that? We're all very tired, and I'm sure Xochitl can't . . . can't deal with the ritual right now."

Relief filled me. She had given me an out.

"Lo siento, Xochitl," he said, and his eyes were deep wells of sadness now, so dark that I thought I could pitch myself into them and never come out. "I would not ask you if it wasn't important."

Emilia gazed in my direction. What was that look on her face? Concern? Fear?

"You don't have to do this, Xochitl," she said.

"Please, cuentista," Eliazar begged.

Emilia left his side, came to me, and pulled me from him, far enough so that no one could hear us. My heart raced a terrible rhythm.

"I get it now," she said.

"Get what?"

"Why you're doing this. Why you want to go to Simone."

My eyesight blurred. And it was such a silly thought, but I couldn't help it: *Don't cry, Xochitl. You need every drop of water to survive.*

I wasn't sure I wanted her to see my face, to see how much her empathy affected me. "Why now?" I asked.

"They all want something from you. This is how it's been, hasn't it?"

"All the time," I choked out.

"And you have to lie to everyone just to get through the day."

I did.

"Especially to yourself."

I breathed in the hot air of the desert. I breathed in that *truth*.

"If you don't want to do this, I'll support you, Xochitl."

I faced her.

"Whatever your decision," she said, and her lips turned up in a smile, "I'll support you."

I breathed that in, too.

I had taken so many stories. In a couple of days, this power would be taken from *me*. It would be over, sooner than I could possibly dream of.

Something was wrong with Eliazar, and I could help him.

This is it, I told myself. *The last story I will take.*

"I think I have to do this," I said. "Just this once."

"Estás segura?"

"Sí," I said without hesitation. "Keep the others busy, can you?"

She nodded, then walked off. She spoke briefly to Rosalinda, and the two of them looked at me. Emilia guided them from me, and I was left with el viejo.

I walked toward him.

He cast a tender gaze upon me. "Cuentista," he said, "may I?" Eliazar dropped to the ground, his knees scraping against the earth. He held both his hands out in front of him, his palms facing down, waiting for me.

A pain stabbed me in the gut again, but it was not a cramp from anything usual. It was the surge of fear: Lito's. Marisol's. Mine.

I saw them in my mind: Lito reading the letter to Julio, Marisol holding her breath as los sabuesos hunted in Solado.

What did he have to tell me?

"Everything is as it should be," he said, still holding his hands out, still gazing at me with hope and longing.

A part of me resisted. Told me to deny him again. Told me to preserve my energy, to think about myself first, to remember all the stories within me that I still had not given back. They woke again and fought for space, and I clutched my stomach. I breathed through the pain and . . . and . . .

It was instinct. I knelt down beside him, then crossed my legs under me. I raised my hands, palms up, and I slid them underneath Eliazar's, and I smiled back to him.

"Breathe, señor," I told him, and he did so, and I pushed those stories down, forced them deeper into me.

The spark hit me, and his sadness rushed down my arms, straight to my heart, surrounding it and squeezing it, and all I managed to get out in time was a choked request:

"Tell me your story, Eliazar."

Let me tell You a story, Solís.

Eliazar never wanted children. He never desired anything more than Gracia, his love. They had met many years before, back when Eliazar's aldea was tiny, insignificant. They lived far, far to the east of Obregán, out where the deserts gradually gave way to las dunas, then to the endless expanse of El Mar. Eliazar was so much younger then, his hands not yet haunted by the ghosts of pain and tension that gripped his joints, that slowed his legs. He made a living as a pescador, and his life was simple and focused before he met Gracia. He used to make the daylong trip to and from the shoreline of El Mar, where he used his handmade nets of intricately tied twine to catch seafood to sell en las aldeas he passed on his trek home. Then, with just enough pescado for himself and his aldea still in his cart, he would guide his horse and his catch back home.

Gracia and Eliazar met for the first time on the road to El Mar. She was walking toward him, a woven basket balanced on her head. When he passed her, she gave him only a glance. He would later swear to Solís—to anyone who would listen to him, really—that he had never seen a woman so beautiful in

his whole life. He stopped his horse, jumped down from his
cart, and called after her.

Her hair, which cascaded down to her ankles, swung back
and forth behind her when she spun to look at him strangely.
He had believed he was being charitable and kind when he offered to take her the rest of the way, but she refused, simply
and quickly. "No gracias," she said, then turned back and kept
on walking.

"But how can I get to know you?" he yelled.

Without hesitation, she said, "Walk with me, then."

He left his horse in the shade of a patch of boojums, whose
brushlike trunks stretched up to the sky, and then he walked
alongside her as she went home. He asked her questions the
entire time—her name, where she was from, what she did
with her days, what she looked forward to in life—and she
gave short, terse answers. But she kept giving them, along
with quiet smiles every time he made a silly comment to her
about what she had said.

When they arrived en la aldea an hour later, she thanked
him for the company. "You made my walk enjoyable today, Eliazar. The time passed much quicker than usual. If you would
like, I leave again in two days. You are welcome to join me."

"I would like nothing more," he told her.

And so, for the next month, Eliazar's routine changed: He
would meet Gracia on his journey to El Mar. Sometimes,
he would walk her to the next aldea—where she sold las camisas and serapes she made with her father. Sometimes, he would
walk her back home. This decision extended his trip to El Mar,
but it was worth it. Gracia was *always* worth it.

The day she agreed to ride in Eliazar's cart was the day he
knew that she finally felt the same affection for him as he did
for her.

He was so happy with her, Solís. They moved together to a tiny aldea that hugged the coast, where Your heat waned and the land was not so impossible. Here, the homes were distant, scattered along the coastline haphazardly. Together, Eliazar and Gracia created. They hunted. They *thrived*. Eliazar brought Gracia's parents to El Mar to live a better life. When Gracia's mamá bothered the couple about the promise of grandchildren, they gave the same answer: They didn't need anyone else. They had each other.

It happened so suddenly, so inexplicably, as these things often did. Years passed, and Gracia's parents had long since returned to You. She had grieved, but with her love beside her, she carried on. Their small home next to El Mar may have been weathered and worn, but it was *theirs*. Eliazar, whose joints had begun to cry out whenever he moved too fast, finally stopped visiting the shore to spread his nets into the unpredictable and violent waters. He did not have the strength to pull them back in. He instead took it upon himself to deliver la ropa that Gracia still made by hand. The pains had not visited her in her old age.

It became a new routine. Eliazar would load up his cart with la ropa, would bid her goodbye, and then would travel west. He would be back by nightfall, so he could curl up next to the one he loved, beneath the starlight that twinkled overhead, that cast such a haunting glow over El Mar.

One morning, he awoke, and Gracia was not by his side. She was not at la mesa where she did her work, either.

He knew something was wrong.

She sat by the ocean on her favorite rock, a dark slab on the white sand, and she dipped her toes in the surf as it came upon the shore.

"Gracia?" He approached gingerly, terrified of the future that was unfolding.

Her skin was pale, waxy, and she wiped at her nose.

There was red on her hands.

"It's time," she said calmly, plainly, as if she were stating the weather. "I've known this was coming."

He reached out to touch her.

She recoiled. "Don't," she warned. "I don't want this happening to you, too."

"Gracia, please," he said. "What is happening?"

"We all have our time upon this earth, Eliazar. Mine has come to an end. Maybe a day or two from now." She smiled, dug her toes deep into the wet sand. "I want to die looking at El Mar." Gracia's eyes bored into Eliazar's. "Will you allow me that, mi amor?"

He didn't respond.

He quickly pushed himself to his feet, his joints protesting, and he headed straight for his horse, an old mare he'd grown close to over the years. Once atop her, he climbed the rise that ascended from the coast. At the crest of the hill, he looked behind him, down toward the home that lay at the bottom, one of only a few built tight against the stone cliff.

She sat upon the rock, which meant there was still time to save her.

Eliazar made the journey with what haste he could on a horse that was probably as old as he was. He pushed the mare as fast as she could go, meaning she sometimes slowed to a trot, and together they weaved through the grove of boojums, then over and down ridges and rises.

Eliazar was determined to save Gracia.

He made it to the next aldea a few hours after he had left

El Mar. He didn't even tie up his mount; he was sure that she was so exhausted she wouldn't go anywhere. He left her next to a large trough of water, and he ran. And ran. And ran. Dodged around those of the aldea who knew him both as el pescador viejo and as the man who delivered Gracia's colorful creations. He had none of these goods with him today, and his body ached terribly as he ran, ran straight to the cuentista, whom he had not spoken to in many years. There was never a need; he had been honest and happy with Gracia.

No longer.

The hut belonging to Téa was crowded, but Eliazar ignored the cries of the others as he pushed inside. "Téa, Téa, *please*," he called out, dropping down before the cuentista in supplication.

They had their hands out.

They were in the midst of taking a story.

Eliazar apologized, tried to explain that it was an emergency, but they shooed him away. "*No*," they said harshly, and their brow was furrowed in anger. "You cannot interrupt this."

Eliazar waited outside, embarrassed but undeterred. It was nearly an hour later when Téa exited the hut. Their black hair was shaven clean on the side, but left long on the top, and the dark coal they wore around their eyes had smeared.

"Eliazar," they said, holding aside the curtain in the doorway, "come within."

When the others protested, Téa held up their opposite hand. "This will only take a moment."

He shuffled in, tried his best to ignore the complaints from other aldeanos, then dropped to the ground once more, though not to give a story.

Eliazar was there to beg.

"Mi cuentista, te necesito," he began.

Téa drifted to the back of their hut, seemingly interested in other things. They crushed herbs in a mortero, poured water over them, then mixed them into a paste.

"Téa?"

They stilled where they stood. "Eliazar, you are not here to give me a story, are you?"

"I need your help. It's Gracia."

Eliazar could see their head shaking. "I don't think I am what you need, amigo. Or what *she* needs."

"But you must know someone. Someone who can help her with the sickness she has."

Eliazar moved closer to Téa. "Can't you ask Solís for help? Just this once?"

They spun around, anger twisting their features. "You know that's not how it works. It *never* has."

They sighed, then reached out to put a hand on Eliazar's shoulder. "Lo siento," they said. "Maybe there is someone out there. Some sort of cure. But I can't hand out favors. I can't get Solís to change the world. Each of *us* is responsible for that."

Eliazar did not feel disappointed as Téa rejected him. He had an idea.

He rushed homeward, pushing his mare harder than he should have, and when he dismounted at the cliff face, she collapsed. He didn't care. He *couldn't* care. He knew she would have taken too long on the narrow trail down. So he shielded his eyes from Your light, peeking over the edge of El Mar, and he searched for Gracia's rock.

He saw the waves that El Mar spat onto the shore, furious and frothy.

He found the rock.

And the body slumped over next to it.

Eliazar walked slowly down the decline, then up to the body, saw how Gracia's skin was sickly, pale, shriveled.

She had a smile on her face.

He bent down, moved her hair off her forehead, kissed her. "I'll be back, mi amor," he said.

Kissed her again.

"I'll find you a cure this time."

His fingers danced over her cheek.

"Volveré por ti."

Eliazar stood. Gathered some supplies. Made the climb back up the cliff face. Ignored the mare, who had not recovered. He walked to the west again, and he stopped in every aldea he found, asking for a cuentista or a curandera. If he did not find something to help Gracia, he thanked the people and moved on.

Eliazar traveled west for a long, long time, meeting new people, seeking out a cure. A few days ago, he arrived in Obregán, and he was overwhelmed by El Mercado. But he rushed past the curanderas, past the centers for healing, and he headed straight for the northwest corner.

CUENTISTAS.

He spoke to one. Another. Another. They shook their heads; their faces slumped in pity; some even returned the money Eliazar gave them.

One of them—dark coal spread over her eyes, a red veil with a dark hood hanging from her body—offered to give Eliazar what he wanted.

He told her what he desired.

And even she tilted her head at him, let go of his hands.

"Señor, you must let go of that," she said.

"Of what?"

"There is not anyone here who can help you get her back," she explained, returning to her booth. "You cannot cling to this."

He shuffled from one foot to another in that spot. "Thank you for trying," he finally said, and he left El Mercado de Obregán.

It has been over a year since he first left El Mar, Solís.

He is still walking.

He was breathless. "Gracias," he said to me, and this time, he steadied me as his story, his never-ending grief, became a part of me. I was a storm, a flood that ripped through the desert and toppled the saguaros and the ironwoods, ripped the bushes from the ground and sent them tumbling.

I coughed.

I nearly lost all the stories—because Eliazar's was so *powerful*.

Then it settled, as the others had before.

I was getting *better* at keeping these stories inside me.

"I had to tell you," he said. "I shouldn't have left her behind. I shouldn't have been so slow." He smiled, that same sad grin I'd seen so many times over the past day. "I'll help her this time."

I placed a hand low on my gut, felt as Eliazar's story settled in deep.

But Gracia was *dead*.

There was nothing to return to.

That was the story he wanted to give me?

Eliazar allowed me to lean on him as we walked back to the group. Emilia had water ready for me, and an affection swelled in my heart.

It passed, though. As I drank the water down, wishing it were cooler, I saw Eliazar speaking excitedly with Rosalinda. He looked so *pleased*.

I recalled Ofelia and her misguided anger.

Or Omar, and his refusal to change his behavior. His face sparked in my mind: I saw his expression as he finished telling me his story, as he knew that he'd been cleansed.

And now there was Eliazar, who believed so wholly that he had done his love wrong that he *apologized* for it.

If I had done as You asked of me—if I had followed the rules as I had been taught—I would have wandered out into the desert, dropped to all fours, and spewed the bitterness into the earth.

Then I would have forgotten.

And Eliazar would never know how wrong he'd gotten it, how his grief was preventing him from seeing the truth.

Emilia rubbed my back with an open palm. "Take as much time as you need," she said.

I drank more water, and the group looked at me expectantly.

No—not expectant.

There was another look in the eyes of Rosalinda, Felipe, y Eliazar.

Reverence.

Because to them, I was once again a cuentista.

Nothing more.

"I'll go slowly," I said, "but if you're all ready, we should start walking."

There were murmurs of agreement. Warm faces. I gazed at Eliazar again, and he seemed lighter, stood up taller, and I knew that I had done something good for him. But that was only temporary; he was walking the land to find a cure that did not matter. His Gracia was *dead*. There was nothing *left* to cure.

Each of us a desert, solitary and vast.

No. Not just that, but:

Solo quiero ser vista.   I only want to be seen.

Maybe that's all these people wanted. To be *seen*.

Slowly, we reached las bajadas de las montañas. There were more árboles and bushes here, more flowers in bloom, more signs of life than Emilia and I had seen the last time we crossed over unas montañas. A large lizard, green with black specks, stood off the side of the trail. Its tongue darted out and snatched a large black beetle, and then it scampered off.

We rested in the shade of the mesquites, and I couldn't resist. I craned my head back.

La montaña towered above.

Standing there, looking up at that giant before me, terror was born anew. I couldn't imagine something bigger than this.

"I need a break," I said, my voice too loud, pitched too high, then added, "To relieve myself."

"Take all the time you need," Emilia said. "We'll be ready to go when you are."

I made for a dense clump of ironwoods, and once I felt I was safely hidden, I pulled out las poemas. I had put them all into a single leather pouch so they would be easier to carry, and then stuffed the empty pouches at the bottom of my pack. There were four poemas now, and even though I knew each one by heart, I needed to remind myself why I had left home.

I held the pouch containing them all tightly, clutched it to my body. I couldn't show these to anyone. Not yet. Maybe someday. But they were too intimate to share with people I had just met.

I crouched, spread them out on the ground next to one another, touched each of them and looked up—

The skull was enormous. It had been picked clean and bleached by the sun, but even then, I recognized the shape. Its snout was long and came to a point, and its jaw was lined with teeth, sharp and pointed in the front, flat near the back. Two horns jutted out from the top sides, curving up toward the sky. And those vacant eye sockets seemed to be staring at me. *Directly* at me.

Un sabueso.

Out *here*? How? Had someone defeated a sabueso tracking them like I had? Or had it suffered a different fate?

I examined it, but not for long, as I couldn't shake the feeling that soon, one of estas bestias would be chasing *me*. So I picked up las poemas, hid them in my pack, and strode away from that monstrosity. I said nothing to the group as I joined them again, only smiled as if I'd taken care of what I needed to, and they were satisfied. Another lie. Another story they bought.

Except Emilia. One of her eyebrows went up.

She suspected something, but she said nothing.

I took another drink of water, hoping it would soothe my jittery nerves.

It did not.

Emilia led us out of las bajadas, said that she knew our camp for the night was on the other side, and I hoped she was right. She hadn't been wrong yet, but I still did not understand who or what guided her.

We followed.

We climbed.

And climbed.

And climbed.

It was not a gradual incline, not like the one I had conquered before reaching Obregán. The packed dirt trail pitched up sharply at first, so much so that I nearly got down on hands and knees to crawl. I pushed myself up, breathing deeply with each step, and then looked back to make sure those behind me weren't faltering as much as I wanted to.

Eliazar surprised me. He had his hands behind his head and a smile on his face. He patted me on the back as he passed me and took the lead. Emilia was next, and she smiled again at me as she passed, but there was an edge to it. She knew I had lied to her about what happened, didn't she? But I merely returned the smile and she continued on.

Rosalinda and Felipe were last, and Rosalinda stood at my side as her son struggled up the steepest section.

Sweat stained the front of Felipe's camisa, and he panted loudly. An awful image filled my head: el sabueso panting in Chavela's refuge, staring me and Emilia down.

"Felipe?" I held out my hand and pulled him up the last bit. "How are you feeling?"

"It's so hot," he said, his voice tiny and weak. "Has it ever been this hot before?"

I wiped at my forehead, and my hand dripped with sweat. "It doesn't feel like it," I said. "When was the last time you had agua?"

He shook his head. "At the bottom."

"Drink more." I thrust my water bag at him. "Not a lot, just enough to wet your throat."

"Lo siento, mijo," said Rosalinda as he drank. "That we have to do this."

He smiled at her despite his clear exhaustion. "We had to." He coughed, then spat into the dirt. "Come on, Mami. You're so slow."

Had to? I pondered that. What drove people to leave their home and venture out into such an unforgiving expanse? I sought a change, a freedom I *needed*. But it seemed that Rosalinda and Felipe had a need, too. What was it?

The trail rose higher and higher, and I looked behind me, down into el valle, back into my past. Even if I could have seen clear out to Empalme, it was too far.

I was too far from *it*.

I faced forward, refused to think about that for too long.

I had been stuck in a recurring sequence that blended into itself— walk forward to the next turn in the trail, glance back down, continue ahead—when I collided with Eliazar, who braced himself on the sheer wall of earth to his left. I was about to apologize when I saw that he was helping tie something around Felipe's head: a strip of cloth.

"It'll help keep you cool," he explained. "Let me know when it dries out, and we'll refresh it."

"Gracias," said Felipe, and when Eliazar stepped out of the way, I saw the redness spreading over the face of that boy. The sun was *burning* him. We still had a couple of hours left in our climb. How was he going to make it?

But You were now on Your decline to the west, and I tried to give myself hope that this wouldn't get worse. Another pang hit my lower stomach, and I let everyone continue on so I could quickly relieve myself at the side of the trail. It was a bright yellow trickle, and I frowned. I needed more water. When I stood, though, the pain continued to needle at me. Was I still bleeding? I hadn't seen anything on my padding, but I dug my fingers into the cramps, trying to will them away.

The moment passed. I took another long drink before I increased my pace to catch up with Rosalinda and Felipe.

It never ended. At least, it *seemed* to be perpetual. Each switchback led to another one, each rise brought us only a tiny bit closer to the summit. The heat bore down on us, and the endless cycle of it all began to erode my hope and replace it with a sick sense of futility. *I'm never going to make it*, I thought. *I'm going to die right here, and I will become part of the earth. I will be forgotten.*

El olvidado.

It was a strangely comforting thought, and somehow, it kept me going. I thought about how I could return my own body to the earth, giving not just the stories but my entire self over to the living things that would feast upon me.

No one else saw it. If I had not looked down, if I had not teetered around that steep turn and seen the dark shape to the side of the trail, all of us would have passed it by. How many others had done so?

I'd seen dead cactuses before, their hollowed bodies brown and shriveled, but the shape of this one caught my eye. I walked to the edge of the trail, stared down into the patch of barrel cactuses, saw the arms of the cactus wrinkled and—

Fingers. They were *fingers*.

I cried out. To You. To the others. The group was above me on the trail, and Emilia's head popped over the ridge. "Xochitl, what is it?"

I couldn't speak. I lifted a shaking finger.

Felipe was at the top of the next curve, and he misinterpreted my scream as something exciting. "¡Yo quiero ver!" he exclaimed, and I wanted to warn him, to stop him from seeing this, but my gaze fell back down to the body, as if I couldn't pull myself from it. The corpse had been cooked in the heat, but most of the torso was picked clean. The mouth was wide open, as if the person had died screaming, and even the teeth were discolored, rotten.

Felipe stared. He said nothing.

This person had died trying to . . . what? Where was their destination? Were they going to Solado, too? What were they hoping to find there? I knew nothing of them, of their reasons for leaving home and risking their life for this unforgiving journey, the same one all of us were making. The sadness—Eliazar's sadness and mine—spiked in me.

I saw Gracia's body in my mind: pale and lifeless, splayed out in the sand.

But this person at our feet had no story. They had *nothing* in death.

"Raymundo," I said softly.

"¿Qué?" Felipe backed away, his face wrinkled up in confusion. "Who is that?"

"I'm naming them Raymundo," I said. Then I repeated their name aloud. "Raymundo."

Felipe was now tucked behind his mami. "Who is Raymundo?" he asked.

How could I explain this to him? How could I tell him that there was so much sadness swimming within me, that not all of it was my own, and that I needed this person to have *something* to be remembered by?

"I'm giving them a story," I said, my voice wavering. "And you can't have a story without a name."

Eliazar, who looked upon us from the rise above, made the sign. "And we honor the dead by remembering them," he added.

I lifted an eyebrow at him, but he smiled, his face peaceful and calm.

There was a brief silence as we stood next to the remains. Emilia squeezed my hand.

I squeezed back.

Felipe tugged on Rosalinda's hand as we continued up the pass. "But we know nothing about that person," he said. "How can we give them a story?"

She ruffled his hair as we made another turn, and Raymundo dropped out of sight. "Well," I said, "what does that name make you think of, Felipe? What do you see in your head?"

"I don't know. Maybe . . . a blacksmith. Someone who uses fire to make things."

"What sort of things?" I asked, hoping to keep him talking.

"Swords, maybe." He gasped. "¡No, puñales! Those ones that hang at your side and you put them in sheaths, and you can whip them out like *this*." He stopped walking and imitated it.

Felipe didn't even realize that he had given Raymundo a story. The blacksmith from Obregán, who had tried to find hope in the north, who died looking up at You.

Felipe continued to talk excitedly about puñales and weapons with Rosalinda as we walked at a steady pace. But the farther we moved up la montaña, the more noise we made. Our feet, tired and weary, scraping against the dirt. Panting. The rustling of our clothing, rubbing and chafing. The conversation died, and la montaña surrounded us with silence, leaned in, waited for us . . . for what? For us to become a part of it? To perish as Raymundo had?

Exhaustion folded over my body. I was still in the rear, and my legs were heavy, as though weighted down with stones. It was the stories. It *had* to be. The closer I got to You, the greater my guilt and shame. I kept moving, though, because I knew that as soon as I stopped, I wouldn't be able to start again.

I looked toward the summit. Had it gotten farther? I pushed forward and pounded my fists into my thighs, willing them to keep moving.

Delirium was close.

I could sense my mind slipping away from me—with the next step forward, I was going to lose it all. I was never going to be the same again. I was *changing*. My body was becoming something else, gnarled and shriveled, violent and evil. I was drying out. I was desiccated. I was *empty*.

I was becoming a desert. Alone, unsheltered, the product of disappointment, hatred, and spite.

I was *You*.

I was exactly what You wanted me to be, what You believed I was. Vacant and isolated. Nothingness.

And as quickly as this raging panic had gripped me, so did the top of la montaña arrive beneath my feet. The sun was well past halfway to the west when the trail very suddenly flattened out. But if I had not seen the others crumpled on the ground before me, I might have kept walking to maintain my momentum.

But there was Felipe, sprawled out on his back between Rosalinda and Eliazar, his pack tossed beside them.

"I'm never walking another step," he said.

I put my pack down next to his, ready to allow my body to fall to the ground as well, but the sight beyond the edge of la montaña, in the desolate valle to the north, pulled me forward. A light breeze blew over me, the first of the entire journey, and it raised bumps over my skin.

"Solís help us," I said, "what is *that*?"

The flatland below us shimmered in the air, like some of the blown glass I had seen in Obregán. There were structures jutting out of that brightness, sprinkled like pimienta y sal over maíz, like las estrellas in the night sky.

It *looked* like a city, but broken. Forgotten.

El olvidado.

I covered my eyes, trying to block the brightness, but it was unending.

"I have no idea," said Emilia. "We didn't come across this on our journey south."

There was a pounding in my chest.

"Emilia, where *are* we?"

"I . . . I thought we were going the right way," she said, and it was the first time I had heard it in her voice: uncertainty.

"But how do you *know*?" I demanded. "Is Solís in your mind? Your heart? Telling you where to go?"

"No! It's not like that!"

"But we're supposed to believe that without a map, you just *know*?"

"Niña," said Rosalinda, and she tried comforting me, her hands on my shoulders. "Cálmate. She's gotten us here, hasn't she?"

"You're not the one with a destination," I snapped, and I immediately regretted my tone.

I put my face in my hands. The only reason I had agreed to this journey was so that Emilia could guide me to Simone. What would happen if she couldn't even do *that*? What would become of me? Of all these stories?

They buried themselves deeper.

"Let's head down," I said. "Get as far as we can, and then find somewhere to set up for the night."

"Then what?" Rosalinda demanded, pulling Felipe close. "What if we don't find somewhere to sleep?"

"Xochitl is good at this," Emilia offered.

"At *this*?" I gestured to the strange ciudad below. "I don't know what that is! I don't know what I'm doing!"

Emilia pursed her lips. "That's not what I meant," she said. "Just that you are good at being out in the desert."

My exasperation bloomed. "Let's go," I said. "I'd like there to be some light left."

Our descent was quiet, unnerving. We did not speak to one another, and we should have been overjoyed to finally be walking downhill. Instead, we let the numbness swallow us, tear us apart. No glances at one another, no conversation, nothing but the steady sound of our feet against the ground.

La ciudad gleamed.

It seemed *impossible*.

Rosalinda got a cramp in her lower back after an hour, and it was only then that we took a break. She stopped to drink, and I caught up to her, helping her to rub out the spasming muscle. "You're losing water," I told her. "Sweating it out too quickly. Drink more."

"Wait until they start to get cramps," she said, laughing softly. "They're not used to them like we are."

I chuckled. It was funny, and I welcomed anything other than pain or exhaustion. I had to, because another thought was racing around my head:

What if I turned *back*? What if I went back to the life I had been given? I could be a dutiful cuentista, exactly as my parents and Empalme wanted me to be. I could take the stories, and I could return them to the desert, and I could forget them, and I could live my entire life as it had been intended.

No.

I looked back at what we had climbed.

No.

I had seen too much. Los sabuesos, Obregán, las cuentistas . . .

How could I go back without knowing if this was possible? How could I return to that life, now that I knew so much?

The resolution spread through me:

I would rather make another terrible decision than live knowing that I hadn't tried.

So I kept going. We all did.

In las bajadas on the north side, lit softly by the setting sun, there was a row of paloverdes that were flourishing. They were a reminder of survival. The grove gave way to what was an endless flatness interrupted only by the ruins of la ciudad in the distance. Even the cactuses petered out as we marched toward those structures.

Who had lived here? What had caused the fate of this place? I could see some sort of building, half of it collapsed, an ironwood growing out of the center of the rubble. We moved closer, stepped over the remains of a low stone wall that stretched in either direction, crumbled and rotted before us. Structures had come to rest against one another—gray stone, mud, wood, rusted metal, all of it gnarled and twisted, decaying and lifeless. But there were patches of greens and yellows where plant life bloomed, thick stalks of grasses and mesquite bushes competing for the available space.

I ran my finger along the edge of one of the stone buildings.

It was covered in a black ash.

And the answer arrived in me, suddenly, uninvited, terrifying.

La Quema.

"Solís burned this place," I said, not meaning to do so out loud, but once it was out, a silence blanketed us, as if all sound had been smothered by this place.

There was not much light left shining on la ciudad, but I tried to make out what I could. A large stone pillar lay across the road that seemed to split la ciudad in two, and I don't know what it used to hold up. A building? Some sort of monument?

A rustling noise broke the silence.

I held my breath.

We all did.

I made a tentative step toward it, my arm out to protect me in case there was something there.

There was a scrabbling in the dirt, and then they scurried out from the eastern side of the road, squat creatures with horns on their heads and long, shaggy brown fur covering their bodies. I had no idea how they survived in the heat like that; they had to be creatures of the night. The lead one looked back at us, and their eyes flashed red in the setting sun. We all stood as still as we could as a lip curled up and tiny, needle-like teeth were bared in our direction.

Then it led the pack away. They scampered over a pile of rubble and vanished.

An awful sensation passed over my skin, and I had never felt so exposed in my life, as if a million eyes were focused on my body.

I turned to look behind us.

They stood there.

A line of them. A *wall* of them. From one side to the next, from far in the east stretching to the edge of sight in the west.

The dead.

Clothing in shambles, limbs missing, skin desiccated and rotting, bodies torn apart, torsos eaten and hollowed.

Most were burned to a crisp, nothing more than human shapes of coal, and they stood there, staring at us, their eyes glowing white.

Felipe cried out, but Rosalinda clamped a hand over his mouth.

"Who *are* they?" asked Eliazar, his voice shaky.

"The punished," one of them answered, and they stepped forward, their skin crackling with each movement. "Those who were eliminated in La Quema. The original inhabitants of esta ciudad."

And then, in unison, in one horrific rush of sound, they all took a step forward. Then another. *Then another.*

"You must move through," they said. "You must learn the truth."

The truth.

Oh *no*.

Was this what Roberto y Héctor had experienced? Was this what we'd been warned about?

Felipe screamed, and then he was the first to run. He made it to the pillar and cleared it in no time. We all ran, as Felipe's reaction woke us from our terror, and my own muscles felt like they were tearing apart as I did so. Still, I pulled myself up and over and I followed after the others, desperate to know if this would all be over if we made it to the other side of la ciudad.

I looked back.

They—the *dead*—were in *front* of the pillar already, a single line, moving ever forward, making sure we could not leave.

I ran in the other direction as fast as I could.

The remains of la ciudad were like the bones jutting out of a carcass that was half buried in the desert, that las bestias had picked clean. We moved through a corpse, dodging piles of basura, pushing through bushes that had sprouted up in all this death. I caught up to Eliazar, who was struggling to keep up with the other three.

"Go on ahead," he said, digging his fingers into his side. "Please."

"No," I said, looping his arm over my shoulders. "We go *together*."

The sun set further. The shadows became longer. The shuffling dead pushed behind us, but I would not turn around to gaze at them. Instead, I *heard* them, a persistent trudging forward.

We couldn't run anymore. I heard a whimper next to me. Rosalinda. She clutched Felipe's hand now.

Emilia looked from side to side as she urged us to continue, staring into the shadows. She beckoned us forward. "We're almost there!"

Had we made it?

I ducked through the remains of some large stone gate, and on the other side, I could see it.

The buildings, growing smaller, spreading out.

More ash, more destruction.

The debris of the northern gate.

We were almost there.

Another whimper, to my left.

But it wasn't Rosalinda or Felipe.

The shadows twisted.

Then grew.

Reached out.

I shouted and fell to the side, scraping my leg on a pile of jagged stones.

"Xochitl!"

The dead were still to the south, climbing over debris, moving toward me.

Emilia grabbed me under the arms, pulled me up, but then it came for *her*.

The shape groaned, and Emilia yanked me north and—

"No."

There was a woman there, her body one enormous shadow that took shape, twisted into reality. Wide nose, long black hair, wrinkles jutting from the corner of her eyes.

She wore a light brown tunic, but there was a stain, slowly growing, overtaking the center of her torso, and it kept spreading.

Red.

Blood.

Emilia sobbed. "It wasn't my fault," she insisted. "I couldn't stop it."

The woman said nothing. She stared at Emilia as the stain now covered everything, dripped from the bottom edge of the tunic down onto the dirt.

"But it wasn't my fault," Emilia cried, her hands on her face. "It was Julio. *He* did this. I couldn't stop him!"

I knew then who she was.

La mujer de La Palmita.

The first person that Julio had killed.

Emilia backed into me. "Make her go away," she said, grappling for my hand, squeezing it tight.

"Just ignore her!" I said, and I tried to get Emilia to come with me, to get out of this place, but she wouldn't budge.

"I can't," she said. "What if I could have helped her? Why didn't I stand up to him before?"

"You're being unfair to yourself," I said. "Trust me. I know. *He* did this, not you. He was the one who killed all those people in La Palmita!"

The woman held her hands beneath her stomach, and then she screamed as her entrails fell forth, and then she was pushing her insides back into the gaping hole, and red blood oozed through her fingers.

It rained down on Emilia: black ash from the sky. La mujer de La Palmita growled, and her mouth opened, impossibly wide, and she pulled a blade out of that chasm, and it was covered in her own blood.

But Emilia became rage, became *rejection*. She roared and Emilia shoved *through* the woman, who now spat ash at Emilia, and then the shadow was *gone* and Emilia was scowling, saying something over and over—

"¡No soy mi papi!"

And he sprang up behind her, stretching terribly from her shadow, and his long arms grasped her from behind, and he was *cackling*.

"Did you think you could escape me?" he roared. "I can find you just as well as los sabuesos, mija!"

She thrashed about, and I dived for her, but my hands went through Julio's arms, right to Emilia's skin.

"Eres una asesina," he cooed into her ear, and his teeth grew, longer and longer and he sank them into the flesh of her shoulder and tore at it, sinews and blood dripping from his mouth. "¡Una asesina como yo!"

She cried out.

She fell back.

Tears streamed down her face, but she wrenched herself upward and began to pummel him with her fists, her voice raw, vicious. "I am *nothing* like you!" she shrieked, and each fist pushed him back, until her hands began to sink into his flesh, began to reshape his form, and then his head tipped to the side, plummeted to the earth.

She *crushed* it.

"I am nothing like you," she wheezed out again, and Julio's ashes burst up into the air. "I will *never* be that."

Someone screamed behind Emilia. "No, *leave us alone!*"

Another shadow had grown.

There was a man, tall, his arms thick with muscle, on his knees in front of Rosalinda, his hands up, pleading with her. "Mi amor, take me back," he begged, and he looked so *real* now, no longer a shadow given form.

Una pesadilla. Made *whole.*

"I miss you. I miss our son. *Felipe.*"

"Mami, stop him." Felipe backed away from the man, right into me, and he latched on to my arm as he did so. "Xochitl, how is he here? Is he going to take us back?"

"No!" shouted Rosalinda at him, furious and righteous. "We left you behind. We are *never* going back!"

He sprang up from the dirt, from the bones of this dead city, and his body grew, twisted, stretched in unimaginable directions, until he towered over the whole group, and he unhinged his jaw, letting forth a bellow that vibrated through all of us. *"You're worthless! I never loved you! I'll just see Adelina again, and she'll give me what I want!"*

Felipe howled as the apparition continued to berate his mother. *"Why did I ever marry you? Why did I ever have a son?"*

Rosalinda did not flinch. She did not cower before that manifestation. She stretched her body taller, and when she screamed, spit flew from her mouth, her eyes flared with fury. "I will *never* let you hurt us again."

"But you waited so long to leave," he teased, his words both slimy and sharp. "You couldn't do it. You wanted him to suffer with you, so that you didn't have to experience me alone."

"Stop talking," she said, and she threw her hands over her ears.

"Mami?" Felipe's voice sounded so small, so terrified.

"It's true, Felipe," crooned his father. "She's worthless. She didn't get you out soon enough."

"No!" she shrieked, and she shoved at the man so hard that he stumbled. "I didn't know *how* to leave! I never would have married you if I knew what you'd turn out to be."

"So you'd give up our son for your own peace?"

Rosalinda smiled, and it left me awestruck, fearful.

"I would choose Felipe over you *every time.*"

His face twisted up in anger, and at first, I thought he was going to turn on her. But then Felipe balled up his fists and started shaking next to his mother. "This is *your* fault!" he said. "Why were you always so *mean* to Mami? Why couldn't *you* love her?"

And then he stood in front of Rosalinda, who watched on with the rest of us.

"I love her, Papi. You have to get through *me* to get *her.*"

He put up his fists.

And Rosalinda spat on her husband.

The shadow shrank, crumbled before Felipe y Rosalinda, and then it was so small—barely larger than a stone. La pesadilla raised its tiny hands, but that was not enough to stop the stone that crushed it, that Rosalinda had hefted up and dropped on that shadowy form.

No sooner had that terrible image left us than a howling began. It was low at first, then higher in pitch. Was it the dead?

No.

I saw them.

They were motionless.

Watching.

Silent witnesses to the truth.

"Mi amor, mi amor . . ." He sang it to her, and there she was.

Gracia.

Flowing, drifting, in a long white robe.

And she was so beautiful, Solís, as Eliazar had said.

He was on his knees, his arms reaching up to her in reverence. "Volviste a mí," he said.

She came closer.

"I knew you would."

Closer.

"I'm still searching, mi amor, I promise."

Her fingers grazed his face.

And then her skin went pale, slowly at first, and blood trickled out from one nostril, and she still wore the same smile as it all sloughed off her, and Eliazar was screaming, and she was dead, the smell wafting through the air. I coughed hard and spat into the dirt, and Eliazar was shaking his head.

"No, I can *save* you!" he said. "I left our home to find a cure!"

She was ghastly, skin clinging to bone, but her voice was still soothing. "I am gone, Eliazar," she said, and tears prickled my eyes. "You have to let me go."

"But it isn't *fair*!" he cried out. "I don't know how to live without you, Gracia."

He pushed himself up from the ground, stood directly in front of her rotting face. "It makes me feel close to you to do this," he explained. "If I'm suffering, it means you're still here."

In an instant, she was normal again. "But love is not suffering," she said, and she reached out and touched his face, ran her fingers through his beard. "I know you want me back. I know you want to see me again. But this is no way to honor me."

"Please come back," Eliazar croaked, his cheeks damp with tears.

"You know I can't. Deep down . . . you've known the whole time."

"But I don't know how to do this," he weeped. "I don't know how to do any of this without you."

"You already have been."

She stepped back. "I am gone, Eliazar."

His shoulders drooped.

"I know," he said. "You died."

Gracia smiled at her love.

She faded, became a thin dust of ash, and then she was gone.

Silence returned.

The dead watched us.

And the four of them stared directly at me.

I was all that was left.

But there were no shadows. No pesadillas. No sounds. *Nothing*.

"Is it over?" said Felipe, and there was the smallest hint of hope in that voice, the tiniest spark of potential.

Emilia moved closer to me, and I was surprised when I felt her hand brush against mine, felt her fingers interlock with my own, and I didn't care that anyone could see us.

She understood me, didn't she?

It was still silent.

"Mami, what's happening?" Felipe asked. "Why is it so quiet?"

"Maybe they are sparing Xochitl," said Rosalinda.

"She is a cuentista, after all," said Eliazar. He brushed the tears off his face.

I let go of Emilia's hand. "We should leave, then," I said. "If this place has nothing for me, then we shouldn't stick around."

I walked forward, heading north, and then—

I couldn't.

I stilled, and it was as if the very will to move had been ripped from me. I tried to turn around, but I couldn't. "Emilia," I said, and the terror went up my throat, came spilling out. "I can't move. Something's happening."

She moved quietly around my rigid body, floated right in my eyesight, her brows furrowed. "What do you mean?"

I could move my eyes. Only my eyes.

Nothing else.

And so I saw them coming.

They advanced from the north, as if they were going to join the dead behind us, and panic pressed my lungs, made it hard to breathe.

"What do I do? Am I—?"

"Mami, who are *they*?"

No. *No.*

I knew them.

Lani. Omar. Ofelia. Soledad. Lázaro.

They all woke up inside me.

"When will you tell them?" Lani said as she approached. She sneered at me. "Or will you continue to let them think you are one of the chosen ones?"

"Are you judging us now?" Omar asked, and he circled me as the others stepped back. "Do you think you're better than us because you know what we've done?"

"No!" I cried out.

But was that *true*?

"You defied Solís," said Ofelia. "How are you any better than us? How are you not *worse*?"

Soledad laughed as she came upon me. "You knew what I had done, and yet you still thought of yourself as superior. You thought you were *pure*."

And then there was Emilia. Something was wrong: there were those cold eyes of hers, the ones that were so uninterested, so uncaring. They were not part of whom I had come to know. It was the *old* version of her, the one I had despised.

"You've been keeping our stories," she said. She smiled, pure malice and spite and hatred.

They began to rot, slowly at first, their skin turning dark, then bubbling up, then falling off, and I held back a scream as I watched them fall apart. Their bodies crumbled, revealed who had been standing behind them.

Rosalinda. Felipe. Eliazar.

"Is it true?" said Felipe. "Did you really keep them?"

"How many?" asked Rosalinda. "*How many?*"

And then Eliazar was there, his mouth downturned, and more so than anyone else's, his expression broke my heart. "I know you did not have time to complete the ritual, but . . . were you going to keep mine, too?"

"I had to," I said, but it lacked all confidence. "I had to keep the stories. I would have forgotten what Lito . . . what he . . ."

They didn't know anything about Lito. Or Julio. Or Empalme. None of that mattered to them.

I remembered that afternoon in the center of mi aldea. How they all turned their backs on me once they'd discovered what I had done.

It was happening again, wasn't it?

"Why?" asked Felipe. "Why would you do that?"

I knew the answer. But I was still stuck in that spot, unable to move, unable to escape their gazes.

"Tell the truth, Xochitl. Say it aloud."

Emilia. She touched me. Once she made contact, I nearly collapsed, free from the terrible force that had bound me. The others took a step away from me, as though I were something to be feared.

The dead remained, watching.

I sucked in a deep breath and choked, and then it all came out. All of it. I told them of that first story, the one Lito had given me, of what I found in Soledad, of the promise of Simone. And then I paused—Emilia nodded, urging me on—and I told them why this was so important.

"Once I kept a story, I saw what it did to the others," I explained. "How it gave them the freedom to make the same mistakes all over again. How I was nothing to them but a means to an end. And when I found out there was another cuentista in the world—one who had actually *left* their aldea—I had to know more. I had to know how he left his home and had *survived*."

But . . .

I chose this. It had not merely happened to me.

And I did not regret it.

So I said that aloud, too.

"And I need to end this," I added. "I know our world values las cuentistas, but . . . this life is so *exhausting*. I have no choice about what I am to do for the rest of my life. *This* is what was forced upon me, and I kept the stories for . . . for . . ."

I sighed.

"I kept them for myself. So I could find my *own* story. So I could rid myself of this power. That's why we're going to Solado. For a curandera named Simone."

The sun was gone, and the soft glow from the stars began to illuminate the earth. I stood there at first, dirt all over my clothing,

stuck to my skin where I had been sweating, and I swayed. I wanted
to give up, to collapse back down to the earth, to let it consume me.

I looked up.

Dos estrellas, right above me, fat and bright.

They twinkled, as if they knew they were being observed. This
had always been a time of celebration for mi gente, for mi aldea, but
since Your eyes were absent, *theirs* were now on me, examining me.

Judging me.

There was a shuffling behind me.

The dead were leaving. I watched them as they climbed back
the way they had come, as they left us alone.

Each of us a desert.

"Vámonos," I said, unsure where I was heading, unsure if I was
worthy.

But I had chosen to do this, and I would do anything to see it
through.

Night arrived.

And the others did not abandon me, as I expected them to.

Did they hate me? Despise me? Were they silent as a punishment? I considered every possibility, and in that act, I assumed the worst of myself. How could I *not*?

But as we walked away from my secret, now spilled forth for all of them to consume, Rosalinda gripped me by the arm, a gesture of tenderness.

"You have been through a lot, chica," she said. "I cannot imagine what it was like to take so many stories for that length of time." She offered me a smile. "I cannot judge you for what you want to do. I would probably feel the same."

"I had no idea," Eliazar added. "I thought you were like Téa. That you took a story only every now and then."

"Are you sad, Xochitl?" Felipe looked up at me with that round face of his.

"Sometimes," I answered. I shook my head. "More than I like to admit."

"Will this Simone you are seeking make you happy?"

I gazed at Emilia; she nodded.

"I think so," I answered.

"Then you should do it," he said. "Sometimes I am sad about

Papi, but I'm much happier with Mami, even out here in the desert."

I like to think that Rosalinda felt comforted by that. That Felipe was thankful that Your gaze was gone. That we were together under las estrellas.

We passed out of la ciudad, left its bones behind.

And as soon as we were beyond it, Eliazar crumpled into a heap on the ground.

He dropped so quick that none of us could have stopped it, both his fall and what followed after it.

He gasped for air, and Rosalinda was at his side, and it wasn't enough. "Breathe, Eliazar!" she cried out. "You're okay. Just *breathe*."

He *laughed*. His elation cut through the quiet night, and he didn't even try to get up.

"Leave me here," he said. "I am not taking another step."

"Eliazar, don't say that!" Rosalinda pulled her canteen out and tried to hand it to him.

He pushed it back. "She loved me, you know? She always loved me."

I knelt at his side. "And you loved her," I said. "Get up. Finish the journey. For her."

"I already did."

He gazed at each of us, peace and acceptance soothing his features.

His eyes were glass.

He went still, then he fell to the side, slowly, inevitably, as if he knew the earth was waiting for him to return.

And Eliazar died with a smile on his face.

Rosalinda broke out in sobs, hit his chest, asked him to stop joking, screamed that this wasn't funny, and Felipe was crying, too, and I fell back on my hands.

A shadow.

Above.

I looked up.

Dark shapes blurred out las estrellas. They swooped around and around, and I could hear the air in their wings. We scrambled to our feet, and Emilia yelped in alarm as one of them nearly landed on her head.

They descended in droves, their wingspans enormous. Their necks were wreathed in white feathers, the rest a terrible shade of black, as if they could devour any light that shone around them. And those beaks, so awful and sharp, snapped open and shut, the creatures anticipating the meal that awaited them.

I had seen them only once in my life, when someone had died hunting outside of Empalme.

Zopilotes.

They swarmed around him until we could no longer see his body.

Could no longer see the smile on his face.

"We have to go," I said. "We need to find somewhere to camp."

The feathers ruffled, and I tried to ignore the ripping, tried not to think what that was.

We were weak and frightened and so very tired.

We left Eliazar behind.

And once again—we suffered.

You were silent. You answered no prayers, sent us no signs of any sort, did not comfort us once.

We walked away from Eliazar's body, and doubt consumed me—permeated our whole group. One of us had *died*. Was any of this worth it if one of us didn't make it? My journey, las poemas, my decisions, *all of it*? Was this a punishment? Did You hand those out and hope we knew why they had occurred?

But You said nothing. So all I had was my imagination.

I imagined many things.

What if Simone was not real?

What if Solado was a mistake?

What if las poemas were a cruel trick, meant to tempt me and torment me and drive me far from home, from my duty?

Or maybe the zopilotes would follow me on the path to Solado, would descend upon my body to feast upon it—but while I was still alive, still breathing.

Or I would return to Empalme, and the gate would be locked. My entrance denied. They had found another cuentista, and I was no longer needed. No home, no purpose anymore.

We were so alone, Solís. We had discarded our previous lives to find something else, somewhere else, and here we were, placed in the hands of someone we barely knew, who had lost her sense of where we were supposed to go, a sense that *You* had previously given her. We were without help, without a means of salvation if something went horribly wrong.

It already *had*.

Each of us a desert, each of us a *curse*.

We could all die, and no one would ever find us.

So we walked to our fate, and I stopped praying to you that night. You couldn't help us anymore.

No.

You *wouldn't* help us anymore.

Las estrellas settled in the sky, and because of them, I could see the distant outline of yet more sierras in the north, and it tired me, Solís. I did not want to climb again; I did not want to push my body further than I had ever pushed it. I wanted more than anything to cease, to give myself over to the inevitability of it all.

But I didn't.

I kept going.

The world came alive around us, and I began to scope out areas that seemed safe enough to set up for the night. Creatures skittered in the underbrush. Felipe nearly stepped on a snake, golden stripes on its vibrant scales, and we all watched as it slithered into the shadows.

We did not know what caused most of the noise; the creatures darted off when they heard us. I occasionally caught a flash of light in the irises of some bestia, some terrible thing that might have been stalking us. Were we the rare prey that had wandered into the hunting grounds of untold monsters? Las estrellas sparkled, enough for us to have suitable visibility, but without you, it was still a land of shadows.

Each of us a desert. Each of us alone.

Especially me.

I was the first to notice it: a crumbling structure that blended in with the rolling hills behind it. I held out a hand to tell the others to stop, and I focused on the structure, trying to discern more details, and I realized it was much bigger than I had first thought.

"What is that?" Emilia asked.

I kept my hand raised.

It was a *wall*.

Much like la ciudad we had passed through, the wall was a mess, a pathetic echo of what it had once been. A ghostly image. The gray bricks and stones seemed to have crumpled long ago and lay in chaotic piles on the ground.

"Not a very good wall," said Felipe. "You can walk through it."

A whisper.

Faint.

Impossible.

"Stop talking," I said.

"Why? It's not like—"

"*Stop. Talking.*" I hissed at Felipe, and I knew I was being harsh, but I had heard it again.

Felipe shrank away from me and into the arms of Rosalinda, who scowled my way.

What was out here? What had we stumbled into?

"Emilia," I said softly, my eyes locked on the remains of the wall, scanning it for any sign of life. "Did you come across this place on your travels?"

"No," she said. "I know we traveled far to the west before we headed south. I think we missed it."

"How do you know that?"

"I can feel it again. Solís guiding me, that is."

I faced her. "You're going to have to explain that."

"We came from that direction," she said, pointing ahead of us, toward las montañas in the north. "But I remember descending in the morning and—" She thought for a moment, then turned her body to the west and pointed. "—we definitely went that way, *then* headed south."

I had no time to react to that. As soon as she stopped talking, I heard something new: the scrape of stone on stone.

We stilled.

A head poked out from behind a pile of rubble. All I could make out in the starlight was that the figure was small, with black hair and dark skin. "Eduardo?"

What?!

"No," I said. "I'm Xochitl. Who are you?"

The person stepped out from behind the stones, and Rosalinda cried out. The piece of the wall behind them was at least three times their height.

It was a *child*.

They came from behind the wall and rushed up to me, but stopped an arm's length away. They were indeed young—perhaps much younger than Raúl, who was twelve—and then they scowled at me. "Why are you here? What do you want with us?"

"Us?" Emilia said.

I couldn't help the sound I made, the cry that erupted from my mouth. They appeared from all over, tiny heads and faces from behind the ruins, from *inside* the piles of stones and brick, and they swarmed up to us. Some held stones, and others held weapons crafted from the ruins, from wood, and I saw one girl with a rotted arm of a saguaro jammed over a wooden stick, the needles jutting out threateningly.

"There are more of us than you," the boy said. "What do you want?"

Rosalinda dropped down to her knees. "Ay, Solís, this is all too much," she said, her head craned back, her prayer spitting up into the sky. "Please, help us, Solís."

"What did you need help with?"

This came from a girl, whose face was stained with some sort of reddish ink in a rough pattern. She held a stone in her right hand, and I completely believed that she could hurt me with it.

"We need a place to stay," I said. "We were looking for a place to make camp, but . . . well, we found *you*."

She examined me. Moved closer. Let her arm down. "What do you think, Pablo?"

"We vote," he said.

All the weapons dropped.

"Who thinks we should not let them stay?"

Silence.

"Who thinks we should let them stay?"

Hands shot up in the air.

"Then we are in agreement?"

In unison: "¡Sí!"

Pablo stepped forward and brushed the hair out of his face. "Bienvenidos a La Reina Nueva," he said. "Our home."

The reaction was instantaneous. The children did not care that we were such a horrible mess. The girl with her face painted marched up to me and extended her hand. "I'm Gabriela," she said. Her eyes were dark like Emilia's, like Papá's, and she was so thin, as though she hadn't eaten in a long time. "We protect La Reina Nueva, so we had to do that."

"What do you mean?" I said, my mouth agape, but she didn't explain further. She dragged me forward, and I looked back to the others, but they were swarmed by children, too. "What does that mean? Who is 'la Reina Nueva'?"

"I didn't name it," said Gabriela. "Supposed to be about some 'reina' who ruled here long ago. Would you like something?"

What were they *doing* here?

"Are you hungry? Thirsty?" Gabriela asked me, and I let her lead me without any resistance. I was too tired, too confused.

"Marcos found some prickly pear fruit today, and we were saving them for whenever Eduardo arrived."

I struggled to keep up. "Who is Eduardo?" I asked, then tried to find Emilia or any of the others. That name. *Eduardo.* Where had I heard it?

I couldn't find the others; there were too many children, and they climbed over the ruins, surrounded my compadres, and I called out to Emilia. Rosalinda. Felipe.

"How do you *not* know Eduardo?" she said, as if the statement were obvious, something I should have known. She brought me to a portion of the wall that was still intact. "You've been walking in the sun all day. Eat! Drink! We always take care of the people Eduardo brings."

Who is this girl? I thought.

"But what about you?" I asked. "How are you—where do you—?" I threw my hands up in defeat. "I don't understand this place. How are you all not *dead*?"

"We stay underground during the day," Gabriela said. She pointed, and I looked to the hollow space there in the ground at the base of the wall.

"You all *really* live here?"

Behind me, a gasp echoed out, and I faced Rosalinda; the children of La Reina Nueva had gathered Emilia and Felipe as well.

"I don't understand," said Emilia. "Where did you all come from? And who is this Eduardo you keep talking about?"

"El coyote," I said, and I watched the epiphany hit Emilia.

"Soledad wanted to send us to him," she said, nodding her head.

Large stones were hauled to us. We were told to sit. No one answered our questions, and then more children arrived—Were they different ones from those we'd seen before?—carrying baskets woven from sticks and reeds, and I could smell the prickly pear fruit. A basket was thrust in front of me.

"Eat," Gabriela said, thrusting the basket nearer toward me. "They're pretty fresh."

Skinned prickly pear fruit glistened in a pile in the basket. I'd had it only a couple of times in my life, and I didn't hesitate. I picked up a piece of the deep red fruit, its flesh sticky against my own, and I shoved it into my mouth greedily, the juices flowing down my chin.

What was this place? How could it exist?

"This is delicious," said Felipe as he devoured a handful of fruit. "But . . . this is really happening, right? I'm not imagining it?"

"Solís help us," muttered Rosalinda, who was now sitting next to Felipe as a group of children swarmed her, offering them both fruit and water, asking her if she was staying.

One voice out of that group cut through the noise.

"Have you seen mi mami? Is she coming back soon?"

Rosalinda whipped her head in the direction of the one who had spoken. She was also terribly thin, smaller than she should have been, and it looked as if a layer of dirt covered the clothing she wore, its edges frayed and tattered.

How long had these children *been* here?

I thought of Raúl, of his bushy hair, and was tormented by guilt. I had not thought of mi hermanito in days. Was he that meaningless to me?

No, I told myself. *I love him.*

I tried to imagine him here, among these jovencitos, all alone in the desert without anyone to take care of him. Nausea pushed up into my throat, and I gagged, coughing repeatedly until Emilia was at my side, handing me her canteen. I drank the cool water down, then leaned my head back, my eyes focused on all those stars around us.

"What is this place, Mami?" Felipe asked.

Rosalinda didn't know what to say. I saw her mouth open, then shut, and she looked to me. I had nothing for her. No explanation, no reason.

How was this *real*?

The child named Pablo approached me. "Sorry about that," he said. "We have to be careful now that Carlito is gone."

I shook my head. "Carlito? Eduardo? Who are these people?"

As I ate, Pablo sat in front of me to explain. "Carlito was our leader," he said. "He was the first person Eduardo brought here."

"*Brought?*" I nearly choked on the prickly pear. "He left you here on *purpose*?"

Pablo nodded, and he curled his feet under him, sat up straight. "Me and Gabriela, we took over after Carlito went missing."

"Ay, what do you mean by that?" Rosalinda groaned.

There. It flashed across Pablo's face.

Fear.

In the light of las estrellas, he was a child.

Then, it was gone, and he addressed Rosalinda as if they were both adults, both ruled by responsibility and duty. "We haven't seen him in a couple of weeks. He went with the guardians to help protect La Reina Nueva, and none of them ever came back."

The four of us stared at one another. Rosalinda and Felipe must have known that this was a bad omen, for they both looked terrified.

I had to know.

"Protect you from *what*?"

Now the children stilled, as we had done earlier. They looked to one another, then to Gabriela and Pablo. She nodded, and they scattered, disappearing into piles of rubble or beneath the wall. It was sudden, almost as if it had been planned. The first of them returned, hair shorn unevenly, face gaunt and desperate, and held it out for me—and I fell off the stone I sat on.

A skull.

A skull like the one I'd found before, when I was alone.

Long. Horned. Impossible.

Yet here it was.

Rosalinda started praying to you as Felipe whimpered. Emilia reached out to it, ran her fingers over the clean bone of the horns.

"Un sabueso," she said.

"They started attacking us," the girl said. "The guardians protected us, but they came to us not too long ago, said that they knew where they were coming from." The rest of the children went quiet, and the girl continued. "Carlito insisted on going. That was when we last saw him."

"But why are all of you *here*?" Rosalinda said, her voice loud, echoing off the ruins. "No adults, no parents . . . where are they?"

Gabriela beamed. "Oh, they're up north! In Solado. Eduardo took them there."

"*¿What?*" Emilia yanked her hand away from the skull.

"Our parents couldn't take us with them, so we stayed here."

Pablo rejoined us and with him came many of the others, some of them carrying skulls of these horrible bestias, but most carried random objects.

Una cobija.

Un rebozo.

Serapes.

Little items, things that someone could leave behind.

Things that reminded the children of who had continued on.

Without them.

"Eduardo promised that as soon as he could, he would come take us back to them," explained Pablo. He opened his hand to me. A small stone, a brilliant green, shone there in the starlight. "This is his promise," he said. "That he would come back for me."

"But *why*?" Emilia asked. "Why would they go there?"

"For work," said Gabriela. "To build us a new life, and then invite us there when things are ready."

Emilia had her hands on her temples, and panic flooded her. "Xochitl," she said, "they can't go there. I barely *escaped* from it."

"You're *from* Solado?" The one who had brought us the first skull lit up. "Can you bring back our parents?"

Emilia's eyes went glassy.

She turned and ran off, past the wall and into the darkness.

"Go," said Rosalinda. "I'll talk with the others. *She* needs you."

I followed after her, my eyes still adjusting to the surreality around me. I hopped over a section of crumbled wall, hoping she had not gone far. Even with the starlight above, I was in an unfamiliar place. The shadows taunted me with untold horrors lurking just out of sight.

"Emilia?" I called out softly. "Please talk to me."

I saw her outline, a dim shape not far from me. I came up behind her and I fought the urge to smother her in an embrace, to kiss the back of her neck, to tell her that everything would be fine.

I did not know her like that.

I probably never would.

So instead, I stood next to her, and we stared out across that vast expanse, that empty desert that stretched so far in front of us, out toward the towering montañas we would have to cross the next morning. I existed in that silence there, wondering so many things. What awaited us in Solado? Had los pálidos maintained their hold over la aldea? How were we ever going to find Simone?

And what if Simone wouldn't help me?

I swallowed down my anxiety, unsure once more if it was my own or if it belonged to one of the stories in my belly.

"We have to go back," she said, her voice soft but certain. "Not just for Luz. Not just for Simone. But for them, too."

I laced my fingers with hers.

"For all of them," I said.

And I meant it.

"I don't know what I'm going to do, but we can't let this go on."
She squeezed my hand.

I squeezed back.

"I am not sure what we'll find in Solado, Xo. And I can't promise it'll be easy."

"I never thought this was going to be easy," I countered, smiling.

"But . . . los pálidos," she said. "I know where they live, and I know how to get into Solado, but . . . it's going to be *really* hard."

"It's worth it," I said.

And I meant that, too. Maybe not in the way she did, but I did. It could not be easy to be around me, but she still was. That had to mean something, right?

"Let's head back," I suggested. "Get some sleep. We'll figure things out in the morning."

"Yes," she said. "In the morning."

She guided me back.

The whole time, she held my hand.

The children suggested that we sleep outdoors. They had not done so in a long time, but they felt safer with us around. Rosalinda was concerned it would be too dangerous. "What of the attacks?" she asked. But they said that there'd be some of them on patrol. We'd be fine.

The idea was too strange to me, but they wouldn't accept any arguments. "We know what we're doing," Gabriela assured me, and she lifted her chin up when she said it.

To refuse her would disrespect her, so we accepted.

I spread out my sleeping roll not far from the underground

entrance, then found a spot nearby to relieve myself. I covered up my waste, then ran water over my hands to clean them. When I turned back, Emilia was sitting on her own sleeping roll next to me.

"Eat something else," she told me, and she held out some dried cabra for me. "Even if you aren't hungry."

I begrudgingly took the food and bit off a piece. Then I collapsed onto my sleeping roll, chewing.

"We should make it to Solado tomorrow," said Emilia.

Tomorrow.

Only another sunrise before I found the person I was looking for.

Another sunrise before this was all over.

Before my life changed forever.

I hoped.

"And then what?"

My question hung there between us, pushed us apart. At least I thought it did. But I heard her roll over, felt her hand on my arm.

"We could figure it out," she said, her voice low, deep. "Together."

I liked the sound of that.

The echo of her words reverberated inside of me, waking Emilia's story, but only for a brief flash. All of them—they settled.

They waited.

Because soon, this would all be over.

They came in the middle of the night.

I saw only the muted glowing of their eyes, first a single pair of them, then another, until the section of the wall I was next to was surrounded by them, dim yellow spots and nothing more. They made no other sounds. Just watched me, countless pairs of eyes so still in the night. I hoped they were guardians, not the terrible creatures that had tormented the children of La Reina Nueva.

They did not move, did not come in for the kill, so I relaxed, but only a little. Was I unworthy? Uninteresting?

I thought of waking Emilia, of trying to find the others, but I worried that any movement at all would set them off. But they never made their presence known otherwise. I watched them for a while, and then they began to wink out, to fade into nothing, until we were by ourselves again, and I drifted off to sleep.

I dreamed of nothing.

The howling woke me up.

The terrible, mournful sound ripped me back into consciousness. I was upright a moment later, and my eyes took a little while to adjust in the fading starlight. Dawn was coming soon.

Emilia still slept. Somehow, during the night, one of us had moved closer to the other. Maybe we both did. I rose as quietly as I could, not wanting to alarm Emilia. My stomach ached again, but the pain was different this time. Not a cramp. Something deeper. I had not been eating much on this journey, and perhaps my body was telling me so. I stood there in the silence, my hand on my belly, willing the pain away.

Another howl ripped through the early-morning darkness.

I walked toward the wall, stood next to it, gripped the cold stone in my hand.

Crickets chirped. Silence filled the space between their calls.

I waited. I opened myself up to the darkness that grew before dawn, to the desert, and it responded.

Rustling.

Thumping on the ground.

They were coming.

I rushed back to Emilia, threw myself down onto the sleeping roll, began to dig through my pack for la pala, wishing that I'd thought to bring a weapon, and—

But it was Pablo. He climbed over the rubble, breathless. "Xochitl," he said, huffing.

"What is it?" I whispered harshly. Emilia stirred beside me.

"They've come back."

"Who is 'they'?" grumbled Emilia, rubbing at her eyes.

He didn't answer at first. He bent over so that his hands were on his knees. "We're surrounded," he choked out.

Emilia sat up. "Surrounded? By *what*?"

"They're all around the camp," he explained, still hunched over, his curls bouncing when he looked back up at us. "The guardians."

The eyes. They hadn't been part of un sueño. They had surrounded *me*.

"They're asking for you," he said. He straightened up, put his hands behind his head, still huffing. "I don't know what they want."

We left our belongings behind and followed Pablo, climbing over a ruined section of the wall, and a thick, nervous sweat ran from my underarms. Just into the next clearing, I saw the others. Rosalinda raised a finger to her lips, waved with the other hand, and we slowly approached them.

"I've never seen guardians like this," she whispered to me. "Big. Dark fur. Casi como gatos, pero . . . no."

"Ours were ositos," Felipe said, his voice even lower than that of his mother. "I think I like them better than these."

I twisted around and around, trying to see what they were staring at. "I don't see them," I said.

"You don't need to," said Rosalinda.

"But I—"

"*Listen.*"

I didn't hear it at first. It was so low, so present, that it nearly faded into the background. But as we all remained unmoving, it filled my ears: a humming, rumbling and deep, that seemed to come from every direction. It varied in pitch every so often, a slow, horrific *growl*.

We really were surrounded.

I tensed up, and it was there again: Emilia's hand in mine. I pulled her to my side.

I waited.

And waited.

And waited.

And waited.

Until one of them finally revealed themselves.

They came from the south, and they made no sound as each of their black paws gripped the soil. One step, then two, then the creature sauntered into the clearing, teeth bared, and in the newborn light of the morning, I saw that some of those teeth were stained red. Blood. It was probably blood.

But *whose*? Whose life had been taken?

They towered there, the monstrous bestia with black fur sleek and shiny in the early-morning light that reached up beyond the horizon in the east, and they stepped closer and closer, and I dared not move. I knew then that the slightest mistake could end in my death. So I kept my eyes locked on them, on their yellowed pupils, on the massive jaws that hung open.

They strode right up to me, and Solís help me, I was *shaking*, trembling right there in that spot, and they sniffed me, then *glared*, brows angling toward each other.

I heard something trickling into the dirt next to me, and slowly, achingly, my gaze dropped to a puddle on the ground. Felipe's leg shivered in terror.

Do you know why we are here?

The voice was a rumble, neither masculine nor feminine, but something in between, something like you, Solís.

And it sounded in my head.

I focused on those yellow eyes. "You are the guardians of La Reina Nueva."

"Who are you talking to?" Emilia asked, but I raised a hand for her to be quiet.

We are, cuentista.

"You protect this place."

We do, they said. *We also protected La Reina many years ago, before it was lost in La Quema.*

"La Reina?"

You passed through it before you arrived here. It is la ciudad of truth.

I nodded. "We were tested."

No. They put their head down, pawed at the ground. *The truth is never a test. It is only the truth.*

"Then why? Why show us all that? Why make us go through it?" I couldn't hide the anger in my voice. "What if the others had rejected me like my own aldea did? The truth could have *harmed* me!"

The lead guardian gazed into my eyes and would not break contact. *You have a journey ahead of you.*

I laughed at that, and I didn't even care that the others were staring at me, wide-eyed. What must that have looked like, Solís? To see me speaking to a guardian, *laughing* at them like that?

"You must be mistaken," I said. "I've already been on a journey. We're almost done."

It was as though they didn't even hear what I said. *We lost Carlito, but we found something else. We have taken care of it, but there is a last piece. You and the other—the one from Solado—you must play your part.*

Those words could have been spoken to me by Tía Inez. Mamá. Papá. Any person in Empalme. It was what I had done my entire life: play my part.

I, the obedient, faithful daughter, la cuentista de Empalme, had done everything that was asked of me.

No. I was *done* playing that part. So how could they ask this of me?

"I am going to Solado to help Emilia," I said. "And to find Simone. That's all."

There was silence once more, and someone shifted nearby. Gabriela and Pablo approached us.

This was their guardian. I could see the reverence on their faces.

"Amato," Pablo said, and they smiled wide, joyful. "It is good to see you again."

Amato bowed to them, brought their head close to the ground, then looked back to me. *Eres cuentista*, Amato said.

"I am."

Then you will be needed.

I considered them. The other guardians sat behind Amato, all with their gaze to the ground, unmoving. But then they each brought up their head, their yellow eyes piercing me.

We know what you are trying to do, Amato said.

"Are you going to stop me?"

No. The guardian licked a paw. *This will be the last thing we ask of you.*

One more.

It was *always* one more thing, wasn't it?

My stomach rumbled, both from hunger and from the stories rousing from their slumber.

But . . . I could take one more, couldn't I?

One more, and then it would be over.

Forever.

"I'll do it," I said. "Just this one, and that's it."

We accept, Amato said, and then the guardian bowed to me. *Gracias, cuentista. We will keep you safe as you journey to Solado.*

I nodded and twisted to face Emilia. "They're all coming with us," I explained. "To protect us as we enter Solado."

"That makes me feel better," she said, "but what's going on?"

I addressed Gabriela and Pablo. "They haven't found Carlito, but apparently, everything has to do with Solado."

"Then we should get going," said Emilia before the others could speak. "If I've learned anything from you, then we want to be far along the trail before Solís is directly above us."

I looked to Rosalinda for confirmation, but she was frowning at me. "I can't," she said. "I can't risk it anymore. This is so much harder than I thought it would be, and . . . " She sighed. " . . . we can't. We're staying."

"Staying?" said Emilia. "*Here?*"

"I already talked to Felipe about it," she said. "We have been trying to find a home for weeks now."

"I'm tired," said Felipe, and his face drooped with sadness. "I don't want to leave you, but . . . " He reached out, and Pablo was suddenly at his side, holding his outstretched hand. " . . . I made a friend last night. I think I want to stay."

"Rosalinda . . . ," I said, and the urge to convince her to come with us, to tell her that we could figure something out, it all died once I saw that she'd made up her mind. Felipe moved to her side and held her tight, and in his face, I saw Raúl.

"They need someone," Rosalinda said. "They've survived this long on their own, but these children need *help*. We can build something here, Xochitl. Are you sure you don't want to stay?"

"I have to keep going," I said. "A little bit more."

"You're always welcome here," she said. She hesitated. "And I understand why you did what you did, Xochitl. I think you need to hear that."

She truly wasn't leaving.

And I had to accept it.

I hugged Rosalinda, then Felipe, and I was surprised by the well of emotions I had for them. How long had I known them? Two days at best? And yet I was sad to leave, and that sadness found companions within me: Lito. Omar. Emilia. Their stories were still eager for someone to join them, to understand them. Eliazar's spoke loudest to me, and the image of him climbing the hill from his home, refusing to look back, to see Gracia's body behind him on the beach, filled my mind. I shook it off, disturbed at how easy it was to recall what others had lived through. Their memories were still more like my own.

I knew it was not a good thing; I would not mention it to anyone.

We packed quickly. Quietly. Refilled our water bags and canteens. We said our goodbyes to those children who were awake, and they waved at us as we walked north. I looked back at Rosalinda and Felipe, the ones who had chosen to stay behind, and there was an anticipation on their faces, as if they expected me to change my mind, to rush back to them and stay.

I kept walking.

Emilia and I walked beyond La Reina Nueva, into a morning that was warming up, into a future that was unknown.

The guardians followed us.

They did not speak to me.

A spike of pain tore into my abdomen, sharper than ever before. I pushed it and the stories back down.

What was I *doing*?

Emilia and I found Carlito not much later.

We came upon his body, splayed between two tall saguaros. Amato sat near Carlito, and I can't explain how, but I *felt* their sadness, and that's how I knew this was the missing leader of La Reina Nueva.

I don't need to tell you what I saw, Solís. Would you suddenly care? Would the details of a dead child suddenly spark your interest? You must have seen him. You must have known. And yet, you still did nothing.

No explanation of that violence would make Carlito more human for you.

I looked away quickly. I didn't want this to be my only memory of this poor young man. The horizon blurred, the ground swayed, and nausea tugged at what little water and food I'd had in my stomach. There was a hand on my arm, another pulling my hair back as I gagged. Emilia's fingers, cool and certain.

Lito. It was Lito all over again. A body torn, potential lost.

Her affection buzzed over my skin. I didn't understand it, how her nearness had grown to be such a comfort.

As a cuentista, I knew that we formed connections with everyone whose story we took. Is this what happened when a cuentista kept a story? Were we more raw with each other, closer together because she had shared her secrets with me?

I had been a cuentista for half my life, and I still did not feel as though I knew anything about it.

I opened my eyes, blinked away tears. Amato gave Carlito one last bow of reverence, and when they finished, they flashed bloodshot eyes in my direction.

This is what's waiting for us.

More violence. More tragedy. More death. That's what Amato meant, right?

We have to keep moving.

I had not stopped since I had made that fateful decision in Empalme. And now I felt so hollow, so empty, so vast.

You have a long climb today. Up Las Montañas de Solís. It will be hard. But you will be almost done after that.

Each of us becomes the desert.

It is important that you make it, cuentista. You must be there.

Each of us so terribly alone.

Amato moved up close, their eyes yellow again. They rubbed their massive head against my own and purred.

Follow me, cuentista. This is the last thing before the end.

I followed because I believed there was no other choice.

Did that count as a lie, Solís? I did not know whether the guardians could lie to others. Were they trying to quiet the panic and terror in me? Were they trying to give me hope?

Did you even care?

I started lying when I was very young. I knew years ago that I had been trapped into a life I did not choose. I couldn't recall the first time that I dreamed of an existence beyond the gates of Empalme. But I still knew to keep those thoughts to myself, to bury them like the stories in my gut, because to speak the truth was to speak the truth of you.

I don't know how many lies I was told either. And did those count if the people who said them did not know that what they told me was untrue? The stories of las cuentistas and las pesadillas were core to our beliefs. So were las estrellas that came out at night, that surrounded us, that granted us freedom from you. Maybe our belief is what gave it all power, what shaped our reality for us.

But where did that leave the others?

Julio, who chose to have this power, and then corrupted it.

Soledad, who yearned for the power and ruined lives because of it.

Téa, who was the sole cuentista for so very many people and could not help Eliazar when he needed it.

All our myths were different.

Did that make them *lies*?

Or were we simply trying to understand the horrors that you had given us?

I had spent most of my life within a lie, and now, when I was so horribly far from home, the truth was revealing itself.

You sat up there, and you did nothing.

Said nothing.

Fixed nothing.

You gave some of us a power meant to cleanse humanity, and then you sat back, and watched it all unfold.

The lies.

The chaos.

The suffering.

I had to keep going, Solís. Do you understand that? I was unattached. How had Mamá put it? *Estás inquieta*, she had told me. And she was right.

And now I was in your desert, which you created when you burned the world, and I was desperate to be free.

It was all worth it.

I had never been so tired, so desiring of rest. We walked as you continued your path through the sky, and your heat smothered us. I tried to drink more water, knowing that the last part of the journey was here, hopeful that I could stave off another pounding headache caused by the heat. I tore at the sleeves of my camisa to make two strips, and I tied them together at either end, making a loop, and I fitted the loop around my head to keep the sweat from my eyes.

It reminded me of what Eliazar had done for Felipe.

It felt as if he had died a lifetime ago.

My feet were stones, and my legs were on fire, both beneath the skin and over the surface of it. I had never been so scorched, so crisp, not since I was una jovencita, when I had wandered outside at mediodía while Mamá was making la masa in the house. She did not notice that I was gone until too late. By the end of the day, my skin was red and warm to the touch, and she had to spread the inside of an aloe vera leaf over my skin to cool me down, to make it stop screaming at me.

I missed her touch. Her laughter. Her temper. Those sharp, dark eyes. Her braids.

I wish I could tell you more, Solís. You always ask for it all, but that day blurred into itself. We walked and walked and walked,

and the guardians kept pace, but we did not talk. Emilia took the
lead, and I assumed that meant that you were still guiding her.

I drank water.

I ate dried strips of meat.

I relieved myself, my urine still too dark for my liking, but I
couldn't do anything about it.

I walked

and

walked

and

walked

and

walked.

Until I was certain I would burst into flames, that I would com-
bust under you, that I would get so close to my destination but still
end up like Raymundo, like all the others claimed by your heat.

And yet, I kept going.

One last story remained.

One last climb.

I would make it.

I *had* to.

Time slowed.

Time sped up.

Time meant nothing.

You were already cresting to the west when la montaña was within reach. Las bajadas at the base of Las Montañas de Solís were short and fierce, a dense collection of thorny árboles and dark bushes, the raised arms of the saguaros pointed toward the sky.

How long had it been since we left La Reina? I looked up at you, at your arc across the sky, then squatted low to the ground, my eyes closed, and I shoved it all down. Panic. Fear. The mixture of stories, churning, living, desiring.

"¿Estás bien, Xochitl?"

Emilia put her hand on my back, but I kept my eyes closed, let the wave pass. I thought of Papá, of how often he asked me that question, never as small talk. He *truly* wanted to know if I was well.

Perhaps Emilia did, too.

You're so close, I told myself. *Don't give up now.*

But I was so terribly afraid, Solís. Afraid that I'd made a terrible choice, afraid that I was barreling toward nothing, afraid that this was all pointless.

The guardian spoke to me in my mind. *Cuentista*, Amato said. *You must rise.*

I opened my eyes slowly, and the burning light hurt. I blinked away tears.

"Xochitl . . ." Emilia's voice was tentative.

Worried.

I expected to see the leader of the guardians in front of me.

Instead, there was a *person*.

Their hair was long, tied in thin braids that fell from a brown wrap on their head. I could only see their eyes: Dark. Nearly black. They were tall. Thin. What skin I could see under their flowing clothing—baggy breeches, a light cloth like mine bound around their torso and then cascading back into something like a cape, dark boots—was similar to my own.

Emilia guided me upright with her hand under my arm, and I looked around frantically for Amato, the guardian who had been speaking to me.

And was surprised to watch them walk up to this stranger's side and nuzzle their leg.

Cuentista, Amato said.

But not to me.

"Who are you?" I called out, my throat parched.

They are with us, Amato said. The other guardians—their coats differently colored but still brilliant in your light—gathered behind the stranger.

"Ximen," they answered, and they stepped forward, slowly at first, then crossed the space between us. "I think we should talk."

Emilia gripped me tightly. "I don't like this," she said. "We should go."

"I'm like you," they said.

I was too tired to be polite to this stranger. "No, you're not."

They unwrapped their face to reveal full lips, long lashes. "We are both cuentistas."

That got my attention, but I still teetered in place from exhaustion, and Emilia steadied me. "I gathered that. But why are you here?"

Then, turning to the guardian, I asked: "Is this what you needed me for?"

No, Amato answered. *But you should hear what they have to say.*

"I am from far, far to el norte," they said, brushing a braid out of their face. "Beyond Solado. Beyond the land of ash."

I felt Emilia stiffen.

"Beyond?" she said.

"Sí. Far beyond. Where the land is covered in árboles, tall and green," they said, and I could hear an accent on their tongue that was unfamiliar to me, one that smoothed out all the parts that would be harder in my own mouth.

"Then why are you here?" I asked. "Why leave that place?"

"Because I had to."

I held my breath.

My own words, echoed back at me.

"Do you ever feel alone in a crowd, cuentista?"

I exhaled.

"Do you ever believe that the people in your life see you only as a means to an end?"

"All the time," I said.

"Then you must understand why I left paradise," Ximen said. "Because even paradise can be tainted by what we are."

I stepped toward them. "And what are we?" I asked.

They smiled, flashing white teeth at me. "We are an answer. To a question no one has asked yet."

A new line of sweat broke out over my brow. I looked to the guardian nearest Ximen, but they were occupying themselves with cleaning their sleek coat.

"So what are you doing *here*?" Emilia asked.

"I'm just passing through. I met the guardians a few days ago, when I first reached the land called Solado and passed over it. We had many conversations about what life is like in the north. It is very different from here in the south."

"And where are you going next?" I asked.

There was a part of me that wanted to ask them to come with us. I had so much I wanted to know, so many things to ask.

"I don't know," they said, and they began to wrap their face up again. "It frightens me, but I find it exhilarating. For the first time in my life, I feel *alive*. I feel like I can choose who I want to be every day."

La poema came to me:

> cuando estoy solo   when I am alone
> estoy vivo   I am alive

"You can be alive, too, cuentista," they said, and then they started walking, moved right past us, then turned to raise their hand in farewell. "Perhaps we will cross paths again."

Had I just met—?

The thought spread through me, and I was so tired, Solís, and I tried to will my legs to run after them, to call out their name.

Is that la poeta?

No.

No, it didn't make sense.

But they did seem to understand me.

Can it be?

There was a low growl behind me.

Come, cuentista, Amato said, their voice reverberating in my skull. *We have a final climb before us.*

I watched Ximen disappear.

Solo quiero ser vista.   I only want to be seen.

Maybe that was *them.*
And maybe la poeta wanted me to feel seen.

And so we climbed.

The road was wide, worn with ruts from the carts that had used it for years, but it narrowed as we pushed through las bajadas, squeezing us together, closer. I traced its path, up and up and up, and even if I could have followed it, even if it didn't snake into ravines and rolling inclines, it was impossible to see the top.

This is it, I told myself. *One last climb.*

So much weighed on each of us. Emilia and I ascended side by side, panting in turn, and we continued in agonizing silence. We were pushed to our hands and knees when the trail became sharp and vicious, and I crawled upward, closer to you, closer to the truth.

When we reached the first plateau, I dropped to my knees and threw my head back, gasping for air. I breathed deep as the muscles in my thighs twitched, threatening to cramp, so I drank water and rolled my fists over my legs, urging Emilia to do the same. I'd learned that move from Papá long ago.

Papá.

Was he worried?

Disappointed?

Had he already forgotten me?

I bent over in a deep stretch, running my fingers over the muscles in my legs, digging them into the cords and tendons, the pain and soreness flaring in protest. I breathed in and out, tried to slow my galloping heart, then raised my arms above me. When I felt that I had regained control of my body, I opened my eyes, let your light pour into them, adjusted to the terrible brightness and—

On the trail.

Farther down.

Right in the middle.

Un sabueso.

It didn't move.

I watched el sabueso's lip curl up, heard the low growl that escaped it, and I tried to scramble away, but my feet couldn't get a grip on the dirt road, and I slipped. I lashed out with both hands, desperate to hold on to something, but I slid down, down toward that gaping mouth, toward the bloody teeth, toward—

"Xochitl!"

Emilia had me under the arms, and it snapped me back, her terror flowing into me, and I stopped falling, stopped plunging into—

It was gone.

I blinked. Sweat broke out anew. I rubbed at my eyes, so sure that I was about to be devoured, but *it wasn't there.*

"Drink," she said, and she held up her own water. As I gulped it down, washing away the bile that had risen in my throat, she asked, "What did you see?"

"See?" I choked.

"If you don't get enough agua, Solís makes you see things," she said. "Remember? You taught me that."

I swallowed more water, shame rippling over my face, heating it up. "It was nothing," I said, even though I knew she was probably right. I had been walking for a long time; my last full meal was two days ago. "Nothing at all," I added.

Do you need help, cuentista?

Amato came forward and pawed at me. I wondered if the guardians cared about me, too.

It is important you make it to Solado, they said.

I gave the guardian a brief scowl. Perhaps they didn't. "I'll be fine," I said. "Emilia?"

She helped me up and steadied me, and a warmth coursed in my fingers, up to my shoulder, like what I felt before I took someone's story. But it was gone as fast as it had arrived.

Did she know the effect she had on me?

I settled my pack onto my back, wiped the sweat that threatened to sting my eyes, and I began to walk.

And I walked.

And walked.

And walked.

You climbed in the sky.

We climbed closer to you.

And you punished me. That's what I believed as my water got warmer. As the cramps throbbed in my lower back and at the bottom of my abdomen. As the stories stretched out and fought for room. As the summit stayed in the exact same spot, never moving, never getting any closer. Was every moment a penance I had to pay, a price torn from my skin and from my mind?

I lost track of time as it stretched out, became everything and nothing all at once. My water was rancid in my stomach, but I knew I needed it. I became the desert, more vacant and alone than ever before, as if you had hollowed me out, replaced me with exhaustion and suffering. I was no longer whole. No longer real.

I slowed again close to el mediodía. I thought I was better at this, and shame rippled through me. I poured hot water over my head, enough to soak my hair, and it ran across my scalp, gathered in the band of cloth around my head.

"Are you as miserable as I am?" asked Emilia.

My tongue stuck to the roof of my mouth as I spoke. "It's like everything has slowed down. I can't seem to remember anything but walking."

"Ay, Xo, take a break," she said, and she dropped her bag next to me. "Más agua," she said.

"Mine is boiling," I said. "It's too hot."

"Let me see," she said, and I handed her my water bag. She tipped a bit of it into her mouth, then shook her head. "Xochitl—"

"I know," I said. "But I don't have anything else, so it'll have to do."

"No, it's *cold*."

She took my hand, let some water trickle over my hand.

It *was* cool.

Rest, Amato ordered. *You are getting worse.*

A spark of disagreement burst in me—was that Ofelia, deep down inside, her spite and ire ripping through me?—but my body simply would not move. I accepted it, and I lay back in your light, let the darkness rush in at the corners of my vision, then shut my eyes, granting the shadows a home inside me.

I heard their voices—was it the stories? Was it Emilia?— swirling about, but I wouldn't open my eyes. *Couldn't.* I wanted to stay here, to stay in the darkness and rest and sleep and never return.

Mamá was here. I heard her, then Papá, and was that Raúl's laughter, too? Were they all here?

"Xochitl!"

My eyes burst open and light poured in. There was a pressure at the back of my skull, and it throbbed, pushing into the back of my eyes. I coughed again, and each outburst sent flashes of light into my vision.

You must not fall asleep, not now, Amato said.

Emilia was there, her hand behind my head, cradling it.

"Where are we?" I blurted out.

"We've pushed so hard," said Emilia. "All of us. And it's catching up to you. You closed your eyes, and then you were just . . . asleep."

My head was a hazy mess; it was as if I'd been under for days. I gazed at the guardians who rested around me, most panting in the unbearable heat.

So it wasn't just me.

We were *all* suffering.

Each of us a desert.

I drank more water, then asked Emilia to help me up. My head did not spin when I did so, and it was enough to get me moving. I ate a piece of dried manzana at the urging of Amato. *You need more energy*, they said. *It is not much longer.*

I craned my head. That didn't seem true.

When we began to walk again, Las Montañas taunted me. At first, the distance seemed impossible. After making a few switchback turns on the trail, the summit was closer, closer than before. Hope blossomed like the flowers that bloomed during the night, under las estrellas. Then it seemed to stretch away from me.

You sank in the sky.

My shadow reached toward the horizon where night would fall first.

Amato stuck close behind me as Emilia led me up. She slowly undid her braids, let her hair fall back. The other guardians padded along in a procession, Emilia and I the head of a strange serpent.

Look, they said.

I glanced up the trail.

It widened.

It *ended*.

It crested the top of la montaña.

I tried to take it as a good sign. We were almost there. Our future was on the other side.

My future was there.

Would I find what I was looking for?

Nos estiramos por siempre   We stretch forever

I pushed harder and harder, ignoring all the signs that my body was ready to stop. The pain. The cramps. The needles in my stomach. The dread. The higher I ascended, the worse it got; the more that I wanted to get on all fours, push those stories out of me, expel that bitter refuse into the earth.

But I couldn't give them back. Not yet. I was too close.

Emilia reached it first. She stood at the trailhead, hunched over, then she was suddenly upright. I propelled my body forward at the sight, my huaraches digging into the dirt, and I rounded the last switchback, and I stopped dead in that spot. It was too much. Terror. Panic. Rage. Elation. Grief. I no longer managed to differentiate between what was mine, what was theirs.

Solado was so close.

This would be over.

The guardians rushed past me; their paws pounded in the dirt of the trail.

I pushed myself over the last rise. A burst of wind hit Emilia, and that long hair of hers flowed toward me, as if she floated in water, and I reached forward, closed the distance, and our palms were sweaty, filthy, but we did not care. We were both breathing hard, my head light and airy, and my vision swam with dizziness.

We had made it.

We had made it.

"Come," said Emilia. "Just a bit more. Let me show you my home, Xo."

I let her guide me.

The guardians fanned out on either side, and they all remained silent as we pressed forward.

I saw the shadow first. At least, I *thought* it was a shadow, cast in the wake of something I couldn't see. The darkness spread, and then the flatness of the top of La Montaña de Solís gave way, and my heart was in my throat, racing, throbbing, and I could not speak.

The earth yawned before us.

The landscape was blackened, torched, an endless vacancy of ash and destruction and decay. There was nothing in either direction: No árboles. No saguaros. No ironwoods or mesquites or paloverdes. No pájaros. No living creatures of any sort.

It was all death, everywhere I could see.

The stories of La Quema that I had grown up with were always that: stories. We were told of how fiercely you scorched the earth, but now I was seeing it for myself. I was seeing what you had really done to us.

And it terrified me.

"We have to go," said Emilia. "Rest a moment, have some agua, but . . . we have to go."

"I know," I said. "I just . . . need to take it in."

Emilia stood next to me as I tried to accept what my eyes were seeing. Everything within view was . . . gone.

Everything.

"This is actually the first time I've seen it in daylight," she said. "I guess we both share that."

She made the sign.

I did not.

I *couldn't.*

Because standing there, looking at your judgment, I had one realization:

There was nothing we could have possibly done to deserve this.

We rested, and then continued.

I cannot say that it was easier. As we descended into el valle de las cenizas, it began.

All the stories woke up.

All of them.

I still wonder if you did that, Solís. Was it out of spite? Had you been silent this whole journey, only to finally speak up? Was this your means of communicating with me?

It was like a war in my torso. I grimaced viciously as we descended on the trail, and thankfully, Emilia did not look back. I kept up a good pace, but those stories tore at me. Begged for attention. Begged for release. I couldn't tell what they wanted. Companionship? Did they require other stories to latch on to? Or were they imploring me to drop to the earth and return them all to you?

I thought I did not understand what was happening to me, but . . . I knew. I knew exactly what it was. How long had I known? Must have been a while. I had not admitted it out loud, but it was right there, all along.

I kept my mouth shut.

I kept the stories in.

I kept walking.

There was a point, more than halfway down, where we met the ashes. Whatever happened during La Quema had been so intense that a good third of la montaña was scorched, too. Each step sent ash up into the air. I briefly crouched and picked some up from the trail.

They crumbled, then wafted into the air. No smell. Only a thin dusting of blackness in my palm.

All that remained of those who had not gone underground, who had perished in La Quema.

I pushed myself onward, wondering if I would survive this, too.

Emilia led us down into el valle, but it was the guardians who led us into Solado.

By the time we reached the flat expanse beyond las bajadas, light was still pouring over us, but the heat had waned. Shadows stretched longer and longer. Emilia told me that we should not stop, that we should get below ground as soon as possible, but the guardians stopped in front of the two of us, blocking our path.

No, Amato said to me, the first they'd spoken in hours. *You must tell her to follow us.*

Emilia shook her head as I relayed their message. "I'm the one who grew up here," she countered. "Mami taught me how to leave, remember?"

This place is not what she thinks it is.

I twisted to stare at Amato, unsure if I should share what they just told me. "What do you mean?"

You must trust me. The final piece is here.

"What final piece?"

Maybe I was too exhausted to entertain any politeness.

Maybe I didn't care about whatever mystical journey these guardians had planned for me.

Maybe I wanted to find Simone and be done with this entire nightmare.

"Why can't you just speak *plainly*?" I yelled. "Are you afraid if you tell me the truth, I won't want to follow you?"

The guardian bristled, and its yellow eyes flashed red.

You have known the truth all along, and yet you yourself deny it.

"So why don't you tell me the truth if I already know it?"

My head throbbed on the last word, and a darkness grew at the edge of my vision.

"Xochitl, what's happening?" Emilia asked, her voice high and worried. "What are they saying?"

"For some reason, this one *insists* that you follow them."

Emilia frowned. "Do they know about Simone? Maybe they mean to take you to her."

I looked back at the guardian.

Please, Amato said, and for the first time, their voice in my head was soft, pleading. *There is one last thing we need of you.*

One last thing. I had come so far to free myself of this curse and escape my life of isolation. Could I really turn back *now*?

Your answers are here, Xochitl, Amato said. *Please. Come.*

It was the first time Amato had spoken my name, had not referred to me by a title I had not asked for.

"I think we should trust Amato," I said, letting my breath out with the decision.

And so we did. The guardians took us through the ashes. My feet sank to their ankles in them, and I did my best not to think of what they were before.

How much farther was it?

Was I close to Simone?

What would the future be like?

She fidgeted next to me, kept biting her bottom lip.

"Emilia," I said, as the guardians kept us moving forward.

Her piercing eyes focused on me.

"We can do this," I said. "We have the guardians on our side. We will find Luz, we will find Simone, and then we'll get out."

"I'm not worried about that, really," she said, and she twirled her hair around a finger. "I mean, I am. It terrifies me."

The ashes crunched beneath our feet.

"Then what is it?"

"You should ask them about los pálidos," she said. "The people in the white cloaks. How are we going to get past them?"

I took a step forward.

Another.

Another.

My skin prickled all over, as though something were passing over me, and it caused me to shiver from head to toe, and then it, too, was gone.

Emilia stepped up next to me. "You feel that?" she asked.

I nodded.

The guardians stilled in front of us.

We are here, Amato said, and he must have said it in both our minds, as I heard the air leave Emilia.

The guardians parted.

And I stared into a gaping hole in the ground.

It was about ten paces ahead, a terrible, dark thing, as if some huge being had reached down and tore the chasm out of the earth. The edges of it were jagged, and the maw opened to reveal . . .

. . . darkness.

Our fate is down there, Amato said. *We will lead the way once more.*

"Wait!" I cried out. "What about los pálidos?"

Amato's reaction was brief. They swung their head, pawed at the ground. *You will be safe. We promise.*

"What did Amato say?" Emilia said, her voice high in terror. "Are we going to be okay?"

I nodded. "They said we will be safe."

"Xochitl."

My name dripped off her tongue, and Emilia shook next to me.

"I don't know what we will find down there."

Neither did I. And Solís, it terrified me.

The guardians—all of them, their muscles rippling—poured into the hole, one by one, until the leader was left.

Follow us.

Then Amato was gone.

I reached down, traced my fingertips over Emilia's, and her hand opened. I took her fingers in mine, and we walked together into the darkness.

It enveloped us, closed in, held us tight, and panic gripped me when I realized I could not see more than a few paces ahead of us.

She gently tugged me forward, and our footsteps echoed within the passageway. My eyes began to adjust, and I could make out the edges of the tunnel. I ran my fingers along the cool rock, impressed at how smooth it was.

This is what the people of Solado had done to survive.

It filled me with awe.

We picked up the pace soon after that. "I know where I am," Emilia said, breathless, excited. "We aren't far."

We passed other caverns. Passageways. Rooms carved into the stone and dirt, with furniture constructed of rocks and mud: sillas, mesas, estufas built into the wall.

Another room to my left. It arced upward. There was a small hole at the top, and what little sunlight was left was pouring through it, illuminating the rows and rows of something that had once grown but was now wilting, dying.

A passage veered off to my right. I could see more entries to homes, recognized them from the stories that Marisol and Emilia had given me.

Another home. Furniture strewn about.

"Emilia . . ."

She rushed forward, let go of my hand, ignored me.

My eyes continued to adjust to the limited light belowground. Where was it coming from? I saw no torches, no fires, nothing.

A room opened to my left.

A trunk, upturned, contents spilled everywhere.

"Emilia!"

A stain.

Dark, spreading from the debris and over the ground.

The stench hit me next: bitter and sharp.

I had smelled it before.

Outside Chavela's.

At home, when it fell from the sky.

When el sabueso brought part of Manolito back.

I looked up and Emilia was gone. Panic tore into me, but there was a guardian—their coat a dull brown, their eyes a piercing yellow—who stood at the end of the passageway. They sped around a corner, and I ran after them.

I heard her yelling first. She called out, her voice high, echoing throughout the various chambers and passages. I rounded another corner, right behind one of the guardians.

"¿Hay alguien aquí?" she screamed.

I was closer.

More rooms.

More destruction.

More stains.

Another turn in the passage.

She stood at the edge of a large cavern, and beams of light fell from above her, poured over the ground, revealed the columns of maíz, their leaves browned and dry and dying. To our right, stalks pressed against the ground, as if something enormous had landed on top of them.

The stains were everywhere, and in the light of the setting sun, they had a color I could not see before.

A terrible dark red.

"Emilia?" I approached her carefully, avoiding sudden movements, unsure if I should touch her. "What's going on?"

"Gone." Her arms hung at her sides, limp.

"What do you mean?" I asked. "Gone?"

"They're all gone," she said, a whisper to the dying fields, to me, to herself. "Everyone is gone."

"How is that—?" I began.

She spun to me, and there were lines of tears dripping down her face. "Xochitl, they're all gone. And we came here for *nothing*."

She collapsed on the spot, and I stood there, numb and useless, staring at the remains of Solado.

We wandered from room to room, our eyes dancing from every terrible stain to the next, from every bit of proof that those who had lived here were now gone. There was clothing piled about the floor, seemingly at random, the red blotches a stark glimpse of some horror that had transpired. We came across more areas where small crops grew in limited sunlight, and everything was limp and dying. How long since they had last been watered? How long ago were they abandoned?

Emilia ran her hands over the walls.

She knelt to touch the bloody camisa left behind in one hallway.

She sobbed the entire time.

I stuck close to her, my own body numb, unsure how I could help.

We had so much to grieve.

Emilia brought me to a large cavern, the ceiling stretching high above us, and here was a gathering place of sorts. Long mesas of stone stood in front of us, and food rotted on ceramic plates. A swarm of flies flew off as Emilia picked up one of the dishes, then she let it crash to the floor.

The sound echoed around us.

No one responded.

We were truly alone down here in Solado.

Come, Amato said, and they came into the cavern and strode right up to Emilia, rubbed their head against her leg. *Your answers are close.*

"Did you *know*?" I said, fury boiling to the surface. "Did you know that this had happened?"

They ignored me, and instead sauntered off down the passageway.

"I thought I knew what I was doing," Emilia said, still gaping at the death before her. "I thought Solís was guiding me here."

"Maybe They still are," I said. "Maybe there's a reason the guardians brought us here."

She wouldn't look at me, though. I couldn't blame her. My reasoning was pathetic and useless. Why would you give her so much suffering? What possible explanation could comfort someone in so much pain? So I understood why she headed after the guardians, leaving me there in that cavern, alone, afraid.

What did this place once look like? I had seen it in Emilia's stories, and even less of it in Marisol's. But it didn't feel real anymore. Those images were distant, blurry.

I gave the hall one last look, then followed after the others, followed after the sound of Emilia crying.

The passage twisted and turned, and if it weren't for Emilia, I would have gotten lost. Solado felt endless, a labyrinth with no sense or organization.

I had never been in a place so *empty*. What of the original inhabitants? Or los pálidos? Could *all* of them truly be gone?

I should have been distraught, but I was too exhausted to be anything but numb.

I slammed into the back of Emilia; she was rooted to the floor, unmoving, stone still. It nearly knocked the wind out of me, so I huffed in air as best as I could while I tried to—

I recognized this passage.

I saw it again as it awoke within me:

Emilia, held by the arms and legs, stolen from the darkness. Luz, behind her, fighting Julio's men.

The guardians had brought us back to Emilia's home.

"Emilia, maybe she's still alive!" I said, wheezing. "Emilia, we have to go in there."

"No, I can't," she said, and her hands trembled. "I can't have come this whole way just to—"

Emilia.

I heard the voice in my head, like Amato's. But this was a new one.

"Luz?"

Emilia staggered there, her sobs breaking out anew as she called out her guardian's name.

"Is that you?"

There was a pause.

In a manner of speaking, she said.

Emilia rushed forward, down the passage, around the bend, and I followed. Maybe this was not so hopeless as I had thought.

The guardians gathered outside Emilia's home. Amato rubbed against my leg and spoke as they did so.

It is not as she thinks.

Amato, do not be so cruel, Luz said, and Emilia reached out, gripped my arm. *Emilia, I am sorry you traveled so far for me. Please, come into our home and learn the truth.*

Emilia walked slowly forward, past the line of guardians, into the doorway, and I was right behind her.

The room was empty, rid of all the details from the story that Emilia had told me. Empty except for a chair.

A guardian.

And a man, seated beside them.

He was young, perhaps only a few years older than I was. His skin was waxy with sweat, and he barely moved, staring at us with dark eyes that seemed overjoyed to see us by our arrival. His hair was matted against the side of his head, and as we approached, tears fell down his cheeks.

"You made it," he said.

The time has come, said the guardian next to him.

I recognized her.

It *was* Luz.

But something was wrong. She seemed to be both here and not here, existing in between life and death, light and shadow.

You can see the truth, cuentista, she said to me.

I moved forward. I couldn't stop myself. I knew that look. I'd seen it more times than I could count.

Eduardo, said Luz. *You know what to do.*

Eduardo.

It was *him*.

He smiled at Luz, then at me.

He stuck his hands out.

Palms down.

"Luz, what *is* this?" Emilia cried. "What happened to Solado?"

Luz did not answer her.

"Cuentista," said Eduardo. "Will you take my story?"

I hesitated, and he smiled again.

"Was it worth it?" Eduardo asked.

"Was *what* worth it?" I asked.

"This journey. The choices you made."

My lips parted, but I kept the answer to myself. I did not know this man. And I did not know how *he* knew.

"I ask you because this will be the last story you will ever need to take," he continued. "Once you do, you will understand why. You will have freed me from a terrible burden. And you will be able to make your *own* decision."

"Luz, *please*," Emilia said. "Tell me what is going on."

She moved toward her guardian.

And Luz *growled*.

I cannot, she said. *We must not make contact.*

Emilia began to sob, and I hated the sound, the sharpness of her inhalations, and that I could not help her. Luz backed up a step, but still stayed at Eduardo's side.

"Please, cuentista," said Eduardo, and his eyes implored me. "Uno más."

But it wouldn't be the last one for me, would it? There was no Simone; there was no means to get rid of all of this; there was nothing here for me. How could this man be so sure of what he had said?

Someone or something brought me here, though. Was it you? I wondered. The guardians? Something greater?

I let instinct take over; I ignored Emilia's screams; I fell to my knees in front of Eduardo, and my leather pack slid off my back.

I placed my palms under his.

I felt the surge.

And then I *knew*.

Let me tell you a story, Solís.

Eduardo was raised to believe that he was nothing.

As long as he could remember, his mamá, Sofía, was distant. He wondered if she secretly despised him, too, because he looked so much like the man she married, a man she *truly* hated. Was it because he and Fidel had the same nose, the same dark eyes, the same long, flowing hair? Did he remind his mamá of the man she mistakenly chose to trust? At a young age, he began to daydream about finding his mamá in another aldea, much, much later in life, when she had left Fidel behind and married someone else, and they would reconnect and love one another again, far from Fidel and his infidelities and excuses.

It was a dream that could never come true. Eduardo's family moved frequently from one aldea to the next, sometimes in the same month. Fidel was a blacksmith, but he never lasted long whenever he was. In their first aldea, he was caught stealing ore from his boss, and so he moved them all to another one after a hellish two-day journey across the desert. There, Fidel learned how to assist the local mercado, keeping track of all the shipments, all the food and supplies. He was good at it. He *excelled* at it. But after a year, Fidel woke his son and wife in the middle of the night, urged them to pack what belongings they could, and then told Eduardo that they were going on an adventure. It was only when the men started chasing them out of la aldea, shouting out *that* word over and over again, that Eduardo realized what his father truly was.

Ladrón. Ladrón. Ladrón.

This was their life. They would flee from one place to another, resettle, integrate slowly into another community, and then it would begin again. Late-night escapes, days gone hungry, and stories crafted so that the next aldea would take pity on them, would take them in, would believe that they were helping a poor mother and father escape the vicious guardias of the previous aldea.

And Eduardo's mother took it out on him. She never hit her son, never laid a finger on him, but she lashed him with her tongue, told Eduardo that he was useless, that he should have been earning his keep at home, that he should have stopped his father from drinking, that he should have forced Fidel to change. Eduardo tried, but his father was impenetrable, unmovable, convinced that he was the victim, that everyone he met only wanted a scapegoat.

He had no one to talk to. He moved so much that he never got close enough to a single cuentista, and thus had no one to whom he could tell the truth.

It all caught up with them in Obregán. Eduardo was seventeen when they left the last aldea and became a part of La Ciudad de Obregán, and it was there that Fidel was finally captured. He had angered so many people, had stolen so much from every aldea he had inhabited, that a band of people had formed just to track him down.

Fidel woke them up one last time.

Ordered them out of their small home on the southeast edge of la ciudad.

They packed what they could, which was not hard because they had learned never to own too many things, since they would inevitably leave them behind.

They ran.

They hid in an empty building, one managed by una vieja with flowing white hair, whose name Eduardo never learned, who allowed them space as long as they needed it.

They did not need it for long.

When they came for Fidel, it was the next night, and las estrellas shone brightly through the windows. The men burst into the building, yelling Fidel's name, and the other inhabitants hid underneath the floor.

Sofía held her son back. "Let them get him," she said. "He deserves it."

When he told his mamá that they couldn't let the men take Fidel, she merely said, "I'll let them take you, too. You're not any better than him."

Fidel, who had spent the day getting drunk, was barely conscious as the men beat him. When his nose broke, his blood spilling to the floor, he merely moaned. When his arm was wrenched backwards, his elbow snapping loudly, there were only tears running down his face.

And when they pummeled his head, over and over again, he simply stopped breathing.

Eduardo watched his father die. Fidel didn't defend himself. Sofía, however, spat on the bloodied body of her husband. She cast one last look at Eduardo. "You're old enough now," she said. "I don't need to raise you anymore."

She left him behind with these strange men, and one of them lifted him from the floor as he sobbed in grief and terror, and he put his hand under Eduardo's chin, pitched his face upward.

"His debt is now yours," he said. "You start working it off tomorrow."

They left him there. Eduardo considered running away, but where would he go? He had no idea where his mamá had wandered off to, and they had only been in Obregán for a week. But la vieja came out from her hiding place beneath the floor and cleaned him up. She told him he could stay as long as he needed to. She guided him to a small bed in the rear of the building, ordered him to rest, and assured him that she would take care of the rest.

He dreamed of another life that night. Of being wanted, of being needed, of being useful. Of not always running.

He awoke the next morning and could not find his father's body. La vieja said she took care of it. She told him again that he could stay as long as he wanted. And she offered him acceptance and peace.

But that is not what you gave him, Solís. Those men returned later that morning, dragged Eduardo out from under the filthy cobijas where he hid, ignoring la vieja's screams, and they took him away. Away from Obregán, out into the endless desert and the saguaros and the heat, and it was there that they trained him, showed him how to find water and to memorize maps and routes, taught him how to get people to follow him out into the desert, to hand over their money and their belongings, all out of their desperation to find a place that valued them, that would give them hope, that would offer them a chance at a better life.

There were many coyotes in Obregán, but the collective Eduardo was forced into cared less about the people they guided and more about making money. Most were not like this, and coyotes were a much-needed force within your world, Solís. Eduardo wished that he had found work for the other collectives, but . . . well, the realization came too late. Eduardo was told that if he wanted to pay off his debt within a year, he needed to be one of the best coyotes Obregán had to offer, that the other groups would never pay as much as Danilo did. So he was trained, the lessons overflowing with cruelty and suffering, and it all made Eduardo stronger, more ferocious, more willing to do what he had to in order to survive.

And then they showed him the truth.

It took them three days to reach Solado on his first trip there. His coyote, his mentor, was Danilo. He was lanky, all toned muscle and spite. They walked during the day, rested at night, and it broke him. Danilo did not make it easy for Eduardo. No one did, but this man possessed a mean streak that never seemed to end. Eduardo had never felt that kind of exhaustion, that kind of thirst before. But Danilo let him experience it all, told him that it would build him into a better coyote if he knew how much the human body could suffer. Eduardo watched other people shrivel and shrink on their journeys. He watched them turn on one another, watched them imagine bestias in the daylight, watched La Reina torment them when they tried to pass. His own pesadilla formed out of the remains of that ciudad, two beings of bones and rotting flesh, and they tried to devour him, all while blaming him for the very act itself.

And when they had made it down Las Montañas de Solís, when they had crossed that final stretch to Solado, Eduardo saw them waiting in the expanse of ash. They were impossible to miss: their cloaks were white, and they were a horrible contrast to the blackness that surrounded them. They wore masks with long, protruding snouts, and every part of their body was covered. Nothing was exposed to the world outside.

The travelers were handed over to these men.

They paid their price.

And then, one by one, they took a step forward and, in an instant, vanished.

"You can never tell anyone what the cost is," Danilo had said when the last of the men in white were gone. "They will not come if they know what price they have to pay."

"Where did they *go*?" Eduardo asked. "What is this place?"

"Solado," Danilo told him. "Es mejor en el otro lado."

"What's on the other side?"

Danilo grinned. "You don't need to know."

Then he handed over a cut of the money.

It was more than Eduardo had ever seen in his whole life.

He promised himself he would guide people to Solado only until he had enough money to escape, to pay off the debt his papá owed, and then he would go south, far away from Obregán and los coyotes. To be himself, alone, instead of something forced on him. He met a woman in El Mercado de Obregán, a cuentista, who told him of a place in the south that she had come to love, and he made it his mission. He would work as a coyote until he did not have to.

Then he would be free.

So he took people north, over las montañas, through los valles, and he kept them alive as best as he could. He lost someone on his second trip; a man made the mistake of believing the illusion of water that you, Solís, so often gave those who crossed your deserts. They were near the end when one of the travelers became convinced that he had found El Mar, and he ran off the trail, deeper into the desert to the east, and by the time Eduardo chased him down, he was shoveling handfuls of dirt into his mouth, swallowing it, and then he pitched forward, and he was dead.

Four people turned back at that point.

Then, when he reached La Reina, he tried to go around the western side of la ciudad. He did not want to torment those who had seen one of their compañeros die. Danilo had explained that cutting through La Reina saved nearly half a day, but Eduardo was positive he could make up that time and spare everyone from what La Reina showed them.

But there, at the western boundary of La Reina, Eduardo met a line of the dead.

They forced the group of travelers into la ciudad.

And once again, his entire party gave up.

Eduardo's contact at Solado was so disappointed, so enraged when Eduardo arrived alone that he threatened to kill him on the spot. Eduardo wanted him to do it, but then he broke down, begged the man to let him keep working and pay off his debt.

He was given a warning: if he did not bring at least five healthy adults or teenagers every time he made the journey north, he would be slain. Simple as that.

Eduardo then believed he had no choice.

But he wanted to try something different. On his third trip, in the shadows of el maíz that belonged to Jorge, he offered the travelers the truth. He told everyone what was beyond Las Montañas de Solís, he told them the price they had to pay, and he said that he'd rather they know then so that they could make a better decision. He believed that his honesty would keep them trusting and believing in him, willing to follow his lead.

They did not see it that way. Eduardo tried to chase after the people who had decided to head back. He got lost in those fields that night, and returned to Obregán the next morning, dejected.

But determined.

He found seven people by himself for his next trip, and he handed them over to the men in white at Solado two and a half days later.

Seven bodies.

All the more closer to paying off his debt.

So Eduardo got better. Quicker. He found it easy to portray himself as tender, as being deeply interested in the reasons why so many people were leaving their homes and aldeas and heading north. He began to tell more and more people in Obregán of the promises of Solado. "No one ever comes back," he would say. "That's how wealthy they are becoming."

Then he would take more of them across the desert, through La Reina, and those who survived—and nearly all of them did—paid their price. They vanished before Eduardo's eyes. He was given his cut of the fee.

And he went back home to do it all over again.

The money kept growing. The people kept coming, too, and within a year, coyotes were in higher demand in Obregán. Most went to las aldeas to the east and west, but the news of Solado—its jobs, its promise of a bright future, its appeal that seemed to keep anyone from returning—spread far within Obregán.

And no one distrusted Eduardo. The deeper he fell into this role, the more he felt as though he had discovered what he was always meant to do. He convinced himself that en el otro lado, life *was* better. He had never seen Solado, had never made the crossing himself, but he believed the price was worth it.

Two years in, the families started coming, asking for passage to the land of opportunity. Eduardo finally delivered a family of eight to the men in white, but they accepted only seven of them. Solado had started restricting who could enter, and a boy named Carlito was denied passage.

"Find us only those who can work," the man said, his voice muffled by his horrible mask, his accent sloppy and rough. "No familias. No niños."

Carlito had screamed as his parents were taken away, and Eduardo did not know what to do with a *child*. Could he take Carlito back to Obregán? Eduardo only had enough food for himself. He knew the old wall that protected La Reina still stood, knew that there was a stream underground that he had used for water on his journeys. So he convinced Carlito to hide there until he could bring him more supplies, and then he would do his best to reunite him with his family.

But Eduardo learned that people fled their homes for so many reasons: Conflicts. Abuse. Terror. Hunger. A lack of jobs. They fled because they believed that things were better elsewhere, that you, Solís, would bless their desire to take things into their own hands. They kept bringing their children, hoping they could all have a better life.

And Eduardo . . . well, he needed the money.

So he took the children, left them at the wall, and two became six, became ten, became twenty, became . . .

He didn't truly give it too much thought. He would fix this, he told himself.

After he paid his debt.

They first came to him months ago, before Carlito disappeared, before Eduardo began to question what he was told. It was within a dream first: a large black *gato*, bigger than anything Eduardo had ever seen. He was somehow back in his home in Obregán; his parents were nowhere in sight, but he sensed they were just outside the door, whispering about him.

Eduardo, the guardian said. *We have come to you for help.*

He asked them to take him far away from this place, far from parents who did not seem to care about him.

Focus, joven. You have been taking people to Solado. We need you to stop.

He refused. He was so close. *So* close to being free.

They are taking us. They are stealing guardians and corrupting them.

He didn't care. He had never seen a guardian before; they had never spoken to him.

The guardian stepped closer, and he could smell the blood on their breath.

You are sending them all to their death, Eduardo.

He tried to turn away, but could not. His body was stone. "That can't be true," said Eduardo. "They go to work there, to find a better life."

Solado is not what you think it is, the guardian warned. *Their bodies, their minds, their spirits . . . they all go there to die.*

And then the guardian lifted their paw.

Placed it delicately on his chest.

And he suddenly *knew.*

He knew everything.

He saw the people he had delivered to Solado; saw how los sabuesos were used to torment them, to hold their lives in a delicate balance; watched los pálidos reap the benefits from the hard work of a people who were frightened, terrified, who did not realize what price they paid when they journeyed to paradise.

Los pálidos stole what was not theirs, the guardian explained.

*They could not survive in the world that Solís left behind, so they deceived.
They manipulated. They demanded. And now, they thrive from the ex-
ploitation of others.*

And they want more and more and more and more.

Guilt spread in Eduardo, like rainwater rushing over the
dry creek beds. "But they chose to go," he said, and even as
the words left his mouth, he did not believe them.

You do not tell them the truth.

But did Eduardo even know the truth? This was un sueño,
nothing more. What was *really* on the other side? Did anyone
actually know?

*And yet, you keep taking them there, lying to them and to yourself.
If you do not stop, we will be unable to protect the children of La Reina
Nueva.*

"How is that possible?" Eduardo cried.

*They have stolen Solado. They have corrupted what is sacred. And
soon, los pálidos will unleash it upon the world. You have to stop them.*

"But *how?*"

The guardian lunged.

And Eduardo awoke, awash in sweat, his mind and body
racing with terror.

He did not do as he was asked. He discounted it all as
nothing but a manifestation of his fears and his anxieties,
and he set out from Obregán that day with a new group. Six
people, four of them without children, and the fifth was a
mother with a seventeen-year-old son, old enough to work.
They made the difficult crossing to Solado in two and a half
days without incident. At la frontera de Solado, they each
paid their fee.

They held out their arm.

A vial flashed in the sunlight.

The masked men took their blood.

And then they took a step forward and disappeared into their new home.

The mother and son were all that was left. The boy offered up his arm for payment, and upon taking his blood, the man in the white cloak began to shake his head. "No, no, no," he muttered, and he rounded on Eduardo, grabbed him by the camisa with a gloved hand. "I told you, they have to be older. He is too young."

"He's seventeen!" Eduardo shouted, trying to free himself. He'd never been this close to one of the men who ran Solado, and now, he could see this person's eyes: bright green, surrounded by *impossibly* pale skin. Was this man sick? Cursed?

Something *worse*?

"No, he's not!" the man sputtered. "Too young."

He threw Eduardo to the ground, then shoved the boy aside. He grabbed the mother's arm, withdrew her blood, and tried to yank her forward.

She realized what was happening immediately.

"No, no, he comes with me!" she screamed, and suddenly, her son had her other arm.

"He is still a *child*! He is not old enough to work here!"

Eduardo stared at her in alarm. "Did you lie to me?" he cried out.

"He has to come with me," she begged, tugging her son closer. "He's fourteen. But he is a *good* worker and—"

The second masked man ripped the two of them apart.

The son screeched loudly.

And plowed into the man who had separated them.

He began to pummel him with his balled fists, and the man struggled to get the boy off him, and Eduardo stood there, unsure what to do and—

The boy ripped off the mask.

Eduardo heard the gasping first, but then couldn't believe what he watched unfold.

The man's skin was pale, paler than any human he'd ever seen, but only for a moment, as it began to turn red, a deep, terrible color, and the stranger clawed at his face, and the boy rolled off him, horrified.

The man tried to find his mask.

He tried to put it on.

His skin blistered over his cheeks, and the most awful shriek erupted from his pink lips as the skin split and bled and then he collapsed, and the three of them stood there, unmoving, silent, as the other masked man whimpered next to them.

The guardian had not lied to Eduardo. Los pálidos could not survive in the world.

They simply *appeared*. Two of them in full suits and frightening masks, and they raised blades, curved like those Eduardo had seen on Jorge's granja, and they cut down mother and son, their bodies crumpling, severed, and neither made any sound. Eduardo heard their life leaking out of them, heard the desert gulping up the blood.

One of them got in his face, their eyes flaring in anger.

"No children," he said. "Don't screw this up this time."

The other handed Eduardo his payment, short the money from the two bodies he did not deliver, and then they grabbed the corpse of the burned one and dragged it across the barrier.

Eduardo had believed this was one of his last trips. But now . . . he was under his goal. He did the sums in his head: five. Five more bodies . . . and he would be free.

But now he could not deny what he had been told and what he had seen. What else was true? What if *all* of it was?

He made his journey home, more confused than ever before.

The guardians then came to him outside of a dream.

He was just north of the gates to Obregán, having spent two days in a fever state of exhaustion and terror, unable to get the images out of his mind. The blistering body. The family, cut down so savagely. The same gato slunk out of the shadows and stood in his path. Eduardo believed he was delirious from the heat, but then he heard the guardian *inside* his head.

Eduardo, the time has arrived, they said. *We can help you if you help us.*

"You're real?" he asked.

The guardian growled, and Eduardo sensed that there were many eyes on him. He looked up and into the faces of countless other guardians, their pupils glowing.

Yes, we are real, they said. *Get another group. Take them north to Solado. Send them through. And when you have received your payment, step into the barrier and stay between it.*

"Between it?" He swallowed, hard. "I don't know what you want from me."

Your body, they said. *Use your body for something good, to stop una pesadilla monstruosa. We will begin the cleansing. You know where the barrier begins and ends?*

He nodded. He knew the exact spot.

Three days, the guardian said. *You will see us again in three days.*

They ran off into the desert and into the shadows.

Eduardo had made so many choices up until that point because of his papá. Because of his mamá. Because of circumstances he had never asked to be a part of. Because life seemed to force him into one disaster after another. Who cared what he wanted?

Something was wrong with Solado.

It was *rotten*.

Maybe he knew the whole time. Maybe that first instance, when he saw how frightened the people were to give up their blood, he had known. The guilt sank in him. He *had* known this was wrong, hadn't he?

And he had kept delivering them to their death, to a life of unending servitude.

His resolve was swollen with bitterness. He was tired of doing as the senior coyotes asked of him. He was tired of walking across the desert, of handing most of his earnings to men who believed Eduardo owed them something, of letting his whole life have meaning to *other* people.

He was going to end this. He *had* to.

He gathered the five worst people he could find in Obregán that night. He reasoned that if he was going to give them over to Solado willingly, he wanted to do so with the least amount of guilt left in his spirit. And it wasn't hard to locate them: Un ladrón. A cuentista who sold his power for an absurd rate. Two brothers, both of whom loved to cheat their workers out of money. A woman whose cures and potions were all watered down or fake. All of them refused to pay Eduardo's full rate, each for various reasons: He was too expensive. They didn't have enough money. So-and-so's brother in Solado would pay the other half. That one made Eduardo laugh. No one ever came *out* of Solado.

And yet, that was all he could think of when he went to sleep that night. Where *did* all those people go?

He knew now.

They set out the next morning, and Eduardo spoke only when he had to. He gave directions. He warned them when they drifted off course, or when they hadn't drunk enough water.

He stewed in his building terror, but allowed the reminder to flood his heart:

He was choosing this for *himself*.

Sure, he might be helping others, but he was tired of being pushed around, of being collateral damage, of existing only to be the forgotten one.

This was it.

This *had* to be the end.

He delivered them all to the masked men in Solado.

They each paid the price.

They all vanished.

And when the last of the men walked through, when the money was in Eduardo's hand, he took a deep breath, and he stepped forward.

Once.

Twice.

And then he felt it.

His skin prickled, all over, from head to toe, and then it pressed down on him.

One of the masked men managed to get out only a few words. "What are you do—?"

The roar came from behind Eduardo, and then the body to his right hit the ground.

He watched as a guardian—its coat yellow and brown and black—tore at the masked man's throat, ripping it out, the blood spraying all over the arid soil, and the voice rang out in his head.

DO NOT MOVE, EDUARDO. HOLD YOUR POSITION.

The pressure on his head was immense, like stones were being balanced on top of him, each one heavier than the last. He nearly shut his eyes, but another body flopped onto the ground in pieces.

The two masked men were dead.

And the guardians streamed by.

He'd lost count of them while trying to focus on staying still. Tears stung his eyes, and his skull was going to crush under the weight. "Hurry!" he called out. "I can't hold it much longer!"

You have done well, Eduardo, the guardian said. *Do not bring anyone here again.*

But Eduardo screamed, the barrier crushing down on him, and he fell forward in pain. The guardian rushed over to him, licked his hair over and over again. *Get up,* they said. *You are on the wrong side.*

Eduardo panted, his head throbbing. "The wrong side of *what*?"

The guardian nuzzled Eduardo, purring loudly. *The barrier has closed behind you.*

Eduardo bolted upright and thrust his hand out and—

He hit something solid.

He could not see it.

But it was *there*.

He watched as they descended into a gigantic, dark hole in the earth, one that had not been there moments before. "No, wait!" he cried out, and he followed them, down, down, into the darkness, where the air was cooler, and he stumbled, his head still pounding something fierce, and the noise rushed toward him, a terrible din of screams and growls and shrieks, and one of them stumbled out of a passage to his right. Their hands were up in a defensive posture, and then a guardian pinned them to the wall, ripped off their arm, and Eduardo had never seen so much blood, never heard so much violence and pain. The redness stained the white cloak the person wore.

There was so much red.

A horrific roar rumbled in the passageway. He looked up,

farther into the tunnel, saw something monstrous charging toward him, its snout too long, horns protruding from its head, and he had never seen anything like it, never seen teeth that sharp, and he knew he should have run, knew he should have turned around and tried to escape, but the guardian that had torn apart one of the masked people leapt up, meeting the creature in the air, and then the leader was there, the large gato that had spoken to Eduardo so many times, and the two guardians tore into el sabueso, bone and muscle rent apart.

This is what they do to us, they said, their jaw covered in blood and entrails. *They kidnap us, and when they force us to consume the blood of the humans we are supposed to protect, we are corrupted. Why do you think los sabuesos came after the children of La Reina Nueva? It is because los pálidos exhausted all their guardians; now, they have turned to us.*

Eduardo slid down the wall, breathing heavily. "What is this place?"

They stole Solado from the original inhabitants many years ago, said the guardian, cleaning themselves off. *They could not survive the world above after La Quema. The sun of Solís burned them terribly. They moved underground elsewhere, but failed to sustain themselves there. It was only when a messenger brought news back of Solado that they planned to take this place, to use their corrupted guardians for the purpose of control.*

"But who would come here knowing this?" Eduardo sobbed, tears pouring down his face.

And when he said those words out loud, the guilt finally crushed him.

He swept viciously, falling to the floor. "I never told them the price," he said.

You did once, the guardian said. *And what happened?*

Eduardo wiped at his face, spat on the ground. "They all left."

EACH OF US A DESERT   363

You knew the truth then. And yet you continued. For your own gain.

"But I—"

He did not finish it. *But* what? he thought. He needed money? He needed to pay off his debt? So that made this acceptable?

The screams continued in the distance.

It was ending. He had to make this right.

And he needed to bear witness.

"Take me," said Eduardo. "Take me to see Solado."

You should stay, the guardian said, twisting its head as it stared upon him. *This is not for you.*

"But I *did* this!" he screamed. "I brought these people here, and I helped it continue! Shouldn't I at least try to free those who have been held against their will?"

When we are done with the cleansing, you—

Eduardo did not want to hear any more excuses. He lifted himself up, plowed forward into the darkness, toward the sound of death and terror, and he pumped his legs, ignored the pain ripping through them, ignored the bodies strewn about the passageway, and he found the cavern, the light pouring in from the holes above and—

And—

No.

He watched a guardian bend down.

Open their jaw.

Rip into a body.

One *without* a mask.

Without a pale cloak.

Without pale skin.

He cried out, and he tried to run to them, to save them, to stop this horror, but the leader of the guardians hit him from behind, and he dropped to the earth, the breath knocked out of him, and they pinned him down.

This is not for you, they repeated.

"What have you *done?*" Eduardo choked out.

We have done as Solís would have wanted. They once scorched the earth. It is time for Solado to start over. We are cleansing it.

"But won't this turn you into those *things?*"

It will not, for we have chosen this. It is for their own good.

And the screams continued. There, in the cavern where the people of Solado could grow food, Eduardo remained on the ground, listening to the horrible sound of death. It was not much longer before the screams faded away, before there were no more footsteps fleeing the inevitable, and he knew it was all over.

Eduardo cried into the soil and did not move, not even when the guardian lifted their paw from his back. When he finally rolled upright, he was not sure he could cry another tear.

"Take me, too," he said. "Do it. Make it quick."

The guardian hesitated, then rested on their haunches.

No.

"There is nothing I can do for this place anymore," he said. "For these people. There is no penance to make up for what I have done. For what I have caused."

The guardian paused and considered this.

There is one last thing you can do, they said. *To ensure that this never happens again.*

"Tell me," Eduardo said, and he pushed himself up on his elbows, and his throat was raw, but he was willing to do anything. Anything to make this right.

Remain here, they said, *until la cuentista arrives with la poeta. Then you can tell her the story of this place, so that Solís will know what we have done for Them.*

He stood and dusted himself off. "But how do you know that a cuentista is coming? How will they know how to find this place?"

Because las poemas are luring her here and guiding la poeta back, they said. *Their journey will begin soon, and then . . . all this will be over.*

Eduardo coughed, spat up blood and dirt, and then nodded. "Please," he said. "Please let me do something. Let me show Solís that I am sorry."

And he was guided to a room in Solado. There, the guardians told him to remain. He could leave only to relieve himself or to drink water from the stream in the rocks in the cavern across from his.

So he waited.

Two days ago, the other guardian arrived, the one with the black and gray fur. She told Eduardo that it was only a matter of time before la cuentista y la poeta would arrive.

Eduardo waited.

And waited.

And waited.

She sat next to him.

They waited.

And waited.

And then . . .

We arrived.

La poeta.

Las poemas.

Emilia.

Emilia.

She had been with me the entire time.

We had been drawn to one another. And for what?

I struggled with the truth then, Solís. Did you feel it? Did you sense what passed over me as I let go of Eduardo's hands?

Elation. Rage.

The person I had been looking for was *right there*. She had written such beautiful words, had spoken to me across the vast and empty desert, and it explained so much.

Was I drawn to her because she understood? Or because the guardians *wanted* me to find her? Because they *needed* me.

Were they on a mission guided by you? How could they be? If I was necessary to their act, then it meant that they did not have direct contact with you. They were the same as everyone else.

I was a means to an end for them.

Just a cuentista.

Once again.

No more.

I sat back as Eduardo took in a deep breath, one of relief, one of finality. "Gracias," he said, and his face looked so peaceful.

He did not rise from his chair. He twisted toward Emilia, who was sobbing. "I am sorry for what I have done," he said, and his face drooped as he spoke. "But now you know the fate of Solado."

He shifted his weight, leaned back, his eyes red with exhaustion and tears.

"It is time to rest," he said. "I'm so very tired."

"Eduardo," I said, my hands still outstretched. "Please. I still have so many questions." I glanced at Emilia, at her distraught face. "We *both* do."

His eyes bored into me. "I wanted to be free," he said. "I wanted to do something for myself. Was that too much to ask, cuentista? Will Solís understand that?"

He looked to Luz.

Luz inclined her head. *You have done well, Eduardo*, she said.

He smiled.

And Eduardo looked so very young again, almost like he was a child.

He leaned forward.

His body pitched to the ground.

And when he hit it, he erupted into a cloud of ash, black and thick, like those above Solado.

They slowly floated to the earth like feathers in a breeze until they settled peacefully on the packed dirt.

Eduardo was . . . free.

Sweat dripped down my face, and I gazed up at Emilia.

La poeta.

"You have them," she said. "You've had them this entire time."

I didn't know what to say. I didn't know how to react. So I reached over to my pack and turned it upside down, letting the contents fall to the ground, and there it was: the leather pouch full of las poemas.

"Did you really write these?" I asked her.

She crouched down and picked up the pouch. An intense urge flowed through me: I wanted to snatch it out of her hands, hold it close to me.

But the feeling passed as she loosened its strings and opened it, as tears spilled down her cheeks.

"You found them," she said softly.

"I can't explain it," I said. "They called to me."

"They call to me, too," she said, running her fingers over the stitching in the leather.

It all came together then.

"That's how you knew," I said. "Where to go."

She nodded, and then she handed them back to me. As soon as it touched my hand, the surge came back: all those emotions, trapped in the words *she* had written, rushing through me.

There were so many clues. So many hints to the truth. But no answer.

So I asked it.

"Why? Why did you do this?"

Emilia looked from me to Luz, who licked at her own paw but

said nothing. "When we were separated, I had no one to talk to," Emilia explained. "Luz had been my companion for so long, and then, all of a sudden . . . no one."

Lo siento, mi amor, said Luz. *I wanted to be there for you, but . . .* She dropped her head down, down between her paws. She said nothing else.

Emilia moved closer to her guardian, stepping through Eduardo's ashes, and knelt down in front of her. "Luz, why can't I touch you?"

Luz whined, a high, pitiful sound.

Because I am not really here.

Emilia shook her head. "I don't understand."

I came to you when you were most alone, when you had not said a single word aloud in weeks. You turned to me, and you relied on me, and you opened up. You told me stories. You were so magical with words, and I loved every single one of them.

And then you found a new way to express what you had denied, what you had hidden.

Luz sat upright and let out a sorrowful whine, then rose to all fours.

After you were stolen from your home, you began to write your poems. You left them behind once you realized the power they held, and they were your path back here.

Emilia's guardian came so close, her snout hovering over Emilia's chest.

You do not need me.

Emilia and I were not touching, either. But I could tell what it cost her, to not be able to reach out to her guardian.

"Where are you, Luz?" Emilia cried. "Just tell me that."

Luz hesitated. Pulled back. Sat down.

I do not understand the magic, she said. *But I have been gone for a while now.*

And then she looked directly at me.

I knew.

Oh, no.

I *knew.*

"Obregán," I said. "Emilia, she was in Obregán."

It took a moment for the truth to blossom, and then Emilia tucked into herself, brought her face to the ground, and she screamed, wailed, pounded her fists so hard against the earth that clouds of dust wafted into the air.

Luz had been el sabueso that Julio used.

They changed me after you left. One of Julio's men stayed behind to do it, so that Julio could have a force on his side. But it took longer than he thought. He could not find someone to feed to me, and he was not willing to sacrifice himself.

Luz let out a low howl, a mournful, pitiful thing. *They fed me the one you called Simone.*

My world spun.

My world *ended.*

I had come so far.

For *nothing.*

"Lo siento, Luz," said Emilia once she was able to speak. "That this happened to you."

It is done, Luz said.

"Then how are you here? How can I even see you?"

I do not know, she said. *We guardians are as in the dark as you are. The light of Solís has not spoken to us since La Quema, since we were created.*

"How is *that* possible?" I asked. "Aren't all guardians in contact with Solís?"

Do not let the others tell you any different—we may have been expected to be between you and Them. But Solís has been silent.

She howled, a mournful sound that echoed throughout Solado.

And it is time for me to go, too.

She trotted up to Emilia.

You will do great things, mi amor. Please keep revealing your heart to others. It is beautiful.

And then she came up to me.

Thank you for taking care of her, cuentista.

I nodded at her.

It is your turn now, she added. *To tell the truth.*

"What do you mean?" I asked.

Tell her the truth.

Luz bowed her head to the earth.

And as she did, her body turned to ash.

Emilia broke down, and her sob pitched sharply, escaped into the place that had once been her home.

At the same moment, I felt a sharpness in my stomach.

My cry must have been lost in Emilia's, for she did not look to me as I doubled over in pain. As I pressed my hand against my belly. As I felt them *move*.

The truth was impossible to ignore any longer.

These stories were killing me.

I watched Emilia, unsure what to say next.

Luz's last words were said only to me.

She touched the small wooden bed in the corner, then sat on it, running her hands over the edge of the frame. She stayed there, silent, contemplative for a while, and finally I lay back, my eyes on that stone ceiling, and I thought about how we were underneath the earth, so very far from you. I *felt* far from you, Solís, more than I ever had before.

"La poeta was right by me the whole time," I said, breaking the silence. "The only person who made me feel . . . seen."

Emilia sighed—a wave of emotion rushing past—the sound of someone letting loose years of relief in one breath. "I suspected you had them because I could feel their power," she said. "It confused me. I thought I was drawn to *you* at first, that morning in Empalme, and I couldn't figure out why it felt so strong. I guess I believed that Solís was guiding me in the right direction the whole time."

She laughed, and I gazed over at her.

"What is it?"

"That's why I thought I was lost the other evening," she said. "Because you had the poems with you, I knew one was to the west, but I could sense the one en las montañas. It confused me."

"I thought Solís was talking to you or something," I said, and I resumed studying the cracks and fissures in the walls. "That you had something that I did not."

"Do you not communicate with Solís during the ritual?"

I shook my head. "I don't think so. If I do, They do not let me remember it." I paused. "No, I'm pretty sure They've never spoken to me."

"It's weird to talk of Solís," she said. "I had heard Their name so much when I was younger, especially here in Solado. But we did not visit cuentistas as much as your people. And we had so many of them. Not like how it was for you."

"I hope I wasn't disappointing," I said.

She squeezed my hand tighter. "No," she said. "Intimidating."

"*Me?* Intimidating?"

"I didn't know whether to trust you!" she exclaimed. "You seemed so distant all the time, and after you took my story, you at least understood me. But then . . . well, everything happened so fast."

It felt like years ago. Soledad, the chase through Obregán, the journey . . .

And now we were here.

Together.

"I have so much I want to say to you," I said, and then the tears came, pouring down my face. "So many things I want to talk to you about. About your words. Your life. Emilia, I *barely* know you."

She laughed. "Well, we have time," she said. "We have to go somewhere."

But where would that even be?

There was no Simone. No more Luz. I had come this far to have this power taken from my body, but now . . . well, what now, Solís? What was I supposed to do?

"Should we go back to La Reina?" I asked.

She nodded. "At least that far. We have to tell them the truth about this place."

I sighed. "I can't even imagine how difficult that's going to be."

"Well, at least we can do that next."

There was a next.

And it was with *her*.

I pushed myself up, my heart thumping fiercely.

I was here.

Because she was la poeta.

Because she had traveled so far from her home.

Because she used to feel so very, very alone.

This all started years ago, at the bedside of Tía Inez, when the power of la cuentista was granted to me. It had frightened me, but I believed what I was told: that I would be the most important person of Empalme, that I had been given a purpose that would last until the end of my life.

It had also trapped me. Contained me. It made me feel as I would forever remain in that place, that the world beyond our gates would forever be a mystery to me.

| No hay paredes | There are no walls |
| para detenerme | to stop me |

But I had left. I had ventured out into the desert, out into the unknown, and what had I learned?

That the truths that I had been told were *stories*.

It was ironic, wasn't it, Solís? I was not even aware that the rigid rules of my life were *stories*, passed on from generation to generation because that's all we knew. Tía Inez believed it, and la cuentista before her did, too. And so, we gave every cuentista of Empalme the same rules, the same restrictions, and we held them down, and we forced them into a life they couldn't possibly have chosen.

The idea came to me while staring at Emilia, watching her contemplate her new existence, her life without Solado.

I *had* to go back home.

And I had to break the cycle.

I got up and crossed the room to the bed, and I sat next to Emilia, took her hand. She gripped it tight, and then I told her everything.

All the stories I took.

All the lies I had told.

The truth—part of it, as much as I could allow myself to face.

"They're consuming me," I said, and a lightness settled over me. It was not everything, but it was enough for relief to flow. "These stories . . . they were never meant to be kept this long. I can still feel them. They're *alive*."

"So . . . give them up," she said. "Do you need them anymore?"

"I need to go back. To Empalme."

She frowned. "Do you *have* to?"

"I need to be somewhere familiar," I explained. "Have you ever seen the ritual?"

She shook her head.

"It's intense. Exhausting. Kind of . . . violent."

I told her why. I told her of the bitterness that poured out of my mouth, of the way the earth drank it up. I told her of forgetting, of the disorientation, of the lingering sensations that remained.

"Sometimes, I can sleep for ten hours after a story, and even then, I can feel lost. It takes so much out of me."

"I'm sure I can find some food or water," she said. "Or I could—"

"No, you don't get it, Em," I said, and I brought her hand to my stomach and I let her feel it, let her touch the roiling stories as they fought within me.

She jerked her hand away. "Is that *them*?"

I nodded. "I don't know what will happen when I give up all these stories. I've never had more than one at a time."

Omar.

Ofelia.

Lani.

Lázaro.

Lito.

Marisol.

Emilia.

Soledad.

Eliazar.

Eduardo.

Their stories lived on within me.

And they were *changing* me.

Who was I but a collection of their emotions and experiences? They were eating me, desperate for company, and how much longer could I stand that?

And would my suspicion come true?

"Can you last three more days, though?" she asked. "It's a long journey back to Empalme."

We both heard the thudding near the entrance, and they slunk into the space, their black fur blending in with the shadows. I had not seen the guardian since they had brought us here, but the others loomed outside.

Waiting.

We can help, Amato said. *We brought you here. It is only fair that we take you back.*

"But how?" I asked.

Do you wish to return to Empalme, cuentista?

After all this time, could I go *back*?

You will return, yes?

"They have to know what I know," I said.

I rose from the bed and I extended my hand out to Emilia.

Unsure if she would take it.

Unsure if this was the right choice.

But I *wanted* it.

"Will you come with me?"

She didn't hesitate.

She took my hand.

"Let's go back," she said.

Emilia lingered in the entryway of her home. Was she trying to remember it all? To commit it to her mind?

Because it was not lost on me that I was now going to return home, but Emilia had no reason to come back to Solado ever again.

She said nothing. There was so much unspoken grief in her, over her lost home, her lost people.

So we left that dark and terrible place.

I still kept the truth from her, Solís. I wasn't ready to tell her everything. Did that make me a bad person? Or can you understand why I did what I did?

It took me a long time to figure it out, though. As we came out of the darkness, the stars around us, you were gone for the night. We were alone, comforted by the glowing estrellas, and I thought of the nightly ritual in Empalme.

We saw no such thing in Obregán or in La Reina Nueva.

And it was because they didn't need it.

You did not punish them because . . . well, you didn't punish *anyone* anymore.

It all made so much sense to me.

You burned the world.

You gave las cuentistas and the guardians our powers.

And then . . . you left. We were all alone down here. What we did with that power . . . well, that was up to us.

I used it to cleanse Empalme.

Julio used it to mimic what los pálidos had done.

Soledad used it for her own purposes.

The guardians believed they were honoring you.

My people, the people of Empalme, believed en las pesadillas so fiercely that they made them real.

Eliazar's people did not.

Téa helped their community as best as they could.

And Ximen chose something else.

Now it was time for me to do the same.

I could be exactly the kind of cuentista I wanted to be. I could follow my own rules. And I did not have to worry about you.

Because clearly, you were not worried about us.

Knowing that I was returning home, knowing that this journey had a new purpose, it kept me alive. Thriving.

We crossed the expanse of ash, and when we reached La Montaña de Solís, I attacked it with a ferocity: I had pushed my body so hard. My legs were still sore, my head still throbbed.

But I didn't care.

When we approached the line of ash, there was a rustling to my left, and two creatures—their eyes orange, their coats thin and pale, many short horns on their head—shuffled onto the trail, then scurried to the other side.

I breathed in.

Smelled the mesquite.

Let the cool air wash over.

The stories still hurt me, but I was alive.

I would deal with what was coming when it arrived. But for now? I had made it to Solado, I had found la poeta, and I was heading back.

We pressed on, Emilia and the guardians behind me, and we climbed up.

And up.

And up.

It was not long before the excitement began to wane, like your light at the end of the day, slowly at first, and then it was gone in an instant. The pounding in my head reappeared, a fierce, sharp thing behind my eyes, and I kept stopping to catch my breath.

Do you need to rest? Amato came up alongside me, pawed at my leg.

"At the top," I said. "Let's just make it there."

Emilia gave me the last of her water. I tried to refuse it, but she said she could find more. "Where?" I asked. "We're in the middle of nowhere."

"You already taught me how," she replied. "Leave it up to me."

And then she kept talking. Emilia told me stories of Solado, of life below the earth—the sounds and the tastes and the feel of the walls and the people. It was her way of dealing with the loss. She asked me more about Empalme. About Tía Inez. I realized that she was trying to distract me, to get me focused on something other than the climb.

It worked.

The hours went by quickly, or perhaps they blurred together because of how tired I was. The summit arrived, and I stumbled over to a patch of paloverdes to relieve myself, and as I squatted there over the hole I had dug, I nearly fell asleep.

The others did not have to coax me into rest. Emilia spread out my sleeping roll. She made me eat some dried nopales. And when I was flat on the ground, las estrellas dimming as my eyes closed, she kissed me on the forehead.

"Descansa, mi cuentista," she said.

I did as I was told.

I dreamed of Raúl.

He emerged from beneath the wall at La Reina Nueva, somehow older. I knew he had lived there for many years, that his time

EACH OF US A DESERT   *381*

there had aged him. There were lines at the corners of his eyes, stress wrinkles over his forehead, and he had a light patch of facial hair, dotted with white, growing below his mouth.

The sun lit him from above.

No.

It was not you.

It was las estrellas. They burned so brightly that I had to shield my eyes with my hand, but Raúl did not blink, did not turn away, and the starlight grew, brighter and brighter, until I was screaming at him, begging him to close his eyes.

He would not.

He smiled, and there was a darkness in his mouth, and his lips stretched wider, wider, until they took up the entire lower half of his face, and his eyes began to smoke, to smolder, and then the starlight burned them out of his sockets, leaving behind two chasms of shadow.

I could see forever in them.

They pulled me forward.

They pulled me *in*.

I fell into that endless blackness, unable to scream, and slept without another sueño.

Emilia woke me long before dawn.

Las estrellas had not disappeared, so I was focusing on them when she loomed over me. "When you're ready and awake, I have something for you," she said. "Take your time, Xo."

She walked off, and I could make out the shapes of the guardians, who slumbered all around me. Amato was splayed out to the left of me, and they yawned.

We will make it today, they said.

I wasn't so sure about that, but I was too groggy to argue. I brought my hands above my head, stretched my whole body, ignored the searing pain of my poor muscles. I took my pala with me to relieve myself, then returned to my sleeping roll to find gifts upon it.

A full goatskin bag of water.

A small cloth covered in fresh prickly pear fruit.

A leather pouch.

My body told me to take the first two objects, to replenish myself, but my heart was drawn to the third, that tether gripping me, tugging me down and forward, and I braced myself as the surge hit me when I touched it.

Another poema.

I tore the pouch open, careful not to damage what was inside, and in the dim light of dawn, I inhaled the words.

Por encima de la tierra	Above the land
No puedo ver la belleza de	I can't see the beauty of
lo pequeño	the small
Pero soy igual para Solís	But I am the same to Solís
Te elevaste sobre nosotros	You rose over us
Mientras sangro detras de mí	While I bleed behind me
Dejé una pieza con cada paso	I left a piece with every step
¿Quién seré en el otro lado?	Who will I be on the other side?

She stood so silently that I did not notice her there.

"You never found this one," she said. "I thought you should have it."

I read it again.

I said it aloud the third time.

Who will *I* be on the other side?

It was like you were teasing me, reminding me of what I had not shared. I almost told her, Solís. I almost admitted the final truth that I had clung to for so long.

But I smiled instead. I thanked her for the gift, pulled her close with a hug. I wanted so much more, but . . . no. It was not the right time.

We packed up our meager belongings, and we left.

The walk was an endless descent. The muscles at the bottom of my thighs screamed at me with each step. *Stop, stop!* they called out, but I couldn't. I let the momentum guide me farther down, around each corner, and I did not stop. I drank water, I ate more dried fruit, and I kept walking.

It was easier at first. I had a destination, an end goal. I had seen these sights before. And Emilia was there, talking to me, encouraging me to keep going, even though she most likely needed my comfort after what she had just been through. When a new pain shot through me, I would tip my head back, dig my fingers in, massage the spot until it faded. They came more frequently; the stories were restless, terrified, furious.

I ignored them because I had to. Because I had to keep going.

Eliazar spoke to me. I don't know if I imagined it. But he was in my mind as Emilia told me more about Solado, about the isolation she experienced, about how strange it felt to be out in the open air.

That is how I felt, niña, Eliazar told me, his deep voice mournful, singing in my head. *Your heart does not know how to deal with freedom when you finally get it.*

Are you free, Eliazar? I asked him.

Freer than las palomas, he said.

"Who are you talking to?" Emilia asked

I smiled at her. "An old friend," I said.

She went silent.

Eliazar spoke to me. Then Soledad. Then Manolito. I listened to them all, let them construct a poetry in my mind, and down,

down, down we walked, cast in the dawn light. We pushed deeper into el valle, farther from you, closer to ourselves.

I stumbled. Emilia caught me before I could pitch over the edge and slip off the trail and then I would be gone, gone, gone, and when her fingers closed around my arm, I could feel her fear, her concern.

I sent my own back.

I sent more.

She could feel my exhaustion, couldn't she? It had a color—gray, like the stone of the wall of La Reina Nueva. It had a sensation, too. Rounded edges, thick like aloe vera, and she knew.

She knew so much about me when we touched.

What did I know of her?

Her stories woke in me, finally, and I saw a young girl, so eager to explore the world. I saw a daughter, desperate for her father to love her, desperate to know what had happened to her mother. I saw una poeta, a person whose heart could turn feelings into words, into a beauty that could reach across deserts to touch the spirit of someone who needed them. I saw a story, still being told, still *alive*.

She had been through so much. *Missed* so much. Did Emilia still think of Alegría? Did she believe she would one day be reunited with her?

No. I think she accepted that loss. She wove it into the fabric of herself, and she moved forward.

Para adelante.

I couldn't talk anymore. I only listened to Emilia.

There was silence eventually, and then Emilia spoke again, asked me more questions. About what I knew of Obregán. Of the land south of Empalme. Of my childhood. I tried my best to share myself with her, but my answers became shorter. Clipped. Until I was responding with a single word.

Then, nothing.

"No, Xochitl," she said. "You cannot fall asleep. Stay awake."

How?

"Tell me things."

What things do you want to know?

"Where were you born?"

Empalme.

"What is your brother like?"

Silly. Annoying. Curious. He gets that last part from me. I think I made him like that.

"What was Empalme like before we arrived?"

Quiet. Dedicated. We still struggled. We still fought. We still waited for Solís to save us all. Maybe we waited a bit too long. They never showed.

"What are you looking forward to the most?"

Sleep.

"Me, too."

No, that's not true.

"Well, then what?"

I don't remember what I said. But I wanted her by my side, at the end. I wanted *us*, most of all.

Us.

I liked the way that sounded.

I hope I said something about that.

———

She made me drink more water. Gave me her canteen. I guzzled it down, tried to ignore how sick it made me feel, how the stories tried to reject it.

I'm sorry, Solís. I know I have to tell you the whole story, but this part is hard. I remember images, and I remember feelings, but I was slipping away by then. I stuck a hand out to steady myself at one point, and the needles of a saguaro pressed into my palm, and Emilia screamed at me, ripped my hand from the green, leathery trunk of the cactus, but there was nothing there. Tiny pinpricks of blood appeared, but did not run down my skin.

I had so little water in my body that I could not bleed. I just oozed.

I'm sorry, Solís. I don't remember.

She carried me, Solís. By the time we were close to the bottom, I was delirious, babbling about El Mar and stories, and you were so far away, close to the horizon in the east, rising into the world, and I let the darkness in my head get so close to taking me.

Emilia swung her bag around, let it hang in front of her, and then hoisted me up on her back.

She carried me down, Solís.

En las bajadas, she set me up next to a large paloverde, rested my back against it. I don't know if she said anything. I like to imagine that she kissed me on the forehead and told me to rest.

And I did. She stayed awake to make sure we were safe, and she did this all for me. She did this despite the terrible pain she must have been in herself, aching over the loss of everything.

Was I finally not alone, Solís?

Was this what I had been yearning for?

Emilia was on one side.

Amato on the other.

Descansé porque estaba segura.

I dreamed again. Maybe my spirit was trying to make sense of this journey, of finding the person who had created las poemas, or maybe I had been in so much pain that this was how I coped.

I could see inside my own body. The stories were dark blotches in me, each of them with uneven borders and boundaries that collided with one another, over and over again. They were scrounging for space, pushing up against organs and bones and muscle, and each little battle stung and pierced me, sent fiery pain rushing up my body.

Then the first of them got the idea, an infectious one, and it rammed into another, on purpose, crushing against it until the boundary broke, and the two stories became *one*. Whose were they?

Omar.

Ofelia.

Lani.

Lázaro.

Lito.

Marisol.

Emilia.

Soledad.

Eliazar.

Eduardo.

The liars.

The desperate.

The abandoned.

They fused, each embracing the terror and isolation of the others, and it was a comfort: they had found someone like themselves. They had discovered that they were not alone. And they had discovered this *inside* my body.

They grew.

They found Eliazar. His grief. His regret. It felt familiar to them. How much had each person lost? How much did they blame themselves for what had torn their lives apart? He joined them.

They grew.

There was Emilia's story, her longing, her terrible desire to escape, and Marisol held her, told her that life aboveground was possible, and Eduardo knew what it was like to want more for yourself, and they embraced, all of them.

They grew.

And there was Manolito. His *secrets*. They all had them, and they all knew how badly they had wanted to keep the truth from the world. From *themselves*. When they took Manolito in, they offered him pity, then *understanding*.

They grew.

They grew inside me.

I was ready to burst.

Was a body meant to hold all of this? Was one person supposed to contain so many truths, so many stories? Or had I defied my design? Was I the first?

Would I be the last?

The guardians were right. If I did not return these stories . . .

They would consume every last bit of me.

I awoke later in the morning, and the stories were coalescing, waging a war against my own sense of self.

"I can't make it," I told Emilia, but before she could react, Amato had their paw on me.

Look at me.

I lifted my eyes to them as quick as I could, obeying the guardian.

You are la cuentista, they said.

"I am," I replied aloud.

Emilia trembled, grabbed my hand, and I surged again, tried to tell her that we were okay.

You take stories.

"I do."

They do not normally cause you pain.

"I don't know," I said. "I've never kept them so long before this."

Other cuentistas have. Why does this cause you *so much trouble?*

I coughed. "Because I am not the others, Amato."

They regarded me as I tried to drink water. Even that was a struggle.

There are many inside you. Too many.

I nodded.

They are consuming you.

"Sí," I said, and my voice faltered. "I know."

You don't have much time. Perhaps a few days at most.

I didn't bother asking how they knew. "I am almost done," I said. "I need to get home."

Home. They said the word as if they were tasting it, trying to determine its flavor. *Such a strange concept. Why must you wait? Why can you not return the stories now? Would you not then experience relief?*

I couldn't say it. Their breath was warm on my face as they snorted at me. I could sense Amato trying to will me to do it. To say the thing I had known but would not vocalize.

"Xo, what's happening?" Emilia asked.

You refuse the truth.

"I'm scared," I said, and my voice broke.

The longer you deny it, the worse it will get.

"Please," I said. "I am almost there. I am almost done."

You will have to face it, joven. It is now or later, but it cannot be changed. You must face the truth.

"What about *your* truth?" I spat my words at Amato, and they reeled back.

We are guardians of the truth, that which is passed on to us from Solís. Their voice was fiery in my mind as they spoke. *We learned from Them, and we honor Them.*

"Is that why you destroyed Solado?"

Emilia gasped. "Xo, no, we don't have to do this now—"

I cut her off. "When, then? When is a good time?"

"Don't you think I'm furious, too?" Emilia snarled. "My home is *gone*. Abandoned. Everyone I knew . . . they're all dead or gone or somewhere else. I lost it *all*!"

But Solado had to be cleansed, Amato said.

"Did it?" Emilia shot back, and it was clear that Amato had allowed their voice in her head. "You couldn't root out los pálidos and spare the rest?"

Amato dropped their head down, and it was the closest thing to shame I had seen in one of the guardians.

"You didn't give them a choice," I said softly, my throat raw and arid. "Just like no one gave me a choice about being a cuentista. No one ever let me *choose*."

Amato was silent for a long while, and we sat there in the paltry, useless shade.

We had not thought of things like that, they admitted. *We only knew one way.*

I grunted in response to them. Had anyone thought about what it was like to give an eight-year-old girl the power to take stories? Had anyone thought about how constrained and suffocating my life was?

No.

"Let's get going," I said, leveraging myself up with the paloverde trunk. "I want this to be over."

And I wanted to choose something different.

I had not relaxed long. We continued, bound for La Reina Nueva.

Time is short if we are going to make it today, Amato told me.

"There's no way I can make that journey in less than a day," I said. "It's not possible."

Not alone.

I did not know what they meant until I heard the musical sound behind us.

She whinnied to let me know that she was here. Emilia and I spun around, and she was *beautiful*, like the color of goat's milk, with patches of brown the same shade of my skin. Her coat shone brightly in the morning light as she moved from side to side, her plodding anxious, eager.

She is ready for you, they said. *She will make an exception.*

"Gracias," I said. "But I've never ridden a horse before."

Amato said nothing.

I exchanged a look with Emilia, then shrugged.

We had both seen stranger things in our lives.

Emilia had ridden before, so she hoisted herself up, then pulled me up next. "Hold on to me," said Emilia, and I gripped her around the waist, my face in her long hair, and she smelled of the earth, of sweat, of flowers.

We begin, Amato said.

MARK OSHIRO

I nearly fell as soon as the horse began to trot, and my distance from the ground was even more frightening once we were moving. I bounced up and down on the back of that beautiful creature, and Emilia laughed, an infectious, joyful noise. "You're too tense, Xochitl," she said. "Relax. Trust her. She knows what she is doing."

Your love is wise, Amato said. *Perhaps you should listen to her.*

My *love*. Why would Amato say that?

I braced myself first, not listening to their advice, but it only made it worse. I learned my lesson quickly. The earth passed in a blur, the wind whipping at my face, blowing Emilia's scent into my nose, and I let my fear go. I leaned into her, still clutching her waist, and I watched the guardians, galloping all around us, their paws gracefully digging into the dirt as they ran.

We thundered along, the only sound in the desert. From my vantage point, I looked out at the land, watched as the saguaros rushed by, the tops of their tall hides covered in white flowers with yellow centers. All of them had bloomed, tiny beacons of hope and beauty that guided us south.

I could see that beauty this time. I didn't remember much of the surroundings from even days earlier, but with my feet off the ground, my hands locked around la poeta, I could take it in. I saw the long shadows cast from the saguaros, how they stretched across the ground as if reaching for one another. The dark bark of the mesquites we passed glistened in the sunlight.

And her hair was so smooth, so shiny and perfect.

The day before, this trip, from La Reina to las bajadas, had taken a quarter of a day. The crumbling wall came into view so much faster than I expected, and a nervous energy thrummed through me. We had left people behind, and I had accepted that we would probably not see them again. But there—to the east, tucked behind a pile of rubble—a head popped up, whistled, and then they came out, a few at a time, and then Rosalinda was there, her jaw dropped open, too, and I climbed down from our horse, hit the ground hard.

"May I talk to them?" I asked the leader.

Do not take long. We have far to go.

I walked up to Rosalinda, whose hands were up to her face, and her eyes were red in the morning light. "Ay, niña," she said. She gazed wide-eyed behind me. "What have you done?"

This was not an accusation. It was a celebration. She pulled me into a hug, and I saw Felipe behind her, his own eyes wide in disbelief, too. I hugged him, too, held them both long and hard.

"What is this, Xochitl?" she said. "Who have you brought with you?"

"It's time for me to go home," I said. "To face the truth."

The children of La Reina Nueva gathered around, brought fresh nuts and prickly pear to us, and a fire was started. One of the girls had managed to catch a rabbit, and she wanted to gift it to us, the ones who had saved their guardians. I tried to explain that this was not the case, but she would not hear it.

And I told them everything I could. I had to. It felt good to do so at first. The children listened intently, never interrupting once as Emilia and I took turns explaining what had happened on Las Montañas de Solís. We told them of the journey, of entering Solado, of finding Eduardo y Luz, and they all hung on to every word.

"Did you find our parents?" Gabriela said, her eyes alight with hope.

That part was the hardest. I held Emilia's hand as we talked, as we took turns filling in the final gaps of the story, as we revealed that the guardians had cleansed Solado . . . and had cleansed everyone who lived there, too.

I will never understand it, Solís. And it made me question it *all*.

How was it fair that you had done the same thing so long ago? How many truly innocent people had you destroyed, just to make a point?

A shame spread through me. I had believed your story so wholly, Solís, so willfully. And I saw that unwavering devotion and hope in those children, in how they expected us to succeed.

But we didn't. Their families were gone. And all we had for them was sorrow and pity.

Some of them cried, perhaps Pablo the hardest. Others were numb, and yet others took this revelation as if we had merely told them something mildly irritating. Everyone grieves in their own way, and Rosalinda—who sat Pablo in her lap, caressed his hair as he sobbed—had a difficult job ahead of her. But she wanted it. She was *made* for this.

"What will you and Felipe do?" I asked her.

Rosalinda set Pablo down on the ground, and he scurried off. "We don't know," she said. "We have to discuss this with the children. Felipe wants to stay, but that's a lot of work. A *new* aldea."

"Building one here?" asked Emilia.

Rosalinda nodded. "Or we could make the journey together back to Obregán. Find new homes for them. But something tells me they won't want to do that."

She smiled, then sent one of the children, a young girl with tight braids down her back, to wash herself. It was so natural for Rosalinda. And she had *chosen* this.

And now it was time for me to do the same.

"I am happy for you, Xochitl," said Rosalinda. "What will you do when you return to Empalme? Will you continue to be a cuentista?"

"I don't know what else I *can* do," I said. "It is the only thing I know. My whole life was decided for me."

"We all decided to come on this journey," she reminded me. "You get to decide how to end it."

But did I *want* to end it? If I returned to Empalme, to home, and I performed the ritual, would I continue? Would I keep doing what I had been taught to do?

My struggle with this was obvious. Rosalinda wiped her hands and stood. "Mija, you do not need to make these decisions now. You have time. Go *home*. I am sure your family will be overjoyed to see you. They will understand in time, even if at first they do not."

"And I will do what I can to help," said Emilia. "If you want me to."

I considered telling them all the final thing, the one truth I couldn't quite accept. But I smiled, and I told them that it was time to leave, that our guardians wanted us to go. I bade them goodbye—once again uncertain I would ever see them again—and we climbed upon our horse.

Amato spoke briefly with Pablo, assured him that the guardians would all return shortly. That idea—that I would be done with everything so soon—sent a nervous energy through my body.

You are conflicted, Amato said, staring up at me with piercing eyes.

"I'll make a decision," I said.

You do not have much time, they said. *If you fail to act, you will die.*

We left La Reina Nueva as fast as we could.

The dread hit me when I remembered what came next.

I was taught as a child that all things rot, that we become a part of the earth as time passes. The first time I saw a dead body outside of Empalme, the coyote had perished many weeks before. Most of their bones had been picked clean by scavengers, but I never forgot the discoloration of what little fur remained, or how I could see remnants of what they used to be.

Eliazar had not been dead nearly that long.

I told myself to keep my eyes straight ahead, to avoid looking to the earth, because perhaps I would miss it, and I would not have to be scarred by the memory of his corpse.

I would have missed it all if Emilia had not cried out, had not pointed to the east.

There, not far from us, was a brilliant patch of green and yellow and pink, a burst of life in the soil that had not been there before, each of the prickly pear barrels vibrant in color, and, floating above one of them, some sort of pájaro, tiny and just as colorful, its wings beating so furiously that I could not see them.

"Do you know what they call those?" she asked me.

I shook my head. It landed on the top of one of the trunks of the prickly pear, leaned its tall, thin beak into a flower, drank.

"Un colibrí," she said. "They are a sign of good luck."

It sped off into the distance.

I stared at the patch of prickly pear.

It was the spot, wasn't it? The last I had seen of it, it was covered in zopilotes.

"Maybe he is in a better place," she said, "and this is how he wants us to know."

I wanted her to be right. Was he at peace? Was he finally resting? Had he reunited with Gracia? I wished I knew what happened after we left your world, Solís.

I wanted so many things at that point. I desired hope. I desired an answer. I desired *rest*.

"Come," Emilia said. "We must keep moving."

There was a part of me that wanted to stay there forever.

But we moved on, and soon, in the midst of the hottest part of the day, our eyes found the bones of La Reina, of la ciudad that had been punished, wiped of life like the rest of the world.

I thought of the dead that had followed us. Before, I had been terrified of them, had believed that they were ready to harm those of us who had not told the truth.

But what if I had gotten it all wrong? What if they wanted those who passed through La Reina to bear witness to what had happened to them? They were cleansed as Solado had been. They were full of stories that had gone untold for years and years and years.

They awoke in me. A single mass. A single story.

We slowed as we approached, and Amato could sense my hesitation.

Why are you afraid?

"I do not know what this place will show me," I admitted.

You survived it once. Surely this means it will be easier for you to face it again.

The sun pressed on my skin. I held Emilia tighter.

"Vámonos," I said.

We moved forward, tentatively at first, the guardians prowling serene at my side. Emilia sat tall and sure. "You will be fine," she told me. "You have told the truth. You have nothing to hide."

She was wrong.

Amato stopped. Our horse neighed softly and stilled. A prickle ran over my scalp, down my back, and I shuddered.

"Xochitl?" She clutched one of my hands, the one pressed against her soft belly. "What is it?"

He has arrived, Amato said, looking behind us.

I twisted my torso until I saw him.

The blood.

The wound.

The sadness.

"I warned you, Xochitl," he said. "And you went anyway."

"I had to, Lito," I said, and I faced forward. I gave the horse a gentle kick, and she started moving.

"I'm proud you did," Lito said, and now he was walking to my right side. His stump still bled, his torso was still torn apart, and his face was a terrible mess.

"But you haven't admitted the truth, Xo," he said.

Emilia said nothing. Did not look at him. I don't think she could see or hear him; she kept her eyes straight ahead.

La Reina had something just for me.

I was angry, resentful that this place had decided that only I deserved the truth. Images of Lito's letters filled my mind, his anger at the rejection—

No. That was . . . Ofelia, wasn't it?

I shook my confusion off of me.

"There is not much time, Xo," Lito reminded me, still shuffling alongside us. "You can't wait."

"I know," I said. "I'm almost ready."

He went quiet, shuffled through the dirt, and we crossed La

Reina. Whenever I looked back, he was there, moving along at the same pace, his body bloody and torn apart. At the other side, the next pass waiting for us, Emilia cleared her throat. "Well, that wasn't so bad, was it?"

One last look behind me.

Manolito had followed us, but now, he could cross no farther.

"Tell her," he said.

He was whole again. For a moment, he was the Lito that I loved. His boyish face, his mustache, that glow that resonated from his kind eyes. He had appeared like this before, on the first day of my journey, and I smiled at him.

But it did not last. I did not tell her the truth.

We kept going. I knew what I had to do, but I still couldn't find the courage. I focused on the journey, tried to quell my racing heart. But each movement forward brought me closer to the inevitable, closer to the truth I could not ignore.

The pain returned. Reminded me. Tormented me.

I had to push on.

Our ascent was long, and the sun was dropping out of the sky. It was faster than on foot, and our horse did not complain as she carried the two of us up, up, and up. I hung on to Emilia with one hand and used the other to pull out a water bag for us.

We did not say much at all, and neither did the guardians. They formed a line behind us, snaking down the trail, and it was the only time I got a sense for how many of these gorgeous creatures were following me. I couldn't see the end of them. They stretched far behind us, a procession of power and mystery.

We crested the hill in the late afternoon, and the drowsiness brewed behind my eyes. My stomach rumbled. Was it hunger? Nerves? Were they awakening again?

They had been quiet since La Reina, and I don't know if that comforted me, or if it unnerved me.

Maybe it was both.

La Reina shone brightly behind us and I shielded my eyes as I looked upon it. It was so small from here. I dismounted and walked to the edge again. Was Manolito still down there? Would I ever see him again?

His story shuddered in my stomach, sending a wave of revulsion through me. Why had he cheated on his—?

No.

No, that was Omar.

Definitely Omar.

The nausea twisted my gut, and I bent over again. Emilia ran her hand over my back. "Are you well? How bad is it getting?"

I brought myself upright, breathed in deep. "Estoy bien," I said. "Just a quick rest."

I needed more than that, but . . . no, I couldn't do it.

Not much longer now.

It hurts so much, Solís. Please, listen a little bit longer.

You were disappearing. We descended.

It sat in the distance, and it was odd seeing them from this side: a smaller rise, then, farther in the distance, Obregán. I remembered that first night, upon la montaña, and how enormous Obregán seemed. It was still so far away, but la ciudad burst up from the earth, beyond the other ridge. It was a sign of hope that we were even closer to home.

What would that home look like? Would Empalme seem different because of my absence? I remembered the morning I left, how mi aldea had taken a new shape, twisted by what I had seen and what I had done. It couldn't be the same, could it? The miles and miles of tunnels underneath the ground . . . would they look any different?

Our horse made good time down la montaña, as she was far more comfortable descending. Emilia had to work hard to keep me awake; I kept leaning into her, and my eyes were so heavy.

"Not yet, Xochitl," she said. "Tell me."

"What do you want to know?"

"Tell me about your friends. Someone. *Anyone*."

I told her about Rogelio first. I don't know why I thought of him, but that led to Doro, led to Ana and Quique, and I asked Emilia if we could find them someday. El Mar first, then Obregán. I wanted to see them again.

Would they want to see me?

Then I told her about la señora Sánchez, about el guisado she loved to cook, and how I would help her offer it about at our celebration because of her bad arm.

"Her bad arm?" Emilia said, leaning back into me.

"Sí," I said. "You know, since she hurt it in Obregán."

Emilia bristled, but did not explain it.

I imagined my return to Empalme. The look on Raúl's face. Papá gazing up from his book and acting as if I had been gone for only a few hours. Mamá, with her braids draping down the front of her, asking me if I had found what I was looking for. That's all I wanted: for them to accept me as I was, nothing more. To ask less of me—to let me be my own.

And then the stories awoke again. There was no complicated shape to them. When I reached down, ran my fingers over my stomach, I could *feel* it. A hard mass, something solid and horrifying and *not* my body. It had grown, hadn't it? It had gotten bigger, had fed off my fear and shame. Just like Lani's. Why had she read Julio's mensaje? Why had she disobeyed him?

Emilia sensed something, and she squirmed in front of me. "I have an idea, Xochitl," she said. "Can I give you something? Something to help?"

"We will reach Obregán soon," I said. "And then it's not much farther."

"It'll only take a moment," she assured me.

I leaned into her back, used our connection to tell her that I trusted her.

She gave the horse a kick, and she broke into a gallop. She took the corners with such mastery, Solís, and I held on to Emilia tight, our comfort flowing back and forth.

You will have to tell her soon, Amato said, bounding behind us. *We are getting closer.*

"I know," I said.

Soon.

She took us to the west once we reached las bajadas, arcing away from las granjas and from Jorge's home.

The guardians were panting by the time we reached it: la huerta, the long grove of árboles that stretched up and out from the earth, rows and rows of them in even order. All of them paloverdes, all of them twisting out of the earth, casting thorny shadows. "This is where I camped with mi papá and his men for a while," she said, hopping off the horse and moving off toward los árboles. "Papi was a monster, but he was clever. He knew this would keep us in the shade and that there'd be a source of water nearby, enough to keep us alive until we found the next place to go." She smiled. "I met Chavela the week after that. Did I ever tell you what I did?"

I shook my head as she helped me down.

"It was a test," she said. "Papi wasn't paying attention to me, so I took the horse I had been on, and I rode to the lights in the distance. I didn't know what it was; I had never even *heard* of Obregán. That's how I met Chavela. I left una poema here, not long after that. Chavela . . . she inspired me."

She knelt on the ground near the edge of la huerta, and then she dug into the soil with both hands, flipping it to the side. The guardians gathered and watched her, silent, their eyes glowing bright in the growing evening. The leader looked to me, interest in their eyes, but they said nothing.

Emilia came to me, her hands outstretched, her gift in her palms.

A leather pouch.

How could I not sense this one? Was my connection fading? Or did it not matter anymore?

I hurriedly opened the little pouch as Emilia stood next to me, her hand on my leg, pushing warmth into me.

It was in my hands.

It was real.

She is real.

I read it aloud:

Mi esperanza es un pájaro	My hope is a bird
que vuela sobre la tierra	that flies over the land
Y en la distancia	And in the distance
tú brillas más brillante que	you shine brighter than
las estrellas	the stars
más brillante que el sol	brighter than the sun
Te seguiré solo si	I will follow you only if you
me sigues.	follow me.

"I didn't know what Obregán was that first night," she said. "It was just this glowing light in the distance, and . . . I don't know." She ran her hand up and down my leg. "I imagined it was a sign, from Solís. Meeting Chavela. Discovering Obregán. So before we left, I wrote that."

"It's beautiful," I said, and my throat ached, the tightness threatening to set loose my tears.

"But a sign wasn't enough," she said, grasping my leg tighter. "I was so tired, Xochitl. So tired of hoping for a better future. I wanted to believe in Solís, but . . . well, I also wanted Solís to believe in me."

"'I will follow you only if you follow me,'" I repeated.

She nodded. "I hope it helps," she said.

"Gracias," I said. "For stopping."

I ran my hands over the drawstring pouch. Was this how love began? Is this what it felt like? Eliazar woke in me; whatever was left of him recognized what was surging through my body, and I saw him, hand in hand with Alegría, sitting around the fire, his face full of joy.

Emilia helped me up on the horse first, and then she claimed her spot in front of me. "I think we can make it over the next pass tonight," she said, "especially with the guardians protecting us."

We took off at a brisk gait, and their leader was astride, keeping pace. *She is an interesting one,* they said. *She surprises us.*

"She surprises me," I said.

Then you must tell her.

"Not now," I said. "She can't know now, not after that."

The hum hit me, and it dislodged the stories in my stomach. I winced and held back a cry, waited for the pain to pass.

"Hold on, Xochitl," said Emilia. "We're so close."

Tell her.

Soon. I would tell her soon.

We passed by Obregán that evening. We did not pass through it. We joined the few traders and merchants who were leaving or entering la ciudad that late, and they gave us a wide berth as we passed. They nodded their heads, a sign of respect for the guardians, and then they went along with their travels.

I wanted to stop. To come back. To visit El Mercado, to tell Soledad about her son Eduardo, to taste all the foods I had never tried before. I wanted Emilia there at my side, and I wanted—

No, I couldn't. I sucked air deep into my lungs. One more pass. One more climb. We would probably make it home by morning.

I did as I had imagined Amato had done so earlier. I tasted the word "home," rolled it around in my mouth, and I wasn't sure I would be welcomed, that I would be wanted, that I could find a place there. My daydream from earlier twisted in my mind. What if Raúl thought I was a monster? What if Papá believed that I had become corrupted? What if Mamá resented me for what I had done?

I had kept my first story in Empalme, and in the span of those days, a change took place, like the cocoons that sometimes hung from our doorways or on the ceiling, bursting one day to reveal some new creature, one unrecognizable from what it used to be.

That is what waited for me: a transformation. I did not have to be what others wanted me to be. I could be *free*.

Soy libre.   I am free.

I knew as we began our climb, that final rise, that I could never be the person I once was, not for anyone.

At the top of the final ascent, the whitethorn still stood proudly, its trunk a stark lightness against the backdrop of night and las estrellas.

I was shaking then. The pain tore at me, and Emilia had to guide me carefully off the horse, who still remained gracious and kind throughout it all. She trotted off to the edge of the vista to the south and began to munch on grasses.

The leader came back to me. *You are running out of time, Xochitl*, they said, and they pawed at my leg, pushing me into Emilia. *What is your decision?*

"Let me rest," I said. "Let me rest for a few hours, and when the sun rises in the morning, it will happen."

Emilia looked to me, her hand on my back. "What are they saying to you?"

"We'll rest," I said. "Not long. And then head out at dawn."

She nodded her agreement, and she took my sack from me, started to set up camp. The guardians were on the north end of the vista, curled up close to one another. I walked over to them, wobbling as I did so, and I called out. "Why did you come?"

Amato turned around, their eyes flashing in the darkness. *You can change the world, Xochitl*, they said. *You can choose something different.*

I walked closer to them. "But I'm afraid."

All change is frightening, niña, they said. *We still remember La Quema. Many of our kind perished that day, too, and those who hid in caverns en las montañas mourned for days and days and days.*

But we kept going. We chose to adapt. We chose to be something different. And now look at us: we thrive. We are feared and respected. We protect the land, and the one you call Solís protects us.

"Do you believe that?"

They did not answer at first. As I was about to turn back, their voice was in my mind. *Sometimes it is easier to believe*, Amato said. *It gives us comfort. It makes us feel like we are a part of something.*

"Each of us a desert," I muttered.

Yes, they said. *But you do not agree. You question. You wonder about your place. You challenge Them.*

They all rose in unison and faced me, and their eyes were so gorgeous, so utterly horrifying, and they sent an energy forth, floating amidst that hum of intimidation.

We admire you, Xochitl. You ask things that others are afraid to say.

You ask Them if They watch our suffering.

You ask Them if They care.

You ask Them if They are listening.

We obeyed.

You challenged.

They knelt then, bowing their heads to me, and the tears rushed from my eyes. I choked back something. A cry? A sob? A story?

You challenged us. You made us reconsider what we have done. What it means to have these powers.

Xochitl, you can change the world, Amato repeated. *Choose something different.*

They curled up again, their eyes closed, and all those yellowish dots of light were gone. I turned back to Emilia, saw her smoothing out one of the sleeping rolls, and I went to her. I let myself fall at her side, and when I did, she was staring at me with eyes that were dark in the starlight, but oh so beautifully warm.

And alive.

I reached a hand out to her face, ran my fingers down the line of her jaw, over her sharp nose, and then I leaned in, and I brought my lips to hers, my tongue to hers, and I kissed her because I had to make a choice. I knew then exactly what I was going to do, and it filled me with an unrelenting terror. But the flash of fear was gone, and I allowed myself to submit so fully to her kisses, to her fingertips on my cheeks, on my breasts, on my legs.

I crawled close to her, everything touching, both of us on the same bedroll, and she embraced me with her body, with her affection. We were warmed by the light of Obregán to the north, the stars around us in the sky, and we were warmed by the existence of each other.

They did not wake me. I woke myself, surrounded by the darkness of night, by the gentle haze of starlight. I carefully untangled myself from her arms, from her legs, so smooth and muscular and strong, and I rose, stretching deep, and I ignored the roaring pain in my torso, ignored that it had spread, that it was now pressing on my lungs, and I ignored the guardians, too, who stirred softly and began to wake up.

I walked to the edge.

I gazed upon Obregán in the north.

It was still an explosion from the earth.

An impossible eruption of light and possibility.

It was still exactly the same.

La Ciudad de Obregán was uncaring. Uninterested. There were so many people who lived there, whose lives were complicated and messy and impossible to define, and *la ciudad thrived*. It lived beyond death, beyond birth, beyond everything in between.

My life had changed so much in such a small span of time.

Obregán had not.

The indifference comforted me, and the last piece of the puzzle fell into place.

You were indifferent, Solís. I believed you were there, that you had burned the earth in anger and rage, that you had given us the power of la cuentista.

And then you left us alone.

You were never coming back.

You observed us from up on high, and you watched us struggle with the chaos born of violence and destruction, and you did nothing. You never sent us signs; you never planned for anything; you just watched your creation.

Vast.

Alone.

A desert.

I decided then, Solís, that you *could* hear me, and that there was only one thing left for me to do.

I woke her up, and she turned over, smiling at me, her lips full and delicious and I wanted to kiss her again, but I was so heavy, Solís. I was so full, and it was time.

It is time now. I'm almost done. Please wait just a little longer, Solís.

"Come," I said. "I have something to say."

I held her hand as I guided her to the south, and there, on the edge of that vista, Empalme was somewhere in the distance, shrouded in mostly darkness. Here, at night, there were only a few dancing lights, fires and torches lit to the south.

They must have kept the nightly celebration going.

They kept going, I realized.

Without me.

Was that even Empalme? Could I even see it? Was I imagining it?

Yes. This was what I needed to do.

"We're almost there," Emilia said. "I bet we could make it before your family goes to sleep."

"No, Emilia," I said. "I'm sorry that I didn't tell you. I should have told you everything."

Those same words again. Manolito had spoken them to me, not far from where I stood. Would he be down there? Would he be gone forever?

"Tell me what?"

"If I go home, I need to be empty," I said. "These stories . . . I can't do it anymore."

She held my hand, squeezed it. It felt so good, Solís.

"I support you, Xochitl. I already told you that."

"They're killing me," I said.

I expected shock. Maybe anguish. But she nodded her head. "The pain," she said. "How you keep touching yourself. I knew it was bad, but I . . . I understand."

"I don't know that you do," I said, and I let go of her, not because I didn't want to remain in physical contact, but because I needed to say this aloud, not through this strange power that neither of us understood.

"We were not meant to keep these stories," I said. "I didn't figure it out until after you told me about las poemas, about how you wrote them, and then discarded each one as you went."

"But I had to—"

I raised a finger to stop her. "No, I have to say it all to you. It makes it real if I do."

There was a scraping against the dirt. I glanced behind me: they were there, all of them, sitting proudly behind me, waiting to hear it, their eyes glowing.

Go ahead, señorita, Amato said. *The world is here to listen. We are here to listen.*

I smiled.

"I think I know why this is happening," I began, and once it left my mouth, it was a flood, like the ones we got during the terrible rainstorms once a year, washing out the desert floor, cleansing it all, and it cleansed *me*. "Solís didn't just want to protect others, to give them a means to tell the truth. They wanted to protect *us*. Las cuentistas. No one body is meant to hold so much . . . so many . . ."

I faltered, not because I didn't know what to say, but because the moment had arrived.

We hear you, the guardians said. *Please make your choice.*

I kept going.

"I have it all inside me. Every emotion. Every feeling. Every possible pesadilla, every imaginable hardship, but none of them are *mine*.

We are all so very alone, Emilia, and these stories have now found one another, have merged together, and they're nearly a part of me."

I breathed out, and with it went all my fear, all my hesitation.

"I know it's happening. I keep trying to ignore it."

She breathed in deep. "What do you mean?"

"I'm mixing it all up," I said, choking back a sob. "The stories."

"You said something earlier. About la señora Sánchez. I just assumed that you were . . . tired."

"I am," I said, letting that truth guide me forward. "I am so tired. But these stories . . . they've found one another *inside* me. And they're becoming one *thing*, one living cuento within me."

"Xo, are you—?"

"I'm giving them all back today, Emilia. Every story. Including my own. And then I'm never taking another one."

There was no hesitation on her part. She threw her arms around me, and I wanted to tell her to stop, that there was one more thing left, the *big* thing, but Solís . . . she felt so good. No, she made *me* feel so good, and then the tears rushed forth, spilling down my face, and I pushed her gently.

"No, Emilia, you don't get it," I cried.

"Xochitl, I will support you through *anything*," she insisted, and she moved toward me, but I moved back, farther from her.

And it was right there.

The tip of my tongue.

It was time.

"I'm a part of them. Which means when I give them back, I will lose myself, too."

Her head cocked to the side, shook lightly. "I don't get it. You always give the stories back, don't you?"

"And I forget them. Solís strips them from my memory, and I can never remember what I was told."

She shook her head slowly as it dawned on her. "And if you give Solís *your* story at the same time—"

"—I will forget," I finished.

It grew, slow at first, like your light in the morning, spreading faster and faster until her face was twisted and uncomprehending. "No, that can't be right," she said, but I could see it in her eyes: she knew it was true.

"I don't know how much I will lose, Emilia. It could be the past week or two. It could be most of my life. Where does my story begin? Where does it end? How much of it was claimed by the others, by the ones that have been eating away at me?"

She was crying now, too, but she wiped at her eyes, and her fury was defiant. "No, I don't accept that," she said. "Solís can't be that cruel to you, not after everything you did for Them."

"I don't think they can do much of anything," I said, and a calmness settled in my body, a clarity I had not possessed before. "I don't think they ever planned for someone like me."

She laughed, and when she hugged me, I did not reject her. Our emotions flitted back and forth, and then the humming began, the low growl, and los gatos joined us, and Amato leapt onto their hind legs and roared, a glorious, rebellious sound, and I kissed her, Solís. I kissed her because I wanted to, because she was la poeta, because I *could*.

"Oh, Xochitl," she said. "I know this must be hard, but I want you to know that I will be here regardless."

"Really?" I said, and I wiped the tears from under her eyes. "You mean that?"

"I think it's my turn," she said, "to become a cuentista."

I opened my mouth to disagree, to refuse her, but she kept talking.

"Not like that. Not like *you*. There is *no one* like you, Xochitl."

She kissed my forehead.

It hurts, Solís, please. Wait just another moment. I'm almost done. I promise.

"We are the stories we tell one another. That's what las poemas were for. I needed to tell my story to *someone*, and *you* found them. You brought them back to me."

Another kiss, between the eyes.

I'm almost there. *Please.*

"So, let me tell *you* a story," she said, her eyes red and watery. "Or two. Or a thousand. I will remember all of this for the both of us, and no matter how many times you need it, I will tell it to you all over again."

On the lips.

"I don't know what we are. I only know what we *can* be. Is that good enough?"

A smile.

"It's perfect," I said.

She stepped back, an arm's length from me, and she was still crying, but they were not tears of sadness.

No.

I think she was proud of me.

She wiped at her face. "I'll wait for you to be done," she said. "I'll be right here."

"Lo siento," I said.

She shook her head. "You have nothing to apologize for, Xo. Never apologize for being yourself ever again."

I left her there without another glance because if I didn't go right then, I could have stood there forever, staring at her, her beautiful hair, her face of angles and sharpness.

I walked toward the whitethorn.

I knelt before it, underneath all of las estrellas.

I began.

And now I am here, Solís. That's all of it. That's why I left. That's why I kept the stories, and why I am kneeling here.

The sun is out now. You have burned away las estrellas, and I hope you have been patient as I told you all of this.

I've never done this part. I have given you every story before this, and I don't even know if this is going to work. But I have to try.

I hope you understand. I hope you grasp why I had to tell you everything, why I waited so long, why I am willing to give it all up. It's not just for her. I promise. She is important. She means everything to me.

But this was all for *me*. It always was, and I am not afraid to say that anymore. I chose this for myself, and if you took my whole life from me, if you sent me back to my birth, I would do it all again.

Every last decision.

It hurts. I can feel them quivering in me, anticipating the inevitable, and they're latching on to everything as they prepare to leave my body. How much of me will they take? How much of this will I forget? Will you take all of me? Will I be an empty shell?

A desert, empty and vast.

I don't think you can. I don't think you care. I think you sit up there and you hear us. You observe, and then you move on.

I believe that there is too much of me for you ever to take. I believe I am more important than the role you cast me into, and when all of this is over, I know I will never take another story from anyone.

Instead, I will tell stories. I will listen to them, too, but not *take* them. And unlike you, I will do something about them.

No more obedience. No more bowing before someone who does not bow back.

See the truth. Believe the truth.

Because the truth is . . . we should not have this. No child should be granted this power. No one *person* should have this. What good has it done us?

Maybe that's what was missing. Maybe when this settles, if I still remember, I'll tell the world that we need a change. That las cuentistas are overburdened and overwhelmed. It's time for a *new* honesty, one that cannot be corrupted by greed or ambition or fear.

But I know you're there. Waiting. Watching.

I'm ready. The bitterness is here, in my throat, waiting to pass out of my mouth and into the willing earth.

The price is worth it. I am not ashamed of who I am or what I did.

I just hope that you have been listening.

Because this is the last story I will ever tell you.

Acknowledgments

Thank you.

To my agent, DongWon Song. You have been a force of support, love, inspiration, and creativity in my life. You encourage my ridiculous ideas (and trust me, there are so many more to come), you told me to write the book of my heart to follow up *Anger,* and you have gone beyond the call of a literary agent to make my life better. I would not be here without you.

To Miriam Weinberg. I handed in a horror novel set in a dystopian landscape to you over two years ago. You loved it, but you had the courage to tell me that I had written the wrong book, that the story I had given you was a scathing polemic, but was this *really* the novel I wanted to release next?

It wasn't, and we set out over 2018 to drastically change this manuscript, which went through two complete rewrites. You pushed me to write fantasy. You pushed me to throw caution to the wind and compose the most complicated, ambitious book I'd ever attempted. When I told you that I realized that Xochitl's voice would work best if the entire novel was a single prayer, you didn't shut me down. Your eyes went wide over plates of French pastries, and you ordered me to do it.

Over and over again, as we have worked tirelessly to make this book the best it could be, you pushed me to be better. And every time, you were right. *Each of Us a Desert* does not exist without you, and I love you for that.

Thank you.

To the women of Deadline City, Dhonielle Clayton and Zoraida Córdova. You invited me into your lives through a Madcap Retreat (and one well-timed visit to a hot tub), then made me a part of our little office community in Harlem. We have spent many late nights together, all on deadline, complaining about the things our industry does wrong, making terrible, terrible jokes, stealing tiny spoons from Jeni's Ice Cream (ZORAIDA), and you have both seen this book take shape into what it is now. You even took me with you on your trip to my second home: Hawai'i. I don't think I would be where I am without my work wives. I adore and love you both.

To the homies: Adam Silvera, Arvin Ahmadi, Tiffany Jackson, Justin Reynolds, Ashley Woodfolk, Patrice Caldwell, Jalissa Corrie, Saraciea Fennell, and Kwame Mbalia. Thank you for making me feel like I could survive in New York City. In the world of Kidlit. As a writer. I cherish all the time I've spent with each of you, either at writing retreats, writing dates, French fry crawls, or cutting it up at festivals. I love you all.

To my incredible team at Tor Teen, who have been so deeply supportive of me, my work, and my vision: thank you. To Saraciea Fennell, my superstar publicist, who keeps me organized and is one of the reasons my debut book was as successful as it was. To Sanaa Ali-Virani, editorial assistant extraordinaire. To Anthony Parisi, Isa Caban, Eileen Lawrence, Devi Pillai, Renata Sweeney, Zakiya Jamal, Lauren Levite, Lucille Rettino, and all those who played a part in making this book (and *Anger*) a reality: you have helped my dream come true, and I'm indebted to you all.

To Project LIT, for the incredible support and community. I can't wait to see you all grow.

To PEN/Faulkner and Lambda Literary Writers in Schools

programs: thank you for putting my very queer books in the hands of students. It's beyond my wildest dreams as a kid who grew up closeted in a small city near the desert to see children get to be their truest selves and express that through literature. You're all changing the world.

To all the librarians, educators, teachers, students, booksellers, bloggers, Booktubers, bookstagrammers, and readers who have influenced someone reading my work: You are my everything. You have also helped make my dream come true, and I am appreciative of you all.

To the wonderful Mark Does Stuff community, for your patience as I continue to balance being a book/TV blogger *and* an author, for sticking with me for over a decade, and for allowing me to finally get revenge on all of you for every shocking plot twist you got me to experience. Here's to another decade of being unprepared.

To all the authors I have befriended in the past three years: I won't list y'all because there are too many, but I feel so privileged and honored to be in the children's literature space with so many brilliant, empathetic, and kind creators. Thank you to all the authors who hosted me, were in conversation with me on tour, who gave me advice, who stayed up way too late at festivals and encouraged bad decisions, who made me feel like I belonged.

Thank you.

To Sarah Gailey, for brainstorming, our trauma bonding, your incredible advice for this book and others, your humor, your generosity, your brilliance, and for all the cursed things you send me. I owe you everything.

And finally.

To Baize White. In early 2017, at a writing retreat my agent hosted, I got to watch you read the first outline/synopsis for the book that would become *Each of Us a Desert*. I have experienced few things as satisfying as watching you get to the massive plot twist that was in the original draft of this book. I loved writing to impress you, and I so deeply wanted to impress you for the rest of my life. Then, a couple months later, you drove me (frequently well over the speed limit, I might add) to the Sonoran Desert so that I could spend days wandering in the heat, documenting the desert as part of the research for this book. Xochitl's journey would not be what it is if you had not done this for me.

Then I wrote the book over most of 2017. You read it at the beginning of 2018, loved it, and gave me some wonderful feedback. I rewrote it once. And by the time I got to the second rewrite, my first book had come out in the world, and my dream had come true. Unfortunately, our dream was starting to crumble, and it was during that second rewrite—when Miriam insisted that Xochitl have someone her age on her journey, that perhaps the book needed some romantic tension—that I struggled with tension in *our* relationship. We were far from home, I could not figure out *why* these two characters should even *like* one another, and you and I were having such an awful time communicating, being present, making things work.

And that's how I figured it out. I thought of you.

And then I wrote you.

Emilia and Xochitl are you and I, written *backwards*. I saw these two characters, unable to communicate, unable to see who they truly were, and then I designed a journey for them that was our own. I guided them to the place where you and I began. Because at the start of our relationship, you traveled an ungodly distance to be with me and tell me that you loved me.

And no one had ever done such a thing.

You read a draft of this last summer. You cried. You told me it was the most beautiful thing I'd ever written. I was pleased because it meant I impressed you.

I wrote nearly all of this right after that. Which means I've reached the point where this has to change tense. Because you didn't make it this far. You didn't get to see this book set free into the world. And I have struggled for months with what I was going to do with these acknowledgments. Do I keep all this? Do I tell the truth?

I would like to think that my fiction does that: it tells a truth. And the truth is that I cannot divorce you from this book. You are written into the very fabric of it, and it does not work without you.

So.

Thank you, Baize. I wrote this book as my love letter to you, back when we were still together, back when you were still alive, and that's the truth of it all. But I also hope that this accomplishes something else. You left your own legacy behind, in your work, in your kindness, in your originality, in your podcast. You don't need me to add to that. Rather, I would like to do something else for you, to honor what you have done for me.

Each person who picks up this book, who makes it to the end, who reads these final words, will hopefully then think of you, even if they never knew you, never got to experience your energy or your beauty. Literature has a way of granting immortality, and so I hope that *Each of Us a Desert* has a long shelf life.

Because then that means you get to live forever in the minds of others.

Thank you, Baize, for being my Emilia, and for letting me be your Xochitl.

Mark

About the Author

MARK OSHIRO is the Hugo Award–nominated writer of the online Mark Does Stuff universe (Mark Reads and Mark Watches), where they analyze book and TV series. Their debut novel, *Anger Is a Gift*, was a recipient of the Schneider Family Book Award in 2019. Their lifelong goal is to pet every dog in the world.

🐦 @MarkDoesStuff
📷 markdoesstuff
f facebook.com/markdoesstuff
markoshiro.com